PRAISE FOR

"Fresh, exciting, and necessary. A
—Taylor Jenkins Reid, author of the *New York Times* bestselling
novels *Carrie Soto Is Back*, *Malibu Rising*, and *Daisy Jones & the Six*

"Palmer tells a story like a girlfriend over lunch."

—*People*

"Funny and clever . . . a real crowd-pleaser."

—*Publishers Weekly*

"Palmer is a witty, charming writer."

—Refinery29

"A nice, warm snack."

—*New York Journal of Books*

"Palmer deftly covers the complicated ground of family and hometown
loyalty."

—*Booklist*

"Honest, humorous, and whip smart . . . impossible to put down and
so much fun to read."

—*USA Today*

"Funny, fresh, and frank . . . Snappy and smart."

—*The Oklahoman*

"Palmer's authentic humor carries the message with a hint of parody."
—*Publishers Weekly*

"Funny, painfully honest, and hard to put down."

—*Kirkus Reviews*

"In a word: genuine."

—*Herald Sun*

FAMILY
RESERVATIONS

ALSO BY LIZA PALMER

FAMILY RESERVATIONS

A NOVEL

LIZA PALMER

LAKE UNION
PUBLISHING

Published by Lake Union Publishing, Seattle

www.apub.com

Amazon, the Amazon logo, and Lake Union Publishing are trademarks of Amazon. com, Inc., or its affiliates.

ISBN-13: 9781662517174 (hardcover)
ISBN-13: 9781662517198 (paperback)
ISBN-13: 9781662517181 (digital)

Cover illustration and design by Sarah Congdon

Printed in the United States of America

First edition

For Juanita and Leila

The history of the table of a nation is a reflection of the civilization of that nation.

—*Auguste Escoffier, from the preface to Larousse Gastronomique*

CHAPTER ONE

Julienne Winter will say that *"something deep within"* drew her into the kitchen that morning. She will tell Richard she felt something was off and then will pause, stare off into the middle distance, run her pale fingers through her long golden hair, and remind him how in tune she is with the universe and what a perpetual burden this is for her to bear. He'll agree with her, as he always does. Richard decided long ago that Jules believing she controls the universe is less taxing than arguing with her about it.

Breathing an exhausted yet benevolent sigh, Jules smooths down her bloodred wrap dress. The expensive silk hugs her every curve in exactly the way she meant it to.

Shoulders back, she bravely pushes open the door to the kitchen.

Athena Winter hunches over the side of pork, her intense gaze focused in on perfect one-inch pork belly sections when an idea comes from nowhere and everywhere at the same time. The crowded 184-square-foot kitchen of Northern Trade melts away around her, explosions of "Behind!" and "Corner!" fading into the background. Athena's calloused left hand tightens around the stag-bone handle of her favorite knife. She pushes her thick, black-rimmed glasses up with her wrist and sets her rebellious sights on the pork loin and the mouthwatering pork chops that lie in wait there.

Without hesitation, she slices.

※

Sloane Winter steps into the main dining room of Northern Trade. She takes in a deep breath and closes her eyes, listening to the wide planks of the original quartersawn oak floor creak and moan underfoot. The fragrant logs crackle and pop from the fireplace as she guides her staff in braiding and intertwining Northern Trade's seven individual wooden tables to make one long community table down the center of the room. A burst of crisp air wafts in through the open front door, accompanied by the familiar aroma of woodsmoke from the dual firepits at Northern Trade's entrance that signal the countdown to when guests will arrive.

Sloane wraps her snowy-white cashmere shawl tightly around her shoulders as she steps into the foyer, treading carefully over its irregular terra-cotta-tiled floor. She picks up a basket from the low-slung leather Spanish chair and meticulously straightens the stacks of the full Maren Winter library of cookbooks displayed atop the simple Stickley table.

After tonight, this could all be hers.

※

As Jules slides in next to her younger sister, the kitchen staff melts back into their original positions, having worked as a unit to surreptitiously clear a path for one of the esteemed members of the Winter family.

"May I steal you for a moment?" Jules asks, eyeing the stack of pork chops. Athena leans back against the kitchen counter and considers her sister's request. Smiling, Jules leans in and whispers, "Don't worry—I'm sure you'll get right back to sabotaging our beloved mother's annual New Year's Eve party in no time."

Athena straightens to her full six-foot height and smooths her black hair back under the gray bandanna knotted tightly at the top of her head, the loose ends making it look as though she has little bunny ears. Athena's height is brought up in almost every article about her: At well over six feet, Athena Winter's presence as the newly anointed head chef in her mother Maren Winter's iconic Michelin-Starred kitchen cannot be ignored . . . and For someone so tall, Athena Winter's grace and agility in the kitchen are undeniable yet couldn't be further from her mother Maren Winter's pint-size fierceness. Or Jules's personal favorite from a couple of years ago: At just thirty-five years old, Athena Winter does not simply stand—she looms. But no matter, she stands firmly in the ever-present shadow of her extraordinary mother, culinary pioneer Maren Winter.

It appears Athena's height is not the only thing notable about her.

Athena sets down her knife and wipes her hands on the towel tucked tightly into the back of her apron. She tells her staff she'll be back, listing exacting tasks ranging from how to fix a too-runny sauce to patiently challenging her poissonier to dice the rockfish in more uniform half-inch pieces. The kitchen responds in a chorus of "Yes, Chef."

As Athena and Jules reach the door, Athena spies her newest intern grab the lid of a pot and burn his fingers. Fingers that are not yet calloused and flame retardant from years of losing battles with the hot surfaces and open flames in a kitchen. Athena scans the immaculate counters and shelves and finds the cork from the 2004 Schramsberg Reserve the staff opened late last night for their own celebration of the New Year. She plucks it from the high shelf, walks over to the intern, and shoves the cork under the lid's handle. Looking directly at the stunned intern and then back to the lid, she wordlessly picks up the lid by the cork, thus not burning her hand. The intern's mouth hangs open.

"Most times the fixes are simple." Athena taps the cork. "Just not that obvious."

"Yes, Chef," he says, his voice shaking. Athena gives him a quick nod and follows Jules outside.

Built in 1852, Northern Trade was one of the original trading posts, complete with an attached boardinghouse, which sprang up during California's gold rush. Sitting on 1,800 wild acres, the historic landmark was abandoned for more than a hundred years.

Until Maren Winter saw its potential.

Sloane walks down the gravel road in a dreamy haze, past the Northern Trade Inn that Maren renovated from the original boarding-house, and continues down the hill past the root cellar and on down toward the gardens and greenhouses. Scanning the hay-colored rolling hills and valleys, she looks out over California's North Coast and beyond to Tomales Bay, with all her luscious oyster beds. The natural symphony around her tunes and blows—the leafy hush, the far-off birdsong, and the distant white noise of the bay.

Sloane inhales, trying to devour just enough of the surrounding tranquility to tamp down the building tension inside her. Always able in the past to manage expectations and squash her deepest desires for the good of the family, Sloane worries she's gotten way too attached to her own idea that tonight is the night her mother will announce to their nearest and dearest that she, the eldest Winter sister, will be taking on more leadership opportunities within the Winter Group.

Sloane crafted the phrase "taking on more leadership opportunities" in the shower one day and decided it sounded far more gracious than the more straightforwardly expressed goal of fully taking over the mul-timillion-dollar culinary empire her mother built over the past forty-five years. As most women know, being ambitious—even being thought of as ambitious—is a trait one must keep well hidden under layers of breezy politeness and effortless smiles. Because for a woman to be a leader, she must also appear as though power is something she's never worked to obtain.

As Maren Winter has aged into her midseventies, the whispers of her retirement have become louder and louder. And as they grew louder, Sloane assured the public and the Winter Group's board of directors that her tireless work over the last twenty years has been in service of only her mother's legacy, never letting on that she has any aspirations beyond that. And when she finally does ascend to the throne (i.e., "take on more leadership opportunities"), she will burst with performative surprise at the great honor that she definitely did not plan for or see coming.

Notably, the one person not talking about retirement is Maren Winter herself. But Sloane is hopeful that her mother's recent remarks about wanting to explore the world, along with giving Sloane more autonomy and greater responsibility within the Winter Group, could point to Sloane finally taking over the company once Central Trade, Maren's first new restaurant venture in forty-five years, officially launches in the coming weeks.

The spitting image of her mother, Sloane neatly tucks a rogue bit of mousy brown hair back into its proper place as she wanders through the gardens scanning the immaculately tended rows. She brushes her fingers along the blowsy and leafy greens, saying a warm hello to Penny Ahn, Northern Trade's master gardener.

Five years Maren's junior, Penny was the pantry chef at the restaurant in San Francisco where Maren Winter first became head chef, when she was twenty-seven years old. She partnered with Penny when she started Northern Trade back in 1977, but not as a chef. It was Penny's brilliant gardening mind Maren wanted. It was why Maren had been drawn to those 1,800 acres of abandoned property. She knew Penny would thrive in a sandbox so wild and free. And she was right. The way

Penny saw food was . . . different. A parsnip wasn't just one ingredient; it was fifteen components and thirty different taste profiles, and after ten years, what would it be then, and what if you pickled it and added it to this or that—what would happen? A lot of what Northern Trade had become known for in the forty-five years since it opened came down to Penny's ability to turn Maren's—and now Athena's—ideas into reality, seed by seed, jar by jar, garden row by garden row.

Nine years ago, Penny Ahn pitched *From Penny's Garden*, her very own gardening show, to the local public television station. After several rounds of development, they picked the show up straight to series. And since then, her popularity has grown exponentially, through two bestselling gardening books, a major brand deal, and a thriving speaker series in the sustainability space.

As Penny worked to grow her reputation beyond the greenhouses of Northern Trade, she began training her only child, Hana, in earnest, preparing them to take over as head gardener. There was never any doubt that Hana Ahn loved gardening as much as their mother—their little ladybug watering can was a staple around the Northern Trade grounds throughout their childhood. Even so, Penny and her husband, Yunho—a professor at Stanford University—made sure that Hana went to college, interned at a variety of businesses, and even took a gap year traveling and seeing the world, from which all they brought back was a little ladybug watering can tattoo and the resolve to follow in their mother's gardening footsteps.

Passing on her gardening expertise was one thing, but when Penny announced that Hana would also be inheriting her seat on the Winter Group's eight-seat board of directors, it sent a very clear message: Penny Ahn was ready to start growing her own empire.

The first week Hana apprenticed, they simply referred to Sloane as "the scary, pointy one," telling their mother that both Sloane's physical features and personality felt almost serrated. Which was when Penny delicately reminded Hana that without Sloane's advocacy and relentless championing of the now-thriving Northern Trade internship program, Hana would be quite without a regular salary, on-the-job training, and full benefits.

Unfortunately, Hana Ahn isn't the first person to be oblivious to Sloane's myriad accomplishments. And while one would expect such naivete from a twentysomething kid, Sloane's own mother seems to subscribe to the same breezy erasures. Forever envious of how plainly conspicuous Athena's skill and talents are, Sloane Winter comforts herself with the knowledge that, at least in this family, staying in the shadows could be a good thing. But just once she'd like to know what the spotlight feels like, rather than admiring it from afar.

Penny and Hana follow Sloane past the field of onggi semiburied in the fertile Northern Trade soil. Row after row of patinaed, dark-brown earthenware containers lusciously filled with Penny's legendary kimchi. Sloane steps into the greenhouse, where she immediately eyes the raised beds that hold her mother's signature green orchids. It was Sloane who gave Maren Winter her first green orchid for Mother's Day more than thirty years ago. Maren loved it so much, she commandeered the plant without ever acknowledging Sloane's role in its illustrious origins. Sloane is hoping she might be able to jog her memory.

"I want them all for tonight's party. Every last one," Sloane says, her voice breathless with possibilities.

Penny nods but shares a look of deep concern with Hana. "But they take so long to rebloom. I'm sure Maren wouldn't want the entire crop to be decimated for one night. How about—"

"Oh, it's a celebration! Let's just go for it!" Sloane says in an overexcited voice so desperate, Hana is compelled to look away by sheer awkward force. Sloane will accidentally overhear Hana talking to the other interns later about this very interaction. She won't be able to hear much, but the words *She's just so cringe* seem to echo through the hills above Tomales Bay with particular clarity.

"Sloane—" Penny starts, trying to find a gentle way to pull her back from the edge.

"I think she'll like them. Don't you think she'll like them?" Sloane asks, her face barely masking the yearning that spills off her. In that moment, Penny sees the little girl she's known for forty-one years, along with a lengthy montage riddled with far too many unsuccessful attempts to reason with Sloane when it comes to her mother.

"I think she'll like them, but—"

"Great! Then we agree!" Sloane blurts out before Penny can add her pleas for restraint. Penny nods, her shoulders slumping forward as her heart crumples like a soda can in her chest.

As Penny watches Hana nervously shift a heavy basket laden with today's crop back and forth, Sloane loses herself in the vision of what tonight's centerpieces should signify as they trace down the New Year's Eve communal table. Her voice grows louder and louder as she unspools her verbal manifesto to Penny and Hana: tonight's arrangements "should draw a collective gasp from the crowd for the awe-inspiring future of the Winter Group," and everything "should be undeniable, impressive, and show Maren the ongoing vitality of the brand." In the end, she says, one should feel "as though this is just the beginning of the Winter renaissance and that the Winter Group is in safe hands with the next generation." As Sloane hurries back up to the restaurant, Penny turns to Hana and tells them to hide ten of the green orchids in the back of the greenhouse.

Just as Sloane is about to head into the restaurant, she pauses as she sees their oyster vendor's little blue pickup truck crest over the south hill. Sloane looks toward the restaurant, counting down to when Athena will stride out to inspect the delivery herself. Instead, she spies her two younger sisters talking quietly outside the kitchen. Immediately suspicious, Sloane walks over to them.

Jules will tell Richard later that she *"felt a dark presence"* and that when she turned to investigate, she saw her eldest sister marching toward her. Both Jules and Richard will break out in hysterics mimicking Sloane's famous militaristic charge of a walk back and forth on the deck of their Stinson Beach home. As they do so, neither will admit that the time they seem to be the most besotted with each other is when they're eviscerating someone together.

As Sloane approaches, her sisters step back, leaving a space for her to comfortably settle into their conversation. To the untrained eye, this looks like sisterly affection and the almost cosmic understanding one sibling has for the space the other takes up in their life. But everyone who knows the Winter sisters will see that this is more about the scientific phenomenon where magnets with like poles repel each other rather than attract.

"The oysters are here," Sloane says, gesturing over her shoulder to the idling pickup truck in the far background. As she does so, the poissonier rushes past the Winter Sisters, having already been directed by Athena to check the oysters in her absence.

Athena just stares at Sloane. "Oh, is that what that is?" she asks.

It doesn't last more than a second, but within that impossibly small moment, there is a negotiation at the speed of light between Athena and Sloane about how messy this exchange is going to get. With sisters, every conversation—no matter how insignificant—has the capacity to contain all the elements of a yearslong, silently held grudge that'll be revealed only when it is brought up along with all the others in a reckoning that will rival world wars.

"So where are we on these preparations?" Sloane asks, recalibrating her voice to send a clear message that she, unlike them, must rise above these petty sisterly squabbles now that she could be on the cusp of being the new head of the Winter Group.

Athena crosses her arms across her chest and laughs. "Is that your big-girl voice?"

"What? No," Sloane says, hating that that was, in fact, her big-girl voice.

"Well, where we are is that Athena here has decided to make pork chops for tonight's festivities instead of Mom's pork belly," Jules says.

"No, you are *not*," Sloane blurts out, her voice cracking. Both Jules and Athena look over at her.

Athena takes a deep breath. "A simply prepared pork chop better highlights the pig I raised and the meat that doesn't need Mom's super-eighties, low-cal-obsessed pork belly with—" She can barely bring herself to finish the sentence. "With sun-dried tomatoes, for Chrissakes."

"Mom wrote on her menu for tonight that she wanted to serve the pork belly. You will not ruin this night for me . . . her. Us." Sloane stumbles. Jules laughs.

"This isn't some personal vendetta," Athena says. "This is about which dish will taste best for the specific guests who are eating in our restaurant tonight. As head chef, shouldn't that be my priority?"

Sloane yearns for the old days when she could pull Athena's hair and pin her down until she agreed to do it her way. Oh, to be young again.

"You have no idea how much like her you are, do you?" Jules asks, looking down at her phone. Jules knows this will hurt her youngest sister and looks up just in time to see her gut punch of a comment register on Athena's face. Athena falls quiet, hating that Jules somehow always knows exactly how to neutralize her.

Jules forces a musing smile as she scrolls through the restaurant's social media, but as she absentmindedly blocks and reports a man who commented More like Northern Fade lol on her newest Northern Trade post, she grows more and more agitated. Athena has long been Maren's favorite, and their connection has been the one thing Jules couldn't manipulate or charm her way into—and not having it has grown from a harmless, adolescent grievance to an overripe, exquisitely tender obsession.

"You can't do this. There must be a way to fix it. I can't have this happen tonight of all—"

"Oh my god, you're so pathetic," Athena says, interrupting Sloane.

"I'm pathetic because I want our mother's New Year's Eve party to be perfect?"

"No, you're pathetic because you think 'our mother's New Year's Eve party' has anything to do with you. You've got it in your head that tonight is an elaborate backdrop for some top-secret retirement announcement—"

"And spontaneous coronation . . . of only you, apparently," Jules adds, hitting the word "you" with prolonged and sneering vocal fry. Sloane shoots her that classic sister look of, *Wait, I thought you and I were ganging up on Athena, not you and she ganging up on me?* Jules shrugs and looks back down at her phone with a breezy smile. Sloane is just about to speak, but Athena cuts in.

"Mom's not handing anything over to you," Athena says. Jules points to her and nods in agreement.

Rather than exploring her own misplaced rage, Sloane harnesses it to shatter Athena and Jules's fragile—and wildly inconvenient—temporary alliance. "Yeah, well . . . she's not handing anything over to you either," she says to Athena.

Jules Winter clocks that no one feels the burning need to clarify that their mother won't be bequeathing any part of the Winter Group's vast holdings to her.

"I know. I—" Athena sputters.

"Do you? But aren't you the one who's made the entire party's main dish about you, or am I missing something?" Sloane asks, barely containing her anger.

"No, it's about the pig," Athena says.

"No, it's about you," Sloane says.

"There was a really easy pig joke there, and I can*not* believe no one said it," Jules says.

"You always liked low-hanging fruit," Athena says.

"Is that a dig at my husband?" Jules asks. Sloane smiles.

"No, but that's amazing that you think it is," Athena says, laughing.

"God, I hate you sometimes," Jules says, her voice definitively no longer breezy.

"Love you, too," Athena says.

Sloane is first to hear the whine of that tinny snare drum of an engine as it climbs the gravel road leading to Northern Trade's entrance. As the color drains from her face, Jules and Athena grow quiet as they, too, see that ancient gray Land Rover come to a stop in front of the dual firepits.

Maren Winter has arrived. And she's brought a guest.

CHAPTER TWO

As the grinding metal of the old Land Rover's doors opening and closing reverberates throughout the hills and valleys of the Northern Trade grounds, it's as if some unseen puppeteer has pulled the strings taut on each of the Winter sisters, unfurling them to full attention. One can only marvel at how quickly three women so at odds moments before are now completely unified in their submission. Until a wide smile breaks across Jules's face.

"What are you smiling about?" Sloane asks.

"Nothing good," Athena says, fighting the urge to duck into the kitchen before her mother sees her. She knows the choice to make pork chops was the right one, but she also knows her mom won't see it that way. As doubt begins to bloom in the pit of her stomach, Athena reminds herself that she's doing this to protect her mother's legacy by evolving some of her more dated recipes. It's the only way Northern Trade remains relevant—the only way Maren Winter remains relevant. But what Athena can't yet admit is that it's also the only way she herself remains relevant.

"Between Sloane's retirement conspiracy theories and Athena explaining the pork chop thing, it's like Christmas morning, you know?" Jules beams, trying to pull back some of the power she previously lost.

"Like the Christmas morning you ate all your stocking candy and threw up before Mom served her World-Famous Breakfast and she made you eat it anyway? Like that kind of Christmas morning?" Athena asks.

"Haven't been able to eat a candy cane since," Jules says with a sigh.

"What a trial life must be for you," Athena says.

As Maren hops out of her car and continues to make idle conversation with her as-yet-unknown guest, the Winter sisters' chronic bickering is quickly eclipsed by their mutual and pressing need to analyze Maren's echoing speech patterns.

The sisters had to master the ability to instantaneously assess their mother's mood based solely on the far-off tonal inflections and timbre of her voice. Excelling at such a skill means they're able to, by the time they come face-to-face, transform into whichever version of themselves is most agreeable to the now-determined parental state of mind.

Just then, the three women are interrupted as Penny and Hana come thundering up the gravel path pushing their almost Paleolithic-looking garden cart. The cart is overrun with every last—*minus ten*—green orchid from the greenhouse, just as Sloane commanded.

Maren's voice stops abruptly.

Athena and Jules's faces are creased with confusion, and then they see Sloane. They know that look. The color draining from her face, the panic to find someone to blame, and the paralyzing terror as their mother gets closer and closer to unraveling the whole thing and, moreover, her singular role in it.

"Is this that 'more leadership opportunities' thing?" Athena asks in a rare moment of kinship. Sloane nods, allowing Athena's question to begrudgingly pass through all her defenses. Her face softens and her shoulders slump, and with a long exhale, all she can manage is the unfiltered, dangerous truth.

"I just wanted her to see—" Sloane cuts herself off before finishing her sentence. Instead, she inhales sharply, gulping the unsaid word deeper still.

Both Athena and Jules look away, unable to bear witness to the desperate yearning they loathe yet recognize in themselves.

Maren strides over to where her daughters stand, a young woman at her side. Penny and Hana come to a clamorous halt at the top of the gravel road. It's imperceptible, but somehow all six women understand that they must now wait. Whatever comes next is up to Maren Winter.

Maren takes her time inspecting the scene unfolding before her. Sloane's slumped shoulders. The cart full of green orchids. The slightly concerned look on Penny's face, her salt-and-pepper hair wafting in the wind as she tucks her hands into the bib of her linen overalls, kicking at the gravel with her hot-pink clogs. As the Northern California winter wind picks up, Maren zips up her well-worn black puffer vest and secures her willfully ageless mousy brown hair. Unhurried, and seemingly unmoved by the expanding silence, Maren takes off the glasses she refuses to admit are bifocals and tucks them into the pocket of her vest; her worn-in Tretorn sneakers gnash into the gravel beneath her feet. Her face is unreadable. The Winter sisters brace themselves. Finally—

"Lola Tadese, these are my three daughters, Sloane, Julienne, and Athena." Lola greets each of the Winter sisters. "Lola is from the *San Francisco Chronicle* and is writing a retrospective about me in the run-up to the Banquet's Lifetime Achievement Award ceremony."

The Banquet Conference started in the 1980s as a yearly culinary and gardening conference held just outside Oxford. But over the years it expanded into a thriving foundation, multiple schools, and an awards ceremony that has celebrated the restaurant world's best and brightest. And this year, the most best and the most bright is Maren Winter.

Lola's eyes slide over to Maren in that subtle yet intentional journalistic way that signals she's observed something her subject is oblivious to but that is both dangerously off the cuff and defining.

Lola pulls a notepad from the leather messenger bag slung across her body and slides her nub of a pencil out of the pad's spiral. Her perfectly tended vintage look is so out of reach, it's almost off-putting. From the tortoiseshell cat-eye prescription glasses to the retro woven houndstooth, double-breasted coat, all the way to the extremely rare Hermès scarf tied loosely around her swept-up locs. It's an outfit that is unafraid of being out of style simply because the person wearing it is in her youthful prime and is clearly setting a trend. Not desperately clinging to an old one.

"I'm so pleased this worked out," Jules says, making sure everyone is aware that this interview was her doing. She enthusiastically reaches across to shake Lola's hand—to really hammer their "bond" home—but is met instead by Lola's engaged, furious scribbling. So Jules must wait.

And wait.

And wait—her extended hand hanging perilously in the air between them for an interminable amount of time.

"That's where I recognized you," Hana blurts. Everyone turns. Jules takes this opportunity to lower her hand, thinking no one will notice. Everyone does.

"I'm sorry?" Lola asks, finally glancing up from her notebook and threading the pencil through the worn spiral without looking.

"You're *Lola Tadese*. Lola Tadese," Hana repeats adoringly. This does nothing to clarify the situation. Lola waits. At barely twenty-seven years old, Hana Ahn is every person over forty's worst nightmare: unabashedly confident and full of wonder, dangerously capable, and able to get out of bed in the morning without grumbling about back pain. "You wrote that great article on the rise of the pop-up. She talks about you in it, Athena!" Athena does not look at Lola, and Lola does not look at Athena. Maren, however, studies them both. "Congratulations on the Pulitzer, by the way."

"Thank you," Lola says. Before Hana can continue, Maren steps forward and, using her decades of experience in hospitality, elegantly guides the conversation back to the original topic: herself.

"And this is Hana's mother, Northern Trade's master gardener and my oldest friend, Penny Ahn. Back in the seventies, Penny and I were known for throwing the best underground dinner parties in the city from our tiny kitchen on Arguello. We made ten-course meals for anyone who could pay five dollars, as long as they helped clean up." Maren waits for the laugh this line always gets. Lola reluctantly obliges. Maren continues, "After one particularly successful dinner party, Penny and I walked over to Golden Gate Park, sat on the smallest blanket in the entire world, and sketched out a dream on the back of a utility bill envelope. We dreamed of a place with a crackling fireplace, creaky wooden floors, and fresh, good food made for hungry people who needed a warm place to sit. A place where the kitchen was filled with good and talented people, rather than temperamental bad-boy geniuses who usually hazed and bullied people like us." Maren gestures around at the idyllic empire she's created as she finally concludes her well-trod origin story, which everyone but Lola knows by heart.

"My mother and I watch *From Penny's Garden* religiously. We're huge fans. Mom even bought a pair of your iconic hot-pink clogs," Lola says to Penny.

"That's lovely to hear. Thank you," Penny says. Lola smiles.

But as they greet one another warmly, Maren Winter struggles to navigate a moment not centered on her. She settles in next to Penny, and her fingers curl around the lip of the garden cart, her knuckles whitening.

"And those are your signature green orchids, if I'm not mistaken?" Lola asks, eyeing the cart. "Getting ready for tonight's festivities?" As Maren answers Lola's seemingly harmless question, Sloane Winter realizes she is holding her breath, the pressure building in her chest while her shoulders inch higher and higher.

"Yes, we love to see all the orchids in the beautiful winter light and choose"—Maren's fingers deftly meander through the tiny forest of orchids as she speaks, her focus mimicking that of a high-powered camera lens, zooming in and out on each of the orchids' flaws—"only the very best." She handpicks two green orchids, handing each one to Sloane as it makes the cut.

"Thank you. These are beautiful," Sloane says, relieved that Lola's presence has pushed Maren to remain civil. Finally exhaling, Sloane takes the two perfect green orchids in each hand, trying to keep the dirty pots away from her perfect snowy-white cashmere shawl. But as Sloane is about to delicately hand the two orchids back to Hana, Maren glides back over to the garden cart and chooses a third flawless green orchid.

Athena's eyes lock on the third orchid, as do Jules's. Lola asks Hana and Penny the origins of the orchids, and their animated conversation, along with the hushed sound of wind whipping and wandering through the surrounding trees, forms an idyllic backdrop to the slow-motion horror of what comes next.

Maren strolls over to Sloane with the third perfect orchid, still engaging with Lola, Hana, and Penny, reminiscing about Northern Trade's humble beginnings. Midsentence, Maren dangles the third orchid out to Sloane, her wrist limp with a warning that she will drop it if Sloane doesn't find a way to hold it. Athena hitches forward, unable to keep herself from trying to step in and take the orchid. But the gut punch of a look Sloane and her mother give her as she does stops Athena in her tracks. While she's quite familiar with Maren's displeasure at her chronic insubordination, it's Sloane's unspoken but desperate plea to let her take this bullet that causes Athena to slink back to where she was. Athena looks down at the ground, shame and rage coating the inside of her brain like honey.

Maren's gaze slides over to Jules, preemptively questioning whether she, too, wants to attempt something remarkably stupid. The memory of her hand hanging in the air for a millennium still thick in her throat, Jules smiles at her mother, casually flipping her long golden hair as she laughs way too hard at something Lola said in an attempt at seeming aggressively obedient. In the fading laughter, Jules chokes down the shame—sucking on it like a lime after a tequila shot.

Steeling herself, Sloane winches one of the orchids she's already holding against her body, balancing the dirty pot tight against her, and reaches for the third orchid with her free hand.

"Thank you," Sloane says once again, the dirt staining her shawl.

"You're welcome," Maren coos as she settles back in next to a furiously scribbling Lola.

To the untrained eye, what transpired could be written off as yet another example of a wealthy person not valuing her possessions, the dirt on Sloane's expensive shawl a mere inconvenience, for Sloane must surely have a closet full of cashmere. But Lola is not an untrained eye. And while she can't yet fully grasp the scope of what she has witnessed, she understands, at that innate human level, that something is off. In her notes she simply writes "the pot thing" and underlines it twice.

Penny and Hana return to the gardens and greenhouses with their cart full of Maren's signature green orchids, as Maren suggests a brief walking tour of the extensive Northern Trade grounds to Lola. Sloane, Jules, and Athena fall in line, ready to be among the royal subjects of whom Maren Winter takes pride of ownership. It's only Athena who catches that the only notes Lola takes during this tour are when Maren explains how each of her daughters' names is a reflection of Maren's own life: Sloane for Maren's maiden name; Julienne for the culinary knife skill, the first Maren learned that made her want to be a chef; and Athena for the strength and wisdom Maren needed to call on as her fame grew. What Athena doesn't know is that Lola Tadese scribbles something else down that crisp winter afternoon: *Where was the father in all this?*

Finally, the group circles back to the dual firepits at Northern Trade's entrance and Maren excuses herself to greet Aunt Josephine, who's just arrived.

Josephine Winter is not anyone's real aunt. She's the older stepsister of Maren Winter's dearly departed ex-husband. An ex-husband who inconveniently left all his shares—and his seat on the Winter Group's board of directors—to his now eighty-seven-year-old corn husk of a sorta-sibling when he passed away from a heart attack thirty-four years ago. The fact that he didn't leave his shares and seat to his children, or even Maren herself, was disappointing but not surprising. Bennett Winter was better known around the Northern Trade grounds as "the mouse that roared." A small man with a fragile ego who couldn't stand living in the shadow of his successful wife. When Maren heard of Bennett's passing, there was a brief unguarded moment when she was beyond relieved that she wouldn't have to spend her life constantly negotiating and apologizing for her bigness. It was as if Bennett's last breath marked the moment Maren Winter finally stepped into her full power.

Married in 1981, Maren Sloane was hesitant about taking Bennett's last name. Penny argues that this was the moment things turned. Maren disagrees. She says things went south when she agreed to marry some-one she hated. But Bennett was a successful attorney with whom Maren had gone to UC Berkeley back in the day. And she thought getting married to him would stop the newspapers and food critics from calling her "a workaholic still searching for The One" or "a single woman who gloomily makes her living cooking expensive dinners for happy couples," or her personal favorite: "an aging home cook who should be focusing on starting a family of her own."

Maren Winter was thirty years old when these articles were published.

Maren and Bennett divorced after five years, when Athena was just one week old. It was Maren who asked for the split. The girls never really knew their dad and know Aunt Josephine only through her wild card meanderings on their board of directors and the haunting tea par-ties she used to invite them to. Tea parties that consisted of staggeringly old black tea that tasted like the lukewarm water that dribbles out of an overheated garden hose, watery cucumber sandwiches on pita bread (fewer calories!), and an ancient King Charles spaniel named Brandy who had a raging—and largely ignored—incontinence problem.

Needless to say, no one rushes over to join Maren in greeting the dinner party's pseudo-familial guest.

Sloane, having taken her filthy shawl off and draped it over her arm, is shivering so violently from the cold that she seeks solace in the heat of the dual firepits. Seeing both Sloane's and Maren's absence as a lucky break, Jules sidles over next to Lola.

"I'm so excited you decided to accept my invitation to join us for tonight's festivities," Jules says, always looking for an opportunity to be not only seen but seen in exactly the way in which she's preordained.

Behind them, another car appears over the hill, and from it bolt Sloane's three children and her wife, Lærke. The little ones run to the restaurant, as the staff usually have candy for them, and Lærke rushes over to find her tiny bird of a wife huddled over a fire like some kind of cavewoman. She immediately takes off her coat and places it around Sloane's shaking shoulders.

"Yes, I'm very much looking forward to it, thank you," Lola says, offering a surgically polite answer. The look that Lola's response earns from Jules is one of game recognizing game. Never one to sit back on her Machiavellian laurels, Jules pivots to another tactic.

"I was such a fan of your 'rise of the pop-up' article, Lola. It's very exciting to have you here. Once again, I'm over the moon you responded to my email . . . *emails*, really," Jules says, looping her arm through Athena's, in a move that's designed more to send a clear message of happy families to Lola than the result of any sort of real affection for her younger sister.

"It was actually Athena's pop-up that inspired it—inspired *me*. Her Southern Trade offerings set the bar for how fine-dining restaurants should have handled the pandemic. I don't know what you did to those hot dogs, but . . . something about them—" Lola cuts herself off, realizing the trauma from those dark years is far from resolved. As the emotion grabs and pulls at her throat, she debates whether to continue, but Athena Winter and those stupid hot dogs got her through a really hard time. "You just knew what people needed."

"If ever there were a time for a good, cheap hot dog and a can of beer," Athena says, allowing a small, proud smile. "Or three."

Lola barks out a laugh. "Between your hot dogs, Rafael Luna's fish sandwich, and Jenn Nishimura's doughnut stands, the entire Bay Area was super well fed during a ridiculously hard couple of years. I think the article was me wanting to say thank you," she says, listing the other two fine-dining chefs featured in her article.

At the beginning of 2020, fellow superstar chef Jenn Nishimura quickly pivoted away from Hills and Valleys, her impossible-to-get-into, three-Michelin-Starred modern Japanese kaiseki restaurant, and opened up little doughnut stands—adorably called Mounds—all over the city. Soon enough the students at SFSU had developed an app documenting which stands had which flavors, with the stand located just outside her restaurant in the Castro the most popular, as that was where Jenn often featured her signature hibiscus tea cream-filled doughnuts. Lola described the stands in the article as "magical points on a map that gave you the strength to keep going."

Over in Sausalito, Chef Rafael Luna pared back Lobo, his brand-new premium seafood restaurant, to only takeout, but within weeks, the Pobrecito—Rafael's riff on a po'boy—became the main draw. Soon enough, he opened a walk-up window that sold the now-infamous sandwich, along with a cocktail kit served in a red Solo cup Rafael simply named the Te Amo—which delivered tenfold on its promise to have you slurring your declarations of everlasting love for those brave enough to order it. Lola wrote that Rafael's food was so embracing it could, "however briefly, transport you beyond the unprecedented times we've been tasked with surviving and into the warm kitchen of someone who loves you."

But even among those greats, it was Athena's Southern Trade that got the most attention. A simple menu that included three versions of Athena's original-recipe hot dogs, homemade rosemary potato chips served in a brown paper bag slick with grease, and icy-cold cans of handcrafted beer from Hella Coastal, a local brewery based in nearby Oakland. The lunch special—which Athena simply called the Hangry—could get you a hot dog, a bag of chips, and a can of beer for a flat five dollars, a price Athena chose as an homage to the cost of Maren and Penny's infamous underground dinners on Arguello way back in the '70s.

In the beginning, it was just Athena holed up in a glorified Airstream in downtown Petaluma of all places, sweating her days away and coming home smelling of rosemary. As the months—and years—passed, one glorified Airstream turned into two, then three—until little

Southern Trade Airstreams were cropping up as far down as Palo Alto. And once the tech bros and Stanford student body got a hold of those hot dogs, Southern Trade officially became a full-blown viral moment, and Athena's original hot dog recipe was hidden away, kept under strict lock and key.

Because of the whole venture, it was this hot dog recipe that most intrigued Sloane. As the popularity of Southern Trade grew, she saw an opportunity in mass marketing the hot dog. It's an idea that's at the top of her list of things to do once she gets "more leadership opportunities."

"Just being mentioned alongside those two is a privilege, so thank you, but I'm definitely grateful to finally be back where I belong," Athena says, looking back at the Northern Trade kitchen and her awaiting stack of pork chops.

"Speaking of," Jules cuts in before Athena can continue. "Rafael Luna is—"

"What's this about Rafael Luna?" Maren asks, rejoining the conversation along with Sloane, still with her wife's topcoat perched on her shoulders.

"Oh, we were talking about Lola's pop-up article, so I was telling Lola that Rafael Luna will actually be joining us tonight." Jules's voice crackles with excitement.

Maren's mouth tenses in a thunderous flat line. Athena and Sloane freeze—pausing to ensure that they've properly arranged their faces as it becomes clear that while Jules has talked of nothing but the famous guests she's added to tonight's festivities to Athena and Sloane, somehow she has failed to run these new attendees by her mom.

Maren remains unreadable, nodding and smiling along with Lola and Jules, going back and forth at how cool it is that *the* Rafael Luna will be in attendance tonight, but Athena and Sloane know their sister. Her bright stripe of a smile is tight. She doesn't seem to know what to do with her arms all of a sudden. And every two seconds her ice-blue eyes flick over to Maren as if she's standing on a subway platform and the train is running late. The situation builds to a jittery climax as Jules barks out a laugh so volcanic that its echoes can be heard throughout all 1,800 acres of the Northern Trade grounds.

"Now, why don't we get you inside with something hot to drink? Sloane, can you see that Lola is taken care of?" Maren asks, guiding them toward the restaurant's entrance. Sloane tries to hide the look of sheer relief as she walks away.

Once they're out of earshot, Jules pulls out her phone and begins nervously talking as she scrolls through her contacts. "I reached out to Jenn Nishimura and Rafael Luna because they were both mentioned in Lola's article, along with Athena. Jenn was in Hawaii on vacation, but—" Jules immediately stops talking as Maren slides her gaze over to her middle daughter. Her half-masted, dark-brown eyes bore into her. Having learned her lesson, Athena does nothing.

"Let me walk through a few details in order to better understand. You invited someone I don't know to my New Year's Eve party without asking?" Maren asks Jules.

"It's Rafael Luna," Jules says, biting the inside of her cheek.

"Jules, I need you to focus. Did you invite someone I don't know to my New Year's Eve party without asking?" Maren asks. Her voice softens and melts as she lovingly brushes a lock of blonde hair off Jules's cherubic face.

"Yes." Jules looks down at the ground.

"What was a solution I offered to remedy this impulsive behavior?" Maren asks. Jules's face pales as she looks back up at her mom.

"That I should check with you before making decisions because I am not credible when it comes to my choices." Jules's voice is soft and robotic.

"And did you do that?" Maren asks.

"No," Jules says.

Maren waits.

"I'm sorry," Jules adds, now looking back down at the ground.

Silence.

"I was wrong." Jules's voice is barely a whisper.

A benevolent smile spreads across Maren's face. "Well, we will welcome Mr. . . ." She trails off.

"Luna," Jules finishes.

"Uninviting him now would appear impolite."

"Thank you for—"

"You're welcome," Maren says, cutting her off. As Jules hurries away, Athena says her quick and quiet goodbyes and strategically turns toward the kitchen. Maren stops her with a single sentence.

"Now let's talk about tonight's menu."

CHAPTER THREE

Maren unzips her puffer vest and fishes around the inside pocket while Athena waits. The birdsong, the whispering leaves, and the hurried feet digging into loose gravel fade into the background, and Athena begins to hear only her own echoing, slow breath.

Athena quickly reviews her planned rebuttals to any possible argument her mother could make about the pork chops. From the practical to the emotional, she lists and prioritizes a series of reasons and explanations, finally ending with the rip cord of "apologize and beg for forgiveness." But deep down she's holding out hope that one of these hard conversations with her mother will be welcomed and impactful for a change. Just *maybe* a long-buried fear or a rare and vulnerable moment of candor will bloom rather than fester. Just maybe today will be the day they can connect through food, rather than compete.

Athena knows the pork chop is the right thing to serve tonight, but that her decision is legitimately valid doesn't mean it's correct. Maren's pork belly was great. The dish was cutting edge . . . *in the 1980s.* And with Lola Tadese and Rafael Luna in attendance for tonight's dinner, there's no way Athena is letting her mother serve that dish.

When Athena first started tweaking her mom's recipes five years ago, she argued that the restaurant was a living and evolving organism and that her modifications and additions to the menu could never rewrite Maren Winter's award-winning stack of cookbooks or erase the truly staggering number of magazine articles or TV show guest appearances that Maren has done.

But as Athena's new menu items started to eclipse Maren's, the seeds of paranoia began to take root deep in the fertile ground of Maren's own creative stagnation. She was proud of her daughter in the beginning, but with every swapped-out dish, she couldn't stop feeling as though she, too, were being swapped out. And by the time Athena—and *her* menu—had earned Northern Trade its sought-after second Michelin Star, a slithering distrust began actively whispering in Maren's ear, quite without her permission.

In other words, Maren feared Athena Winter was a chip off the old block.

Maren pulls a folded piece of yellow legal paper from the inside pocket of her puffer vest, along with a stack of receipts. The abrupt zzzzzip brings Athena back to reality. Writing on legal pads is the lone habit Maren retained from her early pre-law days at UC Berkeley. That and her deep and abiding love for winning an argument.

Athena braces herself as Maren unfolds the piece of paper. Her entire fate rests on whether the words "pork belly" are somewhere on that list.

"Did you get my message about the Cara Cara oranges?" Maren asks, squinting down at the sheet of paper filled with her scribbled notes.

"We're doing your bone marrow pudding for the first dessert course, so Emile pitched adding the Cara Cara to that," Athena says, watching her mother absently search for her glasses. "They're there . . . *here*—" Athena reaches over and pulls the glasses from Maren's vest pocket.

Maren laughs, affectionately pats her youngest daughter's hand, and takes the glasses. "The bone marrow pudding is a great idea. That was one of the first recipes you helped with," she says, putting on her glasses.

"You know I love a pudding." Athena laughs as they walk back toward the entrance of the restaurant.

"You used to love those little chocolate ones that come in the—"

"The little plastic cups," Athena finishes.

"I never understood why your favorite part was—" Maren can't bring herself to say it.

"The skiiiiin," Athena drawls.

"You've been saying it like that your whole life. I'll never forget when your kindergarten teacher called in a panic because you kept crying out for skiiiiin during snack time. If I wasn't an outcast already . . ." Maren trails off, looking back down at her list.

"You're welcome for that," Athena says, trying to force her voice to sound relaxed.

"Oh, the oysters?" Maren asks, getting back to business.

"She got here"—Athena twists her oversize gray G-Shock watch around on her right wrist so she can read the time—"about a half an hour ago." Athena is immediately astounded to learn how long she's been out of her kitchen. What was supposed to be one quick annoying chat with Jules has turned into several quick annoying chats with every member of her family. But Athena knows from experience that if she puts in the time now, she'll earn her freedom for the rest of the day. Just ten more minutes accompanying Maren on her rounds, being the right balance of subservient and competent, means Athena can fly under the radar until well after service.

"We're serving the oysters first?" Maren asks.

"Roe first, then the kimchi ceviche dish, the halibut, and *then* the grilled oyster," Athena says. Maren nods, deftly checking items off one by one.

"I thought we were doing the chowder?" Maren asks, looking up at Athena.

Athena takes a deep inhale before she answers. "The halibut was so good I wanted to find something to better show it off." Maren is quiet. "We're doing the dish from your 2003 fish season. Grilled with the coriander and—"

"The yogurt sauce, right. Okay, that works . . . That'll do," Maren says, pulling up a recipe from almost twenty years ago as if she made it yesterday. "Again, confirm before you change the menu." Maren looks back up at Athena and waits for her assent.

"Yep," Athena says, crossing her arms across her chest. She brings her hand up to cover her mouth, in a futile attempt to both physically protect herself and also create at least one obstacle between her building uneasiness and her mother's big night. Athena doesn't mention that she tweaked the halibut recipe as well.

Maren and Athena step inside the foyer, moving quickly across its tiled floor before entering the main dining room together. The loud creak from the wide planks of original quartersawn oak announces their presence. The bustling staff turns around to see Athena and Maren deep in conversation. Their brief and stuttering acknowledgment looks as though there's been a glitch in time and space, everyone frozen in unison for one brief millisecond before getting back to the work at hand.

Maren scans the seven individual wooden tables that now snake down the center of the Northern Trade main dining room and eyes the three perfect green orchids that stand proud sentry. She sees the sommelier and the front of house manager in the corner going over tonight's service and approaches the pair, Athena still in deferential tow.

"Odette, how are we looking for tonight?" Maren asks.

Odette Bankolé has been Northern Trade's sommelier for more than twenty years and even won the James Beard Award for Outstanding Wine Program. The next year Athena would go on to win the Emerging Chef award. Maren did not attend the ceremony but had Jules post heartfelt congratulations on all Northern Trade socials that Maren Winter was over the moon and so proud that Athena was continuing on with "the great Winter tradition" and then posted a photo from the year that Maren won the far more coveted Outstanding Chef award.

"Good. Very good," Odette says, handing Maren her wine list for that evening's festivities. Maren scans the list as everyone waits. Once satisfied, Maren turns her attention to Eleanor Zhou, the front of house manager.

"Eleanor, to confirm—did Jules speak to you about Rafael Luna attending tonight's dinner?" Maren asks. Eleanor's stylish, spiky pixie cut has lulled several unsuspecting Northern Trade employees into thinking they, too, can pull off the hairstyle. The monthslong, awkward growing-out phase has turned into almost a badge of honor around the restaurant.

"Yes, Chef, she did, and I've confirmed both. Did you have a preference as to where they should be seated?" Eleanor asks.

"Both? I'm confused," Maren says, her voice deceptively calm.

"Rafael Luna is bringing a guest, Chef. I can—" But before Eleanor can continue, Jules bursts into the main dining room along with Sloane and Lærke's three kids, all tangled up in a game of freeze tag.

"Julienne, maybe you can clear this up for us," Maren says. Her use of Jules's full name sends a chill through the room. Even the three little kids know to take a step back from Jules out of sheer self-preservation. Jules's entire being deflates as she unravels herself from the game and joins the larger group.

As Jules walks over, Athena's gaze flicks over to Lola Tadese, who is sitting quietly in one of the two black Crosshatch chairs facing the main dining room's fireplace. She watches as Lola sets her mug on the live-edge driftwood coffee table, picks up her notebook, and slides the pencil from the spiral. Lærke and Sloane walk back into the restaurant from just behind Lola. Lærke's arm is tenderly looped around her wife's waist, the soiled cashmere shawl nowhere to be seen. It's clear Sloane has been crying.

Lærke's severe gray bob should feel intimidating, but her overarching goodness alters any room's climate—even one overrun with Winters. Sloane met Lærke when she dined alone at Northern Trade more than ten years ago. It was back when Sloane was the front of house manager and hadn't taken over the general manager job yet. After an entire evening of truly adorable flirting, Lærke slipped Sloane a note—along with her room number at the inn—that she would "love to talk more." Two months later, Northern Trade began using Lærke's ceramics, and three months after that Sloane moved out of her studio on the Northern Trade grounds and into Lærke's artist's loft in Mill Valley. They were married later that year in a beautiful ceremony on the Northern Trade grounds. Their nine-course reception meal—the menu of which is now framed in the kitchen of Lærke and Sloane's home—was designed by none other than Athena Winter. Minnie, Freja, and Krister were born in quick succession.

Athena watches Sloane as it registers on her sister's face what she's walked into. Sloane whispers something to her wife, saying something she clearly does not like. But then Lærke calls to their three children in her native Danish. The children rush to their mothers, Sloane hands the coat back to her wife, and after a quick whispered couple fight for the ages, Lærke and the children say their goodbyes and begrudgingly exit the restaurant. Sloane walks over to the group and stands on the periphery, still trying not to shiver from the cold that has now gone into her bones.

"How can I help?" Jules asks with a sigh.

"Eleanor has informed me that Rafael Luna is bringing a guest. Can you walk me through how this happened?" Maren asks. Jules bites the inside of her cheek.

"Chef Luna has been married over twenty years. I didn't think it polite to not extend an invitation to his wife as well. Especially since it's New Year's Eve," Jules says. Athena clasps her hands tightly behind her back as Jules fumbles with her phone. "His wife is a huge fan of yours, Mom." Jules holds her phone out to Maren. "She even flew down to LA to come to that Now Serving book signing you did." Maren takes the phone and swipes through a series of blurry photos of her sold-out event, images taken from far back in the crowd of a distant Maren Winter, engaging with and bewitching a crowd of hundreds. "Apparently she was unable to get your autograph because the line was too long and is excited to get another opportunity."

Maren hands Jules back her phone. "Okay, that works. Confirm with me next time, please."

Jules nods. "She has a huge following, too, so it really is a win-win," she adds.

Athena checks her watch. She realizes too late that knowing the time only exacerbates her frustration by confirming that she's been out of the kitchen for far too long.

"She's not going to be posting, though, right?" Sloane asks, her voice a polite jab.

"She's verified, Sloane," Jules says, not even looking up from her phone.

"Is that supposed to impress me?" Sloane asks.

"No, to impress you, I would have said she has spreadsheets and filing systems for everything and they're all color coded," Jules says, her voice cruelly dramatic in the most teenager-y way possible. Sloane takes a sharp inhale to respond when Athena cuts in.

"No posts," Athena says.

"Ugh, come on. It'll be good for the restaurant, Teeny." When Athena was first born, Jules couldn't pronounce her name, so instead she started calling her Teeny. It's the last bastion of pure sisterly affection, and Jules wields it like a switchblade. Athena's shoulders lower, and her face softens as she considers Jules's plea. But before she acquiesces (as always), Maren cuts in.

"No posts," Maren says. Everyone turns. "Our New Year's Eve dinner is for friends and family only. I look forward to it every year simply because it's the one time we all get to be ourselves and don't have to be 'on.' So please inform this guest as gracefully as possible that we would be much obliged if she did not post any photos from tonight's event." Maren speaks loudly so the journalist covering tonight's dinner can hear.

Even in her weakened state, Sloane manages a secret, self-satisfied smile just for Jules.

"You know, thinking about it, I actually like this better. Not taking photos is the new taking photos. She'll tell absolutely everyone about what happened here tonight. Can she still bring her cookbook for you to sign?" Jules asks, volleying the secret, self-satisfied smile back to Sloane.

"That should be fine," Maren says.

"I will tell her to be discreet," Jules says. Maren does not respond.

"Chef, if I could circle back. Where were you thinking of having the Lunas seated?" Eleanor asks, finally bringing the conversation back to where it started.

"They'll take Jules's and Richard's seats," Maren says without hesitation. Jules looks up. "You don't mind shifting down to the far end of the table to make way for your guests?"

"Not at all," Jules answers.

"Yes, Chef," Eleanor says, not making eye contact with the snubbed Winter sister before excusing herself.

Lola watches as Athena's irritation builds. She's started scratching tic marks into her notebook every time Athena looks at that giant gray watch of hers. (Four times in the last five minutes alone.) Lola's working theory is that Athena Winter does this when she wants to avoid providing comment on the current conversation. It seems checking her watch both communicates that her busy schedule is pressing and gives her an excuse to avoid the ongoing familial fray with a thoughtful comment or argument due to this clear distraction.

Lola studies the four Winter women as they stand amid the building clamor of the main dining room, untouched in the eye of a storm they've created. They could not be more different, and yet they mirror and move with one another, signaling to everyone that they're family. A subtle hand gesture that perfectly fits the chaotic and charming Jules somehow also works on intense, looming Athena. Maren's cadence of speech as she works her way through the checklist is echoed back as Sloane finishes her mother's sentences. Because while they may see nothing but their own internal familial battles—sister against sister, daughter against mother—to the outside world, it has always been the Winter Women versus Everyone Else.

Athena notices Lola watching as Maren holds court, commanding her troops with ease and confidence, each good little soldier peeling off from the Winter war council with their individual marching orders to prepare for tonight's festivities. And then there's just Maren, her folded-up yellow legal paper that may or may not contain the words "pork belly" and the looming dread that now hangs on Athena like a sodden wool coat.

"I know. You have to get back," Maren says, affectionately jostling Athena's arms loose from their clamped-down position. "We're almost done, sweetie."

Athena nods, her tragic attempt at a breezy smile effectively hiding the deep worry that it'll be all her fault when this temporary fellowship is ruined. "We left off at the halibut," she says, hesitantly moving things along.

"Right, right." Maren scans her list.

"Which goes to the chard and into the flatbread—"

"Served with the liver mousse—"

"Yes, Chef." Athena's knee-jerk formality of calling her mother "Chef" gooses them off autopilot, eliciting a real and actual smile from both.

"Yes, Chef," Maren answers with a wink.

"Then it's the quail, and the pork belly." Maren casually looks up from her list. When Athena doesn't answer in their conversation's exact rhythm, Maren repeats her sentence in an attempt to reboot the cadence and put the discussion firmly back on the rails. "Then it's the quail, and the pork belly."

Caught in a suspended moment between possible annihilation and a stay of execution, Athena freezes. Were she a better, braver person, she'd surely proclaim "pork *chop*," loud and proud, coming clean once and for all. She would argue her case, stand by her decision, and finally take on her mother as an equal.

But today is not that day.

"Yes, Chef," Athena says, her voice cracking under the weight of the lie. She casually nods, attempting a lazy sigh, but the pressure in her chest is taking up too much room in her body for her to get a full breath. Instead, she takes half of a truncated breath and makes everything worse. "Quail and pork belly. Yep." Athena's voice is unrecognizable to her, as all her breath gets compressed into her throat.

"And then we're going right from the pork belly to the bone marrow pudding?" Maren asks, looking at her list and not noticing that her youngest is on the verge of a breakdown.

"Yes," Athena answers, her own trapped breath now almost choking her.

"I'll do my toast there, then. Give guests time to digest before going into the dessert courses. And you'll join us for that," Maren says, scribbling on her folded piece of paper. Athena nods. Silent. Maren scans the main dining room. She takes off her glasses and folds her list back up. There's a split second when Maren tucks her checklist into her front pocket that she thinks Athena had something to say to her. A moment where her youngest daughter took a sharp inhale, only to hold it and then slowly deflate.

"And do you want the entire kitchen staff to join you for the toast as well?" Athena asks, trying to sound as breezy as possible.

"Of course," Maren answers. Athena nods. "Speaking of, I was meaning to grab Odette before tonight's service and pick her brain about the wine we've chosen for next Thursday's Central Trade soft launch."

Athena checks her watch, piecing together the strategic tour her mother has taken her on this afternoon. The gentle hand on Odette's arm, the performative compliments about her pairing for tonight's dinner—all of it in service of being able to sidle up to the impossibly busy, award-winning sommelier and casually demand extra work from her.

And this is not the first time.

Two weeks ago, Maren asked Emile Aguillard, the Northern Trade pastry chef, if he could "help her carry something in from the car." A request that failed to mention that the somethings in question were boxes of pastries Maren was debating carrying in Central Trade. Emile was gone for more than two hours tasting and brainstorming around which local bakery's pastries Maren's brand-new restaurant should carry. He was firmly in the weeds for the rest of the night.

Athena is still wrestling with her ongoing inability to even somewhat delicately suggest to her mother that while the excitement has caused her to spare no expense on the Central Trade building and all its bells and whistles—including a custom-designed Italian glass installation of a single nineteen-foot green orchid with a staggering price tag in the hundreds of thousands—Maren has yet to fully populate this "innovative culinary experience" with anyone, or anything, innovative or even culinary, choosing instead to hire a young staff who are entirely dependent on Maren's guiding hand. Drunk off new plumbing and a kitchen big enough to fit three of Northern Trade's, Maren is finally fixing the things that annoyed her for more than forty years. But from the complete absence of any equal creative culinary voice but her own, it's obvious that collaboration of any kind was just as irritating to Maren Winter as Northern Trade's old circuit breaker that blew every winter.

Maren spots Odette coming down the south staircase with two of Eleanor's waitstaff and says her quick goodbyes to Athena before striding over to the trio with another seemingly harmless request for a "quick chat."

Lola Tadese has tactically positioned herself, hoping that she'll be able to grab Athena as she walks back to the kitchen alone. In a family of people who can't seem to stop giving interviews and telling people their opinions, Athena Winter is the outlier. A culinary wunderkind who's won every award, set every trend, and is always mentioned in every roundup of chefs to watch. But Athena has yet to write a single cookbook of her own or even appear on some cheery morning show gleefully making a dumbed-down Northern Trade dish along with the overly-tanned-capped-teeth hosts.

In a world of people trying to be seen, Athena Winter remains a notorious recluse who rarely leaves her kitchen, lives on the Northern Trade grounds in the old studio apartment Sloane vacated years ago, and slips in and out of local Bay Area restaurants during either off-hours or peak hours—whichever will provide her with the most anonymity. When Athena is approached about interviews, public speaking events, or attending culinary conferences, she consistently tells those inquiring that she "prefers to let her food do the talking." And when she is approached by adoring fans who've traveled far and wide just to taste her food—and get a glimpse of the infamous loner—Athena has been known to get flustered and revert to mumbled thanks and gratitude before hurrying back to the safety of her kitchen.

This is Lola's one opportunity.

"I know you're in a hurry, but I would love to have two minutes of your time for a few questions," Lola says, settling into Athena's much longer stride as she finally returns to her kitchen. Athena's entire body tenses. She takes a deep, long breath, pushes her glasses up with her wrist, and checks the time. Lola feels a pang of guilt that her own request is causing Athena enough anxiety that she's resorting to her old coping mechanisms.

"I would be open to that, but let me assess where we are for tonight's service first," Athena says, her hand on the door to the kitchen. Lola nods. "Come on in."

Athena pushes open the door to the kitchen.

"Chef?" Athena calls out for Salma Das, her chef de cuisine and second-in-command. Lola notices the change in Athena immediately; like a fish that got thrown back in the water, finally able to take deep gulps of breath.

"Yes, Chef?" Salma's slight Valley Girl accent gives away her deep Southern California roots. That and her signature checkerboard slip-on Vans are remnants of the young Salma who almost became a pro skateboarder. Her dark skin glistens in the kitchen's heat, her headscarf pinned and tucked meticulously into her chef's whites.

"Where are we?" Athena asks, shepherding Lola Tadese through the crowded kitchen. As Salma gives her report, all Lola can do is stand back in awe. Being inside Athena Winter's kitchen feels like she's been shrunk down and placed in the very center of the internal mechanism of an old timepiece. Nestled next to the mainspring, Lola can almost hear the metronomic ticking as she oscillates back and forth, moving in total harmony along with a sea of chef's whites.

"Do you want to taste something wonderful?" Athena asks from just behind Lola.

"Sure," Lola says, still in a daze. Thinking she's going to be fed something overly complicated and truly groundbreaking, she turns around to find Athena Winter holding a simple, perfectly peeled Cara Cara orange, a sharpened paring knife gripped tightly in her left hand.

"Mom brought these in today," Athena says, deftly slicing off a segment for herself and one for Lola. "Aren't they beautiful?" Lola nods, carefully lifting the succulent orange section from Athena's razor-sharp knife. "Close your eyes." Lola looks up at Athena, confused. "I know it's . . . an odd request, but trust me."

Every bone in Lola's body fights against Athena's request, forever scarred, as most were, by the brutality of adolescence—a request to close one's eyes and trust someone you barely knew was usually followed by a humiliating prank where one's excruciating innocence was somehow transformed into someone's idea of a punch line.

"I will if you will," Lola answers. Athena beams, then nods.

And there, amid the symphonic chaos of the tiny, overcrowded Northern Trade kitchen, both women close their eyes together and each take a bite of their single section of orange. Immediately, the din of the bustling kitchen staff fades and Lola is swept away by the bright, sunshine bursts of orange coating her lips and tongue.

Has she never tasted an orange before this?

Lola braces herself, gearing up to bite down on the already overwhelmingly lush droplet of sun a second time. She opens her eyes, her taste buds defibrillated.

"What could I ever make that's going to be better than this orange?" Athena asks, juice dripping down her chin.

"Nothing," Lola answers honestly, her voice breathless. Athena smiles.

"A chef's job—her *main* job—is to get out of the way and let the food shine," Athena says, offering Lola another slice of orange. She takes it, closes her eyes, and is swept away again. Athena waits, watches. Lola opens her eyes to Athena smiling, handing her a slightly wrinkled, charcoal-gray Irish linen napkin. She takes it and wipes her face of the delicious juice. "Or at least that's what I think anyway."

"Is that what you've tried to bring to the Northern Trade menu over the past several years as head chef?" Lola asks, effortlessly switching into journalist mode.

"Yes," Athena answers, stiffening.

Lola, fearing she's spooked her uneasy interviewee, flicks her gaze back to the orange. Athena smiles and slices off another section. Lola closes her eyes and drops the segment in her mouth. Lola senses that she has only one more question before Athena shuts down completely. She has to make it a good one. She opens her eyes and holds Athena's gaze intently, orange juice still sticky on her fingers.

"And do you think that's your mother's guiding principle as she launches Central Trade?"

Athena holds the silence. Lola waits.

"I don't know," Athena answers.

Lola doesn't move. She needs more.

Athena shifts her weight from one foot to the other, resituating the knife in her now slippery hand. Her fears about her mother's blind spots are thick in her throat. Finally, Athena continues—

"Okay. Um . . . okay . . . years ago, I . . . I was once meeting one of our vendors over in the East Bay. I tend to get places early, so I had almost two hours to kill before they showed up." Lola's face bursts into a smile and Athena laughs. "I know. It's ridiculous. But I found this little taqueria, bought a couple of tacos and a horchata, and snagged a seat by the window, and I remember going from feeling so lost to just . . . being found, if that makes sense." Athena stops. Lola nods. "I feel so lucky that I get to feed people and provide shelter and a warm place to sit where you can feel found, but I also recognize that Northern Trade isn't a place most of the world can experience. Southern Trade and those hot dogs helped me as much as it helped everyone else during a truly shit time. I missed feeding people. So much. So while I may not know what Mom's guiding principle is in launching Central Trade, what I do know is that my desire to feed people started with her. I . . . I can only hope . . . think that that is still her North Star."

"So you see Central Trade as part of the family—"

Athena becomes distracted by a whoosh of flame at the grill. She eyeballs the grill chef, who gives her a confident thumbs-up. Athena turns back to Lola, but her attention is now elsewhere, the spell of the orange lifted.

Lola edits the original question and asks again, unsure if she will get an answer. "So you see Central Trade as part of the family business and not a possible threat to all that Northern Trade has built?"

Athena reties her apron tightly around her waist and turns to her workspace. "It hasn't even opened yet, but . . . I guess . . . yeah, I mean, how great would an empire be if it was threatened by its own progress?"

Later that evening, sitting in the calm of her room at the Northern Trade Inn, Lola will circle these words in her notebook.

They will become the opening line of her article.

CHAPTER FOUR

The lyrical choreography of Athena Winter's kitchen is mirrored in the main dining room as the surgical maneuvering around Maren Winter's dinner table reaches its own grand pas de deux. Dueling dances eerily similar in the methodical way they orbit their individual Winter suns. But opposite because one group of planets encircles its star seeking the warmth of validation, while the other is pulled together to build a more meaningful and collaborative system.

Athena tastes a sauce and turns to Salma, who sprinkles in scallions without a word. Jules lobs a setup and Maren dunks on the gathered assemblage with yet another awe-inspiring tale full of dropped names and historical events. Athena watches the pass as each dish is scrutinized and wiped down. Sloane and Lærke share a secret, knowing glance as Richard refills his wineglass, casually draining the bottle Odette chose so lovingly hours before. As the evening wears on, both rooms settle into their own rhythms, each person acutely aware of the role they play tonight.

The last of the quail dishes are served, two in each hand of Eleanor's waitstaff. Salma stops one, wipes down the side of the dish, eyes the brassicas—the perfectly arranged dish looks like an old botanical oil painting, all dark hues, shadow and light. She gives the waiter a nod, and they float out of the room with her hard-won blessing.

Salma navigates back through the crowded kitchen, checking on Emile in his pastry corner as the bone marrow pudding comes together—the succulent Cara Cara oranges now sliced and ready for their moment in the spotlight. Salma and Emile's conversation ends in Salma leaning back and belly laughing about something Emile said. The wheezing and high-pitched riffing that follow take the entire kitchen down into hysterics. Even Athena cracks a smile and tears her focus away from the grill, where Henning Altstädter, the grill chef Athena hired last year, is currently preparing the final dish of the night: the pork chop.

Salma has her hand on Emile's back, and neither one can catch their breath; Henning yells out his unsolicited opinion to a flood of groans and another roar of laughter—his eyes never leave the grill, where each thick chop is nestled tightly within a perfectly seasoned cast iron pan, sizzling in homemade butter. Henning adds pinches of salt as he sees fit, continually moving the chop around the pan, methodically dripping the butter over top as he does so. Pressing his finger into the meat, he tests for doneness. And once he's confident in its perfection, Athena adds the garlic and thyme in those final moments. The smell in the kitchen is heavenly.

Salma finally walks back over to Athena and Henning at the grill and begins overseeing the plating of the pork chop. She places each glistening chop, still slick with butter, on one side of the dappled ceramic plate—a simple vignette.

But as the plates stream out of the kitchen two by two, doubt blooms in Athena's chest, climbing and curling around her nervous system like a vine. She pushes her glasses up with her wrist and eyes the door into the main dining room, unmoving as the kitchen staff seamlessly shifts gears and begins cleaning and breaking down their stations so they can all be present for Maren's toast, a request that was a request in name only. Athena leans down and listens to something Salma is saying, but her reply is off by just enough that the vine of Athena's doubt reaches out, coiling and tightening around Salma's wrist.

"Everything okay?" Salma asks.

Salma's whispered, private question pops the brightness in the kitchen like a balloon. Everyone scans their workbenches, making sure it's not something they did. But when no one can find a tangible explanation for the disruption and Athena's response is only a tight nod and a mumbled "It should be fine," the vines of paranoia begin to spread to the entire kitchen, one planet at a time, tightening and curling around wrists and necks with abandon.

Something is wrong.

By the time the cleared dishes from the last course start trickling in, the tension in the kitchen is a thick, choking fog. Eleanor and Odette push open the kitchen door, expertly navigating the crowded kitchen— vine tendrils groping and swiping at them as they pass—and settle in next to Salma and Athena. The quartet talks logistics and confirms what they'll be using for Maren's upcoming toast, but as Eleanor weaves her way out of the kitchen, she's unable to quite put her finger on why she feels uneasy now. Just as she gets ready to have her staff swap out the wineglasses for champagne flutes, she stops one of her waiters on her way back to the kitchen.

"Was there a problem?" Eleanor asks the waiter. In her hands is one single plate that holds an untouched perfect pork chop. The waiter looks down at the plate, then back into the main dining room before answering.

"She said she wasn't hungry," the waiter says. The waiter doesn't need to specify who it was. Both women look out to where Maren Winter holds court. Observing Eleanor's and the waiter's concerned, fixed stares, Jules excuses herself from the table and approaches the secretive duo. Once there, she needs no explanation as to the root of their apprehension.

"Why don't you package it up and take it home for yourself," Jules says to the waiter. Eleanor nods in agreement, but before they proceed into the kitchen, Jules continues, "Package it up before you take the plate in, please." They nod.

Jules composes herself in the tiny hallway just outside the kitchen, a pocket of neutrality where she can be her own planet for the briefest of moments. She smooths down her dress, making sure to be strategic about where she swipes the newly acquired perspiration onto the dark silk. Taking a deep breath before continuing back out to her seat, Jules prays Maren didn't witness yet another of her impulsive moments of sentimentality.

The conversation around the long communal table is a loose and unpredictable din prompted by the subterranean restlessness that induces an entire group of strangers to eat very little and drink way too much. Richard is speaking too loud, his perfect blond ringlets, once lacquered by expensive hair products, now wild and unruly. Settled back in her seat, Jules places a firm hand on Richard's leg under the table and leans into him—her own face flushed, her teeth sporting that undeniable burgundy hue—to slur everything from prayers to threats in hope of quieting him down. But not enough to send him pouting. At least one of Sloane's children is on the cusp of melting down, and the whispered parental negotiations of screen time versus bedtime are well underway. But both women know the kids have crossed the Rubicon and the promise of ringing in the New Year with the adults will not be easily wrested from their tiny, sticky hands without a fight. They're too close.

The only thing keeping this random New Year's Eve assemblage from completely spiraling is the group's shared communal disdain for Valentina, Rafael Luna's wife—a woman whose sole transgression is not knowing it was her performative and unending silent reverence and gratitude this group wanted, not her actual opinions and real, unfiltered self.

An unfiltered self that had the audacity to come dressed for an actual New Year's Eve celebration, all pink tulle and sequins in a sea of sensible black and understated elegance. Valentina's black hair is up in a messy crown braid, threaded through with flowers and baby's breath. Accustomed to standing out, Valentina regards the dinner party's tight-assed snobbery as she does everyone who has been uncomfortable with her unabashed flamboyance in the past: she doesn't.

Valentina Luna couldn't care less.

But unlike Jules's pleading corrections of Richard, Rafael Luna feels zero obligation to quell or even moderate Valentina's perfectly normal behavior, lazing in his chair like a bored vampire, wearing a deep red velvet dinner jacket, his white collared shirt listing open to reveal a tapestry of tattoos. His longish salt-and-pepper black hair falls like a curtain over his face with detached ennui.

Of course, Sloane and Lærke's children are obsessed with Rafael and Valentina Luna, and the exhausted parents are so desperate to curb the looming slow-blinking tantrums that they oblige their fascination, thus opening themselves up to the same social blacklisting.

But one guest has been using Valentina's disco ball of a personality as cover throughout the evening. Because while everyone else has been focusing on Valentina, Lola Tadese has secreted herself away in bathrooms and dark corners, furtively jotting down her notes and observations from the evening, while also recording mini on-the-fly interviews with anyone she can corner for even a few moments. No one will go on the record, of course—but Lola notices that when they demand anonymity, it's the main dining room they make sure can't hear them, not the kitchen.

As Lola returns, she sidesteps one of the waiters as they thread themselves between Rafael and Valentina, swapping out their wineglasses for champagne flutes while Odette makes her way around the table filling them with bubbling wonderfulness. As this is happening, Eleanor has directed her waitstaff to set out enough champagne flutes on the low console table near the back of the room for when Athena and her staff join the party for Maren's toast.

It's almost midnight.

As the kitchen staff sets aside cleaning and breaking down the kitchen just long enough to make themselves presentable to those in the main dining room, Penny and Hana Ahn enter through the side door, both dressed in what can only be described as "this is fine, right?"

The entire kitchen erupts and the pair is inundated with bites of food, hugs, and ongoing conversations picked up as if no time has passed. Within seconds they're drawn into the kitchen's natural tides.

"We didn't want to go in there by ourselves," Hana says, stealing an off-cut piece of pastry from Emile's workbench. Emile affectionately slaps their hand, only to feed them a spoonful of the bone marrow pudding that he's preparing for the first dessert course. Hana sighs with pleasure. "Dear lord."

Penny laughs with Henning and Salma about how she manages year after year to dodge having to actually attend Maren's New Year's Eve dinner party. The two bow down in awe when Penny only reiterates the importance of boundaries, before she settles in next to where Athena is, off by herself, cleaning and packing away her knives for the evening.

"How you doing, kiddo?" Penny asks.

"Good. You?" Athena answers, mustering up what she hopes will be enough enthusiasm to throw Penny off the scent of her building anxiety. Penny waits. Unblinking. Obviously, it was never going to work. Athena exhales, and her shoulders slump. "I'm tired and am trying to"—Athena stops, pulls off her glasses, and rubs her eyes—"get myself ready to be around people." Penny scans Athena's loud and crowded kitchen. She looks back at Athena. "You know what I mean."

"I do," Penny says with an easy smile. Athena puts back on her glasses.

"It'll be fine." Athena's voice is robotic as she ties her knife bag closed with childlike looped bows.

"You and I both know we have no control about whether tonight will be fine," Penny starts. Athena nods somberly. "But . . ." Penny reaches up to Athena's face and gently brushes her cheek. Athena leans into Penny's soft, maternal touch and finally makes eye contact with the woman she's called Aunt Penny her whole life. "You, my little love, will be fine." Athena nods again, this time attempting a smile. Penny pinches her cheek and gives her a sly wink as Athena leads the exodus out of the kitchen.

As Athena's staff follows her into the main dining room, a vine of doubt loops around Penny's ankle, causing her to pause for just a moment before following the rest of the staff through the kitchen door.

"Ah, come in," Maren says, standing at the head of the table. Dressed in a black-and-gold embroidered tea-length dress, she looks every inch the hostess. "Welcome the real stars of the evening!" she says with the mock humility of someone who knows the people she's just introduced are not, in fact, the real stars of the evening.

Everyone seated around the table turns to look at the assembled "stars of the evening" standing, instead of being seated along with their guests, as they settle in next to the low console table filled with the promise of a much-needed drink. Athena, used to being stuck in the back due to her height, instinctively settles in behind her staff, just next to Henning. Maren remains standing and begins clapping. Which causes everyone around the table to rise and give their new guests a standing ovation.

The kitchen staff stands as they do every year, hands clasped behind them, grateful smiles spreading across their tired, lined faces, hoping this performance will be quick. Because in the back of their minds, they're all itching to retreat to the kitchen to finish cleaning, and they're hoping they can push through the exhaustion enough that they can carve out some time to celebrate the New Year, too.

Athena watches her staff notice Rafael Luna's presence at tonight's festivities. The elbow nudges and whispered asides set off like a fuse through the group, sparking and burning its way through the crowd. It's the kind of chemical reaction that happens only when you have some-one not just famous but infamous in your midst. A fallen king whose daily life has been fully eclipsed by his own mythos. A mythos that, as for Athena herself, is the backbone of any article written about him, lest the public—or he himself—ever forget that he once had a raging heroin addiction and flamed out in an incredibly public blaze of glory.

Back in the midnineties, Rafael Luna was the culinary world's grunge king. At just twenty-three years old, he was an entirely new brand of chef. A native of Los Angeles, he was constantly flanked by celebrities and rock stars as he cut loose at the Viper Room or stumbled out of a party somewhere in Beachwood Canyon. Rafael was just as beautiful and mysterious as they were, and he embodied heroin chic at its finest . . . right up until he personified heroin chic at its most heartbreaking.

Wolf, his first restaurant, was located behind an old dry cleaner's right on the Sunset Strip. It was a fifteen-seat fine-dining restaurant with a private room that was impossible to get into and even more impossible for paparazzi to access. Which made it catnip for Hollywood's elite. His menu was way ahead of its time—highlighting his own Mexican roots in Los Angeles while also thumbing his nose at those who believed Mexican food needed "elevation" in order to be taken seriously in the Eurocentric fine-dining circles that would have him believe otherwise.

By 2001, Rafael was opening his fourth restaurant in the newly minted culinary hotbed of Las Vegas. He was also nursing a full-blown heroin addiction, which was exacerbated by being away from Los Angeles and his family, namely his high school sweetheart and long-suffering wife, Valentina. Months later, it was she who would find Rafael on the floor of that cheap hotel room off the main drag, needle still in his arm and as close to overdosing as one could get.

Within a year of his overdose—and the wild, highly photographed night that preceded it—Rafael and Valentina Luna were bankrupt and living back at home with her parents. He would be in and out of rehab throughout the next several years, finding work where he could—diners, burger joints, and in one particularly humiliating instance, getting recognized at a Hyatt in Oxnard, where he was manning the continental breakfast buffet.

Rafael Luna finally got clean in 2017 and began his climb back by reaching out to an old friend who'd just opened up a fine-dining seafood restaurant on Church Street in San Francisco. He assured his friend he was clean and begged for any position in her kitchen. The friend obliged, first letting Rafael stage for several months before putting him on the grill, where he belonged.

Two years later, Rafael Luna finally opened Lobo, his first new restaurant in sixteen years.

Standing there in all his beautiful weariness, next to his loudmouth meringue of a wife, he's given everyone in attendance what they desire most—their own personal Rafael Luna story to add to the teetering pile like kindling, forever flaming the public's unquenchable desire for another bonfire of extraordinary failure. Because more than money or power, what people crave most is, if and when Rafael finally drowns under the waves of his own demons, to be able to tell people about the New Year's Eve party where they met the tormented genius himself, and how they could sense, even then, that he was on a path of destruction.

Across the sea of darting eyes and whispered asides, the room thick with wine and applause, Rafael Luna gives Athena Winter an imperceptible nod of respect for the meal that evening. Athena responds with a tight-lipped smile, both appreciative of the professional acknowledgment and increasingly paranoid about what his public endorsement might bring forth. Only two people observe the exchange. Unfortunately for Athena, one of them is Maren Winter. And unfortunately for Maren, the other is Lola Tadese.

As Maren jerks her champagne flute high into the air, the effervescent amber liquid sloshes out of the glass in glistening, ropy droplets. Her knuckles whiten as she tightens her grip around the delicate crystal glass stem, her mind a tangle of fragments of conversations, whispers of self-doubt, and ripening paranoid delusions inexplicably knotted together with mangled and corrupted conclusions that threaten to pull her under and into the quiet certainty of her own madness.

That's the thing about breaking points—not even the person who's broken sees them coming.

Maren taps the side of her champagne flute and the entire room falls quiet, hands holding bubbling glasses aloft like some kind of champagne vigil.

"For those joining us for the first time this year, I customarily stand up here and deliver a rousing—often long-winded, sometimes slurring, depending on Odette's wine choice—New Year's Eve toast. It's the one time a year everyone has to listen to me, and you better believe I've exploited the hell out of it." Everyone laughs right on cue. Maren waits for the room to quiet, holding the silence until all eyes are back on her. "But the Winter Group is no longer just about me and the legacy I've built over the last forty-five years. It's about the future." Maren holds her glass up to Sloane, then Jules, and finally over to Athena. Each daughter obediently hoists her glass a little higher as Maren locks eyes with her. Maren then takes a long, purposeful breath and launches into the same speech she delivered earlier that day. "Back in the seventies, Penny and I were known for throwing the best underground dinner parties in the city from our tiny kitchen on Arguello. We made ten-course meals for anyone who could pay five dollars, as long as they helped clean up." Maren waits for the laugh this line always gets. Everyone obliges. Maren continues, "After one particularly successful dinner party, Penny and I walked over to Golden Gate Park, sat on the smallest blanket in the entire world, and sketched out a dream on the back of a utility bill envelope. We dreamed of a place with a crackling fireplace, creaky wooden floors, and fresh, good food made for hungry people who needed a warm place to sit. A place where the kitchen was filled with good and talented people, rather than temperamental bad-boy geniuses who usually hazed and bullied people like us." Those who know this speech by heart recognize the dramatic conclusion of Maren's origin story and absently bring their hands up to applaud. Shocking them all, however, tonight Maren has decided to add one more line. She continues, "No offense, Chef Luna."

Maren's words detonate in the room around her. An unnatural quiet blankets the room—covering some with self-satisfied delight at another's humiliation and others in terror that if Rafael Luna can be a target, then no one is safe. Each person withdraws into their own muffled cocoon of darting eyes and lowered arms, now heavy with the once-celebratory champagne, so isolated in their own private discomfort that no one hears Valentina whisper to Rafael.

"What did she just say?" Valentina asks, getting ready to fight.

"I mean, I've definitely heard worse," Rafael answers, trying to calm his wife with a self-deprecating joke, hoping she doesn't pick up on how much Maren's words stung. Finally, Rafael lets out a bored sigh and looks Maren Winter dead in the eye and smiles.

"None taken, Chef," Rafael says, his voice a velvety yawn. Slightly put off, Maren gives him a quick, sanctifying wink of camaraderie, but just as the room exhales . . .

"So, bucking tradition—something I'm more than a little famous for—I thought instead of standing up here toasting my own accomplishments, I would let the next generation of Winters give this year's toast, since my legacy will soon enough be in their capable hands."

Lærke squeezes Sloane's hand, while Jules smooths down her long golden hair, ignoring Richard completely. Athena, on the other hand, is buried under the guilt that Rafael's nod of approval to her put him in Maren's line of fire. Closing in on herself, she takes a step back from the crowd, searching for an exit strategy that can get her out of what is quickly becoming a waking nightmare.

"As the eldest and our current general manager, I feel it's only right that we should start with you, Sloane," Maren says.

Just as Sloane is about to begin, Maren casually takes her seat, draping herself in her chair at the head of the table. Sloane must now wait—her arm frozen in hoisted celebration—as the guests follow Maren's lead and sit back down. Sloane's arm lowers little by little as chairs scrape against wood floors and cut-glass flutes are set back down on the table. The kitchen staff shifts on the fringes of the festivities, exhausted bodies now seizing and cramping from the drawn-out idleness. Finally . . .

"It's funny—you'd think I'd be used to this feeling of absolute terror that comes from being asked to follow or compete with my mom in any way. But what I finally realized was that it isn't my job to compete with her; rather, it is my honor to celebrate and preserve what she's built for generations to come. Because it's not what she's built that I admire most, it's how she's built it. History has this way of bronzing its most notable people so much that you forget that before they were icons, they were just normal people with an idea. Personally, I think we do it because it makes us feel a little bit better about why we didn't change the world given the time, but I digress. We all know the story of the utility envelope in Golden Gate Park and the spark of an idea, but if you think back to 1977—really think back—Northern Trade should have been impossible. East Bay Soups should have been impossible. And now Central Trade should be impossible—and here we are, yet again, raising our glasses to Maren Winter making the impossible possible." Sloane dramatically lifts her glass. "To the impossible!"

The group toasts as Sloane and Maren embrace, but the tone in the room is notably subdued. Guests take small sips from their champagne flutes, now knowing that they have two more to get through before they can blissfully empty the glass.

Sloane sits and sets down her glass as Lærke whispers gushing praise in her ear before kissing her. They get a millisecond of alone time before being immediately set upon by their children. Ever the canaries in the social mines, the trio of kids' overtired energy is fueled by the confusing discomfort that continues to build and permeate the room. All eyes turn to Jules.

Jules picks up her champagne flute and slinks out of her chair in one slithering, fluid motion. The angles of her soft, round face catch the light, making her look downright angelic as everyone waits for her to begin.

"To say that I've trained for this moment like it's the Olympics would be an understatement. Sloane and Athena have both personally caught and made fun of me for practicing impromptu speeches in front of our bathroom mirror with my hairbrush. So if I could open things up tonight with a big 'I Told You So' to them, I think we can all agree that I was right and that they were wrong. Which, when dealing with sisters, is really all that matters." Jules lifts her glass to Sloane and then to Athena. Both women respond with genuine and unguarded smiles. They lift their glasses to their sister, softening as they always do when it comes to Jules. The guests and Northern Trade staff laugh, loosening and exhaling just a bit, the tension and discomfort from earlier now all but gone. Or rather, as is probably more the case, tamped and buried where it is far more socially acceptable. "For me, I've always felt lucky to have been given this life, this family, all of it really, that my only job—as I understand it—is to just not screw it up. Now, I don't take too much seriously—*obviously*—but when it comes to not screwing up my mother's legacy, I 100 percent understand the enormity of the mission I've been tasked to see through to the end and will give nothing less than everything I've got. I love you, Mom, and here's to me not screwing it all up. Cheers!"

The room erupts in a burst of nervous and relieved joy as they laugh and toast to not screwing it up. As Jules lunges into Maren for a hug, Sloane and Lærke's trio of little ones rejoice in the permission they've been granted by their eccentric Auntie Jules to say a borderline "bad word," and as champagne flutes clink and sparkle, it's their tiny voices that are the loudest. Before she sits back down, and still riding high on the elixir of her mother's momentary approval, Jules quiets the room with a raised hand.

"And because I know my little sister better than anyone and am positive she's spent the entirety of this little exercise trying to figure out a way to sneak out of this room before we get to her turn, I officially yield the floor to Athena—who should probably stop trying to hide behind her poor unsuspecting kitchen staff and step into the spotlight she so deserves. Teeny? You're up."

For as many times as Jules has thrown Athena into the deep end, including the time she literally threw her into the actual deep end of their aunt Josephine's pool when she was six years old, you'd think Athena would be used to it. But for as much pure adrenaline and terror is pumping through Athena's body right now, you wouldn't be able to tell it from her appearance. Hands clasped in front of her, Athena looks the picture of unaffected calm. But Lola Tadese now knows where to look. While Athena's hands may be lazily clasped in front of her, her clawlike fingers fidget with and clutch at her watch with unbridled panic.

Athena's kitchen staff, always aware of exactly how much room she takes up, recedes enough to clear a path for her to come forward. Athena grips her champagne flute and walks the five perilous steps forward. She makes very pointed eye contact with Jules, who innocently shrugs and plops back down in her chair.

"Like Jules and Sloane, I, too, am grateful to be a part—any part—of Mom's life. Sadly, unlike Jules and Sloane, I am not a very good public speaker, so I will do what I am far more comfortable with and let my food speak for me as I toast to my mom." Athena lifts her glass high into the air. "To Mom."

"To Maren! To Mom!" The room erupts in joyful noise, not unlike a classroom of children finally let out to recess.

Everyone counts down to the New Year, more than a little impressed that they timed it all so perfectly. Couples kiss, friends and family hug, and merriment and hope for a fresh start fill the room.

As the gathered guests finally drain their glasses and the din of the room rises with small talk and readying for the dessert course, Maren stands and makes her way over to Athena. The kitchen staff begins to set their now-empty champagne flutes back onto the low console table and start the walk back into the kitchen, the end of a very long night in sight. Maren stops in front of Athena, and Athena loosens her clasped hands and begins to step closer to her mother for a hug. The Winters are not a hugging people, so Athena is awkward as she prepares herself to engage in such an unfamiliar and rare public display of affection. Caught in the echo chamber of her own paralyzing discomfort, Athena fails to notice that Maren has clearly not come to her for a hug. Instead, her mother looks up at her youngest daughter, arms still firmly at her sides, and asks—

"It's interesting that you said that you let your food speak for you. What do you think your pork chop said that my pork belly couldn't?" Maren's question roars like a thunderclap around the room, cresting and rolling through each guest and Northern Trade staff member one at a time.

Athena's arms lower back down to her sides.

One of the single most heartbreaking moments in the pantheon of human experiences is when a person who's lived a lifetime in an environment that demanded they stay guarded finally takes off their armor only to feel the sting of a knife plunge into their heart by the very person they risked it all for. The momentary softness that shone bright in their eyes disappears at an excruciatingly slow pace as the bloodied victim wistfully contemplates that they should have known better.

On one side of the main dining room are tonight's guests, splintered and dispersed around the table, which is littered with drained champagne flutes. Sloane and Jules look on with terror, their loyalty to their youngest sister eclipsed once more by the guilt-ridden gratitude that they were not tonight's targets of public ridicule.

On the other side of the room is Athena's kitchen staff. Arms crossed across chef's whites, they look on helplessly, unable to do anything to help their leader, knowing that such an interruption would only hurt her more. Penny Ahn flushes with rage and, forever protective of her Winter girls, reaches out her hand. But knowing her intervention will only make things worse—a lesson she's learned from years of painful and frustrating firsthand experience—she pulls back. Her hand a twisted fist, Penny swallows and focuses her anger, pulling Hana close. As confusion floods the room, Maren and Athena stand in the stillness at the eye of the storm.

"Nothing. Mom, it's—" Athena's voice shakes as she attempts to de-escalate the situation.

"Nothing?"

"No, I—"

"So, you think my legacy is nothing." Maren steps closer. Athena takes a step back. This pleases Maren.

"Of course I don't."

"I see it so clearly now—"

"I don't think you do."

"The only thing that interests you about the grandness of my legacy is tearing it down, because what could be more satisfying than surpassing someone so celebrated?"

"Being the child of one."

"Don't lie to me, kiddo."

"I'm telling the truth."

"Here's an idea—if you want so badly to make your own dishes, then you should probably go do that at a restaurant that doesn't already have a head chef."

Athena tries to remain calm, but she can't seem to control the panic now shrouding her entire body. Knowing she has only enough strength to regulate her voice for one sentence, Athena chooses her next words wisely.

"But I'm the head chef here at Northern Trade."

"Not anymore you're not."

CHAPTER FIVE

In the agonizing, slowed-down seconds that follow, Athena scans the room. A sea of faces looks back. Not one comes to her defense. Unable to process the full scope of what's happened, Athena's riot of a mind tries to focus on how she can survive the next few moments. The room blurs and muffles around her. Telling herself she has to breathe, she inhales deeply and blinks, hoping that when she opens her eyes again, this will all have been her mother's idea of a bad joke. But as she exhales, eyes fluttering open, Maren turns from her and walks wordlessly away.

Athena lets her head fall, nodding as she pushes aside her own impending breakdown, to focus on making sure her kitchen staff is prepared for whatever comes next. All the while understanding that this decision, while certainly altruistic, also serves her own need to swallow the myriad ways this will most definitely scar her deep into her bones. It's not that she doesn't grasp that she's experienced something traumatic; it's that she understands perfectly and must first get herself to safety in order to let the bomb explode without any collateral damage.

And the clock is ticking.

"Come with me," Athena rasps out to Salma Das, her number two.

Shell-shocked and on the verge of tears, Salma nods and follows Athena through the main dining room and out the front door of the restaurant. Their departure is closely watched through averted eyes. Before they exit, both chefs reassure their staff that they'll have answers for them soon, but now they need to get back into the kitchen to prepare and serve the dessert course. Sloane and Jules have urged the gathered guests to sit back down. Wineglasses are swapped back in, small talk is instituted like martial law, and to those who are hesitant, it's made clear that *they* are the ones making it weird. And it's in this polite and quiet aftermath that Lola Tadese's departure from the table goes completely unnoticed.

Misinterpreting the electric energy in the room, Maren Winter takes her seat at the head of the table, certain that her treatment of Athena has awed and inspired those gathered this evening. Confident that everyone shares her view of tonight's events as Athena disrespecting Maren's great and long legacy, she delights in their reverence at the strength of character it must have taken to dismiss her own child for what was clearly a callous and contemptible plan to usurp her own mother.

As Sloane and Jules crowd around the low console table in search of more bottles of wine, they whisper excuses and explanations.

"She doesn't mean it," Jules offers, opening up another bottle.

"Athena will be back within a week," Sloane adds.

They return to the table knowing both statements are completely untrue. What is true, and left unsaid, is that both Sloane and Jules recognize how Athena's departure could be beneficial to them.

Athena and Salma huddle around the firepits at the entrance to Northern Trade, the brisk cold making every strained breath visible in the night air.

"I don't know how serious this is or how long it'll last, but we have to plan for every outcome," Athena says. Her voice is robotic and hollow.

"Did you . . . How . . . What happened in there?" Salma asks.

"I shouldn't have served the pork chop," Athena answers plainly.

Salma nods, muting and censoring herself from offering any of a litany of alternative pitches she believes have way more merit than Athena blaming only herself for what went down in there. But Athena has always kept herself to herself. Friendly, but never a friend. Working in a group, but never truly a part of it. Salma wants to understand. Say the things. Make her fight. But before she wades in, she must first test the waters.

"What can I do, Chef?" Salma asks, dipping a toe in.

"I'm sure my mother will have her own ideas about who she wants as head chef, but—"

"Wait, you think she planned this?" Salma asks.

"No, I . . . She couldn't have. She didn't know about the pork chop until tonight, so no. I don't think she did," Athena says.

"It can't be all about the pork chop, Chef," Salma says, officially wading in.

"I think it is . . . and isn't," Athena says, still in disbelief.

"But—"

"Look, we don't have much time. Please, just . . ."

"Okay. Okay—" Salma says, backing off.

"Mom won't want to lose our second Michelin Star," Athena says.

"The one you got us. Not her. Got it," Salma says, agreeing but also sneaking in a jab.

Athena presses on. "Our reservations are booked out for the next year. She can't launch both Central Trade and train a new head chef without risking getting bumped back down to one star in the process. She'll need consistency and someone who knows the menu—"

"And what if she doesn't?" Salma asks.

"What if she doesn't what?" Athena asks.

"Maren just fired the head chef who earned her a second Michelin Star—and her own kid, I might add—for a pork chop. A damn good one, too. Do you honestly think she cares about what happens to Northern Trade?" Salma asks, getting more and more angry by the second. Athena takes a deep, slow breath and looks down at the ground, unable to look at Salma.

"Sadly, I am pretty sure Mom will do better by Northern Trade than she did by me," Athena says.

"You sure about that?" Salma asks. Athena is just about to answer when she sees Jules and Sloane exit the restaurant and make a beeline for where she and Salma are talking over by the firepits. Salma follows Athena's gaze, looking behind her to see the approaching Winter sisters.

"Plus, Sloane would never let that happen," Athena adds under her breath, ignoring Salma's question.

"Athena—" Salma's voice is soft and intimate. One last plea. But as Sloane and Jules settle in next to them, Salma watches as Athena pulls herself up to her full height and readies herself for war. Heartbroken, Salma quickly excuses herself as the sisters square off.

Athena shoots first. "If we can try to keep this to a logistics-only conversation and maybe not lead with—"

"That I told you this was going to happen and you ignored me like you always do. 'Oh, silly little Jules doesn't know what she's talking about.' Well, maybe now you'll listen next time," Jules says, shocked by how angry she is.

"Jules, I—"

"What's the first thing you tell your staff after hiring them?" Sloane asks, stepping forward.

"Do you really want to know?" Sloane nods. "That I know Sloane is off-putting, but she does actually know what she's doing," Athena says.

Jules laughs. "Same," she says, giggling.

Jules and Athena's momentary accord enrages Sloane.

"You tell them that a kitchen isn't a place for ego, but rather to be united in service of the menu. What you did tonight was about ego. Plain and simple," Sloane says. Her words hit Athena like a gut punch.

"It's kinda what Mom would have done," Jules says, her voice more unguarded than she's ready for.

"No, that's not—"

"She's struggling right now," Sloane says. "You *know* that. Central Trade is . . ." All three sisters shake their heads in complete and utter agreement. "Not going well. She needed tonight."

"And you kicked her when she was down," Jules adds.

"No—"

"All you had to do was serve the menu. *Her* menu. But you couldn't. And that's why we're here. No, that's why you're out here," Sloane says, anger now burning her throat.

"Okay. I will . . . okay, all of that can be true, but . . . do you seriously not see it? Mom isn't herself and both of you know it. She's paranoid and suspicious, and if Central Trade doesn't do well, it'll bring the whole Winter Group down. This is going to get way worse. I mean, do you honestly think Lola Tadese is writing a puff piece or retrospective, as Mom called it?" Athena asks.

"I mean—" Jules stammers.

"Did you see the way Lola looked at her when she said that this morning? It was brand-new information to her." Athena waits. Sloane and Jules give her nothing. "Do neither of you actually . . ." Athena takes off her glasses and rubs her dark-brown eyes. She puts them back on and takes a long, deep breath. "The piece she won the Pulitzer for? Was all about that elite group of sommeliers who colluded to make sure their little fiefdom remained all straight white dudes. Do you want to know whose quotes were the most damning in her article?" Sloane and Jules are quiet. "The elite group of sommeliers."

"Yeah, but they're bad people. That's not us," Sloane says, completely unironically.

Athena barks out a laugh. "Isn't it, though?" she says, gesturing to the freezing cold into which she's been thrown.

"This is an article that's running in tandem with Mom's lifetime achievement award. What are they going to do—run a hit piece under a classy photo of an older lady pioneer being celebrated? Like, give me some credit for knowing how to do my job," Jules says.

"What something starts out to be can be very different from what it becomes," Athena prods.

"Kind of like how pork belly turned into a pork chop because you were in your damn feelings," Jules parries.

"Just because you make every decision an emotional one—" Athena starts.

"And you don't?" Jules asks.

"This was about the pig," Athena repeats robotically.

"I don't know if you actually believe that or if you're just being obtuse," Jules says.

"'Obtuse' is a pretty big word for you," Athena says.

"There she is," Jules says, smiling. "Nice to see the real Athena Winter finally enter the chat."

"Shut up. Just—both of you shut up," Sloane finally says.

Decades of being told to shut up by their older sister have trained them well. And despite wanting to continue to take out their feelings of fear, shame, and uncertainty on each other, Jules and Athena do as they're told.

"Athena—" Sloane begins, her face lined with anguish.

Athena cuts in. "I know, okay? I figure if I lay low for a while, Mom will cool down. I'll apologize and fall on my sword and—"

"She wants you gone, Athena," Sloane says, sick to her stomach.

"What?" Athena asks.

"She told me she wanted you moved out and that I should start looking for a new head chef," Sloane says. Jules looks at the ground.

"Salma can step in until—"

"There is no 'until.' She told me to find your permanent replacement," Sloane says.

"But—" Jules tries to cut in.

"It's not up to us," Sloane says to Jules, her voice cracking.

"But you could fight for me." Athena looks from Sloane to Jules. "Why won't you fight for me?"

"Jesus, Teeny, we're too tired fighting for ourselves," Jules says, the exhausted truth slipping out before she can censor herself.

"But—"

"But what?" Sloane asks, swiping away a rogue tear.

"But this is my home," Athena says.

"No, this is your job, Athena. You've made it your home."

"Sloane—" Jules starts.

"Don't *Sloane* me. You stood right next to me and nodded along as Mom gave her instructions and didn't say anything, so cut the innocent act and stop making me do all the dirty work." Jules looks down at the ground.

"But . . ." Athena doesn't know what she wants to say next, the word "but" slipping from her mouth in a futile attempt to stave off the inevitable.

"Mom told us to tell you that we'll communicate next steps to your staff, as—" Sloane stumbles on her words. "You are no longer welcome in the Northern Trade kitchen." Her voice shakes with the weight of the words she's been told to say.

"Are these the leadership opportunities you were talking about? Is this really how you want to get what you want?" Athena asks, as the conversation inches closer to the gallows. Sloane shakes her head, not as a yes or no, but more in a futile attempt to loosen the words she's been ordered to say. The words grip the inside of her brain like talons.

"Of course not," Sloane rasps, still looking at the ground.

"Then—"

"Why did you have to do it?" Sloane asks, her voice cracking. "Why did you do it?"

"I don't know," Athena answers truthfully.

There is a long moment when the sisters are quiet. Each one of them coming to the same conclusion as the silence grows. Sloane's shoulders droop as she's the last one to admit to the finality of this moment. There is only one way this is going to go. Sloane tenses her jaw, gnashing her teeth, and continues.

"Despite the law being a bit unclear, if you should decide to capitalize on any recipes you developed at Northern Trade, just know that the Winter Group and its team of lawyers would make that a very difficult and expensive path for you."

"Sloane, look at me. Answer me: Is this what you really want?" Athena begs.

"I don't get to want things, Athena. I do as I'm told. Unlike you," Sloane says, finally looking up to meet Athena's desperate gaze.

"But you don't have to. You could—"

Sloane cuts Athena off as Jules hopes no one notices her swiping a traitorous tear from her cheek, its wetness leaving a dewy trail. "You are to vacate the Winter Group's on-campus housing tonight, as you are no longer an employee of the Winter Group. Just take what you need for the coming week, and we'll pack up the rest and send it along."

"Don't do this," Athena whispers.

"Teeny, you did this to yourself." Jules sighs.

"You are to leave the keys to both the studio and the truck you've been using—also owned by the Winter Group—under the mat upon your exit." Sloane takes in a sharp inhale, and a tiny whimper escapes without her permission.

An unnatural quietness coats the three sisters like oil. Encased and suffocated, they stand in the silence for what feels like hours. With her last remaining shred of resolve, Athena turns away from her sisters one last time. It's only sheer denial at the enormity of what's transpired here tonight that allows Athena to continue to function. Even so, before she leaves, she must say one more thing.

"This is going to get bad," Athena says.

"It already is bad," Jules says, her voice cracking.

"We'll see," Sloane says, wanting the last word.

Jules looks from Sloane to Athena, fighting the urge to say goodbye. But in the end, she decides to keep quiet, believing that saying the words will somehow make it real. Maybe if she doesn't say them out loud, this will all be just a bad dream she can soon wake up from.

And with that Athena Winter walks into the black of the night, focusing only on the task of putting one foot in front of the other.

Everything else feels impossible.

"Sloane, I—" Jules starts.

"Don't. Just don't," Sloane says, desperate to just make it stop.

"Sloanie—" Jules tries again, but this time Sloane is resolved. No more pain. No more choking guilt. No more.

"Maybe this will teach the mighty Athena Winter that without Mommy's recipes, she's just as tragically ordinary as the rest of us," Sloane blurts out angrily. Blinded by her own simmering rage, Sloane fails to notice Lola Tadese standing quietly next to the firepits, notebook in hand.

"She is right, though. This is going to get bad." Jules pivots, falling back into line as she and Sloane stride back toward the restaurant.

"I know," Sloane says, passing through the warm candlelit anteroom stacked high with Maren's cookbooks.

Jules stops Sloane with a firm hand on her arm. "What? You know?"

"The worse it gets, the sooner Mom steps aside. And the sooner Mom steps aside, the quicker I'll be able to set things right. And if she won't make that choice voluntarily, then I'm certainly not going to step in when the consequences of her own actions come due." Sloane forces her voice to sound as sure as she wants to be.

"Okay, I can do that. We can set things right," Jules says, walking back into the main dining room with a wildly different definition of "setting things right" than Sloane. Sloane says nothing as she settles back in next to Lærke with news and whispers of how the talk with Athena went.

Across the table, Rafael Luna is plotting his escape.

He should've left in the chaos following Maren's banishment of Athena but didn't act fast enough. He was swept up in the net of social propriety, graciously taking his seat as if everything were fine. If it had been just him, he could've slipped out, but trying to smuggle his parade float of a wife out could not be done subtly. He envies Lola Tadese, whose exit strategy was far superior to his.

As the bone marrow pudding with Cara Cara oranges is served, Maren asks Rafael where he gets his fish from—hearing through the grapevine that he has the best in the Bay Area. As the conversation between them continues through two dessert courses, Rafael begins to feel the nauseating discomfort that comes from realizing that he and the conversation he's providing are being used to distort the reality of what's really going on. Because what kind of person would interrupt a seemingly casual conversation about fresh fish to demand an explanation from Maren about her behavior toward Athena? As Maren graciously speaks about her own connections with the Tomales Bay Oyster Company, taking sips of wine between anecdotes, Rafael can only sit in wonder. On the surface, there is not one lingering shred of evidence that, less than one hour ago, Maren Winter fired her own daughter as the head chef and all but accused her of treason on her way out.

Maren Winter is good.

It's this realization that finally drives Rafael to act. He's spent too much of his life lying and numbing and worked too hard to claw his way out to slip back into old behaviors while ringing in the New Year of all things. Under the table, he taps "SOS" in Morse Code into the silk and tulle of Valentina's party dress. It's a trick they devised back when they first started dating. And even though they pride themselves on their meticulous tapping, often the distress signal devolves into furious and panicked drumming on the other's leg or arm.

Valentina, currently talking to Aunt Josephine about the weather, feels Rafael's tapping. Her response is immediate.

"Ahhh, well." The entire table turns to Valentina, including Rafael, who's perfected his shocked look over the decades. "I'm so sorry to break up this lovely dinner, but I have a very exhausted sitter to relieve." Valentina looks to Rafael, who sighs and shrugs as if to say, *Welp, guess that's me, too, then.*

"I was unaware you had children," Aunt Josephine says.

"Oh, we don't. The sitter is for our dog, Honey." As the table reacts to this correction, Valentina sifts through her clutch and pulls out her phone. She begins showing the gathered crowd pictures of a giant gray pit bull dressed in every costume and outfit imaginable. "She has over

3.9 million followers, and we have a children's book coming out in the summer."

Maren shoots Jules a look. *A dog influencer. You invited the quintessential bad boy chef and a dog influencer to our New Year's Eve party.* Jules looks away.

As Valentina shows the crowd one last photo—depicting Honey in a matching outfit just like the one Valentina is currently wearing—Maren can barely hide her irritation. She's having a hard time understanding how exactly she pulled the evening back from the brink only to have it scuttled by Honey the Tutu-Wearing Pit Bull.

"Well, it's a shame you must be going. We'll bring your car around," Maren says, waving over Eleanor. She does not stand up or mark their exit in any way. In fact, she very intentionally dives into a conversation with Aunt Josephine as Valentina and Rafael say their goodbyes to the group.

"If you could follow me," Eleanor says, gesturing to the front door.

As Rafael and Valentina follow Eleanor out of the Northern Trade main dining room, through the warmly lit anteroom, and out into the freezing January air, they give each other a look. There's a particular sensation that happens when the realization dawns that the party you so desperately want to leave . . . also wanted you to leave. It's one thing to become annoyed at having to linger at a gathering past its prime; it's quite another to be hustled out by hosts who clearly saw your presence as noxious.

"I forgot my cookbook. She signed it and everything," Valentina says, looking back at the restaurant.

"You're the love of my life, but there's no way I'm going back in there," Rafael says.

"Yeah, I got the distinct impression we overstayed our welcome," Valentina says as the valet rushes out, has a brief conversation with Eleanor, and then heads off in search of their vehicle. Once Eleanor says her overly polite goodbyes and leaves them alone, Rafael answers.

"Honestly, I've never been happier to leave a party," he says.

"Right? What . . . what was that?" Valentina asks. Rafael opens his red velvet coat and pulls Valentina in underneath. He rubs her arm, trying to warm his wife as her somber sigh exhales in front of them.

"From someone who's had his share of meltdowns, that was a particularly ugly one," Rafael says. Valentina looks up at him, the memory of his past still too tender to the touch.

"Happy New Year, my love," she says.

Rafael pulls Valentina close. "Always grateful to have another one." He kisses her. Valentina wraps her arm around Rafael's waist, tucking her head into the crook of his neck.

⚶

Still wearing her chef's whites, Athena walks toward the door of her small studio one last time. A week's worth of belongings, as well as a chaotic mixture of items Athena grabs in a fugue state, are thrown into one backpack, an oversize duffel, and three random tote bags she got from various restaurant vendors over the years. Once outside, Athena drops the bags by the door and pulls the key ring from her pocket. She starts to loop the studio key off the ring but then realizes that the only keys she has open things that belong to her mom. Even the key ring is a little wooden disc with Maren's signature green orchid burned into it. Her shoulders slump as she places the entire set of keys under the mat.

Athena experiences an almost out-of-body weightlessness as she walks away from everything that once meant something to her. With no time—or real desire, quite honestly—to process the loss, nor understand the depth of her grief, all she feels as she loops and hangs her belongings on her body is an all-encompassing, terrifying freedom.

Knowing the only reception is over by the firepits, Athena makes her way up there with a plan to call the cab company Northern Trade uses since no rideshare companies venture so far off the beaten path. As Athena nears the top of the hill, she sees Rafael and Valentina Luna lit by the dual firepits. They're hard to miss, even without the firelight. In that moment, all Athena can do is laugh. It's so comically humiliating; she almost wonders if her mother engineered this, too.

"Oh no," Valentina says, noticing Athena first. Following her horrified gaze, Rafael turns around to see Athena trudging up the hill. "Go help her, my love. But don't make her feel embarrassed or anything. Just—"

"Okay, I got it." Rafael nods, unraveling himself from his softie of a wife.

Rafael Luna knows his way around a humiliating public moment. One of his greatest regrets is that the seminal train wreck of a wild night out in Vegas that ended in his overdose happened while he wore a fedora. The photos from that night always humble him, but it's the fedora that haunts him to this day.

Athena watches as he picks his way down toward her, Valentina's concerned face the only thing lit up in the pitch black. She would almost rather they ignored her, preferred they were as unkind as her own family had been, but their very decency threatens what little composure she has left.

Rafael stops in front of her and, without saying a word, extends his hand. He eyes the three overloaded tote bags. Thankful for his discretion, Athena hands them to him. He loops one over his shoulder and holds the remaining two, one in each hand. He turns around and waits.

"Where's your car?" Rafael asks.

"I don't have one."

"Okay. Where you headed?"

"I don't know." Athena's raspy breath swirls out into the dark night.

"We can drive you away from here if you want?" Rafael asks. Athena nods, unable to speak without breaking. Without another word, they walk up the hill together.

Once at the top, the valet pulls Rafael's car around, confused as to why Athena Winter is not in the kitchen, but rather is climbing into a vehicle with two strangers loaded down with what appears to be almost everything she owns. He stands back, waiting for some kind of explanation, but Athena can't look at him. Can't say it out loud. She walks to the back of the car, still unable to make eye contact with the valet. Finally, the young man hands Valentina the keys and hurries inside in search of answers. Valentina walks to the back and opens the trunk, the taillights washing them in red.

"We're going to give Athena a lift out of here," Rafael says. Upon hearing this, Valentina's face transforms.

"Glad to have you," she squeaks out. Rafael looks at her. "Not that . . . ugh . . . you . . . um—"

"Thank you for the ride," Athena cuts in before Valentina is able to blurt her entire tragic tale in trying to apologize. Valentina beams at Athena, still trying to play it cool.

Athena drops her duffel bag and backpack into the trunk as Rafael carefully sets down the three tote bags. He slams the trunk closed.

"Do you want the front seat?" Valentina asks.

"Oh, uh—"

"You're so tall is all," Valentina adds. Athena nods and smiles, unsure of how to handle someone so good-natured.

"Thank you." Athena folds herself into the front seat as Rafael takes off his velvet coat and sets it down in the back seat. He steps into the driver's seat, pulls his seat belt across his chest, and clicks it closed. And then both Rafael and Athena wait as Valentina and her giant party dress crinkle and shift in the back seat, trying to get every last sparkle and bit of tulle inside the vehicle.

Just as they're about to pull away, a shaft of light at the back of the restaurant bursts through the pitch black, and out steps Salma Das from the side door of the kitchen. Athena's heart shatters as Salma crumples over and, thinking she's alone, puts her hands over her face and sobs. Rafael and Valentina are quiet as Athena watches Henning step out and comfort her, both now overcome. Athena's hand curls around the door handle.

"We can wait, Chef," Rafael says.

Athena knows this is going to hurt like hell. That the smart thing to do would be to drive away, but as she pushes open the door and runs to Salma and Henning, she can't think of what it would be like to continue living having made the safe choice in this moment. This is her team . . . was her team—whatever. It's still her job to make sure they're okay.

The cold air feels like knives in her throat, but her speed quickens. But as she reaches the outer fringes of the light, Sloane appears in the doorway and calls Salma and Henning back inside with that big-girl voice she's been saving for moments exactly like this. Athena immediately recedes into the darkness as Salma and Henning collect themselves and reluctantly follow Sloane back inside to a kitchen that no longer contains their head chef. Closing the door behind them, Athena becomes enveloped in the vast and anonymous dark.

After a span of time that is both unbearably short yet agonizingly long, Athena makes herself walk away. She takes her glasses off, pulls down her sleeve, and swipes at her eyes, trying to regain some level of self-control before getting back into the car with Rafael and Valentina. She climbs into the passenger seat red-eyed, still trying to stifle the telltale sniffling of someone trying not to cry. From the back seat, Valentina offers her a travel pack of tissues. Athena takes them and croaks out her thanks.

Rafael Luna puts the car in gear and pulls down the long road, carrying Athena Winter away from Northern Trade.

CHAPTER SIX

There is an eerie kind of silence that follows obliteration.

As the dust settles, husks of people wander among the ruins, trying to fathom a path forward out of what remains. Some choose denial, positive this new reality is temporary. They mummify themselves, waiting to be made whole upon the return of the life before. For some, panic chooses them as the terror spreads through their bodies like a virus.

And then there are those who see this confusion in the wake of annihilation as a golden opportunity to step into power.

But in those early-morning hours that begin the New Year, there is an almost unwitting act of collusion that happens within each person who attended Maren Winter's big New Year's Eve celebration. In separate rooms around the Northern Trade Inn, on quiet car rides, and in lavish homes peppering the Bay Area, the dinner guests begin to revisit the events that transpired the night before.

It begins innocently enough, with just an attempt to fully remember what happened, which is usually the first stop one makes when they've witnessed something unbelievable. Cataloging the events in their mind to simply confirm to oneself that they did indeed occur.

But along this path of remembering, these same guests must also consider that while the unbelievable was happening, they themselves did nothing. And a great story is only as epic as your own heroic role in it. Which is when it dawns on each person who witnessed the events of New Year's Eve that if they tell this story in all its unvarnished entirety, the obvious response from anyone listening would be, *"And you just sat there?"*

As the bluish haze of a new day cracks through their bedroom windows after a long sleepless night, this realization will thrum and ripple through the entire guest list and staff of Northern Trade. The shame of their own inaction will propel them out of bed. And as they quietly pace the floor, they'll return to their own mental records of last night's events. But this time it's not to confirm the truth of what happened; it's to build a narrative where they remain the "good person" they believe themselves to be.

Which is how the story of Maren Winter firing her own daughter on New Year's Eve transforms into the more palatable version now spreading like wildfire around the culinary world. During a crowded brunch service on the first day of the New Year, a sous chef who's friends with someone who works at Northern Trade will tell one of the waiters that she heard after the big toast, as the guests tucked in for bone marrow pudding with Cara Cara oranges, Athena and Maren were having a hushed, private conversation that no one could quite hear. So when Athena walked out of Northern Trade that night, everyone assumed she was going back into the kitchen. And that when Maren Winter rejoined her guests, nothing in her demeanor could have given them any idea of the magnitude of what had just occurred.

As the news of what really happened during that "hushed, private conversation" spreads, the guests will feign shock and wistfully shake their heads while saying, "I wish I would have known—I would have done something."

Jules Winter watches as the last droplets of her coffee drip into the gourd-shaped, hand-thrown ceramic mug that sits just below. Once finished, she tosses the filter full of freshly ground coffee into the compost bin and wipes down the scale where she precisely weighed out the beans. Beans that were roasted less than a mile away at a small-batch roastery simply called the Rise and Grind. Giving her black coffee a surgical first sip, she scrolls through her contacts, pinpointing those in her circle who have a certain reputation for loose lips. She pulls out the modern, straight-backed dining room chair her designer picked out and uncomfortably settles into a morning of New Year's Day phone calls where she'll just happen to let a few highly strategic sound bites slip out about the events that occurred the night before.

As Sloane Winter moves through her suspiciously quiet home, she tidies up from the chaos of the night before: tiny shoes, toys, and even a pair of little white tights abandoned as sleeping children were carried in from the New Year's Eve festivities. Her arms now full of adorable, deserted detritus, she finds herself standing at the back of the house, staring out the large french doors to their small garden. She has no idea how long she's been standing there trying to work out every possible path forward after what happened last night. The only fixed point in her machinations is her ultimate goal of taking over as the head of all of the Winter Group. Everything else is up for negotiation.

The sound of someone flushing their toilet in the hotel room next to Athena Winter jolts her awake in the early hours of the New Year. There is one fleeting moment where she forgets about last night, her mind so used to processing tweaks to recipes, menus, and lists as she sleeps. She was going to talk to Penny today about the loquats that were just starting to ripen. Sighing, Athena shifts to her side, grabs her glasses off the oversize gothic nightstand, and takes in the ridiculously faux-painted yellow hotel room she was damn lucky to book at 1:30 a.m. on New Year's Day. Remembering she forgot to pack her phone charger, Athena flips over her dead cell phone, relieved that she has at least one item on her to-do list today.

Maren Winter sleeps soundly for the first time in months.

But it's this fraudulent version of events that calcifies into the bones of those who did nothing that fateful night, temporarily giving them the appearance of goodness but permanently contaminating them in the very groundwater of themselves with every evasive retelling. For them, absolution can come only from those who don't know any better. But they know better.

And so does Lola Tadese.

And unfortunately for those who attended Maren Winter's New Year's Eve gathering, Lola knows the true story in all its unvarnished entirety. And she's currently holed up in a coffee shop in the Mission District transcribing her notes from that evening into what will become next week's Sunday cover story of the Food section in the *San Francisco Chronicle*. Lola's editor made this decision so her exposé would no longer run as just another puff piece in the week leading up to the ceremony, but rather as a splashy cover story that would come out the exact weekend Maren Winter received her lifetime achievement award at the Banquet, the preeminent food and gardening conference held annually just outside Oxford.

A conference that, coincidentally, is also boasting a very rare appearance by none other than the reclusive Athena Winter. Athena had agreed to attend in support of and celebrating her mother's grand achievements, but the conference has now become the arena for quite the culinary battle royale.

But because Northern Trade is closed on both New Year's Day and the following Monday, a false sense of calm settles over the restaurant and those who work there. Ignorant to the coming storm, they sink into the stillness that the first day of the New Year brings.

As the early morning breaks into just the regular morning—an interval of time no one names yet everyone knows—a game of chicken begins: Who will be the first Winter to break the silence?

Jules Winter grips her phone in her hand, writing and revising a text in her Notes app. Once satisfied that it hits the perfect tone of serious yet nonthreatening, she presses Send.

⚘

Sloane Winter's phone buzzes as she wrangles little, tired kids to sit down and please eat the breakfast they said was their favorite yesterday, but now apparently hate. Lærke hands Sloane her phone with a raised eyebrow.

"I told you it would be her," she says, wiping peanut butter off Krister's face.

"Jules is nothing if not predictable," Sloane allows, taking the phone. Lærke laughs.

Sloane reads Jules's text: Thought I could come around and we could talk. I bought way too much at Marin Fresh Cheese Co, we could do a charcuterie?

"She wants to come over to talk." Sloane takes the peanut butter–covered washcloth from Lærke and tosses it in the sink.

"And do you want to talk?" Lærke asks. Sloane inhales, ready to unspool all the thoughts she had as she stood paralyzed looking out those french doors early this morning. Her mind swung wildly between polar opposite conclusions. One: she needs to be the peacemaker and bring all parties to the bargaining table and mediate some accord so they can move forward as a family and a business. Or two: she could put herself first for once and prove unequivocally that she could run this company better than anyone if they would just get out of her way.

But in the end, what she settled on was a first step. A chess move that would keep all her options open.

"Right now, I need an ally," Sloane says.

"No, right now, we need to slow down, process what happened last night, and have a conversation about where we go from here. Preferably starting with your mother's appalling treatment of . . ." Lærke mouths the word "Athena" so the kids stay blissfully unaware.

"Honey, I—" Sloane soothes.

"I worry you're going to—"

"Can you please just trust me?" Sloane blurts out, cutting Lærke off before she says something preeminently reasonable. Both women notice their children now watching them, tense and worried as their parents' voices grow in volume and urgency. Lærke takes a long breath, relaxes her face, and gently brushes a swath of white-blond hair out of Krister's eyes.

"You know I trust you." Lærke leans across and kisses Sloane. And in a whisper only her wife can hear, she says, "What I don't trust is who you turn into when it comes to your family."

"It's just Jules. I can handle her," Sloane says, trying to regulate her voice so the kids don't catch on that the adults are gossiping about their beloved auntie Jules. Sloane excuses Minnie and Freja from the table, and the two little girls bolt into the back garden with squeals of delight. Lærke pulls Krister from his high chair and sets him down on the dining room floor so he can play with his sisters out in the back garden.

"For your sake, I hope you're right," Lærke says, following them outside.

Sloane opens her texts back up and, before she can think better of it, taps out, That sounds like a plan. I have wine. 11:30 okay? She hesitates. Lærke's words bang and crash inside her head like a car accident. She allows herself to think ever so briefly of Athena. It's like a phantom limb. Sloane shakes her head. No. Athena made her choice. This is hers to fix, and for once, Sloane is going to let her little sister clean up her own mess. Sloane presses Send.

Jules's phone dings. She swipes it open and smiles.

"Why'd you text first?" Richard asks, leaning against the Carrara marble kitchen counter. Jules looks up from her phone.

"Hm?" she asks, texting Sloane back confirmation of the plan.

"It makes her think she's got the upper hand." Richard sets his coffee down in preparation for what's surely going to be quite the rousing speech on power dynamics.

"Oh?" Jules asks, making sure her voice is strategically breathy and high pitched.

"You should have . . ."

Jules pours the last of her coffee into the kitchen sink with a sigh and turns to face Richard, saying nothing as he lectures her on the art of war, corporate espionage along with just a dash of sports analogies. She nods along, making little "Hm" noises as he threads in the greatest hits of various and sundry motivational speakers before summiting his rousing pep talk with the evergreen scenario that always begins with "Now, how I would have played this would have been . . ."

Having people explain things to her—especially men—has long been the price Jules Winter has had to pay for keeping her intelligence and cunning hidden. It was a price she's gladly paid, finding endless satisfaction in that moment where someone who underestimated her realizes they've been outplayed. But lately Jules's Dumb Blonde disguise has begun to chafe. And as Richard continues to monologue, she's preyed upon by her deepest fears that she made a mistake marrying a man who is getting harder and harder to stomach.

Jules and Richard Hargreaves were set up on a blind date through mutual acquaintances just two years ago. They'd gushed that they'd found someone who was "perfect for her." But as Jules Winter settled in across the table from him that first night, she couldn't help but be haunted by how little these acquaintances apparently knew her.

Because while Richard Hargreaves was successful and handsome, he was also breathtakingly shallow and more than a little bit cruel. But as the dinner wore on and she and Richard shared an intoxicatingly enchanting moment delighting in the very real problems plaguing their mutual acquaintances' marriage, she grew worried that maybe they did actually know her. And that this was the man she deserved.

They were married a little more than a year ago on the Northern Trade grounds. And just like Sloane before her, Athena designed their nine-course meal—the menu of which is now safely tucked away in Jules's desk drawer at work. Richard had declared that framing and hanging it in their modern kitchen would be "tacky."

Jules thought once they got married, she would stop feeling so lonely. Sloane had Lærke and the kids, Athena had cooking and

Northern Trade, but Jules was just Jules. She mistakenly thought her desire to have a good marriage would certainly grant her one. When that didn't magically happen, Jules Winter did the next best thing: she convinced herself that she did and then faked it. Using social media, Jules designed and disseminated the life, the marriage, and the version of herself she'd always wanted. She reveled in the envious and adoring comments of strangers who knew only what Jules's meticulously crafted life appeared to be.

But what Jules didn't bank on was that Richard himself would believe the fantasy. He luxuriated in his internet fame, believing absolutely that he was worthy of the iconic love poems Jules used as captions in the beautiful photos she posted of him. So as Richard spent the first year of their marriage reveling in the fraudulent life his supposedly besotted wife had fabricated, Jules came to understand what true loneliness was.

Refocusing on Richard's meandering halftime speech, Jules smiles and coquettishly tilts her head just so. Richard lets out a conciliatory laugh and continues.

"I know, I know . . . You don't think about any of this kind of stuff," Richard coos, imperiously tucking a piece of blonde hair behind Jules's ear like he's just realized he's been trying to talk to the family dog.

Jules just giggles, as she counts down to being able to extricate herself and get ready for her day with Sloane.

⚓

Athena sifts through her duffel bags and totes, wrapped in a hotel bath towel that covers approximately 45 percent of her body. Holding the tightly tucked towel with one hand and pulling and tugging various pieces of monochromatic clothing out of the bags' dark recesses with the other, Athena finally decides on a pair of black work pants she hasn't worn in years, a wrinkled white T-shirt, and an oversize heather-gray sweatshirt she got as part of the Banquet's swag bag that just says the word Banquet across the front. She slips on her worn Dansko clogs, throws her black hair up into a ponytail, and heads out into downtown Sausalito in search of coffee and a phone charger.

She finds the phone charger at a convenience store three blocks away from her hotel. It takes the entirety of the walk searching for a cup of coffee just to wrestle the charger free of its packaging. She finds an old-school diner down by the water and decides that bacon, eggs, and hash browns sound pretty great right about now. She pulls open the door, tells the waitress she's just one, and is told she can sit anywhere.

She finds a table next to an outlet, plugs the phone in, and awaits the onslaught of texts she'll no doubt get after last night. Waiting for her breakfast and the phone to boot back up, Athena contemplates how she'll respond—not how she should respond, but how she really wants to respond. Because despite Sloane's assuring her that their mother is "serious this time" and even with the added theatrics of making her move out, Athena knows her mother. And there is no way she's going to let even one service dip in quality to serve whatever unintelligible purpose last night's outburst was about. Banishing Athena from the grounds of Northern Trade was dramatic, but banishing her when there were two days without guests or consequences was strategic. Maren could make her point, Athena would come back properly cowed, and Northern Trade would be up and running in time for Tuesday night's dinner service.

But what if Athena chose not to come back so easily? What if this is the opportunity she's been waiting for? She could actually negotiate better terms to return as head chef and demand the full scope of her wants and desires for the future she envisions for Northern Trade.

As the waitress sets down the heavy white mug full of black coffee and an overflowing plate with bright-yellow eggs, perfectly crisp bacon, and a healthy portion of greasy hash browns, Athena wonders if last night was the best thing that could have happened for her.

She takes a sip of her coffee. It's perfect. Her phone begins the process of coming back to life just as she's digging into the hash browns.

Athena decides that she's going to make them wait. She'll go back to her hotel room and craft her response, coming up with a list of demands. With her left hand still curled around her fork, she reaches for her phone with her right. Swiping it open, she wills herself to be brave.

Which is when she sees that she has received not one text.

Maren Winter marvels at how many people are out and about so early. She maneuvers past joggers, cyclists, and overexcited dogs tugging their owners down the Embarcadero. As she hurries past a pack of tourists trying to take a selfie in front of the iconic clock tower that stands sentry over San Francisco's historic Ferry Building, all Maren sees are prospective Central Trade customers.

The decision to take up the lease on the space at the very north end of the property was one Maren saw as easy. Once the hub of the bustling port of San Francisco, the Ferry Building now houses more than fifty different stalls under its impossibly high, soaring rafters. Stalls filled with some of the most delicious food and wine offerings in the state. Busy and humming, the destination spot attracts thousands of tourists and locals daily.

As Maren walks through the Ferry Building's Grand Nave, all she sees are possibilities. Central Trade will become the place you grab a glass of wine before you catch your ferry, it's where you have an inexpensive lunch in between seeing the sights, and it's the necessary stop where commuters pop in for their morning coffee and pastry to go. Most of the merchants at the Ferry Building sell one product, and however well made it is, Maren's betting that the convenience of Central Trade, the one place you can do and have it all, will outweigh the preciousness of waiting in several long lines just to get the most perfect version of the items you need.

Since it's a holiday, there's no construction going on inside Central Trade for once. Which is exactly why Maren decided to make the pilgrimage down here. She wanted to experience the space by herself, thinking she'll have enough time to change or revise any plans for the upcoming soft launch if the need arises. With all the noise and the chaos of construction, she hasn't been able to just be in the space and feel it.

It took Maren Winter a long time to value something as intangible as how she felt about something. She's spent decades challenging the idea that only men could be visionaries, needing nothing more than "a gut feeling" to launch empires.

While she loves to tell the story of Northern Trade being born in the middle of Golden Gate Park on the back of a utility envelope, she learned the hard way that apparently only men were allowed to sketch lofty ideas on whiskey-soaked cocktail napkins and frame them in their corner offices for all to see. No—women needed backers, a board of directors, and several drafts of several different business plans that somehow managed to thread in every note, thousands of comments, and a staggering list of concerns from any and everyone who believed themselves to be far more of an expert than Maren ever could.

Far too much time passed as Maren filtered even the smallest decisions through committee, until her whole life felt like a failed group project that no one wanted to own. Including her.

Get married. Have kids. Be a good cook, but not *too* good a cook. Sure, modern women could have it all, but that doesn't mean you should flaunt it in front of everyone or, God forbid, drop a ball. Starting your own business is too risky; shouldn't you be focused on finding a husband and starting a family first? Don't set your "little restaurant" so far away; no one will come. Don't make the menu too fussy; people won't trust you. Hire a man to be head chef in the beginning to ease people's minds. Every suggestion made "for her own good" sliced into her like a knife.

As Maren tours the quiet Central Trade space, jotting down notes and checking off lists, she remembers that time in her life with perfect, gut-wrenching clarity as if it were 1977 all over again.

❦

Tidying up the last vestiges of a hurried breakfast in her suffocatingly small kitchen after getting called in last minute to work the lunch shift, Maren felt trapped in what everyone thought was best for her. Exhausted, she laid both hands on the cold metal sink as it filled with water. She let her head drop between her taut arms, her back radiating in pain after hours on her feet. Earlier that day, she'd been given the name of a French head chef who'd implied he'd be open to moving to San Francisco if the price was right. It was a real get, one of the backers told her. You'd be lucky to have him, a friend of a friend had said. She said she'd think about it. They told her the clock was ticking.

She felt its vibrations deep in her chest and knew she couldn't swallow it down this time. Trying to dampen the sound as much as possible, Maren plunged her face into the water and screamed.

It felt good.

She pulled her drenched head from the water, took a dish towel off the counter, and attempted in vain to dry her hair. Her long brown hair now dripping onto her sodden shirt, Maren walked over to the phone and told each and every person that what she did with her restaurant was no longer up for discussion. She was going to be the head chef for Northern Trade, and if her "little restaurant" didn't make all the money back within its first year, then she'd quit, get a job somewhere, and pay back every last cent. With every phone call, as she heard herself saying those words out loud, she felt this power surge through her, believing it a little more with every conversation.

After the final call, Maren replaced the phone back into its cradle. She'd given no explanation. She'd given no concrete proof. She'd offered no other more respected opinion to back up her own. She simply said that she knew what was right for Northern Trade and that, in this instance, what was right for Northern Trade . . . was her.

Unable to fall asleep that night, the newfound feeling of power coursing through her, Maren vowed that from that moment on, when it came to her own life, she would never allow anyone to tell her what to do again.

And through the years, that singular vow propelled Maren Winter higher than she could have ever imagined. Because inside every one of her ideas bloomed innovation. Every time she was the first at something, thousands witnessed it and began to believe that they, too, could follow in her footsteps. By not listening to those who doubted her, Maren Winter struck out on a path that no one before her had taken. But that now—because of her—is as bustling as the Embarcadero on New Year's Day.

Maren slides into one of the Central Trade booths by the window and finishes her list, staving off the temptation to send her contractor an email or leave yet another message to the Italian artisans working on her green orchid glass installation that should have arrived weeks ago. Instead, she sends a draft of the email to Sloane, sets a reminder to call the glass installation people in the morning, and takes one last lap through the space and makes her way back to that old gray Land Rover, her mind a riot of lists, plans, and possibility.

She hasn't felt this alive in years.

There's a singular type of energy that comes from feeling that you're good at something. That's what they don't tell you about getting older—it's not the invisibility or the aches and pains that kill you. Instead, it's that incrementally, and over a span of just a few years, you are perceived to be less and less useful to the world. And the belief that you're slipping begins to calcify into the fear that, if you're no longer good at something, then maybe you're not good for anything. And then why are you still here?

For someone who broke glass ceilings and paved new roads, not feeling like she's still masterful is an existence that Maren Winter cannot and will not abide. Central Trade is proof that she's still good for something. It's evidence that she's still useful. And Maren Winter hopes that the undeniability of Central Trade—in all its enormous glory—will send that message loud and clear to all who need the reminder.

⚘

Sloane stands in her kitchen, absently looking into her refrigerator for what to serve while planning a coup. If Jules is bringing charcuterie, she could set out some nice grapes to pair with it. Sloane reaches into her fridge and grabs the grapes, along with a bottle of prosecco left over from an event she can no longer remember. She digs a colander out of the back of the cabinet and rinses the grapes while considering the prosecco.

"Probably shouldn't make it look like we're celebrating," Sloane says to herself, turning the water off and putting the prosecco back into the refrigerator. Instead, she finds a nice solemn Cab. She sets the wine on the table, along with the dewy grapes, a nondescript file folder of her notes, and other pertinent paperwork and continues fussing around the kitchen to give her mind something to do other than play out anxiety-induced, catastrophic scenarios of impending doom. Thankfully, Sloane's phone pings, and this gives her something to concentrate on for even just a few seconds. She walks over to where her phone is on the kitchen counter and sees that it's an email from her mother.

"She's been busy," Sloane says to herself, opening up the email.

Sloane scrolls through what is clearly Maren's punch list for her contractor, as well as a link to a YouTube video of a youngish woman cooking one of Maren's recipes. Sloane clicks on the video and watches just long enough to wonder if her mom has sent this to her so she can have their attorneys send the woman a letter about copyright infringement and fair use because she keeps showing the cover to Maren's first cookbook in the video.

Sloane clicks out of the video and returns to her mother's email. Scrolling through the punch list, she lets out a long groan at her mom having to bump the people making that stupid glass orchid. The ego-stroking, nineteen-foot monstrosity that's going to end up costing more than a half a million dollars. And apparently, it's not even going to be ready for the soft launch. She shakes her head and exits out of her email just in time to hear the beep-beep of Jules setting her car alarm in the driveway.

Sloane walks over to the large wooden front door and pulls it open. She steps out onto the main deck that overlooks the San Francisco Bay and deadheads a few of the flowers planted in various containers as she waits for Jules to climb the three flights of stairs from the driveway to the main house.

"Have I ever told you how much I hate these stairs?" Jules calls out from somewhere down below.

"Maybe your New Year's resolution can be climbing stairs without constantly complaining," Sloane yells down. She looks over the railing and sees Jules sitting on one of the stairs, tote bags full of meats and cheeses littering the ground around her.

Sloane and Lærke's home, like many in Mill Valley, is perched on the side of Mount Tamalpais. Nestled into the surrounding nature, their home is accessible only by an impossibly narrow private road, a death-defyingly steep driveway, and three flights of stairs. But waking up to unencumbered views of the bay—the Golden Gate Bridge peeking out from just under the fog—and living among the lush treetops are definitely worth the trouble. For some . . .

"I'm dying," Jules says, rummaging through one of the tote bags for her bottle of water.

"Don't be such a baby," Sloane yells down. Jules lets out a whimper, takes a long swig of her water, drops it back into one of the tote bags, and dramatically heaves herself up into a standing position.

"You can do it, Jules. Don't listen to your mean sister. I believe in you." Jules pep talks herself all the way to the top of the stairs. Sloane takes two of the tote bags, and Jules follows her inside the house.

"What do you want to drink?" Sloane asks, setting the tote bags down on the kitchen counter.

"Do you still have that great Earl Grey from before?" Jules asks, looking around the house.

"I thought you were doing the whole coffee pour-over thing now?" Sloane asks.

"Apparently I'm in a tea mood today," Jules says.

"They're right there . . . in that cabinet. Just behind the box of Builders tea," Sloane says, flipping on the kettle. Jules finds the tea, grabs a plain white mug with a colorful yet inscrutable painting Minnie did at school and the words "Happy Mother's Day" written in a crayon font across the top. She sets the mug on the counter, drops in a tea bag, and starts unpacking the totes.

"Where is everyone?" Jules asks.

"I set up a playdate with one of our couple friends—"

"What did you tell Lærke we were doing today?" Jules asks, setting out the staggering amount of charcuterie offerings she brought.

"I just said we were going to talk about what happened last night," Sloane says. Jules looks over. "I mean, we don't even know what we're doing today, so . . . it's not . . ."

"Like you intentionally lied to your wife?" Jules prods, pouring the hot water into her mug.

"I didn't . . . I . . ."

"It's none of my business," Jules says, pulling out one of their wishbone chairs and sitting.

"What are you talking about? Nothing has even happened yet. What would I be lying to her about?" Sloane says, sitting across the table from her sister.

"Look, you and I both know that I know my way around stretching the truth a little," Jules says, warming her hands around her mug.

"Are you bragging about being a good liar?"

"I'm not *not* saying that's what I'm doing." Jules blows on her tea.

"I'll tell you what you're doing. You're doing that thing where you think everyone is as manipulative as you are," Sloane says, reaching for the bottle of wine in the middle of the table.

"Ouch," Jules says.

"Are you done? Because I'd like to start mapping out our way forward."

"Mapping out our what? Is that . . . does that mean coming up with a plan? Did you learn that dumb little phrase from the same girl boss book that told you to say you wanted 'more leadership opportunities'?"

"Are you trying to make me regret this?" Sloane asks, letting out a long, weary sigh. Jules holds up her hand in surrender.

Jules watches her sister pour a full glass and take a healthy drink, gulping down guilt, nerves, and a splash of self-doubt along with the cabernet she didn't let breathe. But what Sloane doesn't know is the plan she thinks she and Jules are in the process of concocting together is already well underway. Because long before the events that transpired on New Year's Eve, Jules—like her sisters—saw the red flags with Maren's increasingly concerning behaviors. But unlike Sloane's and Athena's, Jules's methods lean more toward the bloodthirsty. And her plan to destabilize the Winter Group for her own benefit began months ago.

When you are as good at being invisible as Jules Winter, you learn to thrive in the anonymity of everyone's underestimation. But the part that's getting harder is Jules's ability to blame her Machiavellian deceptions on her family's chronic belittlement of her. In Jules's mind, she wouldn't have to deceive, plot, and conspire in the shadows if it weren't for her family's habit of pushing her into the darkest corners of their lives.

Or that's what she tells herself as she fails to circle back to her earlier assertion that she is, in fact, extremely good at her job. And because of this, she absolutely knows who Lola is and that Lola Tadese doesn't write puff pieces.

Lola Tadese writes hit pieces.

Which is exactly why Jules Winter reached out to her several months ago with the opportunity of a lifetime: unfettered access to all stakeholders and properties within the Winter Group in the run-up to Maren Winter's historic lifetime achievement award bestowed unto Lola by someone everyone thinks is too dumb to know she's just let the fox into the henhouse.

Because while everyone in Jules Winter's life has consistently failed to truly see her, she—on the other hand—has studied those around her like an anthropologist, meticulously cataloging every observation, no matter how minute. And over the course of decades, Jules has become quite the expert on human nature, understanding—perhaps because of her own proclivities—the darker sides that those closest to her would rather stay hidden.

All Jules has to do is sit back and watch her little time bomb work. A casual comment about Sloane lying to her wife and then Sloane's own usage of the word "our" while talking about the plan and Jules's detonation will go off at the exact moment when Sloane's guilt about her own deception intersects with the plan's vicious climax. At which point, Jules is positive that Sloane will take the blame herself as Jules slinks back into the shadows . . . far too stupid to have had any hand in what's transpired.

Because is it even manipulation if the people being used brought it on themselves? Without Sloane's primary assumption that Jules is an idiot, this entire plan would've never gotten off the ground.

But here they were at liftoff. Sloane—and Jules, *shh*—will make a plan to instill distrust in their mother's leadership. When Lola's hit piece comes out, Jules will set Sloane up to take the fall. Then Jules, and Jules alone, will finally step out of the shadows and take over the Winter Group.

Jules reaches into her bag and pulls out a small Moleskine notebook, a silver fountain pen hooked to the cover by its clip. She unclips the pen and opens the notebook to the saved page containing her notes.

"I feel like we have to deconstruct this and look at it in phases. Almost like what unlocks what, if that makes sense," Sloane starts. Jules nods in agreement, sets her pen down, and trying to buy some time so she can act like this is a plan she's just thought of, rummages through her purse and pulls out a hair tie. She scrapes her blonde hair up and out of her face, tightly wrapping it into a loose bun.

"We start with New Year's Eve," Jules says, writing that down at the top of her page.

"Okay," Sloane says, waiting for more.

"I know it was terrible what happened, but right now it's the best evidence we have to back up our position that Mom is making choices that hurt the Winter Group."

"You're right," Sloane concedes.

Jules nods and continues. "Okay. So, we start with Mom firing Athena and how, ultimately, it's bad for business. We lean into the impulsivity of it," she says, taking a page out of her own mother's handbook.

"Fired her own kid over a pork chop," Sloane says.

"Her own kid and, more importantly, a world-famous chef that brought in a lot of revenue. I know it feels cold-blooded, but if we're going to plead our case to the board of directors, it means we have to speak their language—which is money. The court of public opinion, however . . ." Jules trails off.

Sloane nods. "Right. I think swinging public opinion hinges on us trying to figure out what people want to think about Maren Winter and how does her firing Athena give them a good reason to act on those feelings."

Jules nods, too. "It's sad, but if a person's success is making people feel badly about themselves—" she starts.

"Not even intentionally," Sloane says.

"And now they're being celebrated with a lifetime achievement award?" Sloane tilts her head. Jules elaborates, "Normal people don't receive tons of awards or get interviewed about every thought they've ever had in their heads. And they aren't then told that each of those thoughts are so interesting and funny and everyone wants to know, like, what's your creative process—like, that doesn't happen to most people. Most people just get lost in doing their dumb little jobs, living their lives, and wishing people could see how special they really are," Jules says, realizing again she's getting way more personal than she'd like to be.

"Right," Sloane says.

"So, here's Maren Winter—super successful at a job she loves, while most people work jobs they hate. And she's making really good money, while most people don't. She's even thin and still looks relatively young? And she's being interviewed, writing cookbooks, and getting all these big awards, and now they hear she's being a big ole bully?"

"Which means she's no longer being super grateful," Sloane says, drawing out the words with dramatic flair.

"And God forbid, she stops being endlessly grateful," Jules says.

"Ugh," Sloane says, looking down at the table.

"Envy is a hell of a drug," Jules says.

"We lean into—"

"We give them what they want." Sloane is quiet. "A good reason to turn on her and, in doing so, feel better about themselves because they would never *ever* do such a thing."

"We use firing Athena as a way to push this egomaniacal thing," Sloane says.

"I mean, it's not even a lie at this point," Jules says.

"And then that can chip away at her credibility and whether or not she can still do the job," Sloane says.

"Which is also true, by the way," Jules says.

"We establish that we had no idea she was going to fire Athena—"

"Another true thing," Jules adds.

"And are actually sick about how Mom treated her on New Year's."

"Also true. We can even—hell, we can say we tried to talk to her, tried to fight for Athena—"

"But we didn't," Sloane says.

"Right, but they don't know that. And if Mom's credibility is under question, her even saying that we didn't won't matter," Jules says.

"We can use the staff as backup," Sloane says, finally.

"How do you mean?" Jules asks, drawing Sloane further out.

"When Mom's over at Central Trade, we set an impromptu meeting with the staff where we disclose that we tried to have the hard conversation with Mom, that we fought for Athena, and that we're trying to make things right," Sloane says.

"I can even anonymously leak what you say to the staff to Lola. Make her think it's coming from one of the staff. Try to smooth over whatever she thinks she may have seen on New Year's Eve. I've got a few burner email accounts," Jules says, scribbling in her notebook.

"A few burner email accounts?" Sloane asks.

"I use them primarily for different social media platforms," Jules says, proving that she does, in fact, know her way around stretching the truth a little.

"I think we should probably try to actually have that conversation with Mom—or at least some version of it," Sloane says.

"Why?"

"Insurance."

"Is that insurance worth her possibly throwing both of us out like she did Athena?"

"I think the more we can hang on these little nuggets of truth, the better. It'll give us those verifiable details—like an actual day it happened, that kind of thing. It'll be more facts she can't deny," Sloane says.

"Fine, but you're going to lead that conversation, too," Jules says. Sloane nods, deciding not to respond by pointing out that Sloane leads every hard conversation and why would this one be different.

"We'll also have to figure out the whole head chef situation—"

"I think for the good of the restaurant Salma Das should step in. She's the CDC. It's the right decision," Sloane says.

"For right now, yes," Jules says. Sloane feels momentarily better about herself for championing Salma Das. Later, she'll pluck this moment out as proof that she's doing the right thing and that the end will justify the means.

"I'll do some digging on the real numbers for Central Trade. I know Mom's been hiding money and spending way more than she says she has. That giant glass orchid for one," Sloane says.

"But we can use the giant orchid to our advantage. It's the perfect symbol of her spending a ton of money on something super unnecessary just to stroke her own ego. And any proof we can provide of Mom putting her own ego in front of the good of the business . . ." Jules trails off.

"So that's the first phase. Then that unlocks the next one—"

"Going to the board of directors," Jules says.

"Assuming Mom already kicked Athena off, that takes us from eight to seven. So, out of the seven of us, we just need to get four," Sloane says, pulling out the list of people who make up the Winter Group's board of directors from a file.

"So, there's the two of us, and I'm sure Odette will vote with us. If she's truly going to represent the staff in her vote, she'd have to go against Mom simply because of what she did to Athena," Jules says, pulling the sheet of paper over to her and highlighting Odette's name in pink.

"The CEO of East Bay Soups will be easy. She's all business, and Mom's becoming a liability," Sloane says, pulling the sheet of paper back over to her and highlighting the CEO's name in pink.

"That's four," Jules says.

"If we can get one more just in case someone flip-flops," Sloane says, scanning the remaining names.

"Penny will go with Mom. I don't think she's necessarily happy with her these days, but . . . there's no way she'd vote her out," Jules says, highlighting Penny's name in blue. "So it's just down to Aunt Josephine . . ." Jules trails off as she looks at the remaining name.

"She'll probably be at the Central Trade launch. I say we feel her out and then proceed with—"

"A vote of no confidence," Jules cuts in.

"The next phase after that would be shutting down Central Trade once and for all—before it takes us all down with it," Sloane says.

"Another true thing," Jules adds yet again.

"I also want to do outreach on what the process would be to get Athena's Southern Trade hot dogs into grocery stores. I'm thinking we can start those conversations with the same company that's doing East Bay Soups," Sloane says.

"Without Athena?" Jules asks.

"If Mom has spent even half of what I think she has on Central Trade, we're going to need a big influx of cash to just break even," Sloane says.

"So you'd just take her recipe?" Jules asks.

"To save the company? To save all of us? Yeah, I would."

"But—"

"This? This you have a problem with?" Sloane asks, her face coloring.

"I thought we were bringing Athena back once we were in charge. Isn't that what you meant by 'setting things right'? She should be head chef again, and you can partner with her on this instead of—"

"Do you honestly think she'd listen to me?" Sloane asks.

"If we are the ones who rehired her, yeah." Jules hits the word "we" with clarifying gusto.

"Let's put a pin in this, okay?" Sloane asks.

Jules recognizes that tone of voice. She's pitched something Sloane doesn't agree with. And rather than compromising or asking clarifying questions, Sloane defaults to "silly Jules doesn't understand hard things." That way she can ultimately ignore what Jules has to say.

"Okay," Jules says, sitting back in her chair. She allows a small smile as the ticking from her time bomb grows louder and louder.

Sloane and Jules Winter spend the next couple of hours hammering out the details, getting their stories straight, and constructing a multi-faceted, many-layered plot to take down their mother.

After they've said their goodbyes, they will each spend the rest of the day figuring out how this multifaceted, many-layered plot might also hide a few well-placed booby traps for their beloved coconspirator.

Across town, Athena Winter sits in her hotel room biting her nails. She sits in an uncomfortable chair, hunched over a small, rickety, gold-leaf table that's pushed into an even smaller bay window. She stares out across Sausalito's idyllic downtown just below, absently spinning her silent cell phone around. Again and again. Again and again. She's been sitting in this exact spot for hours. Unmoving. Paralyzed.

There is a particular heartbreaking brutality to silence. Within the fields of its vast nothingness, doubt and fear bloom because its soil is fertilized with the only tangible thing Athena now knows for sure.

She is utterly alone.

CHAPTER SEVEN

Maren Winter lasted exactly one night as Northern Trade's head chef. The sheer physicality of the job would be a shock to anyone's system, let alone someone who's been out of the game for years. As the night wore on, Maren started taking more time out in the main dining room, making the rounds and chatting up guests.

What Maren knew was that the clientele in restaurants like Northern Trade were pretty much the same around the world. About half the people dining with her tonight were there just so they could tell their friends or post a picture of it on their social media. Eating something Maren Winter made was simply a box to check along the way to becoming a person of importance. Extra points were awarded if you could tell people it was either a once-in-a-lifetime experience or not worth the hype. A few tables were occupied by those trying to impress the person seated across from them, hoping tonight's meal could move their relationship beyond what they feared their own limitations demanded.

Then there were those few. Those who loved food. Who closed their eyes when they tasted something they'd never had before. They were the ones who got it. The ones who made it all worthwhile.

And Maren Winter had missed this. It felt good to feed people again. For so many chefs, success means they don't get to actually cook anymore. Elevated to restaurateur, their daily tasks are more in line with corporate America than anything in the culinary arts.

Throughout the first courses, Maren would stop and lean over parties full of excited diners, giving her lower back a moment's rest in the process. But as the night wore on, she began singling out guests who just happened to have an open seat at the table. And in the final hours of her first—and last—dinner service in more than ten years, Maren Winter ended the evening sharing a bottle of Northern Trade's finest wine with a particularly friendly trio who'd flown all the way in from Singapore.

The guests loved it, of course, and Jules even snapped a great photo of Maren with her trio of new friends, head back and laughing, for Northern Trade's socials. But everyone knew. This was not sustainable. The kitchen staff scrambled to find their rhythm—defaulting to Salma's leadership when Maren was on one of her walkabouts. Then they had to stutter and stop each time Maren tried to rejoin the clockwork precision Athena had so prided herself on.

Sloane and Jules's fragile alliance was tested throughout the evening, while they worked together to comfort the growing number of anxious employees. "Together" being quite the reach to describe the tenuous agreement between the remaining Winter sisters. In the past, it would have been up to Sloane to wade in first, absorbing the first wave of anger and confusion as well as the sticky blame that went along with it. But this time, Sloane made sure that Jules had to endure just as many hard and uncomfortable conversations as she did. *Somehow this is your fault,* they'd say. *Somehow you can make this better and are choosing not to. Somehow yelling at you will ease the shame I'm carrying around for not standing up for Athena on New Year's Eve.*

No longer comfortable with being "the mean one" who's "just so cringe," Sloane made it impossible for Jules to slink around in the liminal space after she'd had a difficult conversation and offer them a soft, pretty shoulder to cry on. Jules's long-practiced method of commiserating with disgruntled employees, dramatically shaking her head as she was forced to agree. *I know,* she'd say, looking at the ground. *Sloane can be a bit much. This must be so hard on you.* And then, just as she's about to get up, Jules would look over at the employee and—with sad, pooly eyes—sigh. *I'll try to talk to her.*

Long after everyone left Northern Trade, as Sloane and Jules got stoned together on the balcony of the second floor of the main dining room, they both knew they could no longer wait to talk to their mom.

But there was also the part that Sloane and Jules didn't talk about. The tiny sliver inside each of them that held out hope that their mother would snap out of this, set things right, and save them from themselves. And as much as they talked about this opening conversation being a strategic one, deep down they also hoped it would be a rescue mission.

Because on top of everything else, if they didn't act fast, there would be no empire to take over. If Northern Trade fell, the Winter Group would have lost its jewel in the crown, and if this happened, it would take very little to topple the remaining house of cards. Of course, neither Sloane nor Jules would allow themselves to repeat Athena's final prophetic words to them as she left Northern Trade that fateful New Year's Eve. But as both women toss and turn throughout yet another sleepless night, Athena's words haunt them: *"This is going to get bad."*

But it's not just her warning that haunts Sloane and Jules Winter. Each of them has long fantasized about what it'd be like to finally be rid of Maren's favorite child. Once and for all. They've each daydreamed about striding confidently around this Athena-less world, respected and envied by all. Powerful and capable, they've each seen themselves as the steady hand the Winter Group has long needed—the steady hand Maren Winter has long needed.

Instead, during Maren's one dinner service as head chef, Sloane and Jules felt perpetually unfinished, always awaiting that third voice that never came. And it wasn't that either woman could properly identify why they were feeling off. The Winter sisters learned long ago that the best way forward in the family they'd been given was to live as unexamined a life as possible.

But as the sun crested over the rolling hills of Tomales Bay early the next morning, Sloane and Jules Winter caught a break. They each woke up to messages saying that Maren was going to be focusing on Central Trade until the soft launch and that Salma Das should step in until Maren found Athena's replacement.

They were both so overjoyed at dodging what could have been an explosively hard conversation—possibly resulting in their own ousting and their entire plan toppling to the ground, to say nothing of the verbal hits that Maren usually throws in arguments such as these—that neither woman took stock of why Sloane had felt the conversation was necessary in the first place. And this misguided bravado would cause both Winter sisters to not fully register the second part of Maren's message—*until Maren found Athena's replacement*—an oversight that could throw a major wrench into their already tenuous plan.

Using Maren's absence to officially begin phase one of their plan, the remaining Winter sisters strode into Northern Trade on the morning following their mother's first and only attempt at stepping back in as head chef. First, they announced to the staff that they'd listened to their concerns and had a difficult but fruitful conversation with their mother.

Standing in front of the crackling fireplace in the main dining room, Sloane and Jules waxed rhapsodic about how they challenged their mother regarding her mistreatment of their beloved sister on New Year's Eve. Jules's bright-blue eyes teared up as she choked out how hard this had been for her, unable to stomach not speaking up for her little sister any longer.

Sloane's mouth settled into a hard line as she patiently waited for Jules to gather herself, an episode that was only hurried along thanks to Eleanor bringing the sniffling Winter sister a steaming mug of jasmine tea. As Jules cradled the mug in her delicate, pale fingers, Sloane announced that they'd asked their mother to step down as head chef effective immediately. It was a declaration that drew actual gasps from the gathered staff. And in those tiny milliseconds, as the air was sucked out of the room, the sound waves from her own words still floating through the air, Sloane Winter wondered if she might have overplayed her hand. But that fleeting moment passed as she scanned the faces of the Northern Trade staff standing in militaristic lines in front of her.

Respect.

She felt as though she were being seen for the first time. Sloane Winter basked in their reverence. And she never questioned that this moment felt so good because it had none of the residue of discomfort that would've come from actually having the conversation with Maren. It was a celebration of an unearned boundary. And it felt amazing only because the other side was oblivious not only to the fact that they'd lost the battle but that there was a battle to begin with. Emboldened by their wafting approval, she went on to explain that they'd told their mother that Salma Das would step in as head chef of Northern Trade until they could bring Athena back home. Jules Winter sneaked a look at her elder sister just after the word "told" cut through the main dining room. That wasn't part of the script they'd agreed upon. Jules sipped her tea, swallowing down her concern along with the warm, spring-green brew. If anybody knew the power of language, it was Jules Winter. The deliciousness of one wrong word was oftentimes too tempting not to spread.

But Sloane continued, her voice growing louder as she listed their final key points: the Great Maren Winter had acquiesced to their demands and would, from here on out, be focusing solely on Central Trade. And most importantly, Sloane and Jules Winter were now in charge at Northern Trade.

None of this was true, of course, but every bit of it was about to be anonymously leaked to Lola Tadese.

Athena Winter sits on the side of her hotel bed, clad once again in only a minuscule, scratchy bath towel as she scrolls through her phone. She's taken to spending her mornings checking to make sure that everyone in her life seems to be thriving and getting along just fine without her.

"Oh, is this a super-fun road trip trying different local cheeses for your newest restaurant that you can't tell us anything about yet?" Athena mocks, her thumb scrolling violently past the happy faces of colleagues she thought were friends, although none of them had reached out to her in the aftermath of New Year's Eve.

She doesn't like being this person.

She doesn't like feeling all that single-minded intensity she once used to feed people innovative and delicious food now turned against her like a fire hose of bitterness and rage. She doesn't like spending her time imagining a bleak future where she works the line anonymously, making someone else's dopey restaurant successful until she's physically unable to do the work and then lives out her final days in a run-down, moldy-smelling studio being delivered Meals on Wheels by a well-meaning young person with their whole life ahead of them.

Not that she's thought this through or anything.

Athena throws her phone on the bed and strides into the bathroom to finish her morning routine. Looking at herself in the elaborate gothic mirror in the bathroom, she notices how tired she looks. No. She doesn't look tired.

Athena Winter looks broken.

She spits out her toothpaste and rinses her mouth, looking away from her own reflection as quickly as she can. And when she walks back into her hotel room, she sees a text on her phone. Her entire body buzzes and tenses as she runs through each and every scenario of who it could be, what they want, and moreover, how she will be able to regulate her emotions in responding to them. She's had fantasies of answering all texts with "What the hell took you so long."

Not that any of these fantasies deal with why Athena herself hasn't reached out to anyone. But it isn't like it was something she meant to do. That first day she was so blindsided she couldn't untangle her feelings long enough to draft a cohesive thought to anyone. And with each day of radio silence, it almost became this sick game where the only way to win was by berating herself for not putting more energy into making real friends and building community. That, ultimately, it was all her fault that she was alone. This was the recurring spiral that woke her up every morning at 3:30 a.m., weighted down with the thick fog of one overriding emotion: shame.

Athena picks up her phone. Braces herself. The text is from Jenn Nishimura. Athena didn't even know she had her phone number.

have an opening at tonight's early dinner service. Would love to have you.

Athena holds her phone tight in her hand.

It's hard to fathom, but somehow kindness is always harder for Athena Winter to process than absolute annihilation. Before she can shut it down—

I would love that. Count me in.

Jenn responds with the details, and after Athena replies with what she hopes is a somewhat normal level of gratitude, she sits on the edge of her bed and tries not to cry.

The day goes by in a haze. Athena tries to keep busy by bagging up all her clothes and walking down to a local Laundromat. It's next door to a small, family-owned taqueria, so as Athena's clothes are in the dryer, she eats some of the best mole poblano she's ever tasted, washing it down with a giant horchata, and feels a little less lost.

Athena gets dressed in an outfit she once wore to a fancy dinner. Staring at herself in the mirror, she thinks she looks almost presentable. She sweeps her bangs to the side, but because they've been growing out and she never made the time to get a haircut, every time she pushes them back, they fall right back into her face. Positive this will be the one thing that finally makes her crack, Athena looks around the hotel room and finds an old binder clip among some papers she grabbed off her desk back at the old studio. It's bright blue, and Athena convinces herself that if she clips the bangs back and is somehow able to hide the metal part of the clip, no one will be able to tell.

This will be one of several lies Athena Winter tells herself that night.

As it becomes time to head into the city, Athena walks down to the lobby in search of the number to the cab company the hotel uses. Athena has long opted for cabs over any of the rideshare options, preferring their anonymity over awkwardly sitting in the back seat of someone's personal vehicle as they earnestly try and ultimately fail at making small talk with her.

"May I help you?" the woman behind the counter asks.

"I'm staying in room 205. Athena Winter. I have to get into the city. Do you have a cab service you use?"

"Oh, sure." The woman pulls a business card from a stack and slides it across the counter. "Have a great night."

"Thank you," Athena says, taking the card and pulling her phone from her pocket.

"Oh, wait. Room 205," the woman calls out to Athena.

"Yes, is . . . that's me," Athena asks as the call connects with the cab company.

"You haven't given us a checkout date," the woman says. Athena quickly tells the dispatcher on the other end that she is in need of a cab and provides the hotel's address. Once Athena hangs up, she turns to face the woman.

"Right. Do you need to know that right now?" Athena asks.

"As soon as you can—that way we can manage our reservations and know when your room will be available again," the woman says.

"Right. That makes sense," Athena says, unsure of what to say.

"Do you think it'll be tomorrow? In a week? I mean, you're not planning on staying forever, are you?" The woman laughs, trying to lighten the mood.

"No, that would be insane," Athena answers, before walking out of the lobby without another word.

Waiting for the cab just outside the hotel, Athena begins to feel trapped. She most certainly doesn't want to be at this hotel for another night. But at the same time, she doesn't want to start looking for her own apartment, because that would mean that this is permanent. And that all this actually happened.

As Athena waves the cab down and crawls inside, she can't help thinking that when her life felt real, it apparently wasn't. And now that it doesn't feel real, it is, whether she likes it or not. She looks out the window, trying to quiet her mind. Unable to do so, she pulls out her phone and takes another tour of Other People's Happy Lives on Social Media. She spends the remainder of the cab ride numbly scrolling.

Athena's breath catches as she steps inside Jenn Nishimura's gorgeous restaurant on a tiny side street in the Castro. When you think you don't get to do something you love anymore, being around someone who's doing it well is sheer agony. And as Athena is led to her table, she notices all the things she took for granted back when she got to have them. Athena looks around at the other diners. They're excited and smiling as they, too, take in everything Jenn has created.

Hills and Valleys is a tiny restaurant made up of dark woods and bohemian pops of color. Clean and sparse, it somehow feels bigger than just its walls. Jenn has created a space that feels both entirely unique but also utterly familiar, as if the design were pulled from each one of the diners' memories of a long-forgotten time. *We've all been somewhere like this. We've all loved somewhere like this. And we've all forgotten how much we missed somewhere like this.*

For each of the diners here, whatever is happening in their lives outside is gone, and tonight will be a culinary experience that will make them feel again, rediscovering each and every sense deliciously, passionately, and electrically. Athena watches as a young man closes his eyes and just breathes in. How long has it been since he let himself just be? Athena turns away. The pain overtaking her.

She once made people feel like that.

"Hey, I'm so glad you could make it," Jenn says, walking over to Athena's table. Athena notices everyone in the restaurant turn and watch as Jenn settles in next to her. Surreptitious photos, excited squeals of delight, and broad smiles stab into Athena's quickly numbing body one after another.

Athena and Jenn know each other only through work, having attended the same culinary events throughout the Bay Area. Although they really bonded at one particular conference as they sat next to each other during a particularly terrible keynote speech where the chef used an asparagus puppet to make a point about sustainability. Sadly, the only thing the large green talking phallus communicated was that maybe the chef should have run his idea by someone before premiering it on a stage before hundreds of his esteemed colleagues.

"Thank you so much for the invitation," Athena says, using every fiber of her being not to make it weird. Jenn smiles and they run through a little of the menu—bonding over their love of Tomales Bay Oysters and nigiri sushi. Athena nods, taking in Jenn's neon-green workman's jumpsuit, clogs, and rainbow-striped compression socks. Her long black hair is pulled back from her face and tied up in a messy bun at the nape of her neck. She looks exhausted, but there's something else.

Jenn Nishimura looks . . . purposeful.

Jenn walks back into the kitchen just as the sakizuke course hits Athena's table. And as each course comes and goes, Athena falls into almost a trance, tasting food as if for the first time—a tiny bite of ripe persimmon just as it's going out of season, a lobster dish that compels her to sit back and close her eyes as she chews, and the most perfect piece of A5 Wagyu beef she's ever tasted. But with every dish she feels a deep melancholia, as if she's working up to bidding farewell to a beloved.

By the time the last course sits in front of Athena, she is—well, completely drunk. The thirteen-course wine and sake pairing (with healthy pours, thanks to Jenn) has rendered Athena Winter altogether plastered. But she has also crossed firmly into whatever stage of grief is represented by attempting to hide that you're trying not to cry while dining alone at a colleague's beautiful three-Michelin-Starred restaurant.

As the early dinner service begins to wind down, Jenn again appears at Athena's table. This time she sits down in the chair opposite Athena.

"That was probably the most beautiful meal I've ever had," Athena slurs.

"You're drunk." Jenn laughs.

"I am, but that doesn't mean it's not true," Athena says, her eyes inexplicably closing for three full seconds.

"I'm glad you could make it," Jenn says.

There is a long pause. Jenn's face softens, her brow furrowing warmly as Athena feels the atmosphere shift in the room. She knows what's coming. She has to act fast.

"I know you know what happened," Athena blurts out.

"Rafael told me," Jenn admits.

"That's where you got my phone number," Athena says, trying to celebrate figuring out at least one of today's mysteries by snapping her fingers. But because she's so drunk, the snap is more of a jerky wave. And in trying to play it off, Athena decides to scrape her hand through her hair, only to pull the bright-blue binder clip loose. Athena examines what can only be described as a rogue office supply in her hands as if for the first time. "How'd that get there?"

"You okay?" Jenn asks.

"Yeah. I'm fine," she lies. Jenn begins to grow ever more concerned, looking on helplessly as Athena tries to refasten the clip into her hair once more.

"Look, it's none of my business, but this is actually a really great opportunity for you. Everyone has kind of been waiting to see what you would do on your own. You know, without . . ." Jenn trails off before stating the obvious.

"Well, what I've done on my own is to turn very quickly into a petty, embittered person that's probably the only James Beard–awarded chef who was fired by their mom," Athena says, adding a forced laugh to cut the sourness of her words.

Jenn can't help but notice that the wallpaper on Athena's phone is a photo of Northern Trade. It just about breaks her heart.

"Athena." Athena looks up. "You've got to have recipes, an idea for your own restaurant?"

"No, I don't—"

"But what about Southern Trade? That was all you," Jenn argues.

"Those are just hot dogs. That's not a menu," Athena says.

"It's the start of one—or at least proof you can build something," Jenn says.

"But that's just it. I don't think I can. I was watching one of those home-decorating shows on television the other day. Right in the middle of the day. Sitting in a hotel—fine, okay, I was lying in bed. Anyway, I think that's when I realized—I just know how to renovate houses, but I don't know how to build them. I don't know how to build. Anything. I just . . . add on. Southern Trade was just an add-on," Athena says.

"That's not true," Jenn argues.

"Mom built the brand. Mom built the goodwill. Mom took the risk. I just made hot dogs," Athena says, looking down at the table.

"But—"

"Look, it's not a fun epiphany to have, coming to the realization that I've spent my whole life being a parasite. Without Mom's recipes, I wouldn't have anything to tweak or innovate. And I never . . . I never looked beyond Northern Trade for what I wanted in a restaurant. It's everything to me. *Was* . . . everything to me."

"Do me a favor," Jenn says, pulling a pad of paper from her apron pocket and scribbling something down. "You're too drunk right now, but maybe tomorrow just start by answering this question." She slides the slip of paper across the table.

Athena picks it up and reads it aloud. "What do I want?" She looks down at the slip of paper and then back at Jenn.

"My mentor asked me the same question way back in the day—when I . . . well, I was pretty lost. And that question got me here. Maybe it can help you, too," Jenn says.

It takes everything Athena has not to blurt that what she wants is everything Jenn already has.

"Thank you," she says, folding the slip of paper and tucking it safely into her pocket. Jenn nods and waves down her front of house manager, telling her to call a cab for Athena.

"I'll see you at the Banquet Conference, right?" Jenn says, standing up.

"Yep. I'll be there," Athena says, trying to stand and then, realizing how very truly drunk she is, leaning heavily on the table for balance. In that moment, however, she's overcome with pride that at least she didn't drunkenly ask if Jenn Nishimura wanted to be her friend. As she regains her balance, she tries to puzzle out how anyone makes a new friend past the age of thirty.

The front of house manager comes back over and tells Jenn the cab is out front. Jenn nods and helps Athena outside, finally pouring her into the back of the cab.

"You're going to be okay, Winter," Jenn says, shutting the cab door behind Athena.

"That's hilarious," Athena slurs just as the cab pulls away from Jenn Nishimura's Eden of a restaurant.

As Athena is driven out of the city, she pulls the little slip of paper out of her pocket and reads the words over and over.

What do I want?

"Please, I just want my life back," Athena whispers, clutching the piece of paper as if it's a magic lamp.

But as they drive over the Golden Gate Bridge, Athena Winter starts thinking about what Jenn has. What she liked most about Hills and Valleys. That feeling of being found. And in her drunken stupor, she lets her imagination take a little baby-deer-wobbly-legged step. She envisions a little shack by the beach . . . fresh seafood . . . a welcoming place where people can be fed and feel a little less lonely.

Her very own restaurant.

And for eight glorious days, Sloane, Jules, and Athena Winter let themselves dream that maybe they could get everything they ever wanted. That this is their chance to actually live a good life that would be far beyond any fantasy they've long held in their hearts and minds.

And for those eight shining days, Sloane, Jules, and Athena Winter actually like themselves. And for these three people, raised in a family steeped in the tradition of constantly moving goalposts so every player on the field never felt good enough, the Winter sisters become terrified at the contentment that cradles them.

With every golden morning that breaks over this new reality, Sloane, Jules, and Athena grow ever more paranoid. And just a little bit more fearful that they didn't deserve such a sweet life in the first place.

Sweetness, to those who've never known it, can feel like a glinting scalpel. The subject is positive that once the blade cuts them open, it will only expose their guile and inherent unworthiness.

CHAPTER EIGHT

Athena Winter opens the door to the rental car place at SFO and steps inside. It's still decorated for the holidays, though the snowflake garlands now droop and sag. The Christmas tree ornaments embellished with employees' names have acquired just enough rips and tears for the place's overall feeling to be less cheerful and way more dismal and pitiful.

Athena waits in line, trying not to look at the old tree. But she's unable to pull her gaze away from its tractor beam of earnest hopelessness. She gets her phone out and finds one of the many word puzzle apps she's downloaded during the past week. They've given her something to do instead of numbly scrolling through social media in search of someone to envy.

After another twenty minutes in line, while violently doing as many crosswords as she can, Athena reaches the counter and finally gets the keys to her rental car, which she's been told is located in parking spot number ninety-six.

"Ninety-six . . . ninety-six . . ." Athena mutters as she walks up and down row after row full of rental cars. At the very end of the third row, Athena spies a bright-orange Prius, shuddering as she looks down at the number painted into the parking space: ninety-six.

"Perfect," Athena says, her shoulders slumping in defeat.

Surveying the giant parking lot and spotting no other bright-orange cars as far as the eye can see, Athena can only laugh as she beeps the tiny tangerine open and folds her six-foot frame inside.

Pushing the seat back as far as it can go, Athena situates the mirrors and sets her phone and the Banquet tote bag full of loan papers, financial printouts, letters of recommendation, and a notebook full of Athena's hopes, dreams, and plans for her own restaurant down on the passenger's seat.

She pulls out of the maze of rental cars and into the mind-numbing traffic that surrounds the giant San Francisco International Airport. Rolling down her window, she connects her phone to the tangerine's sound system and turns up her music as she navigates herself back onto the freeway and toward a much-needed cup of coffee.

After her dinner at Jenn Nishimura's restaurant—what she remembers of it—Athena poured all of herself into answering Jenn's question about what she wanted. That little shack by the beach, the fresh seafood—a restaurant of her own. So she spent the last few days setting up a plan to make that dream a reality.

Athena finds a coffee place on the way to Stinson Beach and the restaurant property she's seeing today. Feeling better than she has in a long while, she also orders a kouign-amann, her favorite pastry of all time. Buttery layers interwoven with caramelized sugar that melts in your mouth as you peel it apart. She breathes in a lusciously long inhale, feeling as though she's in one of those movies where the plucky heroine strikes out on her own and shows them all what she's really made of. Smiling, she makes her way onto Interstate 280 for the hour or so drive toward what could turn out to be the very first restaurant on her own.

As she crosses back over the Golden Gate Bridge, Athena starts feeling a growing weightlessness. It feels like she's almost being lifted up out of her driver's seat by her spine. Thinking it's a passing sensation due to taking the little rental car off the slower, traffic-ridden streets of the city and into the faster flow of traffic now on the Golden Gate, Athena shakes out her hands and sings along with her playlist.

But, as she cruises through Sausalito, the weightlessness is joined by a tingling in her feet and hands, along with a blooming flutteryness in her chest that's started to worry her. That sensation . . . she knows. She takes a long deep inhale and counts to six, knowing now that what's happening is not about a new rental car but rather a buildup of feelings currently intensifying inside her at an alarming rate.

Shaking out her hands again and trying to sing along with whatever song is playing right now, Athena's relieved to get to the much slower and windier US Highway 1 that traces itself through Mill Valley and down the entirety of the rugged and breathtaking California coast. The slower, more intentional pace gives her mind something to do, and the weightlessness and tingling hands thankfully subside.

"Okay, okay . . . we're doing okay. I can do this . . . This is a good thing, remember? This is what you want," Athena says to herself as she tries to pull her shoulders away from her ears.

Athena's eyes dart around the glorious splendor that surrounds her, taking in none of its beauty. She shakes her hands out again as the tingling returns and struggles to take in a deep breath, the shakiness in her chest becoming more and more pronounced. Athena checks behind her for cars. Seeing no one there, she slows her speed down to just twenty-five miles an hour and takes the winding curves of the road slow and steady.

But as she traces her way down the mountain, she feels herself losing control. It's as if she's been wrestling some giant invisible beast for the past hour and is just cognizant enough to know that she's about to be bested. Exhausted and unable to continue to pull her mind back from its catastrophic yet wordless terror, Athena finally pulls her ridiculous orange rental car over and parks on one of the many vista points that dot Highway 1.

The relief is immediate. She takes a long inhale and, after a few tries, finally gets a full and wonderful breath. Sadly, she makes the mistake of looking at the time on her watch and sees that her appointment is in less than forty-five minutes. This ticking clock bursts through her entire body. She turns the car off, unfolding herself from the driver's seat, and steps out onto the dirt of the vista point. Rubbing her hands together, hoping this will put a stop to the tingling, she paces around the vista point, trying to talk herself down.

"This is a good thing, Athena. Why are you freaking out? You were so excited, and this place is perfect for you . . . This is what you want. Remember this is what you want. Please, little love . . . please calm down." Athena leans back to give her trapped breath more room. She checks the time again. Thirty-eight minutes. Next, she tries to give her mind something to do. Grasping at straws, Athena begins to run what can only be described as a diagnostic test on herself in an attempt to discover the origins of this burst of emotion. Almost like her own out-of-control feelings are some kind of cold case it is now up to her to solve. Why didn't this happen in the truly depressing days that followed her New Year's Eve banishment? Where was all this when she was sitting on the side of that awful gothic yellow bed in a tiny towel with nothing to do all day as the silence closed in around her? Why is this happening now, when she finally has something she's excited about?

Athena takes in the expansive view from the vista point. The sheer vastness of it all. Waves of rolling hills undulate all around her as the blue of the Gulf of the Farallones opens up far below and expands into the magnificence of the Pacific Ocean. Weightless once again, Athena takes a deep breath. And in the momentary fullness of her inhalation, a tiny clue emerges as she takes in her environment. She's never truly existed beyond Northern Trade, so her emotions could never get enough oxygen to fully ignite. She's been so contained, so controlled, and so tightly wound that any flinted spark of feeling would be snuffed out before it ever got the chance to really burn.

But out here she is untethered, uncertain, utterly alone, and completely out of control. And that little spark that's been stomped out for decades finally has the oxygen it needs to burn it all down. A growing sick feeling in the pit of Athena's stomach blooms as the height of the vista point fish-eyes around her. Dizziness and nausea sweep over her in waves. She sets her hand onto the warm hood of the rental car, trying to establish a grounded ballast that might keep her from floating away.

"This is real. You're standing on this dirt. You are touching this stupid garbage bag of an orange car. This is real. Athena, please listen to me. You are not going to float away. You are a very tall person. You are real. This is real," Athena whispers to herself.

Athena checks her watch again. Twenty-seven minutes. She marvels at how fast time is moving despite feeling like she's stuck in a looping nightmare. She reaches inside the rental car for her phone, pulling up the map that's guiding her to where she's supposed to be embarking on a brighter future. She has just under twelve miles.

Twelve miles of winding road stand between Athena and what could be the beginning of her next chapter. She focuses in on the map and sees familiar sights and places she's been a thousand times before. She knows these roads like the back of her hand, and to feel so unsafe in this of all places feels like the biggest betrayal of all. She looks up from her phone, taking it all in. Cars speed past. Cyclists zoom by.

Just then, a couple pulls in next to her, getting out of their car and onto the vista point. The soft and curvy woman is dressed in casual clothes, her hair swept up in a messy ponytail. But the lanky, jittery man—currently trying to wipe his clammy hands on a pair of super-formal pants—is dressed a little too nicely for just another breezy drive down the coast.

"Oh no," Athena says, utterly trapped.

And sure enough, after just enough time to make it weird with just the happy couple and Athena on this glorious vista point on this stunning winter's day, the man gets down on one knee and proposes to the love of his life. As the woman cries and accepts his proposal, Athena shambles around behind the car in a truly pathetic attempt to physically crop herself out of their romantic moment. What Athena wouldn't give to be able to jump into that dumb little orange car and drive away from here. Alas . . .

"Hi, excuse me," the man says, his voice shaking from sheer delight. Athena turns around to the happy couple now standing before her.

"Hey, hi," Athena says, her voice shaky and unrecognizable.

"We're so sorry to trouble you, but do you think you could take a photo of us?" the man asks, his face so open and hopeful it hurts.

"We just got engaged!" The woman squeals, throwing her arms around her new fiancé.

"Congratulations—and sure," Athena says, taking the phone from the man.

The happy couple step back closer to the edge of the vista point, so the photo Athena has promised to take will also feature the full expanse of the glorious landscape behind them. As they do so, Athena balls up her hands. They won't stop shaking. And now she has to take a photo that will be featured in this couple's life forever, not to mention posted to social media within a matter of seconds. Athena breathes in deeply and tries to steady herself.

The lovely couple wrap their arms around each other like two puzzle pieces who've just found the right fit. The sprawling landscape opens up behind them like an oil painting.

"You're not going to float away," Athena whispers to herself as she steps closer.

"I'm sorry?" the man asks. Athena steadies her hands. Breathes. She steps closer.

"Oh, so sorry. I said, say cheese!" Athena yelps. The couple smiles and poses as Athena snaps several photos. And as the man walks toward her for his phone, Athena quickly flips over to the photo feed and sees that, thank God, there are miraculously a few good shots in with the other blurry, shaky offerings.

"Thank you," the man says, taking the phone and scanning the photos. The couple peruses the shots. Watching them judge and assess her work while not being able to just get back into her car and drive away is somehow becoming worse than having to take the photos in the first place.

Finally, the couple say their goodbyes and drive off to a bright future that doesn't involve being stuck on this vista point forever. Athena just watches it all, wondering how normal this day seems for everyone else, while she struggles to drive just twelve miles.

Unable to put it off any longer, Athena flips over from the map to her text messages and pulls up the phone number for the woman she was supposed to meet at the little perfect shack on the little perfect beach just outside Stinson. Athena struggles to craft a text that properly encapsulates whatever is going on with her. Finally—

Hey there! Athena rolls her eyes at her own usage of an exclamation point. She keeps it in, hoping it communicates a level of cheerful normalcy she definitely does not feel at present. So sorry to cancel last minute, but... Athena looks up from her phone. Stares over at the stupid orange car. My rental car has... Athena struggles with lying to the woman, but finally she types out, My rental car has broen down and I'm afraid I'll have to reschedule.

Athena's fingers hover over her phone. She reads the whole text aloud.

"Hey there! So sorry to cancel last minute, but my rental car has broken down and I'm afraid I'll have to reschedule," Athena reads in the most forced casual tone she can muster while simultaneously failing to notice her glaring typo. She looks up, hoping against hope that her circumstances have changed. But the world sways and moves around her as she scans the horizon, her chest tightening with every second that passes. Athena lets out a long sigh and shakes her head. Apparently, she's not the plucky heroine and there won't be any inspirational cinematic montage today. She will not be striding back into Northern Trade as the proud restaurant owner of her very own Michelin-Starred restaurant. The only thing she'll be showing people is that her story is becoming more and more of a tragedy each day.

Despondent, Athena Winter presses Send.

As the text swooshes through the ether, Athena's frustration explodes into a deep, guttural scream that bursts out of her like an out-of-control flash flood. She lunges back into the car, hoping to get some sense of privacy as a peloton of cyclists pulls into her vista point for a break. A vista point she's now positive she will never be free of. She looks away from the twenty or so cyclists, tugging at the nicest sweater she owns, having tried to dress up a bit for the woman she was supposed to be meeting.

Much to her surprise, the scream alleviated some of the pressure in her chest. However uncomfortable she was with finally letting her emotions out, Athena tries not to tamp them down as the newfound ability to breathe far outweighs whatever semblance of dignity she was trying to save. The peloton moves on just as the woman she was meeting texts back her concern about Athena being broken down on the side of the road, asks if there's anything she can do to help, and says she looks forward to when they're able to finally meet.

All of a sudden, Athena feels an urgency to get off this vista point, imagining the woman, now having been thoroughly stood up, driving back up the mountain only to see Athena Winter screaming inside a perfectly operational vehicle twelve miles from the restaurant she was supposed to be buying. Athena is finally able to take a series of deep breaths and looks down at the map on her phone. She exits out of the directions down the mountain and instead sets her course for back the way she came. She puts in SFO and is immediately overwhelmed with the distance she has to travel just in order to return this stupid tangerine of a cage she's been trapped in.

Instead, Athena decides to set smaller goals for herself. She remembers a little coffee place in the heart of Mill Valley and sets her map for there. Ten miles and about twenty minutes. She tells herself she can do anything for twenty minutes. Athena reaches behind her and pulls her seat belt taut across her body and turns the car on. The weightlessness pinches her spine and gently begins to lift her up ever so slightly. But with the open window and the appointment with the woman now canceled, she is finally able to leave the vista point and make her way back up the mountain. Checking constantly for cars behind her, Athena is now driving between ten and fifteen miles an hour. And the ten miles that were supposed to take twenty minutes take her closer to forty-five.

She pulls her little orange rental car in front of the coffee place and finds another destination about five miles away, and this is how Athena Winter makes it back to SFO in three and a half hours: stopping and starting every five miles and taking it one deep breath at a time.

As Athena looks out the cab window on the long ride back to that awful yellow hotel, the streets that so harassed her slip harmlessly by in the rainy evening just outside. She catches glimpses of the multiple places she had to stop and can only shake her head at how mind-numbingly normal they all look from this vantage point. She pulls her phone out of her pocket, swipes it open, and finds the text message from the woman she was supposed to meet at the restaurant. She has yet to respond, because how does one breezily communicate that not only will Athena not be rescheduling but she would like to fully cancel the meeting and would really appreciate if the woman forgot about her entirely and maybe act as though none of this ever happened. Finally, Athena texts back: Thank you for understanding. After reassessing, I am unfortunately going to have to rethink the property. I'm so sorry this didn't work out and am grateful for your time and effort.

Athena's fingers hover over her phone, and she finally forces herself to press Send. Whatever happens next, it's not going to be at that little perfect shack in Stinson that she thought she wanted. It just can't be. Not with what happened today. She would never be able to look at the restaurant without remembering getting inexplicably trapped on that vista point.

Athena grips her phone in her hand as the cab drives into Sausalito. As they make their way through the downtown area, Athena sees that awful yellow hotel in the distance. Mustering the last drop of her energy, Athena goes online and finds a little short-term rental to stay just a mile up the hill from there. It's not a hotel, but it's not an apartment either, and at the very least, it'll be a change from what she's got now.

She books it just as the cab pulls in front of her hotel. Thanking the cabbie for the ride home, she strides inside and proudly tells the woman behind the reception desk that she'll be checking out tomorrow and settles her bill. These days it's the little victories.

Stepping back into her hotel room one last time, Athena is overcome with exhaustion. She decides to take a quick shower, hoping it will wash the day away. But as she brushes her teeth and gets ready for bed, she can barely look at herself in the mirror. There are bags under her eyes, and she just looks . . . wrung out. It's clear she's lost weight on account of losing her appetite over the last week of trying to build a future based on a scribbled question on a tiny slip of paper. She started eating these chocolate chip granola bars she found at a nearby grocery store just to make sure her body had some kind of fuel, but that's why the kouign-amann was so notable. Athena thought that maybe she'd gotten her love of food back. No such luck.

She turns off the bathroom light, gets into her pajamas, and slides into that large gothic yellow bed one last time. But Athena can't sleep. Instead, she tosses and turns all night, obsessively listing all the things she needs to pack in a desperate attempt not to have to think about what happened today and what it could ultimately mean for a future that now seems a little less bright.

As the sun rises early the next morning, Athena is already up and around, folding clothes and filling up tote bags and her duffel bag with all her belongings. She shoves the tote bag with all yesterday's bank documents into her backpack, unable to look at it anymore. Muttering to herself to remember her phone charger, Athena contorts herself to reach back behind the heavy nightstand to where her phone is plugged in and makes one final sweep of the hotel room. Satisfied she has everything, she loops her backpack over her shoulders, threads her duffel bag across her body, and loads up each of her arms with as many tote bags as they can manage.

With her new lodgings just under a mile up the hill, Athena decides that she could do with the walk—obviously this choice has nothing to do with the fact that she's an hour early for check in. The brisk morning air feels good, and for the briefest of moments, she forgets what a wreck she's become and steps confidently—and even a little hopefully—out onto the sidewalk and on up the hill.

Athena Winter checks the map on her phone again, wondering how much farther she has to go until she gets there. Duffel bag, tote bags, and backpack straps dig into every part of her as she winds her way through the hills of Sausalito.

At the beginning of this trek, Athena bought a cup of coffee, thinking it would be a lovely treat for the walk. But as she hikes steeper hill after steeper hill, the tote bags keep slipping down her shoulder, jerking the ravaged paper cup just enough to spill the coffee onto her ever-stickier hand droplet by droplet. And because she's now in a residential area, there's nowhere to throw the little burden away. Which is how Athena Winter finds herself sitting on the curb, with all her belongings piled around her, violently swigging down cold, sour coffee in between bouts of exhausted hilarity and gloomy despair 0.3 miles away from her destination.

When she found this converted garage space online, she thought she would stay there for the next month as a stopgap until she figures out . . . Athena's mind trails off. Now more than ever she can't finish that sentence. Is it about figuring out what exactly happened on that vista point yesterday? Is it about processing the fact that she apparently has no idea what she wants? Or is it trying to face that, after a lifetime of being part of a family, she was all but disowned in a matter of hours? Athena lets out a scoff of a laugh as she registers that she may be onto something.

Because how does one "figure out" being thrown out of your own family tree?

Crumpling up the now-empty coffee cup, Athena stuffs the little traitor into the top of one of her tote bags, muttering a string of particularly graphic and colorful swear words. As she rinses her hands using a bit of water still left in her water bottle, Athena is not clear what she's actually "figuring out." She stands up, loops her belongings over her shoulders and arms, thinking that maybe a month will be enough time for her to start by figuring out how to finish that sentence. And something about finally having a goal, however small, gives her enough hope to continue the climb.

Putting in her earbuds, Athena turns on some music, looks at the map, and begins trudging up the hill again. And in just under twenty minutes, she finally arrives at the gleaming white, three-story shingle-style house nestled in the hills just above Sausalito.

There's a black Mercedes SUV parked in the driveway, along with a metallic gray minivan. Multicolored plastic tricycles litter the area, as do strewn toys, scooters, and muddy cleats. Athena picks her way around the children's detritus, hoping no one can see her standing in the dead center of their property looking just a bit worse for the wear. The last thing she wants or needs right now is to have to engage in idle chatter with whomever lives here. Even a well-meaning "enjoy your stay" would send her spiraling.

Athena brings up her confirmation email and reads through the instructions, the first of which is to look for "the small teal bistro table." Athena zeroes in on the small teal bistro table, and sure enough, hidden in one of the garage door panels just beyond are a silver touch pad and a door handle. Athena hurries over to the secret door, her tote bags, duffel bag, and backpack clunking along with her. She enters the code given on the confirmation email into the touch pad and hears a click from within. She tries the door handle, a single tote bag slipping off her shoulder and down her arm as she does so, and almost gets emotional as she's able to push the door open and finally step inside.

The converted garage space that will be her home for the next month is bright and airy. A large Murphy bed takes up the majority of the main space, along with a big sectional couch and a good-size white desk that sits under a huge picture window looking out into the woods just beyond. Athena drops her stuff on the Murphy bed and sighs.

Now unencumbered, she walks around the space, stepping up into the kitchenette and laundry room to see what they have on offer. She scans the homemade granola, high-quality coffee beans, and oats that are displayed in matching glass mason jars at the far end of the concrete counter. There's a mini-fridge with two glass carafes set in the door— one filled with fresh milk and the other cold water. She turns around and sees a full-size washer and dryer stacked in the corner of the space and finds herself getting downright teary about being able to do her laundry. She notices there's no range, stovetop, or even a hot plate. There's something about this that calms her, knowing the decision to cook something is out of her hands. It's one thing to be stuck in a hotel room unable to cook, but stuck in a house without a home-cooked meal feels particularly cruel.

She walks back into the main room and starts pulling her clothes out of the bags, separating them into their proper piles over on the big sectional couch. As she's putting the first load in the washer, she can hear the family who lives in this giant home just beyond the door in the kitchenette. It's early still, and from the sounds of it, they're in the throes of getting everyone ready for school and after-school sports. The normalcy of it all is a gut punch on a day already lousy on the ground with them. But the thing that really gets her is how lovely it is just to hear voices in the house and, however sad it is, to be around a family again. Even if she is just listening in at the door.

As the washing machine clicks and whirs to life, she can hear the family behind the door register that the Woman Who Rented the Garage has checked in. After a symphony of teeny, adorable squeals and scraping chairs on floors, she's positive there's one of the kids on the other side of the door right this very minute. She can see the flittering of the shadows of their little feet dancing beneath the door. Athena tiptoes away, quietly walking back into the main room. And in some misguided attempt at "acting natural," she stands in the middle of the main space, not knowing what to do with her arms. After far, far too long standing like that, she hears front doors slam, car doors slam, and within seconds she is, once again, alone.

Athena sets up her laptop on the desk, signs in to their home Wi-Fi, and checks her email. She deletes all the junk, then sees an email from the head of HR at the Winter Group confirming that they sent the rest of her belongings to the storage unit in Corte Madera she rented out last week. She lets the email sit for a long time. How does she respond? Finally, Athena writes back, thanking the woman for taking the time. Just before pressing Send, Athena deletes the three exclamation points she added to make sure she sounded as fine as possible. She sits for a moment. And then adds just one exclamation point before hitting Send.

Scrolling through the rest, she sees an orientation email from the Banquet Conference, which is now mere days away. Athena's cursor hovers over the email. She stares at it. The thought of seeing her family. Seeing people she's worked with. The questions, the humiliation, the stares . . . She shakes her head and closes the laptop, choosing instead to busy herself by emptying out her backpack. She pulls out all the tiny journals and notepads that she's been scribbling in over these past two weeks, trying to make a plan or just find an answer to all this. Page after page of stream of consciousness, drafts of texts, emails, voice mails that she never sent, a detailed account of how much money she has, and a budget that will get her through the next several months, if need be. She scans the list of possible connections and jobs she should reach out to—something she can't quite bring herself to do because it would mean that all this is real and permanent and that her time as head chef at Northern Trade is officially over.

Athena is also very aware that tonight is the soft launch of Central Trade—an event she hadn't planned on attending because she would have been in the kitchen at Northern Trade, where she always was. She remembers that of all the things that made her anxious about the soft launch, having Northern Trade completely to herself was not among them. She'd been so excited, she'd even brainstormed an entirely new menu to test out, knowing that there'd be no prying eyes. She flicks through one of her notebooks and finds the menu, brushing her fingers along the hopeful black ink.

Athena remembers being inspired by that moment in the kitchen with Lola and the Cara Cara orange. Her mind tiptoes past all the fears about what Lola must think of her and how her article is probably going to blast Athena's worst night out worldwide. She can't think about that now. There are only so many humiliating things she can process at one time or she'd probably still be stuck on that vista point.

Athena reflects back to the Northern Trade menu she was going to make the night her whole family would be attending her mother's soft launch. She catches herself again. She can't believe that's tonight. This is the menu she was going to be making tonight. She shakes her head. The life she used to have feels further and further away with every day that passes. Like this muffled TV show playing in a distant room somewhere in the house and she can't quite make out any words. But it sounds a little familiar every once in a while. Athena looks back down at the kernels of ideas she sketched out for the menu. For once, it wasn't based on her mother's recipes or made from dishes tweaked and iterated off in an attempt to modernize them.

This menu was going to be all Athena Winter.

It started with the question—a challenge, really, to herself—about developing recipes that best highlighted a single seasonal ingredient. She wanted each dish to imbue the diner with a new respect and depth of understanding, so that when they finished the meal, they'd be newly invigorated by ingredients they may not have fully appreciated. But the difficulty in doing anything simply is that the execution must be perfect. And as she began to build a recipe around a lemon, Athena sees her writing become more and more illegible as Past Athena lost confidence with each new layer that was added.

Her chest tightens. That Athena had no idea what was coming. That Athena was just dreaming of making an amazing dinner. That Athena had no idea her world was about to be shattered within a matter of hours.

There's something particularly irrefutable about finding actual evidence of how truly clueless you once were. The blind hope of it just breaks your heart.

She sits at the desk looking out the window for several minutes. Paralyzed by what she should be doing—figuring out how to answer Jenn Nishimura's scribbled question, packing for her red-eye flight to the Banquet Conference and seriously questioning if she should even still go, or maybe doing some light internet stalking as to who will be in attendance at tonight's soft launch—she decides instead to crawl under the covers of the big welcoming Murphy bed. She falls fast asleep within minutes, and the whir of the washing machine and the distant sounds of a family home shifting and settling just beyond one closed door lull her into the deepest sleep she's had in weeks.

⚔

Sloane Winter tugs at her sensible black blazer as she and Lærke wend their way out of Sausalito, through the rainbow tunnels, and across the Golden Gate Bridge. She's still adjusting her blazer even as they inch through rush-hour traffic past the Presidio. Lærke told her it looked good, the babysitter told her it looked good, but Sloane just keeps tugging and pulling, muttering to herself about "the fit." As they continue to sit in traffic, Lærke tries to lighten the mood by joking that they should have just taken the ferry across the bay. But all that gets is a tight smile and panicked "hmpf" from her wife.

Lærke has been here before. Sat beside the woman she loves, watching her spiral about the smallest detail, and helpless to soothe or comfort her in any way. For the first few years of their marriage, Lærke made the rookie mistake of thinking it was really about the small detail—the fit of a sensible black blazer, a chipped nail, or even a threadbare doormat that apparently was "a safety hazard." But what she came to understand was Sloane's spiraling about these small details was just a little red flag that signaled a much larger danger below.

Another mistake Lærke made, when she finally grasped what these red flags meant, was attempting to draw out what was really wrong as Sloane paced around wringing her hands about the doormat. Which seemed to make everything worse because Sloane then turned her pent-up fear at Lærke and the overall health of their relationship. How could she be trying to have a deep conversation now, in the middle of Sloane just trying to fix something trivial? Couldn't she see how bad the timing was?

But the timing was never right to talk to Sloane about her feelings. She was always too busy, in the middle of something, or positive Lærke was connecting dots that weren't there—sometimes, Sloane reasoned late one night as they lay in bed, a threadbare doormat is just a threadbare doormat.

Lærke often wondered if Sloane actually thought that and, despite how obvious it was to her, whether Sloane really didn't see the connection. How could she not know what was at the root of her fear? Could she not put together that these episodes seemed to happen only when she was dealing with her family, and more specifically when her mother was around? Watching Sloane fiddle with her blazer, Lærke tries a new tactic.

"We should take the kids to City Lights Bookstore this weekend," Lærke says as they pass Columbus Avenue. As if a spell has broken, Sloane looks up from her sensible black blazer as if she's completely forgotten where she is.

"Oh . . . right. They'd love that," Sloane says absently. She continues brushing and pushing down the buttons on her blazer. "It just won't sit right . . . It . . . it's pooching." She looks over at Lærke in desperation. And it breaks Lærke's heart. She knows what she should say; she knows what she wants to say. Hell, she talks of nothing else in her therapy sessions except for how to talk to her wife about the dangers of pushing down her emotions whenever it comes to anything having to do with her family. But finally trying to learn from past experience, Lærke presses on.

"There's a little ramen place across the street. We could stop for lunch after," Lærke says, her voice cracking under the sorrowful weight of her own subterfuge. Sloane nods. Lærke notices that her hands are now folded on her lap. It's working.

"Freja loves ramen," Sloane says, her knuckles white with pressure as her fingers tighten around one another.

"We'd have to make sure Krister didn't just dunk his whole hand in the bowl, though," Lærke says, the pit in her stomach growing as a smile curls just at the edges of Sloane's tight lips.

Seeing an opportunity, Lærke reaches her hand across and frees one of Sloane's hands from the vise grip of the other. The warmth of her wife's hand thaws Sloane just enough that she allows her fingers to curl around Lærke's. But with the warmth comes the unwelcomed constriction in her chest.

Without the busyness of fidgeting and perseverating on her buttons, Sloane's fear begins to crawl across her shoulders as the weight of her and Jules's plan takes a heavier and heavier toll. Lærke feels Sloane trying to pull her hand back in a near fit of frenzy. As they make the final turn onto the Embarcadero, the looming clock tower of the Ferry Building sends Sloane into a fit of panic. Lærke steadies herself. She looks over at her wife, willing her face to be easy and calm, and lifts her hand to her lips and kisses it gently.

Sloane's shoulders lower just a little. But Lærke can see that she's fighting back emotion—her mouth distorted and tight as she holds back what appears to be a flood of tears, a primal scream, or some combination of both.

It's not that their plan or the lies she and Jules have told so far are inherently bad. Nor is it that Jules was annoyingly right back on New Year's Day, when she said that Sloane was feeling guilty about what she was and wasn't sharing with her wife. It's that Sloane knows it's going to get much worse. And she also knows she could put a stop to it right now. The overwhelming guilt she's been carrying around has caused her to have these recurring nightmares where she sees herself at a railroad crossing watching as a train barrels down toward a car stalled on the tracks. When she tries to get out of her car to help the faceless person who's trapped within, she realizes her doors are locked and all she can do is stand by helplessly as the stalled car is obliterated night after night after night.

The part that wakes her up in a flop sweat isn't the wreckage or the feeling of helplessness; it's that she can never quite make out who is trapped in that stalled car. And as Sloane wades deeper and deeper into this treachery, the more she fears that it's not her mother who's trapped, but Sloane herself.

And by extension, if Sloane is trapped inside that stalled car, that means Lærke is also inside it. Minnie is inside that stalled car. Freja is inside that stalled car. Krister is inside that stalled car. The soft and gentle homelife she and Lærke have built outside of the Winter Group is trapped inside that stalled car. And as Lærke's hand tightens around Sloane's, it's not comfort she feels, but rather that she's knowingly and duplicitously doomed her own wife to obliteration inside this stalled car. All because Lærke made the mistake of falling in love with someone too weak to stand up to her own mother.

"I won't let go," Lærke says, tightening her grip around Sloane's hand.

Overcome, Sloane can only respond with a curt nod. She fears her wife would think differently if she knew the full truth about what she's done over the course of the last couple of weeks. That while she may have been the most fulfilled she's ever felt at work, she's also been the most tormented. Because in a truly intimate relationship, the ensuing argument won't be about the size of the lie—it will be about the broken trust that Sloane lied at all. Sloane remembers their conversations on New Year's Day, when she told Lærke to trust her. That she could handle Jules. But no matter how much she practices her excuses, argues semantics, or brands the lies as necessary, Sloane's defense will always be undone by one simple question: "But why didn't you trust *me* with the truth?"

So every time Sloane has wanted to come clean, she couldn't bring herself to tell Lærke about her and Jules's plan to take over Northern Trade, regardless of how much she's trying to believe that the end will justify the means. Even though those very means are still something Sloane can't bring herself to say out loud to anyone other than Jules—which is never a good sign. Sloane just wants to be in charge of the Winter Group and have it all be worth it, but she fears that that might be the biggest lie of all.

"Hold on to me, my love," Sloane says, swallowing down the lies and the deceit and the fear that who she's become is not someone who gets to be loved by someone as good as Lærke.

Sloane and Lærke's Town Car pulls up to the front of the north side of the Ferry Building.

"I thought this was supposed to be a small soft launch?" Lærke asks, looking at the oversize floral archway spraying orange, fuchsia, and silvery greens over the front door. A throng of photographers crowds onto the orchid-green carpet, set off by velvet ropes, and out onto the already bustling Embarcadero. Each one trying to get a good shot of the culinary Who's Who currently swarming outside the front of Central Trade.

"I thought so, too," Sloane says, her voice a disbelieving whisper.

"Did you not know?" Lærke asks.

"No," Sloane says, shaking her head.

"Honey, we—" Lærke starts, reaching across to her wife.

"Better get in there," Sloane says, pulling her hand away as she reaches for the door. Just as Sloane's fingers curl around the cold metal of the handle, she plasters an easy, bemused smile across her face. Once the mask is fully in place, Sloane pushes the door open and steps out without a look back at her wife. As the door shuts behind her, Lærke sits in the back seat in the eerie quiet of being left behind. Her eyes dart to the rearview mirror, and the confused eyes of the driver bore into her.

"You okay, ma'am?" the driver finally asks.

"Yes, thank you," Lærke says, unmoving. "Yes . . . okay." With every meandering word, Lærke tries to convince herself that if she keeps saying it, it might become true. Until it finally dawns on her that tonight is not about actually being okay; it's just about creating the appearance of being okay. Lærke, taking a cue from her wife, plasters her own easy, bemused smile across her face and finally steps out of the Town Car to join her wife.

Sloane and Lærke join the crowd lining up to walk the orchid-green carpet. They spot familiar face after familiar face, and within just a few moments, they're absorbed into the horde, quickly transforming into the versions of themselves who appear not only okay but thriving. A persona that requires high-pitched squeals of greetings and "it's been so long," kissing both cheeks and pulling various partygoers in for an earnest tight hug as you struggle to remember their name and where you've met before. Everyone knows this particular Dance of Acquaintances, where the goal is to keep it light, keep it friendly, and most importantly, keep it moving.

But as Sloane and Lærke finally enter Central Trade, it becomes clear that tonight is not about who showed up, but rather who did not. No one has come right out and asked if they can expect to see Athena Winter at tonight's gala. But the sheer magnitude of the not-asking of it hangs over the entire gathering like a pall. Getting fired is one thing, but family is family. Right?

Lærke takes two champagne flutes off a passing tray, hands one to Sloane, and begins to take the space in. She looks high into the rafters, where an elaborate scaffolding of hooks, joists, and support braces dangles above the gathered well-wishers. Sloane follows Lærke's gaze and can only roll her eyes.

"It's for the giant orchid," Sloane says.

"It begs the question . . ." Lærke trails off.

"Who needs a giant orchid? Or where is the giant orchid?"

"Arguments can be made for both," Lærke says, smiling.

"Very true," Sloane says, allowing a little laugh.

"Where did the staff come from? Did you—" Lærke asks, watching a harried manager scrutinize a young waiter as he clumsily opens an expensive bottle of wine.

"Nope. Mom did all the hiring," Sloane says, watching as the young waiter tugs out only half the cork. The harried manager deflates and grabs another bottle, deciding this time to open it herself.

"It's very Danish, is it not?" Lærke asks, taking in the whole space.

"Almost," Sloane says.

The Central Trade space is open and bright, with a wall of huge unadorned windows looking out onto a patio and the San Francisco Bay just beyond. Filled with light woods, sheepskins on the backs of wishbone chairs, and nothing on the stark white walls but a few off-white macramé wall hangings.

"It doesn't have that . . ." Lærke trails off.

"Warmth," Sloane finishes. Lærke nods in agreement.

What both Sloane and Lærke can't quite put their finger on is that this space doesn't bear any resemblance to the other two restaurants in the Winter Group portfolio. Northern Trade is all rustic log cabin, dark woods, and crackling fireplaces. Southern Trade was outdoorsy, bucolic, and felt like you were camping in a national park, warmed by woolen southwestern blankets.

Central Trade stands alone.

Which is exactly what Maren Winter had in mind when she meticulously chose each design detail of the space, hoping to send that very message loud and clear. And Maren is certain this message is one of unshakable power. Power that doesn't need anyone else to succeed. It can stand on its own, just as Maren can. She envisions Central Trade will change the global conversation around food and will, once again, put her—and her alone—at the very apex of that movement.

As Sloane and Lærke scan the room looking for Maren, neither of them notices Jules Winter standing by herself on Central Trade's second floor, overseeing it all. Standing back from the live-edge wooden balustrade that took twenty workmen to hoist onto the second floor, Jules is virtually invisible to all who are gathered below.

In order to be the best at chess, one must take in the full board before making their first move.

Jules sips her wine while she studies the social murmurations of the crowd below with a surgical focus. Who's talking to whom. Which couple is clearly gossiping about another. Who's standing by the bar, nervous to jump in at all. And most importantly, who is everyone avoiding.

Just then, the energy in the room shifts. Everyone feels it.

The two large glass front doors swing open, and Maren Winter walks in to deafening applause. She looks resplendent in a tailored, silk chartreuse pantsuit paired with a hot-pink pointed-collar silk shirt that's open just enough to see the tasteful diamond necklace that lazes around her neck. Her shiny brown hair is wavy and effortless, and her dewy, natural makeup finishes off a staggeringly cool look for the launch.

Maren Winter has never looked better.

Jules watches as the crowd circles and tightens around her mother, a human maelstrom of the culinary elite, all vying for their moment to get happily sucked into Maren's vortex of popularity and approval. To be seen—or better yet, to be photographed—with the great Maren Winter at such an exclusive event provides a benefit that'll reverberate out into the world beyond, socially, financially, and professionally.

Because the secret that Jules knows is an event like tonight's is much more than just a soft launch for an upcoming restaurant. No, tonight's event is one of those opportunities where the elite can affirm their preferential supremacy over the unwashed masses. It's what Jules has not so politely referred to in the past as a high-society circle jerk. An exclusive gathering, full of exclusive people, that's "somehow" heavily publicized. This is to ensure that everyone else knows it happened, but most importantly—that they weren't invited.

So while Jules was surprised at how big tonight's event had gotten, she's over the moon that it did. Because just the act of launching this restaurant with a high-society circle jerk will help brand Central Trade as a backdrop for the rank and file to see and be seen in their hollow, misguided attempt to be accepted as one of the in-crowd. But Jules knows that this particular brand of clout is exceptionally fickle. If even one review chips away at Central Trade's cool facade, then all those fragile wannabe influencer kids will distance themselves from the restaurant, fearing that one wrong move will make them persona non grata.

When it comes to popularity, those who live by the sword die by the sword.

Jules spots Sloane and Lærke as they're set upon by a steady stream of well-meaning guests. The plastered smile on Sloane's face looks like a waxen mask, and Jules can hear her now—*Oh, thank you! Isn't it lovely! We're so proud of Mom!* Politely nodding along as the guests tell her what an icon the woman whose overthrow she's currently planning is.

"I can't believe she wore that stupid black blazer," Jules mutters to herself.

The stupid black blazer in question is the outfit that Jules knows Sloane wears when she's trying to be seen as an authority. It's her big-girl outfit to match what Athena called her big-girl voice. But what Jules never had the heart to tell her earnest cheeseball of a sister is that the stupid black blazer just makes Sloane Winter look like a middle manager who's worked at the same family-owned insurance company for twenty-five years.

Jules sips her wine and laughs at her own joke . . . right up until she sees Lola Tadese talking to Rafael and Valentina Luna in a private corner of the grand, cavernous space. While Lola is here gathering what she needs to finish her article, it doesn't surprise Jules that Maren has invited Rafael and Valentina as well. It's the ultimate power move, and Maren never misses an opportunity to make sure those who've questioned her are present to witness her at her best.

Jules stops sipping her wine as she watches Valentina Luna throw her head back and laugh, touching Lola's arm as she does so. This congenial moment even draws a begrudging curl of a smile from Rafael. Jules definitely doesn't like the level of intimacy that seems to be going on over there. Because as far as she knows, New Year's Eve was the only other place that trio were together. And this level of camaraderie can mean only one thing—they've bonded over what they went through that night and are now growing ever closer by sharing war stories, funny takes, and most importantly, gossiping about the circus sideshow that is the Winter family.

Jules learned—probably during the cesspool of adolescence—that while the deepest way to bond and connect with another was through vulnerability and sharing all of oneself, the fastest way sidestepped all that messy emotion and yielded similar results. Because, she concluded, ultimately most people are wary and resistant to being vulnerable and sharing all of oneself, but everyone loves to gossip.

So while she wants nothing more than to go over to that trio and charm the pants right off them, she does not. She knows if she does, she'll be giving them yet another opportunity to grow ever closer. She has no doubt they'll share a look of communal fellowship at having endured yet another awkward Winter episode. And Jules is certainly not going to give them that satisfaction. Instead, seeing Richard over by the bar, she decides that her first move will be starting this game as a duo, rather than on her own.

Jules Winter learned long ago that a woman by herself automatically started any power negotiations at a deficit. Stepping up to the front lines without the one weapon every woman must have in her arsenal: proof she was chosen by a romantic partner and therefore is clearly valuable and worthy of all society's accolades.

Society allows a single, beautiful woman without children only two paths to walk—either she can be the legendary muse and courtesan to a notable man or she can be the pitiable, workaholic husk who—rumor has it—was cruelly jilted in love and will soon metamorphose into her final form: a calcified old crone.

Jules can't help but slide her gaze over to the open bar, where Aunt Josephine is standing with the CEO of East Bay Soups. As miserable as she is in her marriage, looking at these women who fully embody the latter of the two paths available to unmarried women, Jules Winter tamps down any feelings of despair she may be harboring about Richard and reaches for her favorite lowest-hanging fruit—the satisfaction that comes from making people envious of a life they can only witness from a distance.

Jules sets her wineglass down on the live-edged wooden balustrade, quickly shifting it over from a raised knot in the wood that would have caused the glass to slip and topple right onto the crowd below. She shakes her head, knowing full well Sloane would have never let something like that slide. Checking her makeup in the tiny mirror of her gold compact, Jules picks up her wine and steps into the light, finally making her way down the stairs and officially onto the chessboard.

As Jules threads through the crowd, she gives a good-natured nod to Sloane and Lærke. They're talking to a couple that she quickly assesses is far beneath her notice. Which makes it all the more annoying when Sloane calls her over just as Lærke excuses herself to refresh their drinks.

"Jules, I want you to meet someone," Sloane says. Her voice is forced and urgent in that very Sloane way.

"Sure, hi—"

Sloane cuts Jules off and continues. "Jules Winter, this is Heather Osborne and her husband, Timothy."

Jules shakes their hands and politely greets the couple. Heather is a wiry woman, severe and rangy. She has her blondish hair pulled back in a tight bun. Timothy is someone so utterly forgettable, Jules can't even remember his name one millisecond after he's introduced.

"It's great to meet you," Heather says.

Jules thinks to herself, *Yeah, I bet it is*. A thought that fuels her next question. "So, how do you know our mom?"

Sloane tenses.

"Oh, I was just telling Sloane here that—" But before Heather can finish her sentence, Maren sweeps over to the group—full maelstrom in tow—and interrupts her.

"Ahh, I'm thrilled you've met Heather!" Jules still doesn't understand. Her blank face—and a growing audience—is enough for Maren to expound further. "I've hired Heather as the head chef at Northern Trade."

CHAPTER NINE

Sloane and Jules Winter are at a crossroads.

Momentarily blinded by camera flashes as a bevy of photographers jump at the chance to get a shot of the three Winter women in attendance tonight, they both arrange their faces into easy smiles, trained from childhood to keep up appearances no matter what. So, as their entire plan is threatened, Sloane and Jules hit their marks, leaning into each other, arms wrapped tightly around one another's waists as they play nice for the gathering crowd. Maren tugs Heather Osborne and Whatever His Name Is back into the maelstrom with an excited declaration of introducing her to "absolutely everyone."

"Who is this Heather Osborne person?" Jules asks in a conspiratorial whisper.

"She makes videos for the internet. Mom sent me one attached to an email, and I thought she wanted me to talk to our lawyers because her entire shtick is cooking recipes out of Mom's cookbooks. And you know how you can't show a cookbook cover . . . copyright and fair use and all that." Sloane trails off as she pulls out her phone and searches for the email.

"And you're sure Mom didn't say, 'Hey, I'm hiring this internet person to be the head chef of a two-Michelin-Star restaurant,'" Jules says, now loudly whispering.

Sloane finds the email and scrolls down to the attached video. "I don't . . . I don't think I could have missed that, but . . . I saw Heather milling around the launch and recognized her from the video. She bee-lined over to me and started wittering on about how excited she was to be starting at Northern Trade, and I don't know—I just panicked and called you over," Sloane says, reading through the email more carefully.

"Yeah, thanks for that, by the way," Jules says. Sloane looks up from her phone and sees Lola Tadese talking to Rafael and Valentina over in the corner.

"Oh great," Sloane says. Jules looks over.

"She's just here so she can include the soft launch in the article," Jules says, hoping to push past this detour as quickly as possible.

"But if Mom introduces her to Heather Osborne, what then?" Sloane asks.

"It'll be fine. Her article is a retrospective on Maren Winter. I'm sure her boss wants her to keep it focused on whatever press they're doing for the Banquet Lifetime Achievement Award. Dame Jocasta is not about to be quoted in some tasteless hit piece. She's the pinnacle of sustainable foodie culture and farm-to-table cuisine as well as being the benchmark of class and elegance, " Jules says, taking Sloane's advice and nesting her lie in a nugget of truth.

"And did you have a chance to . . ." Sloane trails off before asking outright if Jules anonymously tipped off Lola to what Sloane said to the Northern Trade staff on that fateful day.

"It's all taken care of," Jules says.

"Okay. You're right. You're good at your job. We've got ourselves covered with the quote, and this will all be fine," Sloane says, looking back down at her phone. Jules knows that Lola's article will benefit their plan in the long run. It will blast all Maren's recent foolishness far wider than they could ever dream. But if Jules is going to take over the Winter Group by herself, she needs to have at least one trick up her sleeve that Sloane doesn't know about.

"So, did Mom say anything in the email?" Jules asks, leaning into Sloane and reading the email herself.

"No, it's just . . ." Sloane shows Jules the email. "See? She just attached the video. Nothing else."

Sloane and Jules fall silent under the weight of what they now must do.

For in this moment, there lies a golden opportunity. Standing in stunned silence, a look of recognition passes between Sloane and Jules. Because while Maren's recent erratic behavior has certainly been bad for business, there is something in it that they can continue to use to their advantage. If they have the stomach for it.

If.

Wordlessly, Sloane and Jules extricate themselves from the party—leaving Lærke behind without explanation as she returns to where they once stood, carrying her wife's favorite cheer-me-up cocktail.

Sloane scans the ground floor for a quiet corner where she and Jules can get their bearings, thread this new wrinkle into the plan, and find a way out of this mess. Putting aside their plan to talk to Aunt Josephine tonight about a vote of no confidence, Jules and Sloane instead decide to make hay while the Heather Osborne sun shines.

An odd calm passes over Sloane, the doubt and guilt now replaced with steely resolve. Because while the first phase of their plan tore her apart, this second phase has filled her with purpose. Lærke will understand. She must do this. There is no other way.

Maren has forced her hand.

Sloane motions for Jules to follow her to a more private spot. Jules takes in a breath, the word "wait" stuck in her throat. A momentary sensation that feels like the time Maren took the girls to the top of the Empire State Building and everything was going fine right up until Jules realized how high they were. She must have been around ten years old and remembers becoming light-headed and having to step away from the edge. It didn't last more than five seconds, but Jules is immediately transported back to that moment as she reaches for a nearby empty table to steady herself. Her recent concealment of Lola's true intentions still stuck in her throat, Jules is on the verge of calling Sloane back. They can stop this right now. They can sit down with their mother and talk it out. They can tell the truth. They can have the hard conversation and let the chips fall where they may. They're reasonable human beings. It's not too late.

But as Sloane turns a corner and disappears into the catacombs of the illustrious Central Trade, Jules thinks back to New Year's Eve. How all it took was a single pork chop for Maren to banish her favorite daughter forever. The look on Athena's face was heartbreaking. But it was Maren's expression that she hasn't been able to shake since. Where there was once warmth, recognition, and love, now there was just suspicion, anger, and . . . Jules can't bring herself to say the last word.

The realization sweeps over her, leaving her cold. What if this rumor isn't a lie? What if their mother's madness is real?

Just as Jules turns to follow Sloane, she locks eyes with Lola Tadese across the crowded room. Jules can't hide her true feelings. So, before she gives too much away, she turns around and follows Sloane into the shadows.

"I really liked Athena," Valentina finishes saying, just as Lola turns back toward their little trio in the corner.

Tonight, Valentina Luna is wearing another showstopper of an outfit—one that Lola is sure is also currently being worn by Valentina and Rafael's beloved dog, Honey. It is a crimson baby doll dress with crinolines that poof out the skirt so Valentina looks like she's a spinning ballerina even though she's standing perfectly still. Rafael Luna stands next to her in a pair of slightly tinted glasses, wearing a black leather blazer over a white T-shirt, his sleeves of tattoos peeking out from just under the cuffs and onto the tops of his calloused hands.

As Rafael and Valentina talk, Lola reaches for her digital voice recorder but realizes she can't say what she's thinking out loud. Instead, she slips her pencil out of the tiny notebook spiral and scribbles down as much as she can of what's transpired in the last twenty minutes. Her article is all but finished—tonight's soft launch was supposed to be nothing more than an epilogue. But instead, she now must rethink the entire second half.

"I know. Athena is exceptional," Rafael allows.

"Yeah, she's great," Lola says absently, as she jots down a few words to describe Jules Winter just before she disappeared behind Sloane.

Despondent. Anguished.

Lola's pencil hovers over the notebook paper, its tiny grid of dots tempting her to continue.

Childlike.

"I've never heard of this Heather person, have you, Rafael?" Valentina asks.

"No, but that's not saying much," Rafael says.

"I know who she is," Lola says, closing her notebook.

"Well, do tell," Valentina says, leaning in.

Lola can't help but smile. "You know that thing people were doing on the internet a while back, where they would cook their way through some famous chef's cookbooks?"

"Right, they made a movie out of it," Valentina says.

Lola nods. "I think Heather said she was a sous chef at a Michelin place in Yountville. I could never confirm it. But people know her mostly from the stuff she's posted online. She has a whole website, hundreds of videos, huge social following. She's even been on a few talk shows and has merch and everything—of just her cooking her way through all of Maren Winter's cookbooks." Lola takes out her notebook again.

"No—" Valentina dramatically starts.

"Right?" Lola responds with an arched eyebrow.

"That's a bit on the nose," Rafael says.

"It is," Lola says, writing it all down.

"But—" Valentina starts.

"Looks like I'm going to be driving to Yountville to confirm Heather Osborne is who she says she is," Lola says, tucking her notebook safely away once and for all.

"I mean, has anyone . . . do we even know where Athena is? I kind of thought she'd be here?" Valentina asks.

"Me too," Lola says, clearly disappointed.

Valentina smiles to herself, noticing Lola's outfit. Tonight, Lola is wearing a deep-purple vintage wrap dress, cinched tightly at her waist with a gold belt. She's paired this look with designer, faux-snakeskin boots.

"You look very nice this evening." Valentina beams.

"Yeah, okay. Fine. Maybe I hoped Athena would be here more than just thought it," Lola says, allowing a small smile.

"I knew it," Valentina says.

"She did." Rafael sighs.

"I told him on New Year's Eve that I thought there was something there," Valentina says.

"How . . ."

"It was just how you looked at her. And how she looked at you. You can tell," Valentina says.

"Well, that's embarrassing—" Lola says, smiling.

"Oh, it is not. It's wonderful," Valentina says.

"Either way, it feels like a pretty good time for me to leave here and get to Yountville before the news of Heather being named head chef gets out. If I leave now, I can get to the restaurant long before closing so I can interview the staff about her time at the restaurant."

"Are we going to see you in Oxfordshire this weekend at the whole—" Valentina asks, waving her hand around.

"The Banquet Conference," Rafael finishes.

"Yes. The Banquet Conference," Valentina finishes, her voice just a hint more "professional."

"I leave first thing in the morning. You?" Lola asks, barely able to contain her excitement at the prospect of speeding the sixty or so miles to the Napa Valley area in search of another journalistic thread she can pull.

"We're on a red-eye tonight," Rafael says. Lola winces. "Do you want to tell Lola why we're on a red-eye tonight?" Rafael's voice is a low drawl as he slowly turns to his absolutely buzzing wife.

"I want to spend a day in London, okay. There's a little restaurant right at the very top of the Portrait Gallery. We had tea there the last time we went to this conference. Sitting right next to the window. It was raining. It was a perfect moment. It was right after—" Valentina trails off, realizing her story has wandered into slightly rocky territory.

"I'd just gotten sober," Rafael adds, letting her off the hook. Valentina smiles over at him, and Lola feels as though she's been entrusted with a very private moment.

"And it's all I've been thinking about ever since. But that's not the only reason," Valentina says, her excitement building.

"No?" Lola asks, as she looks knowingly over at Rafael, who can't help but smile just a little.

"I may or may not have ordered a full tea set that has me and Honey on it, playing off those sets they do for the royal weddings. So it's just—" Valentina turns to the side and strikes a very official wedding pose. "But, like, just imagine me and Honey . . . little heart around us, you get it."

"Not that you're actually married to someone you could put on the tea set," Rafael says.

"But where's the fun in that?" Valentina laughs, pulling him close. He immediately melts.

"No, I can see how this very important errand would be a priority," Lola says, trying not to laugh.

"Right? Well, they said I could see a prototype if I came by the showroom, so obviously—" Valentina bursts, looking over at Rafael, who clearly doubted her.

"Obviously," Rafael repeats.

"Well, if you see me walking the Oxford streets in this same outfit, just know that my last twelve hours didn't quite go as planned," Lola says.

"Is it weird if we swap phone numbers? I like you, and you know, just in case you want to go see the tea set, too," Valentina asks, her knuckles whitening as she grips her bedazzled phone.

"I would love that," Lola says. They swap phones and input their numbers. Valentina goes so far as to take a quick selfie to add to her contact. Lola looks over at Rafael.

"I don't have a phone," he says.

"Of course you don't," Lola says, laughing.

"It totally fits, right?" Valentina asks.

"Okay, let's just—" Rafael spins his finger around. "Move this section of Let's Make Fun of Old Man Luna along."

"But it's such fertile ground," Lola says.

"Okay . . . all right," Rafael says, smiling and fidgeting with the cuff of his leather blazer.

"Until Oxfordshire!" Valentina sighs dramatically as Lola leaves the Ferry Building on her way to race a rumor up through California's golden, rolling hills.

Valentina turns back toward Rafael, but her husband isn't paying attention. Instead, he's watching as Maren Winter pulls Heather Osborne from group to group, excitedly introducing this "huge talent" to the world.

"I just don't get it. The timing . . . all of it," he finally says.

"Oh, I do," Valentina says, without missing a beat. Rafael waits. "She wants to win the breakup, right?"

"What breakup?"

"With Athena maybe?"

"That . . . that doesn't make any sense."

"Do you remember me telling you the story about my first sort-of boyfriend?"

"The kid who had that tippy-toe walk?"

"He did not."

"He absolutely did."

"Don't you dare do it . . . don't . . . Rafael, *do not*—" Rafael walks on his tippy-toes around their not-so-private corner of Central Trade. From afar, his performance looks like a fussy rock star creeping around the fringes of the party. Just to get him to stop, Valentina continues. "Remember how I told you that he broke up with me right before that big party?"

"Tippy-toed right out of your life—yeah, I remember."

"Well, I couldn't let him think he got to me, so I made my mom drive me to that stupid party anyway—wearing the prettiest dress I could find—and acted like I was having the time of my life."

"Yeah, but didn't you tell me that you came home and cried for a solid three months?"

"But nobody saw that part! Sometimes you just have to show people that they didn't win," Valentina says.

"What people does Maren think she needs to show?" Rafael asks, struggling to understand.

Valentina scans the room. "Apparently everyone." She checks the time. Rafael lets out a frustrated sigh. "We should get going. We've got to pack Honey's bag and get her over to the sitter."

Sloane and Jules Winter have no problem efficiently navigating the full scope and sweep of the event. Hopping from clique to clique, as if each tight-knit circle is a stone placed strategically across a rushing river.

By the time Rafael and Valentina finally reach the exit, the swift undercurrent of Central Trade has found a new vortex—the choppy waters now orbiting the two Winter sisters as they begin to pull everyone under.

CHAPTER TEN

Just as Athena Winter pulls the door of the garage closed behind her, a dark-gray minivan pulls up the driveway, its lights blinding her as they close in. Knowing she's fully lit up, it takes everything Athena has not to dart down the driveway to where the Town Car the conference hired for her should be arriving any minute. But like a deer in headlights, she is trapped again . . . into making small talk.

She pulls her duffel bag up on her shoulder, situating it snugly over her backpack strap. Taking a few steps forward, she forces a small wave and smile as she does so. The headlights shut off and darkness engulfs her. As she tries to blink her vision back, she hears car doors slam, an excited child hopping down onto the cement of the driveway, and then, much to her horror, little tappy footsteps bearing down on her. Fast.

"Serafina? Sweetie, please—" The man's low voice cuts off as he hears his teeny daughter nearly take Athena out at the knees with a bear hug that she thought was going to be a bit higher up. "I'm so sorry, Ms. Winter. Please . . . just . . . I'll be there in one second."

Athena looks down at Serafina, her natural hair up in two puffs on either side of her head—little purple plastic balls tied tightly around the base of each poof. Athena can hear Serafina's dad trying to calm a baby, who's vocalizing as he struggles to free them from their car seat. Serafina tightens her grip around Athena's knees, looks up at her, and—

"Why are you so tall? Why are you staying in our house? Are you going somewhere? What's in your bag? What's your first name? Do you have a family? Do you play tetherball? Are you a fast runner? Do you like purple?" Serafina asks. Athena looks down at the little girl and doesn't know where to start.

"I do like purple," Athena says. Serafina pushes off Athena's knees and steps back, getting a better look at her.

"But is it your favorite color?" Serafina asks, nonchalantly pulling her tiny purple, frilly sweater up over her belly.

"Okay, honey—that's enough." Serafina's dad finally walks over, holding the roundest, chubbiest baby Athena has ever seen. "Why don't you go tell Daddy we're home? I am sure he is going to want to hear all about your day." Serafina takes one final look up at Athena, her eyes narrowing. But the promise of telling her dad about her day is too much for Serafina to pass up.

"Okay! Bye, Dad! Bye, Tall Lady! Purple is my favorite color!" Serafina announces, climbing the stairs to the front door, where a tall man dressed in an apron that reads KISS THE COOK awaits her. She leaps into his arms, and they disappear inside the warmly lit home.

"I'm so sorry. She's been wanting to meet you ever since you arrived. I'm Justin, and this is Zeke." Zeke is a bruiser of a baby, all dimples, food stains, and chubby rolls. Zeke squeals, his arms outstretched to Athena.

"I'm Athena," she says, bobbing and weaving to avoid the incoming sticky-handed baby.

"It's lovely to finally meet you, and if you need anything, all our numbers are in the desk drawer. There's a folder there with everything you'll need," Justin says, pulling Zeke back just before he gets a swipe at Athena's glasses. "He loves glasses, so . . ." Athena resituates hers higher on the bridge of her nose as Zeke watches intently, drool tracing down onto a little handmade bib with polka dots on it.

"Oh, thank you—I'm heading to London . . . actually Oxfordshire, just . . . outside. Yeah . . . it's for a conference for cooking. I used to . . . Anyway, it's for a few days, but I'll be sure to reach out if I need anything,"

Athena says, seeing the headlights from her Town Car pull up just behind Justin. He turns to see the car as well. Zeke points.

"That's a car. Car," Justin says, turning back around to Athena. Zeke squeals something that he probably thinks sounds exactly like the word his dad said.

"Okay, well, it was nice meeting you . . . both of you . . . um, all of you. You have a beautiful . . . uh . . . home," Athena says with an awkward wave.

"Thank you, and nice meeting you, too," Justin says.

Athena steps past Justin and Zeke before carefully walking down the driveway to where her Town Car is idling. As she loads her bags into the back seat, she sees Justin trying to teach Zeke how to wave goodbye, finally just taking his chubby little arm and waving it for him. Athena crawls into the back seat by her bags and watches as Justin clambers up the stairs to his front door, hefting Zeke higher on his hip as he climbs.

As her car winds its way down through the Sausalito hills, over the Golden Gate Bridge, and on toward SFO, Athena nervously fidgets with her backpack so she doesn't have to relive that three-and-a-half-hour drive through hell in that infernal orange car. Instead, she checks and rechecks that she has her passport, her ticket information, and her headphones. Finally confident she has everything she needs and without anything else to do but sit in this back seat, Athena swings wildly between replaying little snippets of her cringeworthy conversation with Justin and catastrophizing every possible detail that could go wrong at this upcoming conference.

She should have canceled. She really should have canceled. If pressed, Athena will say that she didn't want to let Dame Jocasta down and be a no-show at her own widely publicized Q and A session. But the truth is much more complicated. A dash of avoidance, a smidgen of denial, and a whole lot of hope and fear that maybe everything will go back to the way it was—if she can just talk to her mother and set this right.

Because without the usual demands of her job as head chef of Northern Trade, Athena has spent the last couple of weeks coming completely undone, one deeply held belief at a time. Before New Year's Eve, Athena thought she was a pretty together person—capable and reasonable, she believed she knew herself. But now, Athena knows that that certainty was not grounded in her. Rather, it was rooted in the soil of Northern Trade. Because without her job, her home, her mom's menu, her staff, and her family . . . it took just over a week for Athena Winter to have no idea who she is. And these recent little discoveries only serve to paint a picture of a slightly too intense, awkward loner who has a hard time mustering the courage to talk to a baby.

And all this upheaval is happening just days before she has to go onstage and not only try to convince a conference full of her peers that she knows what she's talking about but also somehow manage to side-step prying questions and sad looks while navigating the preeminent event in the culinary world as the woman famous for being fired by her own mother.

Athena picks at her fingernails as she plays and replays a horrific montage of every possible disastrous scenario where she sees her family for the first time since New Year's Eve. She forces herself to stop picking her fingernails before she draws blood. Clasping her hands tightly, Athena wishes she could just be angry at them. She'd do anything to feel the clean lines of rage. Instead, all Athena Winter feels is pain. Every time she thinks about her mom or Jules or even Sloane, an uncontrollable hurt crawls up her throat from somewhere so vast it scares her.

Because truth be told, tonight's awkwardness wasn't because she didn't know what to say to Justin. It was because she couldn't say it without crying.

She didn't want to tell him he had a beautiful home—what she wanted to say was that he had a beautiful family.

But Athena has not become so nostalgic over the course of these days and weeks that she is unable to see her own family in all their complicated glory. That's why this loss was so tectonic. Athena's entire life was not only about being a part of the troublesome Winter clan; it was also about the energy spent problem-solving and monologuing about how to handle Sloane's control issues or trying to outmaneuver Jules's chessboard of sibling rivalry. But most of all, it was about trying to figure out how to be good enough for Maren. Every action, every motivation, every waking breath was always taken in service of proving to her mother that she was worthy. And that journey, more than being the head chef of Northern Trade, became Athena's purpose.

But now that she finds herself without this North Star, Athena Winter doesn't quite know why she's waking up in the morning anymore.

It's one thing not to know who you are. It's something else entirely to have a lifetime disappear within a matter of days.

Until now, Athena Winter has known herself only as a small branch of the Winter family tree. Every definition of herself began in relation to them—she was Maren Winter's daughter. Sloane and Jules Winter's little sister. She was a part of the long-standing Winter tradition of head chefs. She has her mother's eyes but her father's height. She laughs like Jules but likes cherry pie just like her grandfather. Like all Winter women, she became vigilant about getting yearly mammograms when, after Grammy's passing, they learned the hard way that breast cancer ran in their Winter genes. Christmas mornings were spent at Sloane's house, Christmas Eves were spent at Jules's, and Christmas dinner was always made by Maren. They were a family of famously hardheaded women who explained to outsiders that it was simply the Winter Way.

So, who is she now? Who does she laugh like now? Where will she spend her Christmas mornings in the future? And is it really charming to boast about being obstinate and stubborn, if it's just you and not some adorable family mantra?

But more than anything, who will tell her when she's good enough? What is her purpose now?

Athena has played and replayed that fateful night over and over in her head. Looking back on that singular moment where she decided to make that stupid pork chop, and how Jules tried to protect her against herself. And even Sloane warned her to change course. But she wouldn't listen. She knew better. Or more likely, she thought her sisters' motivations in trying to dissuade her were selfish and slippery. How could she know, after decades of competing and undermining one another, that this was the one time her sisters actually tried to help her—whatever their methods.

The Winter Way.

After being stuck far too long in the confines of the quiet back seat of that Town Car, Athena finally arrives at SFO. Unloading her bags, she thanks the driver and heads inside the crowded and bustling airport. But as Athena struggles to weave her way through the crush of humanity, she is forced to see herself and what she's become over the course of just a few years as head chef at Northern Trade. Disappearing into the convenient blur of busyness, Athena became reclusive to the point of obstruction. And as she finally finds her gate among the rushing chaos, she begins to interrogate why she would craft such a life.

As Athena settles in three full hours early for her flight, Sloane's words burst and crackle inside her head: *No, this is your job, Athena. You've made it your home.* She told herself it was passion and determination and true commitment that drove her to be so single-minded. But now that she's been cast out, she's been punched in the face with the daily reality from the harder truths lurking just underneath this oh-so-convenient narrative.

Because what she sees now is Sloane was right. Athena has no friends; she had work colleagues with whom she was friendly. She has no home; she had a place to stay. She has no menu; she had a hot dog recipe born out of necessity, one other hollow attempt that was undone by a lemon, and Maren's original recipes that she tweaked and then congratulated herself for. And she had no restaurant; her mother did.

As Athena slumps in the uncomfortable airport chair, cradling her backpack on her lap, the dots finally connect.

She has built nothing. She has risked nothing. And maybe the reason she's struggling to know herself is that, without her family, Athena Winter is nothing.

The one good thing about having a full mental breakdown in an airport is that you are never alone in that endeavor. Surrounded by people coming and going, an airport holds within its labyrinthine walls a singular assemblage of pilgrims overloaded with their own unstable baggage of fear and expectation. As Athena scans her immediate area, she counts no fewer than three other people staring hollow eyed into the middle distance right along with her. Something about this comforts her. Because while Athena may have just come to terms with how truly alone she is in this world, for right now, at least, she's not alone as she begins to process it.

Athena takes off her glasses and sifts through her backpack. She's in search of the sneaky microfiber cloth that somehow always manages to separate itself from her glasses case. Digging into the deepest, darkest recesses of her bag, she manages to find the balled-up microfiber cloth nestled in a nice pocket of granola bar crumbs. Shaking the cloth clean, Athena sits up in her chair and begins cleaning her glasses.

"Athena?" A woman's voice.

Athena looks up, squinting into the snarl of humanity, and sees a hot-pink, blurry blob next to a fuzzy all-black rectangle standing in front of her. Athena quickly finishes cleaning her glasses and puts them back on just in time to see Valentina and Rafael Luna exchange a look of deep concern at the state they've found her in.

"Hey," Athena says, pulling and pushing her baggage closer to her in a way that she hopes looks welcoming.

"May we sit?" Valentina asks, eyeing the open chairs just next to Athena.

"Oh, sure," Athena says, shifting over in her chair. Valentina settles in next to Athena as Rafael sets his bags down just next to his wife.

"I'll be right back," Rafael says, disappearing into the crush of the airport.

"He's not a very good flyer. But we've learned that something about those little airport stores calms him down. So he'll come back a little bit calmer with some giant bag of candy, a random magazine, and a bottle of water that he'll somehow manage to hold on to throughout our entire trip." Athena laughs and Valentina smiles, proud that she's managed to lighten the moment.

"You headed to the conference?" Athena asks.

"Yeah, Rafael has a talk on sustainability and fish and all that. You?" Valentina asks.

Valentina knows they're both bound for the same place, and Athena knows full well—and in incredible detail—what Rafael is being asked to do at the conference, as both were given a full schedule, along with a massive marketing campaign that features both Rafael's and Athena's faces plastered all over it. Sometimes the need for a conversation is not about clarity; it's simply about connection.

And as for Athena, reconnecting with someone who saw her on the worst night of her life is a delicate balance. Acknowledging the gut-wrenching circumstances, while trying not to relive them, navigating her embarrassment and vulnerability at being seen in such a state, but also trying to build something new on the foundation that Rafael and Valentina were there for Athena when she needed someone and in the most profound ways.

Simply, she knows they are good.

Not so simply, she comes from a family that doesn't really keep company with such people.

"They wanted me to talk about Southern Trade, pop-ups, what fine dining learned from the pandemic, and all that," Athena says, picking at her fingernails.

"Oh, so something light and fun," Valentina says. And Athena barks out a laugh that echoes around the cavernous airport. Her face immediately colors, but Valentina couldn't be happier. Seeing the slightest of open doors—

"We're going to London first. That's why we're subjecting ourselves to the red-eye," Valentina says.

"Me too. I changed my ticket. I mean, what else am I doing, right?"

Valentina doesn't know how to answer. She's not well versed in Athena's dry delivery or self-deprecation just yet. The slight delay when Valentina is slow to respond makes Athena want to gather her things, say her farewells, and walk out into the crush of traffic just outside the airport. But then—

"Well, currently we're both trying not to notice how that dude over there just took off his sandals and is now sitting in a public airport fully barefoot," Valentina says, jerking her head toward the offending man.

"I thought I was the only one who noticed," Athena says.

"The listening to videos at full volume is probably not helping draw attention away from him, I must say."

Before Athena can think better of it, she takes a sharp inhale and speaks, her voice loud. "There's this restaurant . . . restaurants, really . . . I have a whole list, but the one I really want to go to is this Korean barbecue place right by the New Malden Station that . . . I've been dying to try." Athena pauses, gulping down her terror. "Do you two want to come?" She clasps and reclasps her hands on her lap.

"Only if you come with us to the Portrait Gallery. It just reopened and there's a restaurant right at the tippy top. It's kind of corny, but you can sit by the window and drink tea, and it's wonderful. I love it there," Valentina says.

"That would be great," Athena says, unable to keep from smiling.

Valentina looks up and sees Rafael walking back toward them with an armful of candy, random magazines, and a bottle of water. He's in deep conversation with Jenn Nishimura. Jenn has her huge headphones resting around her neck and is wearing a hand-knit granny square afghan coat, a black short-sleeved workman's jumpsuit, and some Birkenstocks with pink and blue compression socks. Athena straightens up in her chair, hoping to signal to Jenn that she's no longer quite the wreck who dined at her beautiful restaurant the other night.

"Rafael knows the chef at this tiny mom-and-pop over in West Hendon—we go there every time we're out his way. Do you want to go to that, too?"

"That sounds delicious," Athena says, watching as Rafael and Jenn settle in front of them. Athena stands up. Jenn is one of those sneakily tall people, so she's among the few people Athena Winter doesn't tower over.

"Hey, it's good to see you again," Athena says to Jenn, who smiles wide. Athena couldn't be more relieved. "I didn't know you were taking the red-eye." Jenn nods as she rolls her luggage over to the end of the row of seats and off-loads all her gear, the messenger bag slung across her body, and unravels the headphones from around her neck. Finally unburdened, Jenn Nishimura takes a long deep breath. She turns back to Athena.

"It's why I always go a day early to this conference. I want to play in London, just take my time sauntering through the Borough Market, fondling fruit and veg. Is that odd . . . is this odd, am I weird . . ." Jenn crumples into a fit of laughter.

"The use of the word 'fondle'—" Athena says, smiling.

Jenn laughs. "Then you tell me what it is we do."

"Nuzzle?" Athena throws out.

"Paw?" Valentina offers. They look over to Rafael.

"I was going to say caress, so this . . . so this is not going to get any less uncomfortable for us all." He takes a long drink of his water.

Valentina stands up and speaks to the three exhausted chefs with authority. She holds her bedazzled phone in one hand and gesticulates to the gathered group with the other. She looks like an overzealous camp counselor.

"Okay, so if I could just pitch something amazing. If everyone is up for it, once we land and get through customs and all that, we can check into our various hotels, or I can get us all into the same hotel. That way we can take the same train up to Oxfordshire, and I will handle all that—we'll take showers, get the travel dust off us. Then I say we go to the Portrait Gallery first, drink tea and cakes and get as caffeinated as possible—"

"Not as much as last time, though," Rafael says.

"They just kept bringing me pots of tea. I could see through walls by the end of it. Then we go to the Borough Market, caress our fruit and veg, working up an appetite. That sounds super wrong, but—"

"Here we are," Athena breaks in, starting to settle into the rhythms of this conversation.

"Here we are, indeed. Then we eat a late lunch over at your friend's place in West Hendon, Rafael. Go back to the hotel, take a nap if need be—"

"If need be? Jesus, I'm exhausted just hearing this plan," Rafael says.

"We've got one day, for Chrissakes. We can sleep on the train up to the conference. Then we head over to the Korean barbecue place that Athena wants to try over by—"

"New Malden Station, right?" Jenn interrupts.

"Yeah," Athena says, beaming over at her.

"Ooh, I know the chef. I'll let him know we're coming," Jenn says. Athena smiles, the tension in her chest lessening.

"We can see how we feel, but one of our friends just opened an iza-kaya over in Shoreditch that we can close the night out with," Valentina says, finally looking up from her phone.

"We need more than one day," Jenn says, slumping down in her airport chair.

"We need more than a week." Athena laughs.

"Is everyone good with this plan?" Valentina asks, downright buzz-ing. The three chefs look to one another and finally give Valentina the green light.

"Ahh, this is going to be so fun!" Valentina says, utterly delighted at spending the next hour canceling hotel reservations, making new ones, calling old chef friends, hiring cars, and turning reservations that were for one or two into reservations for four culinary VIPs.

Once Valentina leaves to sit on the floor next to a wall with a free electrical socket so she can charge her phone, Rafael turns to Athena.

"I've been meaning to ask you—I have a pop-up down in LA right after we get back. I'm testing to see if my Pobrecito can anchor a whole new thing . . . I mean, it's basically what you did with Southern Trade. We've got a space in Altadena that we're trying out. I know it's not what you're used to, but I need an experienced grill chef, if you're up for it?" Rafael asks. Knowing what Athena—and the rest of the world—knows about Rafael and the last time he had a restaurant in Los Angeles, she knows his calm demeanor belies the uneasiness of returning to the original scene of the crime.

"I would really like that. That would be great," Athena says, trying to hide her excitement, as well as the absolute relief at not having to spend endless hours and days back at that converted garage with the perfect family.

"We can talk pay and all that, but I did want to throw out—um, we're giving the San Francisco transplants a stipend for lodging while they're down there, but I'm staying with a friend and there's a spare room if you want it?"

"Oh . . . I mean, if they're okay with it, that would be great." Athena shifts in her chair, nervous at the prospect of living in a stranger's home. And it's not just regular living in someone's home; it's Athena in chef mode living in a stranger's home, which she's realizing hasn't really been fertile ground in which to make a great first impression. But if this person knows Rafael, then they must have an idea of what it's like to be around someone like them.

"Okay, I'll email you the details. Excited to have you aboard," Rafael says with an exhausted drawl. Athena smiles but looks away from him and down at her lap, still uncomfortable with showing too much emotion or revealing how much this opportunity truly means to her.

The three chefs fall quickly into silence. Jenn and Rafael both disappear into their phones—the emails, the messages from back at their own individual restaurants—everything that comes with being in charge.

Without a restaurant of her own, Athena is left to simmer in the aftermath of the last ten minutes.

As she starts to analyze and pick it apart, Athena finally sits back in her chair and sighs, thinking that it simply felt nice and to leave it there. She needed nice after the last couple of weeks. Hell, she needed nice after the last couple of years . . . decades . . . how long has it been?

No.

Athena pulls herself back from the edge, tempted to hang little sandbags of fear and doubt onto this terrifying hot-air balloon feeling of belonging that she's currently struggling against.

Feeling good is a dangerous thing to get used to, but as Athena squints to make out the shimmering corners of that miraculous flash of hope, she decides that she can, at least, try.

The flight to London is an uneventful one. Because Athena is one of the special guests at the Banquet Conference, she was upgraded to first class—along with Rafael, Valentina, and Jenn. She told herself she was going to use at least some of the flight to prepare for the conference, scripting responses to questions she knows she'll be asked, as well as jotting down a few key points that she would say to Maren, Sloane, and Jules should she get that chance. In the end, Athena lasted under an hour before turning her airplane seat into a bed, curling up, and blissfully falling fast asleep.

Awakened a full eight hours later by a shaft of light coming from another passenger opening their window, it takes Athena a few seconds to orient herself and remember where she is. Once she remembers she's aboard a plane bound for London, she finds her glasses, sits up, and takes in her surroundings. Just over her shoulder Rafael and Valentina are quietly talking. Valentina is standing in the aisle with her makeup bag and Rafael is newly awake, scraping his unruly salt-and-pepper hair out of his face. Athena gives them a small wave before noticing that Jenn is still fully asleep, headphones firmly over her ears.

Within a few minutes, Athena's packed up her bed, brushed her teeth, pulled her hair back into a ponytail, and is sitting back down in her seat with a much-needed cup of coffee and the promise of breakfast. As Athena waits, she scrolls through the morning news and finds a review of Central Trade in the food section of the *Marin Independent Journal*. Athena's stomach drops as the headline populates her screen: Winter's Central Trade is Centrally Fine.

The lukewarm review is worse than a pan. Everything about the language is middling and beige and . . . forgettable. The critic compliments the beautiful venue, goes into the airy Scandinavian design of the restaurant, but then uses that as a jumping-off point to make the argument that while the restaurant itself is impressive, the same thing cannot be said for the food:

> Winter clearly had a vision for the restaurant, every detail lovingly chosen. What seems to have been less of a priority, however, was the food. What feels like a menu chosen more for quantity than quality, Winter provides something for everyone but at the cost of not making any one item truly singular. Central Trade is the place you end up when everywhere else is booked.

Athena feels both guilty and vindicated that the reviewer picked up on the very concerns she herself raised prior to the Central Trade soft launch. That in trying to be a place for everyone, Central Trade became a catchall of inoffensive, bland mediocrity where most people could probably find something they liked but wouldn't go out of their way for the one thing they could only get there, except its incomparable view of the bay.

The flight attendant settles in just next to Athena's seat and serves her breakfast, as well as a refill of her coffee. Athena shoves her phone back into her pocket, thanks the woman, and tries to shake the feeling that that review was somehow her fault. Was there something she could have done or said or . . . Athena lets out a genuine laugh as she catalogs the number of ways her mother made sure that no one but her made any decisions around Central Trade. That review is because of one person and one person alone. And as Athena tries to take a few bites of her breakfast, she wonders how long it will take for that one person to blame everyone and everything for the choices she made.

Athena watches the map on her television screen, their little airplane getting closer and closer to their destination. Valentina has given her the full itinerary for the day both verbally and via email. And as the group makes their way through customs, Athena reads and rereads the day's events, getting more and more excited with every reading. The group is herded toward the exit and finds the driver with the sign that reads LUNA. They all pile into the car, while their luggage—or moreover, Valentina's luggage—is loaded into another Town Car.

Once in her hotel room, Athena is running on pure adrenaline. Overtired and completely out of her depth, she pep talks herself all through her shower, brushing her hair, and finding an outfit to wear to wildly different events. She plays out scenarios where she says something dumb, does something dumb, or just is dumb. As Athena throws on her sweater, she thinks maybe she should cancel or tell them she's too tired. Clasping her watch onto her wrist, she envisions herself always riding in the front seat because "she's so tall" and craning her neck to eavesdrop on the other three as they laugh and chat away. Finally, as Athena sits on the toile bench at the end of her bed lacing up her shoes, she gives herself permission to just be excited.

Standing up, Athena grabs what she's going to need for the day and makes a rule not to check her phone and to stop waiting for some kind of bomb of an email from her family on the eve of them seeing each other for the first time since New Year's. The conference will be what it is. If it's a train wreck and Lola's article reopens all Athena's wounds, so be it.

But at least she'll have today.

"Just try to have fun," Athena says to herself as she tucks her hotel key inside her wallet. A quick moment to herself and Athena pulls her hotel room door open and steps out into the hallway with a determined "hmpf."

As Athena presses the elevator button for the ground level, she feels that same fluttery sensation in her chest that she did up on that vista point on her way to Stinson. Athena pulls her hand up to her chest and holds it there, catching her own reflection in the shiny surfaces of the hotel's elevator. She sees the smile breaking across her face. It's been a long time since she's seen that. Seeing the wrinkles around her eyes that mark her long-lost joy causes an eruption of emotion and gratitude. And that's when Athena puts it together that this feeling isn't because she's experiencing something good or bad. She has this feeling when she's uncertain.

As the elevator doors open at the hotel lobby, Athena sees the rest of the group gathered and waiting for her. She takes a deep breath, and using the extraordinary energy stemming from the feeling in her chest, she calls out to the group with a loud yawp and is met with laughter and squeals of delight in response. And just like when her great guttural scream alleviated that pressure in her chest so, too, do her own eruptions of joy and glee. Because, for once, Athena Winter feels safe enough to show those around her exactly what she's feeling. And in doing so, she gives those little feelings of uncertainty something to be certain about.

Athena hangs back a bit at the Portrait Gallery. This is all still relatively new to her—having friends, going out, not being a complete recluse. She spends her time at tea listening and laughing to scandalous kitchen stories and relatable tales of demanding customers and impossible standards, adding her two cents in with surgical precision. But mostly Athena sips her English Breakfast and soaks it all in.

As they walk through the Borough Market, Athena begins to shed her armor one hammered steel plate at a time. In awe at the food stalls inside the market hall, Athena is in heaven. Pointing to this stall and meandering over to that one. Pulling Jenn to come taste fresh honey and taking a toothpick with a bit of cheese from Somerset from

Rafael, Athena feels her love of food reigniting. As she feeds Valentina a bit of cheddar, Athena notices that her voice is getting louder. And when she hears the things she says and the stories she tells as they drive over to Rafael's friend's place, it's almost as if she forgot she had all this inside her.

Leaning back in her chair at the West Hendon restaurant, Athena closes her eyes and lets the taste of their transcendent Haleem dish slide down her throat and bring her to tears. The slow-cooked lentils warm her through and through, while each perfect bite of shredded lamb is even more delicious than the last. As lime and ginger are somehow able to finish the warm hug of a dish with a sunlit brightness, she feels herself coming back to life. Watching Rafael speak so passionately to his friend, homing in on the smallest of details, and watching the chef's face light up that someone noticed. It's magic.

While Valentina goes to check out her tea set prototype, Athena takes a two-hour nap before showering again, changing into a slightly nicer outfit, and then joining the group on their way to the Korean barbecue place over by the New Malden Station.

The restaurant is everything Athena dreamed it would be. Their group is seated around the table grill, charcoal glistening just below.

They are greeted by their waiter, but before they can order, bottles of soju are being set down along with the first round of chadol. Athena knows, as the youngest at the table, it's her job to do the cooking tonight. The sheer joy she feels with every flip of thinly sliced brisket on the grill colors her in just a little bit more each time. And by the time Jenn, the eldest in the group, pours yet another shot glass full of soju for Athena, she's the loosest and most free she's ever felt . . . maybe in her entire life. The exceptional staff somehow intuits whenever the group is finishing with one meat and wordlessly brings the new offering just as Rafael uses a lettuce leaf to clean off the grill in mouthwatering preparation for the next course. They blow through the saeng galbi as Jenn drunkenly slurs her love of the thicker cut of rib eye, and by the time the bulgogi comes, Athena is officially running this grill as if it were Northern Trade.

The only lull in an otherwise perfect meal is when the pork belly is served, and even though they try not to, the assembled group can't help but look from Athena to her New Year's Eve nemesis. They wait as her face flushes, and she considers just bulldozing past it as if nothing happened. But then she looks at them. Really looks at them, almost as if the world has fallen into slow motion. Their eyes are soft. And instead of feeling embarrassed, she lets this soft gentleness course through her. She feels held by them. These are friends. Her friends. Athena lifts the first chunk of pork belly from the tray and places it on the grill.

"I wonder if they can do a pork chop instead?" Athena asks with a smirk.

The table lets out a burst of nervous laughter and falls back into raucous conversation. As Athena moves and flips the pork belly on the grill, Jenn reaches over and places a hand on the small of her back, brushing it from side to side as she proudly looks up at her. At the same time, Rafael feeds Valentina a perfectly engineered ssam while everyone tries not to fall into hysterics looking at the photos she took of her custom tea set. The group chooses to forgo their naengmyeon, deciding that a bowl of cold noodles would make it impossible to eat anything else.

And, after all, they still have one more place to go.

Tomodachi Sake is a tiny izakaya in Shoreditch that has no sign and is in a nondescript storefront between a liquor store and a mobile phone store. Stepping inside, Athena feels wonder and awe. And when Jenn looks back at her with a wide smile, Athena feels the warmth of belonging pull her into the present moment with wild abandon. They're led to a back room and slide into a cozy little den in the back corner of the already dark and shadowy bar. The music is loud and they're playing hits from the '90s so that everyone in their party finds themselves mumbling along with lyrics they thought long forgotten.

There's something magical about a really good orderer. But there's something otherworldly about a table full of them, as well as a chef who can't wait to serve you all their favorites. The shared hunger and thirst to taste delicious things is almost seductive in its chase to experience them. And this table wants it all.

Valentina and Rafael's friend comes over to their table, and there are hugs all around. Athena and Jenn are introduced, and that's when the owner starts flooding their table with everything she has on offer. Sake after sake. Tiny plates full of delicious bar food appear and disappear. Athena and Jenn mumble along to '90s hit after '90s hit while cheersing with tiny glasses of some of the most delicious sake Athena has ever tasted. And by 2:30 a.m., Athena is drunker than she was at Jenn's restaurant but can't tell if it's the sake or the soju or just the breathtaking beauty of a day that was so intoxicating.

Crawling into bed in the wee hours of the morning, their train ride to Oxfordshire in a matter of hours, Athena finds herself sighing, smiling, and laughing as she replays the day. When you have a complicated definition of family, belonging can feel like a fairy tale. But today Athena was embraced and accepted and understood for exactly who she is by people who were once strangers. And as she drifts off to sleep, her hotel spins around her.

It's as if Athena Winter is five years old again and is positive she just saw Santa Claus with her very own eyes.

CHAPTER ELEVEN

The Banquet Conference was started quite by accident in the winter of 1982, when four of the United Kingdom's top chefs came together for what turned out to be a drunken weekend at Jocasta Pryce's sixteenth-century manor house nestled in the rolling hills of Oxfordshire.

At the time, Pryce was leading the charge on sustainable, fresh ingredients; seasonality; and nose-to-tail dining at her two-Michelin-Starred restaurant, the Glass House. Located next to the manor house's expansive gardens, the Glass House revolutionized the way diners interacted with the very source of where their food was coming from, even going so far as to take a gold at the Chelsea Flower Show for its container-grown salad and vegetables. Infamous for pulling patrons right out of their chairs to urge them to pick their own greens, Pryce earned a reputation as being a tad eccentric in her commitment to freshness. It seems that the idea of getting one's hands dirty during a meal that cost a month's rent was seen by some as a bridge too far.

Nevertheless, Pryce became a culinary legend—soon expanding the Glass House's ethos beyond the restaurant and its elite on-site cooking and gardening school. Chronically annoyed by just the few receiving accolades for the work of many, she launched the Banquet Foundation and Awards Ceremony in 1983. The Banquet's mission statement was celebrating each phase of a dish's journey equally, highlighting the aspects—and people—of the culinary world who'd long been ignored. Pryce provided scholarships, awards, and education to superstar chefs as well as to community gardens, food scientists, and grassroots organizers alike. Her tireless pursuit made her a dame, after she was appointed Dame Commander of the Order of the British Empire in 2012.

More than eighty years old, Dame Jocasta has turned the reins of her empire over to her two nieces, after having made the choice long ago not to have any children of her own. Preferring to go narrow boating with her beloved husband of fifty-two years, Pryce will still venture into the Glass House's dining room every now and again, tugging ecstatic diners out into the gardens for what she calls "a little bit of dirt therapy."

A longtime colleague of Maren Winter's, Dame Jocasta held off on presenting her old friend with the Banquet Conference's much sought-after lifetime achievement award until she felt doing so would be undeniable and not just playing favorites. But in Jocasta's eyes, this honor is long overdue.

The manor house is abuzz preparing for the arrival of the thirty-two VIP guests who'll be staying in the manor house itself, as well as the three hundred and fifty guests who have registered for the conference and gala. For such a well-known institution, the Banquet is a conference everyone knows about, but very few get to actually attend. Those in attendance at this year's conference are a blend of chefs, gardeners, local growers, journalists, and writers, as well as environmentalists, food scientists, and even a few politicians. What all these people have in common is that they share Dame Jocasta's view that in talking about food, you are talking about the human experience. You cannot, nor should you, separate the two.

As guests begin to arrive on that rainy Saturday morning, on the first day of the conference, Banquet volunteers check the attendees in one by one—giving them their itineraries for the next three days, a map of the grounds, and a full catalog of the long weekend's events. Conference attendees can choose anything from talks on the state of the restaurant industry to exciting innovations in food science, all the way to a walking tour of the Glass House gardens and even demonstrations on how to start a kitchen garden and the basics of Plating 101.

As the star-studded presenters begin to arrive, the atmosphere begins to shift around the old manor house. Banquet volunteers try to keep their cool as they sign in a world-famous chef with more than thirty restaurants around the globe, who's standing in line just behind one of the hosts of a gardening show that's been on for decades. Famous faces with even more famous restaurants crowd around the registration desk as each presenter is handed their key to one of the main manor house's twenty-eight accommodations, where they will find an elaborate gift basket awaiting them, along with an invitation to tonight's opening keynote speech by Dame Jocasta Pryce herself.

Arriving together, Jules, Sloane, and Maren Winter step out of their SUV en masse. Their presence causes a slight hysteria among the conference volunteers and staff. However, just underneath their pristine facade, trouble is already brewing.

The review of Central Trade that Athena read on the plane was just the first in a run of similar reviews. The more esteemed publications won't review the restaurant for another month, but across the board, online food writers who attended the soft launch said the restaurant itself was beautiful, but in each write-up, they mention being wholly underwhelmed by Maren Winter's culinary choices. The reviewers managed to carefully walk that line of respect for a legend, while also holding Maren accountable for what some feared was a "cash grab" or "a misguided attempt to stay relevant."

The most generous online reviewers called Central Trade a "work in progress" and were hopeful that it would "find its stride." However, a few of the newer writers on the culinary scene were far more straightforward with their analysis. One particularly clever meme created by an online food critic simply known as YumTime was a screenshot of the infamous 1988 vice presidential debate where candidate Lloyd Bentsen told his opponent, "I knew Jack Kennedy. Jack Kennedy was a friend of mine. Senator, you're no Jack Kennedy." But YumTime placed the words "Northern Trade" in crude text over the words "Jack Kennedy" and replaced "Senator" with "Central Trade." Maren showed the meme to Jules on the ride to Oxfordshire as if Jules hadn't already seen it. Maren tried to argue that no one would take this person seriously—pointing to YumTime's sad-face-egg avatar as proof of their amateurish tone. Jules looked at the avatar and then pointed out that YumTime had almost a million followers and tried to explain to Maren that while YumTime might appear unprofessional to Maren, their tone and way of communicating were perfectly matched with all things viral on the internet. And she'd strongly advised against dismissing these reviews out of hand because, while they might not move the needle on how the more legacy institutions talk about Central Trade, they would certainly affect whether those wannabe influencer kids flock to the restaurant now that it's been deemed uncool by one of their own. Jules stopped short of reciting the line she repeated to herself at the Central Trade soft launch: you live by the sword; you die by the sword. And sometimes the opponent who lands the best shot is a sad-face-egg avatar who reads you for filth with a forty-year-old political screenshot and a succinctly worded, impossibly clever takedown.

Upon seeing the Winter clan step out of their SUV, the young woman at the front desk radios Dame Jocasta's personal secretary that Maren Winter has arrived. Dame Jocasta asked to be apprised of when Maren checked in, as she should like to greet her personally.

Dame Jocasta's personal secretary comes striding down the south walkway toward the folly where Pryce is currently—as she calls it—"walking the battlements" with her two nieces, Isobel and Cressida. Isobel, the oldest, has taken over all things related to the Glass House. She is the executive chef of the restaurant and, with her two children, also runs the manor house and both the culinary and gardening schools exclusively. While Cressida, younger by just two years, oversees everything related to the Banquet Foundation and Conference, along with her four children.

Dame Jocasta Pryce is barely five feet tall with a shock of white hair. Dressed in a loose black cashmere sweater and pencil pants paired with expensive loafers, Dame Jocasta is the very picture of country elegance.

Holding her beloved raincoat, her personal secretary clears his throat just as Cressida is about to walk Jocasta through the social strategy around the conference and the posts they have scheduled throughout the long weekend.

"Thank you for saving me," Dame Jocasta laughs to him, as he holds out the raincoat for her so she won't get wet in the rain.

"Social media again?" he asks.

"Indeed," she says with a smile, as Cressida swipes her tablet off.

"Maren Winter has arrived," her personal secretary announces.

"Before we go, have we remedied our accommodations for the Winter family to correspond to the state in which they are at present?" Dame Jocasta says delicately.

"We had all four members of the Winter family in each of the four Conservatory Suites, but we have since moved Athena Winter over to one of the Garden Cottages. We feel confident this will mitigate the situation with utmost discretion," Isobel says, her hands clasped in front of her.

"Very well," Dame Jocasta says. Her personal secretary opens his large black umbrella and steps carefully to the entrance of the folly. But before Dame Jocasta follows, she continues, "Should anything untoward happen this weekend, we must be vigilant in protecting our guests' privacy. Is that clear?" Isobel and Cressida both nod.

Isobel helps Dame Jocasta down the wet and slippery steps of the folly, and she disappears down the south walkway toward the manor house. Cressida quickly texts her son and tells him to get to the registration desk to capture the moment Dame Jocasta Pryce greets the great Maren Winter on the eve of her receiving the Banquet Foundation's Lifetime Achievement Award.

Staff from the Glass House rush out to meet Maren, Sloane, and Jules Winter with large black umbrellas. Jules looks back to see their luggage being unloaded out of the back of the SUV—or at least that's what she'll tell Sloane or her mom if they ask. In reality, she's scanning the horizon looking for Athena.

She's planned a speech, of course. Practicing hypothetical speeches is one of Jules Winter's favorite pastimes. She's perpetually worried about tarnishing the sterling public image she's crafted, cultivated, and tyrannized other women with, as this effortlessly perfect paragon of womanhood. But now, the only place Jules can let out her more inelegant emotions—like sarcasm, frustration, or rage—is with her immediate family and during these elaborate monologues that have turned into a daily practice. The sheer combustive energy of the things women don't say could fuel the entire world's electric grid.

"Right this way, Mrs. Winter," a Glass House staffer says to Jules, offering his umbrella.

"Thank you so much," Jules says. She smiles benevolently and delicately tucks herself under the umbrella, nestling into him with surgical adorableness.

But just as Jules is about to take her first step down the flagstone walkway leading to the entrance of the manor house, the Glass House staffer very politely tells her to wait. Jules's eyes flare as she regulates her tone. But before she can speak, her mother swans past, surrounded by a pack of umbrella-wielding Glass House staffers, all making sure that she is the first Winter down the path. Thinking she has the full grasp of what's happening, Jules starts to walk again. And once again, she is told to wait, the wet and cold now creeping into her bones.

"So, is the conference out here, then?" Jules jokes, making sure her voice is properly light and airy. The young Glass House staffer laughs uncomfortably, craning his neck to see if what he's waiting for is on its way.

Jules lets out a sigh, her displeasure punctuated with a misty cloud. She shifts her weight as the rain has gone from coming straight down to more of a diagonal presentation. Jules is on the cusp of either strangling this young man, prying the umbrella from his cold, dead hands, or just making a break for the front of the manor house in one desperate, rage-filled sprint, when Sloane appears with her own cadre of umbrella-holding Glass House staffers. She, too, strides down the flag-stone walkway behind their mother.

When her older sister is about halfway down, the young man hold-ing her umbrella gives Jules the nod and she begins her entrance, know-ing that in the eyes of Dame Jocasta Pryce, she's someone who should be left waiting in the rain to make way for the two more important members of her family. Even with Athena gone, Jules still manages to come in last.

With every step Maren Winter takes toward the imposing entrance to Dame Jocasta's sixteenth-century manor house, she feels the rising tide of two opposing emotions begin to swirl deep within her. Excitement and pride course through her body as she sees the crush of adoring and awed faces of the Banquet volunteers and Glass House staffers alike lining the walkway and crowding around the reg-istration desk. Sneaky photographs, teary nudges to colleagues, and three rows deep of culinary students stand on tippy-toes just to get a glimpse of her.

But for every explosion of fireworks, there's this tiny whisper that very quietly asks, *"Look around . . . shouldn't you have all this?"* Maren takes in the manor house, solid and stable, just like Dame Jocasta's legacy. The sheer number of staffers, students, teachers, gardeners, and hangers-on is staggering. As Maren scans the sea of faces, recogniz-ing Isobel and Cressida among them, the whisper quietly repeats, *"You should have this. You deserve this. You've earned this."* And just as Maren chooses to shoo away these whispers and lose herself in the glow of pride at everything she's accomplished, Sloane and Jules Winter settle in at her side. And as the middling reviews, clever memes, and dismissive quotes about Central Trade ooze and seep around the dark corners of Maren's psyche, the whisper hisses, *"It's their fault people hate Central Trade. They are to blame. They stole this future from you."*

Maren looks over her shoulder at her daughters. And the look she gives each of them propels them to take a step back. And another one. Maren slowly turns back around, just as the sea of chef's whites part in front of her and Dame Jocasta appears, walking down the center of all that she's created. Maren's whispers and hisses subside as she sees her old friend. And she can't help but soften.

So few people understand the singular burden and seclusion of fame. And in this moment, Maren recognizes a fellow traveler. But her desire to speak honestly and bare her soul to someone who gets every facet of this wild and extraordinary existence is twisted by Maren's deep hunger to prove to Dame Jocasta that she, too, has it all. She, too, is just as fulfilled. She, too, is just as powerful. And that she, too, has as solid, stable, and permanent a legacy as any Dame Jocasta could hope for.

Because deep down Maren Winter fears that confessing this rumbling foreboding she can't seem to shake to Dame Jocasta might just shatter everything and reveal a lapse in confidence. How could anyone admire a woman on the cusp of receiving a lifetime achievement award, when she's questioning the lasting impact of all that they've achieved in their lifetime?

As Maren Winter and Dame Jocasta Pryce greet one another warmly in the grand and soaring entrance hall of the manor house, Maren decides that the cost of honesty is too high. She will find another way.

Alone.

As the horde of admirers buzz and swirl around her mother, Sloane Winter quietly steps forward and handles the more pedestrian orders of business. She checks herself, her mother, and her little sister in; gathers all their various schedules and agendas; and collects their room keys, along with a map of the vast grounds. Once this is done, Sloane weaves her way through the crowd and finds a completely sodden Jules sulking over by the large, crackling fireplace.

"It looks like we're all in the Conservatory Suites," Sloane says, pulling out the map of the grounds.

"But there are four. Do you think—" Jules asks, craning to see the map that Sloane is holding just a little too close to be considered "sharing."

"Who do I even ask about that? How do I even ask about that?" Sloane asks, folding the map up as Jules was still looking at it.

"Do we even know if she's still coming?" Jules asks.

"She's still on all the program materials, but those would have been printed out long before . . ." Sloane trails off before explicitly saying "before our entire family blew up." She scans the room for someone to ask whether their estranged little sister has confirmed she will be in attendance or has been seen lurking around their wing of Dame Jocasta's expansive grounds.

"I thought I saw her in the background of one of Valentina Luna's social media posts yesterday. They were at the Borough Market in London," Jules says, pulling her phone out of the pocket of her dress. She finds the offending post straightaway and shows it to Sloane, pulling her phone just a little closer so her older sister must contort her body to get even a bad view of the incriminating piece of evidence. Not wanting to give her sister the edge, Sloane shows no signs of struggle while she evaluates whether it is her littlest sister's back walking with Rafael Luna down the center of the open-air market.

"So, she's friends with them now?" Sloane asks, fighting back her jealousy.

"Guess so," Jules says, replacing her phone in her pocket.

Everyone knows things posted online aren't real. This fact, however, does not stop them from proceeding as though they are.

Sloane turns away from Jules and spots Dame Jocasta's eldest niece, Isobel, quietly speaking to a Glass House staff member in a hallway just off the main entrance hall.

"Okay, I'll go talk to Isobel," Sloane says.

"And you're clear on what you're going to say?" Jules asks.

"It's just like we talked about. I'll reiterate what I said to the staff and, as delicately as possible, drop a few hints of concern that . . . you know," Sloane says, still unable to say out loud that she and Jules want to intentionally sow seeds of doubt that their mother has gone mad.

"Could you be any more uncool about this?" Jules shakes her head, cringing at Sloane's attempt at being cloak and dagger.

"I'm betting I could," Sloane says, and something about this just cracks Jules up. And there is the tiniest, most tragic moment where both sisters pull back from letting themselves giggle like they used to as little girls. Instead, Sloane hardens herself, searching for a concise summation of the events of the last several weeks. She continues, her voice now steeled and unwelcoming, "I'll also ask her about the whole—"

"I'm on the edge of my seat right now waiting to see how you're going to spin the whole Athena thing," Jules says, pretending as though she didn't notice the missed moment. Instead, she catches a glimpse of herself in a large mirror. She smooths her long blonde hair, curling the tendrils around her finger as she meticulously lays them flat on her thin shoulders.

"Just take this and I'll text when I'm done," Sloane says, unloading all the registration materials onto Jules, while she unravels her room key from the pile. Jules struggles to manage the unwieldy jumble.

"Isn't this a conversation I should be a part of?" Jules asks, shifting and stacking the detritus.

"Do you want to be a part of this conversation?" Sloane asks, knowing her sister better than she knows herself.

"I want to be the kind of person who wants to be in this conversation." Jules stumbles.

"Are you that kind of person now?"

"No, I am not."

"So why don't you be in charge of getting that pile of stuff back to our rooms and I'll text when I'm done," Sloane says, repeating the command from just a few seconds ago.

"Fine. Okay." Jules looks away from Sloane, hoping her older sister thinks she can't look her in the eye because she chickened out of the big-girl conversation and not that she's sending her into this conversation like a lamb to the slaughter. From the self-satisfied look on Sloane's face, Jules knows that she has been successful in her deception.

"Oh, can you give me Mom's key?" Sloane asks, her voice light and airy, and just on the fringes of smug.

"Here. Just take it." Jules knows that it appears as if she has lost this round. And that Sloane thinks that she lost it. Having Jules hand over the key to their mother's room is a nice touch—it almost makes Jules respect Sloane a little bit more.

As Jules hands Sloane the large iron key, she finds it almost endearing to watch Sloane's first baby steps into the next level of espionage. Her older sister's little flare of arrogance does slightly ease Jules's guilt at sending Sloane into this conversation with Isobel without all the information she'll need. The sheer naivete of Sloane Winter trusting that her "ditzy coward" of a sister has shared all the pertinent details. And that she, hypothetically, of course, didn't hold back that she'd received a phone call from Lola Tadese. Jules was prepared for Lola to ask for comment from the Winter camp refuting her claims around the truth of what's unfolded over the course of the last several weeks within the Winter empire. The phone call was confirmation that, just as Jules thought, Lola Tadese did what Lola Tadese does best: she'd written a hit piece about Maren Winter to coincide with the occasion of her receiving the Banquet Lifetime Achievement Award.

What Jules hadn't banked on was that Lola was an even better journalist than she could have ever dreamed. Lola confirmed the anonymous quote from Sloane's speech to the staff that Jules herself had planted. Line by line, Jules nodded along as Lola paraphrased Sloane's championing Athena, challenging their mother for her shocking mistreatment of her, and how ultimately the goal was to bring Athena back as head chef.

But then Lola said something that would shock even Jules Winter.

Unbeknownst to both Sloane and Jules, Lola Tadese had overheard their conversation as they stood outside Northern Trade on New Year's Eve. She'd been standing by the dual firepits scribbling a quote into her notebook from one of the dishwashers when she heard Sloane say with perfect clarity, *"Maybe this will teach the mighty Athena Winter that without Mommy's recipes, she's just as tragically ordinary as the rest of us."*

Jules felt like the wind got knocked out of her as she listened to Lola read back Sloane's quote verbatim and immediately connected the dots of what Lola was going to do in her article. Lola Tadese was going to juxtapose what Sloane had said publicly to the Northern Trade staff against what she'd said privately to Jules and then let her damning hypocrisy speak for itself. In a rare moment of softness, Jules began to feel a little bit bad for Sloane and the inevitable internet walloping she was about to get.

But Winters were being picked off one by one, and as far as Jules could see, she was going to be the last one standing.

Naturally, Jules had confirmed both of Lola's quotes but offered "no comment" as her only response. She told no one of Lola's phone call. In Jules's mind, having Sloane be the one to personally communicate their agreed-upon narrative to Isobel, while knowing the real quote Sloane said in private is hours away from going public, is exactly the insurance policy she needs to put her own endgame into motion, tarnishing Sloane's credibility and giving Jules the benefit of her two favorite words in the English language: plausible deniability.

Watching her plan come together, Jules Winter can't help but smile.

"What? Why . . . why are you smiling? What's going on?" Sloane looks around the bustling entrance hall as she pockets her mother's large iron key.

"Oh, nothing," Jules says with a strategically placed sniff. Sloane's eyes narrow. "See you back in our rooms then?"

And just like that Jules Winter is back on the board.

As Jules slinks out of the entrance hall, Sloane multitasks, setting her sights on Isobel, checks on the status of her mother, and scans the horizon for Athena.

Sloane Winter has never felt more alive.

"May I have a quiet word?" Sloane asks, waiting politely until Isobel has finished her conversation with the Glass House staffer.

"Of course. This way," Isobel says, motioning to a closed door at the end of the hallway. Sloane follows and is let into one of the manor house's several reception rooms. Isobel motions to one of two wingback chairs arranged in front of a large stone fireplace that Sloane is sure she could almost stand up in. The wood-paneled room is lined in large windows hung with lustrous curtains falling in elegant puddles on the parquet floor. In the center of the room, there is a coffee table adorned with a spray of beautiful flowers perfectly arranged in a large cut-crystal vase. As Sloane settles into the chair, Isobel calls to a Glass House staffer for some tea.

Coming back into the room, she gestures at the fully stocked bar cart nestled in the corner and asks, "Unless you want something stronger?"

"Only if you'll join me?" Sloane asks.

"Very well," Isobel says, pouring them each a glass of eighteen-year-old Bowmore whisky. She hands one to Sloane and sits.

"Thank you for taking the time. I can't imagine how busy you are," Sloane says, resting her glass on the arm of her chair.

"It's my pleasure." Isobel waits.

"I wanted to check in with you personally and talk through some of the more delicate details around my family's current predicament," Sloane says. Noticing her hand is shaking, and the whisky with it, Sloane tries to steady herself.

"Whatever our family can do for yours, just ask," Isobel says.

"May I inquire if Athena is still confirmed for the event, and if so, where will she be staying this weekend?" Sloane asks, starting with the simplest request.

"We have placed Athena in one of the Garden Cottages. We have also made sure that any talks or panels in which Athena participates or has expressed interest in attending are located outside of the scope of your mother's responsibilities. As to the events in which all attendees of the conferences shall be present, we've made sure to seat Athena as far away from your mother as possible."

"Thank you for your care and sensitivity during this time. Both my sister and I are actively trying to work with our mother to bring Athena back into the fold. Needless to say, we are not on the same page as to how that night should have gone."

"Understood; however, I do want to flag one possible troublesome scenario," Isobel says, setting her glass down on the large coffee table.

Caught off guard, Sloane takes a long swig of her whisky to calm her nerves. "Please, go on," she says, gulping down her anxiety.

"In ongoing recognition for your mother's many accomplishments, we decided to name an award after her for outstanding achievements in innovation and pioneering in the culinary world," Isobel says, her face draining of color. Sloane's stomach drops. "To ensure fairness and transparency, we run all of our awards through a neutral third party." Isobel clasps her hands in front of her. "Athena Winter is up for the award this year, and we won't know if she's won until the envelope is opened onstage."

"And who is presenting this award?" Sloane asks.

"Maren Winter."

"Does my mother know any of this yet?" Sloane asks. Isobel checks the large grandfather clock ticking loudly in the room.

"Your mother and my aunt are set to have a private lunch together in a little over an hour. The announcement of the award is on the list of things to discuss."

"May I ask a follow-up question?"

"Of course," Isobel says, shifting in her chair.

"At what point in the ceremony is this new award being presented?"

"Currently, we have the Maren Winter Award for Innovation going last," Isobel says.

"And when is the lifetime achievement award being presented?"

"Before the final run of big awards, so just over halfway," Isobel says.

Sloane sits back in her chair.

It's very rare to be faced with such a clear crossroads. While Sloane is struggling to fully understand the scope of her mother's corruption, she can definitely recognize a lit match when she sees one. And the prospect of Maren Winter's big moment being eclipsed by having to present an award to her youngest daughter—and greatest rival—in recognition for the exact category in which Maren Winter fears she's lost her edge is as sure a bet as she's ever seen. But just in case . . .

"I'm sure you will handle this situation with the utmost of discretion, but I would offer a word of caution." Sloane sets her drink down on the coffee table and leans forward. Instinctively, Isobel curls toward Sloane, understanding that what comes next is to be handled with the greatest of confidentiality. "I'm afraid to say that my mother has not been herself as of late. I don't know if it's the stress of launching Central Trade to middling reviews, or if it's just her getting older—but her behavior has been growing ever more erratic. That nasty business on New Year's Eve that shocked us all when we heard what my mother had done to Athena and then bringing in—as I'm sure you've heard—this internet person as head chef at Northern Trade. I'm worried, but hope this is merely a temporary slip, rather than . . ." Sloane trails off dramatically as Isobel silently finishes her ominous sentence. Isobel brings her hand to her heart, feeling the weight of what Sloane is saying. Sloane takes a deep, brave breath. "It's been very hard."

"Is there anything I can do?" Isobel asks.

"My hope is that this weekend brings back the woman we all know and love. Maybe even mends some fences—" Sloane stops, surprised by how emotional the thought of things returning to normal has made her. "May I ask how Dame Jocasta handled . . ." She trails off, but Isobel knows exactly where she's going with her next line of questioning.

"Aunt Jocasta had it all planned out. That's not to say that it wasn't without its challenges, but she presented Cressida and I—along with our entire board of directors—with a five-year plan ten years before she retired." Isobel laughs to herself. "It's not often you're presented with a binder full of someone else's plans for your future." Sloane smiles. She would have killed for a binder.

There is a polite knock on the door. Isobel calls for them to enter.

"Dame Jocasta is asking after you," a Glass House staffer says.

"Ah, yes. I'll be there straightaway," Isobel says and the Glass House staffer nods, steps back out into the hallway, closing the door to provide at least a semblance of privacy in their final moments.

The two women both stand, smoothing their clothes and preparing to go back out into the fray.

"Thank you for your counsel and your understanding," Sloane says, extending her hand. Isobel takes it.

"You're welcome," Isobel says.

"Depending on how this weekend goes, I may have to start having some hard conversations with our own board of directors," Sloane says, planting the very last seed.

"Let me know if I can be of any help to you," Isobel says, walking toward the door. Sloane follows.

"I will. Thank you again," Sloane says. Isobel nods and is quickly whisked away by the Glass House staffer.

Now alone, Sloane stands in the hallway as the din of the entrance hall wafts throughout the magnificent old house. Glass House staffers race past. But quite suddenly the noise and the heat from the fireplace and the weight of what she's done begin to curdle Sloane's insides. Thinking she's going to be sick, Sloane finds a door to the outside and bursts through to a beautiful gem of a courtyard lined with soaked-through benches all arranged around a gorgeous burbling fountain.

Unable to sit down, Sloane pitches forward, trying to stave off the nausea. She tries to steady her breathing, her mind a riot of wordless terror—the shame and guilt of what she's doing, now that it's officially in motion, infect her.

"I have to do this . . . She's making me do this . . . I have to do this . . ." Sloane says, her hands on her knees, tears and spit dropping to the slick flagstones beneath her feet.

She forces herself to see any other path, anything else she could have done, and over and over again there are only two options: the path they are currently on and the path Athena is currently on. However much she wishes she had, if Sloane stood up to her mom on New Year's Eve, she would have been packed off along with Athena. And had she and Jules sat their mom down and had the hard conversation after the fact, they both would have been banished and made to watch as everything their family built was run into the ground.

Sloane's breathing steadies as she crafts her argument, that this whole plan would be nothing without her mother playing an active role. It's her own mother who fired Athena over a pork chop. It's her own mother who had no five-year plan ten years before she was set to retire. It's her own mother whose insecurity and self-doubt made her view her daughters as rivals. It's her own mother who wouldn't collaborate or even listen to any guidance around the launch of Central Trade, and it's her own mother who hired some internet sycophant to be the head chef of one of the world's top hundred restaurants, rather than listening to Sloane and Jules about who was best for Northern Trade.

And it will be her own mother who is responsible for the very undoing of herself this weekend. A trap is only as good as the mechanism that makes it slam shut, and Maren's fragile ego is all it will take to confirm Sloane's story and set this whole place on fire.

"They have to see . . . We have to make them see," Sloane says, wiping her face and trying to find an excuse why this takedown had to be so very public.

Sloane is finally able to stand upright. Her breathing steadying. The tears subsiding. The words coming back. But then a whisper. A tiny whisper from somewhere deep inside her.

What about Athena?

Sloane shakes her head, trying to make the whisper go away.

Why does she deserve this?

Trying to quiet the whisper, Sloane takes out her phone and texts Jules that she's on her way to their rooms.

Jules texts back, asking how the conversation with Isobel went. Sloane answers that she'll fill her in when she gets back to the room and pockets the phone before Jules can text back for Sloane to at least give her a hint.

Sloane checks her face in the reflection of the windows around the courtyard.

Why does she deserve this?

Sloane looks away from her own reflection as the noise in her head grows louder and louder. As a desperate last stand, she smacks the side of her head with the heel of her hand. And again. The noise begins to fade, but the lack of completeness in answering the question shallows Sloane's breath as she attempts to put herself back together and reenter the busy main house. Striding so single-mindedly down the long hallway and through the entrance hall on her way to meet Jules back in their rooms, Sloane Winter fails to notice Lola Tadese checking in at the registration desk.

And Lola would be hard to miss, considering she's wearing the same deep-purple dress, with the faux-snakeskin boots. A little worse for the wear, Lola's paired this look with a long puffer jacket and a woolen beanie with the Union Jack on it that she clearly bought at the duty-free section of Heathrow Airport.

But the tragedy of Sloane Winter has always been her inability to see beyond what's right in front of her. Not only did she miss Lola Tadese, but she's also blind to another path she and her sisters could have taken. She was partially correct about there being two current options available to her: the path she and Jules are taking and the path Athena is following. But there's a third option available to all three Winter sisters. They could simply choose to step off the paths forged by those who came before.

Walking solely on someone else's path is both the easiest and hardest thing to do.

CHAPTER TWELVE

In the early hours of Sunday morning, Lola Tadese reads and rereads the proof of an article that's hours away from doing something so revolutionary it'll turn the entire Winter empire upside down.

Lola Tadese is about to tell the truth.

※

As the Banquet Conference begins its second day, Glass House staffers are already hard at work. The culinary team is busy preparing in-room breakfasts, pots of tea, and the pastries and fruit that will be on offer in all the conference's green rooms. The event team is being activated on several different fronts—readying rooms for workshops, panels, talks, and press junkets as well as preparing for tonight's gala award ceremony.

The rain has finally subsided for right now, but with temperatures dipping into the low forties, attendees and presenters alike have chosen to stay in the warmth of the manor house.

Except Athena Winter.

Bundled up from head to toe and carrying a steaming mug of tea, Athena ambles across the misty, rolling hills, letting her fingers brush the dewy tops of the wild grasses and vegetation brave enough to grow during these cold and brutal months. Setting her sights on Dame Jocasta's grand glass house and sweeping gardens, Athena picks her way ever closer. Arriving at the large double doors of the glass house, she tries to get the attention of the handful of gardeners already busy at work, bent over their harvest. As an older woman stands, her long brown hair pulled back from her face with a headband, hands covered in soil, she sees Athena standing just outside.

"May I?" Athena asks, motioning to the woman to ask if she can come in. The woman, recognizing Athena immediately, approaches her.

"Can I be of assistance?" the woman asks.

"Yes. Is it okay if I explore a little?" Athena asks, trying to make her request sound more concrete than just her needing to smell wet soil and feel the rough veins on the backs of delicate leaves. The woman looks to the other two gardeners in the glass house, and they're just as flummoxed as she is.

"Of course. Please, do come in," the woman finally says, brushing away the soil on her apron.

Athena steps inside the glass house and inhales. She's missed that smell. She's missed it so much that breathing it in almost makes her break down and sob. Instead—

"Do you need any help?" Athena asks, eyeing the crop of rocket that is clearly being prepped for today's menu.

"That would be lovely. Aprons and gloves are in there," the woman says. Athena sets down her mug of tea and has to keep herself from skipping over to the shed, attempting to keep some semblance of decorum.

After she joins the trio, Athena loses all track of time. She couldn't be happier. And as she follows the gardeners inside to deliver their harvest, she wonders if Dame Jocasta is hiring and if there's a place for her here. But as she steps into the loud and bustling kitchens of the Glass House, she sees Isobel in the middle of it all. And then she fears it would just be a matter of time before what happened at Northern Trade happened here, too. Can a chef as senior as Athena do well in any kitchen where she's not in charge? Does she even want to do well in a kitchen where she's not in charge?

Isobel gives Athena a friendly wave and Athena waves back. She makes herself leave the kitchen, deflating just a bit with every step.

The guests lucky enough to stay at the Glass House awaken to its singular beauty and serenity. It's the kind of peace and quiet that comes from being in the middle of nowhere. Surrounded by breathtaking vistas and melodic birdsong, guests do their best not to contaminate this all-encompassing grandeur with their own personal demons. Trying to live in that split second upon awakening in the large feather-down bed, the morning light shining through the wavy old glass of the manor house windows, just for a moment, they are weightless. And maybe they can forget the burdens of their own life that they've yet to hang on their already exhausted shoulders.

But for others, the quiet brings with it an unwelcome stillness that feels more like the calm before a storm. Because for some, a moment of peace is just the inhalation before the inevitable primal scream.

And on this cold day in January, nestled in the lush, rolling hills of Oxfordshire . . . those poor souls would be right.

For many, it starts like any other day. The beloved habits and rituals of their mornings are steeped in possibility. Guests and attendees reach for caffeine, nourishment, and the news of the day. And on this quiet Sunday, the news of the day is a front-page story in the Sunday *San Francisco Chronicle* Food section bearing the headline, Has Maren Winter Lost Her Edge?

The headline alone jolts Sloane out of her early-morning fuzziness. This is not the puff piece Jules promised her it would be. Sloane whips off her covers and begins pacing as she reads what is an inconvenient masterstroke of a journalistic hit piece.

In just under two thousand words, Lola Tadese manages to use the interaction she had when she first got to Northern Trade as the backbone of the entire article. She masterfully grounds a decades-long career in a relatable and visceral story of first impressions. Using each small observation from that first day to anchor a story or interview from Maren's past, Lola keeps the reader on the edge of their seat, breathless and careening toward what everyone now knows happened at midnight that very night. The true mastery of Lola's article is in telling the story of New Year's Eve:

she lets Maren Winter herself embody the tragedy of a tortured genius coming face-to-face with the consequences of her own fragile ego.

And then Sloane sees her quote.

> Maybe this will teach the mighty Athena Winter that without Mommy's recipes, she's just as tragically ordinary as the rest of us.

"Oh my god," Sloane says out loud, crumpling to the floor. She reads it again.

She clamps her hand over her mouth. Seeing the quote forces Sloane to see her own cruelty in black and white.

What has she become?

In what will most certainly earn Lola her second Pulitzer, the article compels her readers to examine their own unsteady relationships with those in our world upon whom we've bestowed the moniker of genius. And in so doing, she makes us all complicit in Maren's corruption, thereby bringing her tragedy right to our own front doors.

After reading through Lola's full article—in all its stomach-churning, honest glory—Sloane Winter hauls herself off the ground and, still in her pajamas and robe, grabs her room key, pulls the door closed behind her, and sets her sights on Jules's room.

Sloane knocks quietly at first. Then she sends a text. Then a phone call. Another knock. Then finally a more forceful knock brings a newly awake Jules to the door.

"What is wrong with you?" Jules asks, pulling her robe closed over her wrinkled pajamas.

"Did you know about this?" Sloane asks, holding her phone out so Jules can see the headline. Instead of looking at the headline, Jules walks over to the in-room phone and calls down for breakfast and tea. Sloane follows her inside.

"I think Lola being a Pulitzer Prize–winning journalist who attended our New Year's Eve dinner because she was writing an article about us gave me a clue that she was writing an article about us." Jules languidly hangs up.

"You know what I mean," Sloane says, trying to calm herself down.

"It's the middle of the night—"

"Maybe this will teach the mighty Athena Winter that without Mommy's recipes, she's just as tragically ordinary as the rest of us," Sloane reads, every word breaking her heart.

"Look, she called and asked for comment, but I shut her down and she didn't—"

"I don't believe you!"

Jules sits down in a sunny-yellow tufted chair, pulling up the article on her phone, and tries to calm her nerves.

Sloane continues, "I don't believe you, because it was the smart thing to do. And you have always been smarter than me. You sent me in to talk to Isobel, knowing exactly what was in this article, and now I look like a hypocritical asshole and a liar." She struggles to keep her voice from cracking.

There's a knock on the door. Both sisters immediately shift into their well-rehearsed roles, staying gracious and polite while the Glass House staffer delivers Jules's tray of breakfast offerings. They thank the young man.

As Jules fusses with the breakfast tray, she thinks back to that day at Sloane's house when they came up with their plan. She remembers how many little time bombs she lovingly sewed into every stitch of this scheme, but setting time bombs is very different from having to sit in the front row and watch them explode one after another. The absolute carnage she's wrought on Sloane's psyche with just a few well-placed comments, suggestions, and open questions has left her sister in pieces. Not to mention the sheer unadulterated betrayal at having kept Lola's intentions with her article a secret. Jules was so sure of her little subterfuge. But now, seeing the damage she's caused, she's not entirely sure "little" is even close to the proper word for what she's done.

"Sloane, please—"

"You trapped me just like we trapped Mom. Her ego and my desperation were all you needed," Sloane says, trying to hold back tears.

Jules sets down her tea and stands, walking toward Sloane. Sloane pulls away from her sister, and something about the fear in her eyes sends a chill down Jules's spine.

"We'll get through this," Jules offers.

"No. You'll get through this. I . . . I'm . . . I'm—" Sloane cuts herself off, terror choking her as she tries to grasp the full scope of what's to become of her.

Sloane turns away from her sister and walks toward the door. As her fingers curl around the cold brass doorknob, she turns around. She's positive her sister, who's always got something to say about everything, will offer one last jab or quip. But Jules is silent. Speechless.

This terrifies Sloane and explodes the reality of Lola's article like an atom bomb that's going to wipe out her whole world. And as if broken from a spell, Sloane remembers Lærke, and her entire face drains of color as she pitches forward.

"What?" Jules asks, still picking up her own pieces.

"Lærke . . . Lærke is going to read this and—"

"She was there on New Year's Eve. She knows the truth," Jules offers.

"She didn't know I said that about Athena." Sloane stops and looks down at the ground. "You were right, okay? I lied. I told her I fought with Mom to keep Athena in as head chef. She was so proud of me. Said I finally stood up to her. But I lied. I lied and lied and lied," Sloane says, breaking down.

"Why didn't you tell me?" Jules asks.

"Because I was ashamed of myself," Sloane says, unable to look at Jules.

"But you said you were going to tell her everything. You always tell her everything," Jules says, trying to quell her growing guilt by poking at the ongoing jealousy she's always had for her older sister's marriage. The fact that Richard hasn't crossed Jules's mind once during the entirety of this elaborate plan should be cause for concern. But the thought simply hasn't occurred to her.

"I started to, and then I could see that she was getting worried or annoyed or . . . so I just lied," Sloane says, remembering that night in the

Town Car on their way to the Central Trade soft launch. How Lærke held her hand and said she'd never let go. How could Lærke trust her now?

Because this time, she can't blame it all on her family. This time it was Sloane who made a series of choices that landed her in this nest of vipers. In fact, it was Sloane herself who constructed the nest. Her ridiculous assertion that "she could handle Jules" all but mocks her. And with every bite and hiss, she shared a little less with her loving partner, telling herself that it was all for Lærke's own protection.

Because everyone has certain people in their lives who embody a wholeness of integrity that, in the best of times, can operate as a moral North Star for the many choices we make throughout the day. For Sloane Winter, that person is Lærke.

Was Lærke.

There's a stark simplicity when one finally sees the truth.

As the sun breaks across the rolling hills of Oxfordshire, Sloane Winter realizes she may have lost everything. That it was her in that stalled car on the train tracks. And weighed down with this new reality, Sloane can't get out of Jules's hotel room fast enough. Leaving Jules Winter shaken and quiet in the blown-out rubble caused by the bombs she set off. Jules looks away from the blast radius, ashamed for the first time at how truly good of a bomb maker she's become.

⚕

As Athena walks back to her Garden Cottage after her relaxing morning of gardening, she can't help but notice people's stares lingering on her a bit longer than usual. She's used to a certain level of recognition among the foodie crowd, and with what went down on New Year's Eve, she's even gotten used to the nervous, furtive glances. But this feels different. This feels . . . malignant.

She picks up her pace and keeps her gaze firmly on the ground in front of her and far away from the intrusive stares of staff and attendees alike. Breathless and finally at the front door of her cottage, Athena pulls her large iron key out of her jeans pocket and is trying to thread the key into its hole when she hears Rafael and Valentina Luna's voices wafting from the patio just outside Jenn Nishimura's cottage. The pull to step inside is tempting, but something else draws her toward that patio and the new friends who await her there. Something tells her she shouldn't be by herself when she learns about whatever is causing people to gawk at her. With a violent exhalation, Athena tucks the iron key back into her pocket, steps off her porch, and walks toward Jenn Nishimura's patio.

"Hello?" she calls out over the boxwood hedge. All three voices immediately stop talking. There is a quick hushed conversation, where the only thing Athena can really make out is Rafael Luna's low drawl of a baritone and the high-pitched adolescent whispers that clearly belong to Valentina. Finally—

"Yes?" Jenn Nishimura asks, her voice professional and clipped.

"It's Athena. I just—"

"Oh, well, why didn't you say so—" Jenn starts.

"We thought you were some eavesdropping stranger," Valentina says, popping up over the hedge. "But here you are!"

"Valentina, tell her to come around to the front," Jenn says.

"Jenn says to come around to the front," Valentina says, repeating the command, which was as clear to Athena as it was to Valentina. Athena walks around to the front of the cottage and is met by Rafael Luna holding the heavy wooden door open for her.

"You good?" Rafael asks.

"Okay, what is going on? I feel like people were looking at me so weird, and now you're asking if I'm good. Did my family do something? Did my family draw a curled mustache on my poster in the entrance hall?" Athena asks, stepping inside Jenn's cottage. Rafael closes the door behind her, now weary from the news he must break to her.

"Lola's article came out today," Rafael says.

"Oh my god, of course. I totally forgot. I've been so in my head about . . . everything. Oh no." Rafael starts walking toward the patio, but Athena reaches out, putting her hand on his shoulder. He turns around. "Is it . . . is it bad?"

"For you? Not so much. But . . . for your family? Yeah, it's bad," Rafael says. From someone who's seen his fair share of exposé articles, Athena takes him at his word.

"Okay," Athena says, her voice a whisper as she tries to steel herself for what comes next.

"You can absolutely go back to your cottage and read the article on your own, if you want. Everyone would completely understand," Rafael says, stepping in front of her so Valentina and Jenn are unable to see.

"No, I . . ." Athena trails off. Rather than linger in her struggle to give a reason why not, he cuts in and lets her off the hook.

"Okay, then." Rafael gives her an efficient nod, turns around, and continues out onto the patio. In a daze, Athena follows him.

"So, how do you want to do this?" Jenn asks, pulling up the article on her phone.

Athena thinks.

"Why don't we start with the whole Heather Osborne thing," Valentina suggests, looking around at everyone. Rafael brings Athena a cup of coffee and gestures for her to sit in the fourth chair, covered with a large bath towel to protect whoever sits down from the early-morning dew. Athena takes the coffee and sits.

"Who's Heather Osborne?" Athena asks, the warmth from the coffee helping to calm her nerves.

"Your mom hired Heather Osborne as the head chef at Northern Trade," Rafael says.

"What? But Salma was supposed to step in. I've never even heard of this person. What restaurant does she—"

"Oh, no. There's no restaurant," Jenn says.

"What?" Athena asks.

"Just listen. Lola really does say it better than any of us ever could," Valentina says, her eyes sparkling.

Jenn Nishimura goes on to read the two paragraphs from Lola Tadese's article that center on Heather Osborne, Maren Winter's mysterious, newly anointed head chef of Northern Trade.

To the surprise of no one, the assertion Heather made about being a sous chef at a Michelin-Starred restaurant in Yountville was false. How, then, did Heather have those pictures on her website of her inside the kitchen wearing chef's whites, the rest of the staff gathered around her, all smiling for her selfie? This quote from an anonymous source at the restaurant says it all: "She came in one night for dinner dressed in chef's whites. She told us she'd just gotten off shift over at some restaurant in Calistoga and didn't have time to change. We all totally get the wild schedule, so it didn't even register. When she asked for a selfie with all of us in the kitchen, we gladly agreed, thinking she was one of our own."

"But they must have figured it out when she started getting famous?" Athena asks.

"That's the best part," Valentina says.

"She used a fake name," Jenn says.

"On the reservation?" Athena asks. Jenn nods.

"She knew exactly what she was doing," Rafael adds.

"Lola put together the whole timeline. Heather had already bought the domain name and secured all the socials by the time she took that picture. She even found where Heather's husband . . ." Jenn trails off, forgetting the man's name.

"Timothy," Valentina finishes.

"Perfect. Where Timothy bought the cameras and shooting setup for their videos—some tiny mom-and-pop camera store in Tiburon. It was just a few weeks before the picture." Jenn scrolls through the article.

"Dear lord," Athena says.

"So she creates this entire backstory, uses that picture for credibility in her bio—" Jenn starts.

"But if she made videos of her cooking Mom's recipes, wouldn't that . . . I mean, my mom is a lot of things, but her cookbooks are quite rigorous to work your way through," Athena says.

"It's not her," Jenn says.

"What? How?" Athena asks.

"If you watch the videos, a lot of the skill is seen only in the top-down shots where it's just someone's hands," Rafael says, pulling up one of the videos on his phone.

Jenn continues, "Lola interviewed the woman whose hands those actually are. She's a saucier over at a restaurant in the Marina. That's why the saucier, who's definitely not Heather Osborne, always wears these signature friendship bracelets—"

"That she sells on her website," Valentina trills.

"So you'll look at them and not the actual hands. It's genius, really," Jenn finishes.

"And everything else is just swaps and kind of basic culinary acumen," Rafael says.

"I mean, she's a good cook, but not . . ." Valentina trails off.

"Good enough to be the head chef at Northern Trade," Athena finishes.

"No," Rafael answers.

"God, it's so embarrassing. Why did . . . What was Mom thinking? How could she not check Heather's references? That's basic stuff," Athena asks, watching one of Heather's videos in disbelief. Shaking her head, Athena thinks of the Northern Trade staff. "Poor Salma, I can't imagine how hard this has been on her."

"Lola interviewed a lot of Northern Trade staff, and apparently of the two dinner services Heather was in charge of, she spent most of the time crying in the walk-in," Valentina says.

"Word is she was given a few days off—" Jenn says.

"For self-care," Valentina says, putting giant air quotes around "self-care."

A lull falls over the group as it sets in that the other portions of the article are far more personal to Athena. Feeling this unease, Athena chimes in.

"I'll read the article in its entirety, but . . . is there anything in there that I don't know? You all were at the New Year's Eve dinner; you saw what went down . . . Am I going to be surprised by anything in the article?" Athena asks Rafael and Valentina, barely able to get the words out.

"She goes into that night pretty . . . It's very detailed," Rafael says.

"It was hard to read," Valentina adds, her eyes kind and worried. Athena nods, looking down into her half-full mug of coffee.

"There's a quote by Sloane that's pretty bad," Jenn says.

"I mean, Sloane's pretty bad, so . . ." Athena trails off, trying not to show how upset she is.

"Do you want to know what she said?" Jenn asks, her voice gentle.

"Yeah, why not," Athena says with a long sigh. Rafael, Jenn, and Valentina look to one another. Jenn gives an imperceptible nod of understanding.

"Maybe this will teach the mighty Athena Winter that without Mommy's recipes, she's just as tragically ordinary as the rest of us," Jenn reads.

"I mean, she's not wrong," Athena says, forcing herself to take a sip of her coffee to stem her growing emotions.

Not wanting to make her sit any longer in Sloane's catty yet far-too-close-to-home words, Jenn continues, "It was interesting how Lola built a lot of the article around something you said to her in the kitchen."

"What did I say to her in the kitchen?" Athena asks, panicking about a conversation she can only remotely remember.

Jenn begins to read:

Standing at the very center of Northern Trade's illustrious kitchen, culinary wunderkind Athena Winter naively shrugs off my question as to whether she thinks Central Trade will threaten the very underpinnings of the Winter legacy. Not even looking up from her station, Winter answers, "How great would an empire be if it was threatened by its own progress?" Unfortunately, the story that follows is of exactly that—a once-great culinary pioneer, eroded by time and turned brittle by ego, threatened by the progress embodied by her very own daughters.

"Daughters?" Athena asks.

"Plural," Jenn answers, reading the line again to confirm.

"That's interesting," Athena says, feeling her phone vibrating in her pocket. She straightens her body and wiggles the phone loose.

"There was a lot more in there about your sisters than I thought there'd be," Jenn says. Athena looks at her phone.

"I honestly didn't even know they were that involved in the restaurant," Valentina pipes in.

"Right? I thought their jobs were just for show," Jenn says.

"No, not at all," Athena says, her voice quiet.

"I didn't know it was Sloane who set up the internship, and all those networking events—" Rafael starts.

"Medical insurance and time off alone are revolutionary," Valentina says. Seeing who's calling, Athena takes her black glasses off and begins to rub her eyes.

"She doesn't get nearly enough credit," Jenn adds.

"Neither of them do," Valentina says.

"If more restaurants had a Sloane Winter, it would be a far better industry," Rafael says.

"You know, minus the pretty bad part," Valentina adds, looking over at Athena, who's bent over, her glasses dangling in her fingers as her phone continues to vibrate. "What's wrong? Who is it?"

"It's my mom," Athena says, holding out her phone.

CHAPTER THIRTEEN

The photo Athena chose to assign to Maren's contact information was one of her favorites. It was a picture she took of her mom probably about ten years ago now. Athena would often go down to the gardens when her mom was there and just sit and listen to her and Penny talk. It was the closest thing to a lullaby Athena had ever known.

On this day, it was just Maren in the gardens, and she was meandering through the rows of fresh vegetables. She looked so small in the middle of it all, but it was the look on her face that compelled Athena to take a photo of her in that moment. Maren looked perfectly contented. Her face was soft, and she had this little musing smile of absolute peace. Athena loved that picture.

Loves that picture.

Except for right now. When it appears on her phone screen. The sight of her mom's contented face among her blooming garden fills Athena with a truly stomach-churning mixture of terror and grief.

"Are you going to answer it?" Valentina asks, her voice soft and easy.

"I don't think I'm ready," Athena says, staring at her mother's photo.

"Okay," Valentina says.

"Is that okay?" Athena asks.

"Of course it is," Valentina says.

"Okay," Athena says, watching as her mom's photo disappears from her phone screen and a notification pops up that she now has One Missed Call.

"Are you okay?" Jenn asks.

"I don't think I am," Athena says, letting her head fall back into her hands as her three friends share a look of concern.

⚸

Maren Winter paces her room. None of her daughters will answer her phone calls. Not even Athena. She stands frozen, phone clutched in her hand, staring out through the french doors and onto her lush garden patio.

Even though the article has yet to fully gain momentum, Maren knows it's just a matter of time. Lola's masterful yet damning words will migrate like a swiftly moving plague—*"a once-great culinary pioneer"* coughs all over Europe just before *"eroded by time and turned brittle by ego"* smears its germs all over New York before infecting all of California with *"threatened by the progress embodied by her very own daughters."*

Maren knows the clock is ticking on how much longer she has control of this story. It's still early back in the US, and if she can get in front of this—*"a once-great culinary pioneer"* explodes inside her head. Refocusing, if she can just get in front of this, she can have a statement ready and—*"Eroded by time and turned brittle by ego"* slaps her across the face. Forcing herself to take a deep breath, she brings up her phone, swipes it unlocked, and scrolls. *"Threatened by the progress embodied by her very own daughters"* punches her in the gut.

Unable to concentrate, Maren decides instead to take a shower and get dressed for the day. The last thing she needs is to appear as if any of this has affected her. As she slips out of her pajamas and pads into the bathroom, Maren Winter resolves that she must present as unruffled an air as she can muster throughout what is quickly becoming a pivotal day in the span of her career. Now in full-blown denial, she turns on the water and the rain shower spurts to life. The freezing-cold water forces Maren to take a step back so none of the frigid droplets land on her naked and vulnerable skin.

But as the shower heats up and Maren begins to minimize the possible repercussions of Lola Tadese's article, she remains tragically—and quite voluntarily—oblivious to how an article like this will extend far beyond her career and into the very fabric of her life. And in denying seeing the true impact of the article, but rather relying on the usual regal indifference that tends to protect those in such rarefied echelons, Maren Winter has made a calamitous mistake. A mistake that has the potential to pull her whole house down.

Or more aptly, a mistake that gives someone looking for one . . . an opportunity.

As she steps into the large, tiled shower, now thick with steam, Maren reflects on all the times she's come up against—and coincidentally, come out on top—in situations that she now feels are on par with what's happening to her right now.

"*To* her" being the operative words.

What Maren Winter still fails to grasp while she lathers her body and builds herself up by running through the highlight reels of all the times she fought back, and proved them wrong, and rose above small-minded people is her own crucial role in all this.

She was not responsible when a very famous food critic called Northern Trade Maren Winter's little café that would be fun to bring your wife to. So when Maren quoted that review as she accepted her first Michelin Star, deftly rubbing the food critic's nose in the steaming pile of his own narrow-minded evaluation, she challenged the belief that a woman couldn't be taken seriously in the fine-dining space.

Maren was also not at fault when a bullish celebrity chef called Northern Trade "fussy" during a panel at a book festival. When Maren confronted him in front of the sold-out crowd, asking him to specify exactly how Northern Trade was fussy but his failed restaurant—with its tasting menu inspired by an ayahuasca trip he'd taken the year before—was, and this was an exact quote, "a reverie based on a dream made reality," Maren gave voice to everyone in the audience who'd ever fantasized about standing up to the school bully.

And it also wasn't something Maren did to cause a young, up-and-coming chef to take to the internet and lament that these old-people chefs who insist on not being gracefully put out to pasture are to blame for why there were no real opportunities for the new culinary class. So when Maren told Jules to take a picture of her in the middle of Northern Trade's wild and overgrown fields with only the caption Love a day out in the pasture, she was heralded as a champion for women of a certain age.

As Maren steps out of the shower, now baptized in her own heroism from past attacks, she still doesn't get how this battle is any different from all those that came before.

Because so often a genius is someone who's consistently had to push back on a society that wasn't ready for them or who's stood by an idea that was before its time as it was rejected by those who much preferred—and benefited from—the status quo. How then are they supposed to understand that this time is different? This time it's not society that's wrong or that their idea is ahead of its time. This time they're wrong. This time their idea is simply not that great.

In fact, this time they are now the status quo that's being threatened.

Maren Winter ties the fluffy, white bathrobe tightly around her small frame and steps out into the main area of her suite. She hears her phone ringing on the crumpled duvet of her king-size bed. She walks over and is just about to answer it when she hears a knock at the door. Maren checks her phone and sees that it's Jules calling. Another knock at the door. Thinking it's Athena knocking in response to her last phone call, Maren ignores the call and walks toward the door—revealing Jules with her phone to her ear.

"This was a fun little experiment that was incredibly hurtful," Jules says, stepping inside the room and hanging up her phone. "Who did you think it was at the door? You know what, never mind—don't answer that." Jules walks into Maren's suite and turns to face her mother.

"This isn't the time to be reading into things," Maren says, closing the door behind them.

"Reading into things like you saw that I was calling and ignored the phone call, but answered the door because you thought it was . . . I'm guessing Athena?" Jules asks, walking over to her mother's breakfast tray.

Maren is quiet. That's exactly what she thought. Jules waits as her mother takes just a bit too long to defend herself. She gulps down the hurt by tearing off a corner of a croissant and popping it into her mouth.

"Can we just move on to the problem at hand?" Maren asks, sitting down in a large swivel chair next to the fireplace to warm herself.

"It's funny that you don't see not answering my call as a problem, but yeah—we can move on—"

"To the article," Maren finishes.

"Yes, to the article. I think—"

"I don't think we do anything."

Jules is caught off guard.

Maren continues, "Any comment we make will only give the article credibility."

Collecting herself, Jules plays the next few moves with surgical precision. "Lola Tadese has won a Pulitzer, and it's the *San Francisco Chronicle*. The article already has credibility, Mom."

"Maybe we post—"

"I'm posting that really great photo of you from when Northern Trade first opened. The one where it's just you and Penny and you're in the garden and you're hauling up—"

"That first basket of lettuces. That was our first crop."

"I'm going to turn off the comments, and the caption is just going to be something about celebrating a lifetime of work in preparation for tonight's ceremony," Jules says.

"Fine," Maren allows.

"I'll follow that up with a throwback to when Aunt Penny won her Banquet gardening award back in 2015. I'm hoping it'll throw them off the scent," Jules says.

"That sounds good," Maren says.

"We're getting a lot of phone calls from journalists wanting a comment. How would you like to proceed?" Jules asks.

"No comment. Obviously," Maren says.

Jules nods. She takes in a breath, shocked by the words that nearly escape her tight line of a mouth in response to her mother's dismissive reply, erupting from somewhere so deep, Jules almost feels possessed by them. Her intake of breath is so pronounced that Maren looks up and waits. Jules's temper flares at her own impulsivity, which Maren so reviles, and she forcefully pushes the seven traitorous words back down to wherever they came from.

Why don't you just say you're sorry?

Desperate to course correct, Jules blurts out, "What about Heather Osborne?"

"Fire her," Maren says.

"And . . ." Jules leads.

"And what?"

Why don't you just say you're sorry?

"A-a-and . . . nothing." Jules stumbles.

Jules takes another breath. Another pause that's just a bit too long. Maren waits. Panicking, Jules gives her a tight, efficient nod and hurries out of her mother's now suffocatingly confined suite that is also somehow the largest room the Glass House has on offer.

As Jules hurries down the hallway, she tells herself it's better she didn't say it. It would have shown weakness. It would have shown her hand. It would have ruined her plan. It would have . . . it would have . . . Now struggling to breathe, Jules crumples onto an elegant settee in a small alcove just outside the Glass House's main entrance hall to get herself together. Looking at the situation objectively, Jules recognizes that of all the Winter women, she's the one who's suffered the least from the impact of Lola's article.

But being invisible never feels like a victory for a middle child.

Jules tries to remember when she decided to embrace her lifelong anonymity and started using it to her advantage. But the pain of looking back at those years when she fought and screamed at people to witness her, hear her, and acknowledge her is too much.

Because it was within the Winter household that Jules became the perfect spy and game player. Observing everything, whispering in people's ears, slipping unseen into those crowded and fraught spaces. If they weren't going to see her, they would certainly see the chaos she wrought.

She can craft the perfect bomb. Everyone constantly underestimates her. No one ever notices her. And she's the only one who hears the ticking.

But Lola saw her.

Lola Tadese captured something in that article that no one ever had: the real Jules Winter. The despair. The sadness. The turmoil. Lola saw right past her bravado and attitude at the Central Trade soft launch and in the hallway of Northern Trade as Jules tried to protect Athena from the untouched pork chop that their mother hadn't deigned to eat.

And after decades of being invisible, someone finally seeing her has thrown Jules Winter off her game.

But as Jules threads herself back into the early-morning crush alongside Glass House staffers and fresh-faced attendees getting ready for the last full day of the Banquet Conference, something extraordinarily mundane happens. Life goes on. There are breakfasts to be made, teeth to be brushed, and emails to check. As ever, there is a relentless brutality to the world spinning obliviously on—even as a percentage of her occupants just try to hold on for dear life.

There are panels and workshops and interviews and conversations that have nothing to do with "this business with the Winters," as one attendee politely calls it, scrolling through her phone looking for the newest think piece on Lola's article while also trying to pay attention to Rafael Luna's presentation on sustainable fishing practices.

Lola's article is the elephant in the room at Athena's sold-out talk on the lessons fine-dining restaurants learned from the pandemic. Knowing the elephant would be front and center, Athena told the moderator that she would rather not do a Q and A portion with the audience. Relieved herself, the moderator agreed, and instead of announcing their decision—and thus calling attention to it—she strategically lets Athena's talk run long and then apologizes to the audience for there not being enough time for questions from the audience. The disappointment in the room is palpable.

It also doesn't stop a few attendees from approaching Athena afterward and offering "more of a comment than a question" as she exits her talk.

As the day passes, Lola's article becomes like a pop song everyone heard on their drive in. Somehow both ever present and in the background at the same time, the catchy tune can be heard as it's hummed, whistled, and sung by all in attendance at some point throughout the day. And it is this phenomenon that begins to transform the gala and awards ceremony on the last night of the Banquet Conference into what feels like the hottest concert of the year.

As each of the Winter women gets ready for the evening, Lola's article looms large. But so, too, does the unsettling disbelief that the undoing of the Winter Empire has taken a mere two weeks.

But that's not quite right, is it?

When things explode—businesses, relationships, empires—the tourniquet often tightly wrapped around the gangrenous limb is the basis of argument that the unraveling seemingly "came from nowhere" or that the parties involved were "blindsided." And usually this statement is followed by such flaccid assertions as "I would have done something had I seen it coming."

It's this exculpatory narrative that lets everyone off the hook for aggressively ignoring the writing on the wall, confidently striding past red flag after red flag, and making a series of choices to avoid the hard conversations that are necessary to evolve and grow.

The sad truth is the Winter Empire has been crumbling for decades. The familial rifts have long been stretched beyond their elasticity, until the only things holding it all together were sheer will, flickering hope, and a deep fear of change by all parties involved. The past two weeks have been the reckoning that's been a long time coming.

So as the Glass House's grand ballroom fills up, the excitement in the air is unmistakable, the ambient music quickly drowned out by the din of a chattering, excited crowd. And it is in these final moments that each of the Winter women finally arrives at the festivities.

A hush descends as Maren Winter settles in at the nearest table to the stage on the left and Athena Winter slides into the remaining seat at the nearest table to the stage on the right. Not in line to receive any awards tonight and unable—or unwilling—to communicate to Isobel and Cressida about their last-minute blowup, Jules and Sloane Winter are seated next to each other at a table in the far back of the ballroom. Neither woman acknowledges the other as the lights dim and a large screen lowers on the stage.

Inspirational music fills the room as the movie starts, beautiful slowed-down shots of fresh produce being pulled from the soil, thoughtful chefs fussing over tiny plates, and Dame Jocasta Pryce walking and talking with her two nieces as waitstaff and gardeners alike rush all around them. Dame Jocasta's raspy, posh accent soars over the inspirational music with talk of why she started this foundation and how she hopes to inspire future generations. She talks of legacy, giving back, and her life's work. There are several plays on the idea of good soil, patience, and harvesting one's crops in due time. And as the music builds to a stirring crescendo, the words "Welcome to the 41st Annual Banquet Conference Awards Ceremony" trace across the screen in gold script to a round of applause.

The lights in the grand ballroom come up as the screen disappears and Dame Jocasta Pryce walks out from backstage and settles in behind the podium as the round of applause becomes a standing ovation.

Dame Jocasta is very comfortable with standing ovations and effortlessly waits for the roar to die down. Once it does, she launches into welcoming everyone to the event and makes a joke about whether they appreciated the rare ten minutes of sunshine they got earlier this afternoon. The crowd laughs politely, and Dame Jocasta introduces Jenn Nishimura, who will be presenting the first award of the evening.

Even though the awards are being handed out onstage, the real show is taking place out in the audience. And from where Jules is sitting, she can see the entire scene playing out in front of her. While the crowd may check in on the awards from time to time, everyone is really focusing on Maren Winter. Dressed in bright red and seated right in front, she appears completely unperturbed, scanning the room, smiling and waving at colleagues, whispering and laughing with the other culinary legends sitting at her table. Jules has to hand it to her mother. From where she's sitting, it's as if Lola's article never happened.

This time that noblesse oblige attitude that Maren wears so well seems to be having the opposite effect from what she envisioned. This crowd expected Maren to walk in tonight as someone who'd learned their lesson, someone who was "working on it" or at the very least appeared to be humbled by the contents of Lola's article. Instead, Maren is living her best life, drinking champagne and whispering loudly during people's acceptance speeches. And were it Maren's behavior alone, the crowd might have been able to move on. But despite being at odds, Jules and Sloane are aligned in their contrition, both dressed sensibly in black and going out of their way to look as gracious and penitent as possible.

And then there's Athena. Wearing the same black smock dress she wears to everything, her eyes downcast as she fidgets with her big gray G-Shock watch that looks hilariously out of place at this upscale event. The heaviness of Lola's article evident in every pore of Athena's being.

As Jules scans the crowd, she sees Lola Tadese sitting at a table precariously close to Maren, Rafael and Valentina Luna on either side as if they're her bodyguards. Unable to not flaunt her observations, Jules starts, "I know we're fighting, but—"

"Don't talk to me," Sloane says.

Jules is quiet. Sloane performatively concentrates on the awards ceremony, clapping as another award is handed out. Jules stares at Sloane.

"Jules, I'm serious. Don't—"

Jules scoots her chair closer. "Mom is *not* playing this right," she says, powering through with a conspiratorial whisper.

"Well, you'd know." Sloane forces herself to watch the festivities and not give in to Jules.

"Yeah. I know."

"Yeah."

"Yeah," Jules says, confused.

A pause. Both Winter sisters watch Rafael Luna present an award to a group of Scottish park rangers tasked with protecting their stock of salmon. More applause. A beat. Sloane's shoulders lower. A weary sigh.

"What do you mean she's not playing this right?" Sloane finally asks, always taking the bait.

"She's having *too* good of a time," Jules says.

"But isn't that a good thing?" Sloane asks.

Jules scans the gala attendees. "No. This crowd wants blood. And I don't think they knew who from until tonight." Her voice is serious.

"It depended on who—"

"Came in here acting like the biggest asshole," Jules finishes.

"Confirming that everything in the article—"

"Is true."

"This is bad," Sloane says.

"Bad for Mom, but good for us," Jules says.

Jules and Sloane fall silent once again, politely clapping for the chef who just won an award.

"God, look at Athena," Sloane says, her voice cracking.

"I know."

"She looks terrible."

"I don't know why. She came off great in that article," Jules says.

"Maybe because our mother essentially kicked her out of the family, and I completely betrayed her, threw her under the bus, and said the meanest thing ever and then was maybe going to steal her hot dog recipe for my own gains. But that's just me spitballing," Sloane says, remembering that she's mad at Jules.

"I mean, it's not—" Jules cuts herself off as a waiter comes around their table and fills everyone's glasses. She thanks them and she and Sloane fall silent as they focus once again on the awards ceremony.

"What were you going to say? Besides making sure to dodge any and all responsibility for the last few weeks?" Sloane asks. Jules smiles, having successfully lured her sister back into her good graces. Sloane catches herself. "Ugh, never mind."

"I was going to say that it's not much of a family," Jules says, making pointed eye contact with Sloane. Deflated, Sloane nods.

"Yeah."

As the presentation of Maren Winter's Lifetime Achievement Award nears, the tension in the room builds to uncomfortably suffocating levels. Jules is trying to continue her calculations as to exactly how big this bomb can get. But with every flip of Maren's hair and every head thrown back in rapturous laughter, the audience's hissed whispers and side-eye glances multiply. Until not even Jules Winter can keep up with the necessary computations.

"I really hope Athena doesn't win that award," Jules says.

"Me too."

"For her sake," Jules adds, and empties her full champagne flute.

※

Athena catches a young woman staring at her, scrutinizing her as she fidgets with her watch. As the young woman's gaze slides back up to Athena's, their eyes lock. Athena gets that the woman's intent is to be kind, but the impact of her furrowed, worried brow makes Athena feel even more pathetic. Athena stops playing with her watch, clasps her hands in front of her, and offers a brave smile to the young woman. The young woman smiles back, but there's a distinct hint of "chin up" in it that annoys Athena. Athena looks away. The brief two or three minutes she spends being irritated at the woman's little "chin up" thing feels like a welcome respite from being constantly sad all the time.

When Athena comes back to focusing on the ceremony, she sees a Glass House staffer wending their way through the crowd toward her mother. The staffer kneels next to Maren, and for the briefest moment, Athena can see a little snarl curl cross her mother's face, wrongly thinking the staffer is some kind of interloping fan. But Maren quickly catches herself, smiles imperiously for the staffer, and follows them backstage in preparation for the presentation of her lifetime achievement award.

As Maren and the staffer exit, Athena sneaks a glance back at Jules and Sloane. Looking to her older sisters is a habit she's barely aware that she still does. But seeing that they're also watching as Maren disappears behind a mysterious side door just next to the stage makes her feel like both nothing and everything has changed. Jules leans over and whispers something to Sloane. Their closeness is a dagger to Athena's heart. Sloane stiffens; then both of her sisters turn to look at Athena. The teary speech being given at the podium provides the perfect cover for the three Winter sisters to share a meaningful look, without it also being well documented on the internet by someone in attendance.

It's a lingering look that no one quite knows what to do with. No one smiles or waves or looks away or sneers. Instead, it's simply three people completely frozen in the inconveniently heartbreaking realization that they miss each other desperately. The room fills with applause as the teary speech finally comes to an end, breaking the floating elsewhereness of the moment. Each of the Winter sisters breaks their gaze, and in the brief moment of silence between the last award and the next, they ache just a little with how good it felt to be back together—even for just a short-lived moment in time.

As the lights in the grand ballroom dim, a hush falls over the crowd as the screen flickers to life, inspirational piano music rising and falling with every word that traces across the screen.

Pioneer.

Genius.

Revolutionary.

Maren's own voice drifts out into the crowd.

"I just wanted to make the kind of food I wanted to make, but apparently me doing that meant I had to burn down a few outdated systems in the process."

Despite their best efforts, the crowd is energized by Maren's defiant words and find themselves quite moved to applaud. This reversal of the audience's fealty is both wildly inconvenient and fascinating to Jules.

Voice-over from an endless Who's Who of famous chefs sing Maren's praises as old, grainy photographs tell the visual story of her rise to greatness. In one photo, she's bent over a flaming grill in a tiny kitchen, sweat pouring down her face as she manages a staggering number of orders. In another, a clearly exhausted Maren Winter is seated on an overturned crate in some back alley, smoking a cigarette—her signature brown bob held back in a gray bandanna. And in a third, Maren and Penny Ahn peek out from the back of a large group photo of chefs. Maren and Penny are, of course, the only women.

As Maren's rise to fame grows, the stirring retrospective shows photo after photo of her holding up award after award in her signature pose—mouth open, arm held high as if to say "Here I am!"

Maren's voice cuts through the grand ballroom. "I actually didn't know I did that pose until someone pointed it out to me. What I did know was that I needed to show them I wasn't going to be small for them." The quote cuts off as a photo of Maren accepting her most recent James Beard Award populates the screen. And then Maren's voice continues, "I wasn't going to be small for anyone."

As the rousing movie builds to its climax, the screen fills with a series of truly staggering series of statistics. How many awards Maren Winter was the first woman to win; how many accomplishments Maren was the first woman to achieve; and finally how many cookbooks she's sold, television shows she's been on, and restaurants and businesses she's built into successful enterprises. Being reminded of all these extraordinary and singular facts about Maren Winter seems to be having more and more of an interesting effect on the audience.

In the last twenty-four hours, Maren became human to so many for the first time. Or more accurately, over the course of the day, many felt betrayed by Maren's imperfect humanity. But this movie has reminded those in attendance that Maren Winter, despite being revealed to be as flawed and complicated as the rest of them, is still a legend living in our time. As the movie swells to a truly emotional culmination, what can only be defined as a "hesitantly awed" audience begins to fall fully back in love with Maren Winter.

The movie ends with a single photo of Maren sitting in one of the Adirondack chairs outside Northern Trade. Relaxed and surrounded by lush greenery, she's drinking a cup of tea and looks effortlessly contented. It's a photo Jules took of her mother last month, and something about seeing the warm and affectionate look on Maren's face makes Jules emotional. Because that look was for her.

As the lights come up and the screen disappears once again, Dame Jocasta's voice cuts through the room. "This year's lifetime achievement award goes to the one and only Maren Winter."

The room erupts as Maren strides out onto the stage to a roaring standing ovation. There is a microscopic moment where Maren and Athena Winter lock eyes. Maren is unwavering and defiantly holds her gaze. Athena is the first to look away.

"Thank you! Thank you!" Maren says, trying to calm the crowd down. But this only makes the cheers louder. Hooting and hollering, the audience has apparently all but forgotten the disapproval they had for her just hours before. "Thank you . . . thank you!"

The crowd finally quiets as they sit back down, faces open and awaiting Maren's next words.

"First, I want to thank Dame Jocasta Pryce for bestowing on me this great honor. What I will say, however, is that it's actually her enduring friendship that I will prize far more than any award." Maren looks out into the audience to where Dame Jocasta is sitting, and they share a tearful moment. Hands on hearts, mouthed "I love yous" . . . it's all very touching.

"So here's what they don't tell you about getting old." The crowd laughs. "You don't actually feel old. Don't get me wrong, you *feel* old—all you have to do is try to work a Friday dinner service to remind you that this is a young person's game. But your mind, your soul . . . your heart still yearn for possibility—that flush of a new idea, the buzz of a doomed plan, the late nights, the early mornings, the sheer exhaustion that only comes from doing something that you love. I look at all those old pictures, and I see the same me—the same face, the same drive . . . the possibility. When I heard I was to be given the lifetime achievement award, my first reaction was . . . but I'm not done yet. I still have so much I want to do, so much still inside me and . . ." Maren takes a beat. "And that's when I realized that I can be a pioneer here, too. I can revolutionize and inspire those around me to do the same. I have not lost my edge. I will not go quietly. I will not be put out to pasture. I will determine when this lifetime of mine has finished achieving all that is possible. Simply, I'm not done yet. Thank you again for this great honor, but this is just the beginning."

The crowd leaps to their feet. The applause is deafening.

Despite still technically being at each other's throats, Sloane and Jules share a look of weary uneasiness as they are bested by their mother one more time. Using the article's incendiary headline in her speech was downright masterful.

Turning the tide here at the Banquet Conference—with its high percentage of trendsetters, representatives from every corner of the culinary world, and all-around spokespeople—could very well right the Maren Winter ship in the global culinary conversation. And what Jules knows— the single thought slithering up her spine right now—is if the culinary world makes Maren Winter back into a hero, then they're going to go looking for the villain who made them question their loyalty in the first place.

They're going to want to blame someone. They're going to want blood. And Jules fears that this backlash will hit the person—or *persons*—closest to the turmoil, but not someone with whom the unwashed masses have a real relationship or history. And with Athena being the heir apparent—and a chip off the old Maren Winter block—the blood this crowd is going to want will inevitably be Jules's and Sloane's.

As if reading her mind, Sloane leans over. "She still has to get through presenting the Maren Winter award," she whispers.

"Right, but if Athena doesn't win—"

"We'll cross that bridge when we get to it," Sloane says, focusing back in on the still-applauding crowd.

"You said 'we,'" Jules says, with just the right amount of playful smugness in her voice.

"Don't make it weird," Sloane says, not looking at Jules.

As Maren finally exits the stage, a team of Ghanaian gardeners who revolutionized how to farm cassava come out from the other side to present the next award. They proceed without incident and with enough applause from the audience to convince Jules that should this ceremony continue on as it is, it will be the social gallows for her and Sloane. This conclusion saddens Jules, because she's really liked having her older sister back at her side, even if Sloane is still wary of her. A stance Jules would not argue with, given her . . . *tendencies.*

Not wanting to think too much more about her own brutal nature, Jules checks the program to see how many more awards there are before the Maren Winter Award for Innovation. Her shoulders slump, realizing that she'll be kept in suspense for far longer than she thought.

As the evening wears on, those in attendance blissfully slip back into a world where all is just as it was: Maren Winter is a legend, and the identity they built around her is back to being something they can be proud of. In short, this audience needs Maren to be the hero they think she is, because that means they're the heroes they think they are. If Maren were unmasked as a villain, then what does that make them?

Now, hours into the evening, the audience is positively buzzing, tension building as the ceremony finally comes to its last award of the night. Dame Jocasta Pryce strides out onstage and settles behind the podium one last time.

"I want to thank everyone for coming out tonight and celebrating all of our winners, nominees, and awards and staff alike. We have so much to look forward to in the years to come, and I know that I, for one, feel very excited about our bright future as an industry. Which brings me to the final award of the evening. When Isobel, Cressida, and I got together to think about this new award around innovation and pioneering, we couldn't think of a better person to exemplify those attributes than our very own lifetime achievement award winner, Maren Winter. So, presenting the Maren Winter Award for Innovation is Maren Winter herself." Dame Jocasta steps back from the podium and claps as Maren walks out onto the stage. The two women hug and say a few words that only they can hear. Then Dame Jocasta takes a few steps back and stands just behind Maren. It's not lost on Jules and Sloane that Dame Jocasta has remained on the stage. Looks like they weren't the only ones in suspense at this final award.

"I am so deeply honored to be here and to have this award named after me, but right now I don't think I'm the one you want to be hearing from. So let's get to the nominees." Maren pulls out her glasses and begins reading the names off the back of the envelope. "The nominees for the Maren Winter Award for Innovation are . . . Rafael Luna." Maren waits for applause. "Lala Patel." A huge swell comes from the table where Lala and her restaurant's staff are seated. "JoEllen Redd." An absolute seismic eruption explodes from JoEllen's table. "Jenn Nishimura." Another explosion. "And finally, Athena Winter." Maren's voice gives nothing away as the applause for Athena is deafening. Athena herself offers a smile and a tentative hand in the air as thanks for the ovation.

As the applause dies down, Athena finds herself completely torn. On one hand, she doesn't want to deal with the obvious drama that would come from her winning the award. But on the other—she could really use a win right now. And maybe even by her winning the award, her mother will see herself in Athena, and that the pork chop she made for New Year's Eve was something that Maren herself would have done back in the day. Maybe this award . . . Athena holds her breath . . . maybe this award can begin to fix things.

"And the winner of the first annual Maren Winter Award for Innovation goes to . . ." Maren rips open the envelope and her eye twitches.

"Oh no," Jules says, grabbing Sloane's arm under the table.

"What?" Sloane asks, looking down at her arm.

"Her eye twitched."

"Oh no," Sloane says, biting the inside of her cheek.

Worried, and now fidgeting compulsively with her water glass from the burst of nervous energy, all Jules can do is look helplessly over at her youngest sister as Maren Winter leans into the microphone and says . . .

"Athena Winter."

CHAPTER FOURTEEN

Time stops.

Athena looks around as everyone at her table turns to her, their faces alight and beaming with excitement. Now, somehow completely separated from her body, she feels like she's being pulled toward the stage, not of her own volition. Fear grips her. Each step she takes feels heavier than the last. By the time Athena reaches the last stair before stepping up onto the stage, she feels light-headed not only from holding her breath but from lifting each of her thousand-pound legs, one and then the other. Athena walks across the stage in a daze, the world blurry and muffled all around her.

Athena looks up just in time to see Dame Jocasta take a step toward Maren, as she holds out the award to Athena. Dame Jocasta is whispering something to Maren that Athena can't hear. But whatever it is, Maren nods in acknowledgment, her jaw tightening.

Athena stops in front of Maren, who hands her the award. It's heavy. Cold. Athena looks at the award and then, bracing herself, looks down at her mother for the first time since New Year's Eve.

"Thank you," Athena says. Her mother's eyes are unreadable. Needing to find answers, acceptance, and approval in them, Athena dangerously wades in deeper and deeper. But the undertow is strong and she is swept away into the darkness.

And where Maren sees yearning, she sees weakness. And where she sees weakness, she sees opportunity. Positive the grand ballroom is firmly back under her spell, Maren seizes the moment to squash this burdensome mutiny once and for all. Maren slides her gaze away from Athena's, steps solidly back in front of the microphone, and refocuses on Dame Jocasta. "What do you say, Jo? Kids today have no idea how easy they have it, right? I mean, how hard is it to innovate once someone has already cracked the code?"

There is a stomach-dropping, stunned silence in the milliseconds that follow what Maren surely thought would be an uproarious punch line. It's the kind of visceral quiet that discomforts the whole room because every single human being recognizes that particular kind of stomach-dropping, stunned silence: it's the sound a joke makes when it doesn't land.

Athena's fingers tighten around the award's cold base as she processes hearing her very worst fear about herself being said by her own mother in front of hundreds of people. She resists the urge to just say a quick thank-you and get back to her seat. Or maybe leave England altogether. But as her mom steps back next to Dame Jocasta, Athena forces herself to take a breath. Forces herself to get it together. Forces herself to stand up to her mother like she should have done on New Year's Eve. And if her mother wants to have this conversation in front of an audience, then so be it.

Pushing her shoulders back and lifting her chin a little bit higher, Athena gives her mother a polite smile, and then she steps in front of the microphone knowing full well that doing so will cause Maren Winter to be pushed further into the background. This move is not lost on anyone in the room.

"Thank you so much for this award, Dame Jocasta, Mom, Isobel, Cressida, and all who voted for me. I look out at all the other incredible nominees and the brilliant chefs and those just getting started and know that you and I understand the tricky balance that exists when one challenges the way things have always been done. Innovation and progress have a way of . . ." Athena looks back at her mom and smiles. Slowly, she turns back to the microphone. "Leaving people behind. And oftentimes that desertion can cause a tragic nostalgia loop that pits them against anyone or anything that threatens their comfort or supremacy. But we must press on. Because we are the future, whether they like it or not. So thank you again for this great honor, but this is just the beginning."

"She used Mom's last line," Sloane whispers.

"She sure did," Jules says, leaping up to join the ovation.

As the crowd erupts in applause, Athena doesn't look back at her mother or Dame Jocasta, nor does she try to find her sisters in the audience, or Lola or Rafael or Valentina or Jenn. Chin still high and shoulders still back, Athena Winter steps down off the stage and strides right out of the grand ballroom without looking back.

In the scramble to end the evening a bit less chaotically, whoever is running the gala pipes some calming classical music through the speakers. Moments later—and without giving off the air of being rushed—an announcement cuts in inviting everyone to continue the festivities in the main courtyard, where cocktails are being served. As the crowd buzzes with gossip, their bloodlust finally sated, Dame Jocasta takes this opportunity to take Maren Winter by the arm and pull her close.

"Come with me," she says. Maren nods, still processing what just happened.

Dame Jocasta leads Maren through the backstage maze, bobbing and weaving through the hustle and bustle of postshow hysteria. Staffers and stagehands alike try to clear the way, but in such a cramped space, collisions and traffic jams are to be expected. Dame Jocasta serpentines through the entirety of the backstage area, until she finally pulls open a hidden door in the back left corner of the blackened backstage. Just inside is a well-appointed green room of some kind with lush furniture, fresh flowers, and a banquet of tea, waters, and upscale snack food. Still in a daze, Maren begins to sit down in one of the chairs.

"Not quite yet—" Dame Jocasta says, before pushing open a bookcase, revealing a secret passage.

"Are you taking me somewhere to kill me? Was it that bad?" Maren jokes.

Unsmiling, Dame Jocasta turns around. "We had the king for an event once, and we had to ensure he could get safely in and out without being seen."

Chastened by her friend's solemnity, Maren follows Dame Jocasta down a cramped hallway, before finally coming to yet another well-appointed reception room. This one, however, feels far more private than any of the others. Dame Jocasta motions to the plush and overstuffed love seat and Maren sits. Dame Jocasta walks over to the well-stocked bar cart and dispenses a generous pour of a Dalmore King Alexander III whisky into two cut-crystal glasses. She hands a glass to Maren.

"Thank you," Maren says, taking a slow, smoky sip. The whisky warms her throat.

Dame Jocasta downs her whisky in one swallow. "You fucked up, girl," she says. Her long-hidden working-class accent cuts through the lavish surroundings. Jocasta walks back over to the bar cart and pours herself another glass.

"Did you say 'you fucked up' or '*you're* fucked up'?" Maren asks, shocked by Dame Jocasta's coarse language.

"I imagine one begot the other," Dame Jocasta says, now settling in across from Maren. She waits.

"It was a joke, Jo. It was just a joke. Everyone is so sensitive these days and—" Maren says, trying to shrug it off.

"Mare—" Dame Jocasta starts.

"They're reading too much into it. It'll blow over," Maren says, her voice hardening around her lies. Dame Jocasta takes a long drink of her whisky. And waits. Maren shifts in her seat.

"You had them. That's what's so frustrating. You actually brought them back and then . . . what? You couldn't just win? You needed her to lose, too? Is that it?"

"No." Maren's voice is adolescently defiant.

"Then what was it?" Dame Jocasta asks.

"A joke. It was just a silly joke that—"

Frustrated with Maren's persistent nonchalance, Dame Jocasta stands. Confused, Maren looks around for a reason, other than her own impudence, for Jocasta's unusual behavior.

"As your friend, I'm trying to figure out if you actually believe your own bullshit, and it's dawning on me that you just might." Dame Jocasta takes Maren's glass from her, and the unfinished whisky swirls and sloshes around as she walks back over to the bar cart.

Something about this single act shocks Maren—the lack of propriety, her expert use of profanity, and the swift anger that propelled Dame Jocasta to snatch the glass from her. No one has treated her like that in years . . . decades. She watches in stunned silence as Dame Jocasta slams the glass down on the bar cart.

"Fine. I may have gotten a bit overzealous with the opening of the new restaurant—"

"Over. Zealous," Dame Jocasta repeats. Her voice a violent, mimicking staccato of Maren's ridiculous words.

"What do you want me to say here?"

Dame Jocasta turns to face her longtime friend. "Is the article true?" she asks. Her simple question catches Maren off guard. Maren shifts in her chair, starting and stopping several sentences. Dame Jocasta nods. "I'll take that as a yes."

"It's complicated. You know that, Jo. I—"

"You have systematically bullied and humiliated your own daughters. And from the looks of tonight, you seem to rather enjoy it. We are beyond what I want you to say. The question now is, Are you completely lost on this ego trip of yours and beyond help?"

"Ego trip?" Maren asks, standing.

"You've turned into one of them." Maren shakes her head. "Yes, you have. You've turned into a Giant Ego Baby Chef—isn't that what we used to call them?"

"I have not."

"Oh, but you have. You're throwing little tantrums, you're taking credit for other's people work, you're minimizing other's accomplishments so you can shine the brightest, you're making snide comments that you pass off as 'just a joke.' Now who does this sound like?"

"I haven't."

"You humiliated yourself tonight. I don't think you really get that."

"*They* humiliated me, not—"

"Wrong!" Dame Jocasta shouts. "You're wrong, Maren." Jocasta waits. "Do you have no one in your life who tells you the truth?" Maren is shocked into silence. "*You* humiliated you." Maren opens her mouth to say something but thinks better of it. "So the question now becomes, How are you going to fix it?"

"And what? Our friendship hangs in the balance until I do?"

"Oh, much more than that, my darling, sweet friend. Much more than that." Dame Jocasta turns away from Maren and walks toward the door without another word. The finality of the moment unnerves Maren. She follows her to the door and, unable to catch her, calls out to keep her from leaving.

"Jo . . . it's me." Dame Jocasta turns around. "You know me." Maren reaches out to her old friend, her eyes imploring Jocasta to see her and step back from the cliff's edge of this conversation.

"I don't think even you know you anymore." Dame Jocasta's eyes well up, finally seeing the truth of what her oldest friend has become. Heartbroken, she shakes her head and strides out of the room, leaving Maren utterly alone.

Outside, in the main courtyard, the Banquet Conference attendees are gifted with a beautiful clear night on their last evening in Oxford. They've also been given a shared subject with which to bond and connect throughout the evening. Free from the shackles of small talk and awkward cliques, the after-party is downright buzzing. A string quartet plays over in the corner, the open bar keeps the alcohol flowing, and the luxurious seating areas nestled around glowing orange heaters have made the slate and cobbled courtyard seem enchanted. As waiters and waitresses weave through the crowd, snippets of conversation all orbit around everyone's personal take on what went down tonight: who was right, who was wrong, and what they think it *really* means. Apparently, tonight everyone is an expert on the psychology of interfamilial relationships, and they've got something to say about it.

But the subjects of tonight's lively conversations are having a night that couldn't be further from what is taking place in the main courtyard.

Feeling hemmed in and trapped, Athena finds herself walking through the Glass House gardens, immune to the cold and just trying to get a full lung's worth of air. Talking to herself and running through the evening over and over again, she feels like she's coming out of her skin. One moment, she's the hero of her story, and the very next, she's the villain. Walking down alternate aisles, Athena plays and rewinds what her mother said and then what she said, both getting more and more distorted as the night wears on.

With no one to talk to—or more to the point, with no one she feels she can really talk to—her brain morphs into the main courtyard, a deafening echo chamber dissecting every possible angle of tonight's events. Until finally, she finds a wooden bench on the fringes of a fallow field, collapses onto it, and stares at her trophy. Anger and frustration swirl inside her, but once the sluice gate is officially raised, the tidal wave of pain, hurt, and desperate longing rush in. And in that moment, it doesn't matter who's right and who's wrong—Athena Winter just wants to be sad.

Behind her, Athena hears someone knock over a flowerpot and stifle a yelp of pain. She turns around to see Lola Tadese bent over and holding her shin, her dress now muddy from the collision.

"Lola?" Athena calls out.

"I wanted to see if you were okay, but then the farther you walked, the more it felt like I was an assassin sent to kill you," Lola says, trying to brush the mud off her dress.

"If you could make it quick and painless, that'd be great," Athena says.

Lola smiles. "Do you mind if I sit?"

"Please," Athena says, scooting over on the bench. Lola picks her way over and sits down next to Athena.

"Congratulations," Lola says, eyeing the trophy.

"Thank you," Athena says, letting the heavy gold statuette droop in her hands. They are quiet.

"How . . . are you doing? Are you . . ." Lola trails off.

Athena looks over at her, tries to smile and lie, but instead . . .

"No," she says, in a wrenching whisper.

Lola is unsure what to do. She's never really been a touchy-feely kind of person and knows that any attempt at being one would just feel weird and forced. So instead she unzips her giant puffer coat and pulls from its depths a vintage sterling-silver hip flask. She unscrews the top and hands it to Athena—zipping her puffer coat back up as Athena takes a swig of the smooth bourbon.

"This place is freezing. I'm cold all the time. I've had to strategize multiple levels of warmth, so don't judge," Lola says, retrieving the flask and taking a drink. "I'm actually surprised you didn't hear me behind you, swooshing around." She moves her arms and produces a swoosh swoosh swoosh sound with every sway of her arms. Athena smiles.

"I was too busy talking to myself. And the fact that you overheard that is going to be a wonderful moment to relive at 4:00 a.m., when I wake up in a flop sweat," Athena says, as Lola passes back the flask again.

"Ah, we all do it. Especially after quarantine. I mean, who else were we supposed to talk to locked in our houses for years?" Lola crosses her arms and looks out over the fallow field.

"Is this where I confess I did it long before that?" Athena asks, passing the flask back to Lola.

"Yeah, me too," Lola says. Athena smiles.

They are quiet with just the occasional swoosh as Lola—in her giant puffer coat—shifts on the bench.

"My editor came up with the headline. I need you to know that," Lola says.

"Your article was really good," Athena finally says, cutting through the silence.

Lola blows out a long exhale.

"You're a really good writer," Athena says.

"Thank you."

"I'd been meaning to tell you all day, but—"

"No, I get it."

"Heather Osborne, right?"

"Right? I went there thinking it was going to be this little final detail to confirm and the whole thing came apart in my hands. I barely made my flight," Lola says.

"The friendship bracelet was downright diabolical," Athena says, turning toward Lola. The warmth of her feels nice.

"You know she was selling those for thirty-two dollars on her website? Thirty. Two. Dollars. Had some lady in Denver making them for pennies," Lola says.

"I would marvel at how one gets to that point, but . . ." Athena trails off.

"I'm sorry about what Sloane said," Lola says.

"I think I'd be way more mad if she wasn't right about me," Athena says. Unsure of how to proceed—ever the journalist—Lola decides to offer up some facts to refute Athena's claim.

"Rafael says you're joining him in LA for the Wolf Cub pop-up?" Lola asks, trying to cheer Athena up.

"Yeah, he wanted me on the grill," Athena says, her voice flat.

"And have you thought about what you want?" Lola asks.

Athena turns to look at her, wondering if she's in cahoots with Jenn Nishimura. "You're a really good interviewer," she says, trying to change the subject. Lola is quiet. Patient. Waiting. "I tried to think about what I wanted for a couple of weeks, and it didn't go so well for me."

"Hm," Lola says.

Athena looks over at Lola. Her face says it all. "Go ahead and ask. You have a terrible poker face."

"I know. It's . . . actually something I learned about myself while playing poker, which feels a bit on the nose if you ask me." Athena laughs but waits. "You'd never planned on opening your own place?"

"No. Isn't that the saddest thing in the world? Being head chef at Northern Trade was everything I dreamed of."

"And now?" Lola asks.

"In my brain I know one thing. I know I should have a plan. I know I should think about my own restaurant, and not just the binders full of tweaks to Mom's recipes and scribbled kernels of ideas for recipes that I abandon. But every time I try to do what my brain and I have decided is a good next step and forward progress and all that, the anxiety takes over and pushes me underwater again. And every time it's a surprise . . . Is this . . . Does this make any sense?" Athena asks, like she's coming out of a haze.

"It . . . yeah. I . . . it happens to me, too," Lola says.

"Like while I was in the world's most depressing hotel those first weeks right after . . ." Athena trails off. Lola nods. "I went to dinner at Jenn Nishimura's place—"

"So good, right?"

"So good. But we talked and she basically challenged me to answer one single question: What do I want? Just like you. So I came up with this big plan. Put everything into it—all my energy went from being sad to onward and upward. Even found a place. This really great little beach shack kinda thing over by Stinson. I was so excited to go see it. Rented a ridiculously orange car, got a coffee and a kouign-amann, even talked to my bank. Had my music going, felt the wind on my face, and then promptly had the longest and most violent anxiety attack I've ever had right there on Highway 1. Gorgeous scenery, and there I was just trying to get a full breath . . . and . . . couples are getting engaged next to me . . . it was surreal. It took me three hours to get the car back to the rental place. I had to keep stopping. And I . . . I've been spooked ever since," Athena says, staring down at the fallow field in front of them.

"Oh god, I'm so sorry," Lola says.

"I think what scared me the most was how blindsided I was by it. There was me and then there was it and . . . I know I'm going through something right now, but I didn't know it was that bad, you know? And also, this was a good thing. I was excited and happy. And then all of a sudden, I couldn't feel my hands, I couldn't breathe, and I couldn't make it stop. I felt so trapped in my own head, you know? And I just got . . . I was paralyzed by it." Athena looks over at Lola. Her face is soft and open. Athena exhales. It feels so good to just say it. To tell the truth to another person.

"Yeah. I . . . uh . . . that happened to me at SFO. It was my first big interview for the *Chronicle* and all I had to do was get on the plane. And I couldn't. I couldn't move. And I remember staring at all the people around me, who were just walking by, not frozen from terror and apparently doing fine, and I've never felt . . . so alone. And I'm good with being alone, but something about that particular aspect of it felt like such a betrayal—"

"That's exactly it," Athena says.

"Because it was me against me. And I think I understood that both sides had good points—you know, one was like . . . this is scary and you're going to humiliate yourself. But the other was so excited for the opportunity, and there I was, just caught in the middle." Lola is becoming more and more emotional as she retells what is clearly still a very raw story.

"How did you get out of it?" Athena asks, her voice quiet and gentle.

"I got this woman's attention across from me. She had that look— you know, gray hair, steely gaze . . . She'd already given side-eye to this man talking super loud on his phone. And she felt like one of those super-amazing, capable women who could wade in, you know?" Athena nods. "I told her what was going on, and when it came time to board . . . she pulled me to standing, looped my backpack on, threaded her arm through mine, and walked with me to the gate without a word. I can't remember showing my ticket or passport, but I remember her finding my seat, stowing my luggage, and sitting me down. She even put my seat belt on."

"Did she say anything?"

"Right at the end. She put her hand on my wrist and said, 'You're safe.' She patted my arm, and I never saw her again." Lola unzips her puffer coat and removes her right arm from its warm depths. She pulls up her sleeve, and tattooed on the inside of her forearm are the words "you're safe." "It helps. When I feel it starting again." Lola shivers and puts her puffer coat back on.

"I'm so sorry that happened to you," Athena says.

"I'm so sorry that happened to you," Lola repeats right back at Athena.

"Every time I think about my own place . . . every time I think about officially moving on from Northern Trade . . . from Mom . . . that floaty feeling happens."

"And how has it been here?"

"It's so sick, but I've been fine here. Fighting with my family and being humiliated by my mother is oddly comforting and familiar." Athena looks over at Lola and just shakes her head. "How did the interview go? The one you were so nervous about?"

"Oh. That. Yeah . . . well, we met at this fancy-ass restaurant in London and I was still super dazed, so I ordered what I thought was this breakfast special, but in reality it was just a side of compote."

"Oh no."

"The waiter brings it out, and it's in the tiniest ramekin you've ever seen in your entire life. And he asks again if this is all I want, and I squeak out that it is. 'I love a compote,' I believe is what I said," Lola says, laughing.

"Oh no," Athena says, laughing. It feels good.

"Yeah, and then I proceeded to eat what was a lovely apricot—maybe a peach—compote, definitely a stone fruit. I don't quite remember because I was having a mental breakdown while eating it. But I ate the whole thing with a fork—why not a spoon? I don't know. When I finished it, I think I said, 'Now that's good compote.' Not 'a good compote,' mind you. Just 'now that's good compote.' Thankfully, I remember that with perfect clarity. I can't . . . That one still hurts."

"In your defense, a good compote should be celebrated far more than it is," Athena says.

Lola laughs. "That's the nicest thing anyone's ever said to me," she says, unscrewing the top of her flask. She takes a long swig and passes it to Athena, who takes a long drink.

"Thank you," Athena says, passing back the flask.

"Oh, you're welcome," Lola says, tucking it back inside her puffer jacket.

"Not just for the drink," Athena says.

"I know," Lola says, smiling.

"Would you mind if we just sat here for a while?" Athena asks. Lola unzips her puffer jacket and pulls another flask out of the other pocket. She shakes it around and arches an eyebrow.

"I came prepared," she says. Athena smiles and takes a long, deep breath as she relaxes back onto the bench. Lola shifts over more on the bench, the warmth from her puffer jacket making Athena feel safe.

Over in the main house, Sloane slumps on the edge of her king-size bed in the extravagant suite given to her because she's a Winter, holding her cell phone tightly in her hands. She's left multiple messages for Lærke and has yet to hear back. But so far all her messages were appeals to talk it out and that she could explain it all and that this was all one big misunderstanding. Desperate, Sloane dials her wife one last time, and after being sent to voice mail, she finally decides to tell the truth.

"Hey, honey, it's me. The thing is . . . the stuff in Lola's article? It's all true. I said those awful things about Athena. I lied about the conversation with Mom. I never had it. I should have trusted you. All it did was make me keep more things a secret and do more things I wasn't proud of." Sloane swipes away the streams of tears trailing down her cheeks. "I don't want to do this anymore. I don't want to be this person anymore. I love you and I love the kids and I love the home we've made and I just . . . I just want to come home. I love you. Please call me back." Sloane hangs up and drops her phone onto the bed.

A tightness closes around Sloane. Now that their mother has made a public spectacle of herself, she and Jules can start the next phase of their plan. Fire Heather Osborne. Circle back to the four people they're confident will vote with them. Gather the board of directors. Take a vote of no confidence. Oust their mother once and for all. Cheat Athena out of her recipe and start the process of producing the Southern Trade hot dogs. Shut down Central Trade. Fight their mother at every turn. Fight their mother, cheat their sister, and keep on lying.

Fight, cheat, and lie. Fight, cheat, and lie. Fight, cheat, and lie.

Sloane stands and begins to pace around her suite, thinking about how things will begin and what will happen tomorrow. They'll play happy families for everyone; she and Jules will lie (again) and tell their mother all is well on the long car ride back to Heathrow. Then the two Winter sisters will silently text their mutinous plans while trapped together on the ten-hour flight home. They'll smile and listen to their mother as she makes excuses, makes plans, and continues to suck out every drop of goodness that they have left in them. And by the time they get back to Northern Trade, Sloane will officially be a husk of the person she once was.

Or she could just walk away.

Sloane stops pacing.

She could walk away.

It's an idea so revolutionary, Sloane doesn't realize until she begins to feel light-headed that she's holding her breath. She could walk away. In fact, she could walk away right now. Tonight. No happy families, no more keeping things from Lærke, no silent car rides, no mutinous texts . . . She could feel good again. She could be good again. She could be herself again. Before she talks herself out of it, Sloane scans the suite and focuses on the in-room phone. She dials the front desk.

"Hello, this is Sloane Winter. I'd like a car to Heathrow, please."

"Yes, ma'am. And when would you be wanting this car?" the woman at the front desk asks. Sloane looks around at her clothes, open suitcases, toiletries strewn everywhere.

"Half an hour, please." Sloane can hear the woman quickly typing in the background.

"I would like to note that there are no flights for San Francisco leaving tonight."

"Thank you for that information. If I could just have the car, please?"

"Yes, ma'am. It'll be around front in thirty minutes."

"Thank you."

Sloane hangs up and immediately books a room at a hotel next to the airport and switches her plane ticket home to the first available flight tomorrow morning. Now with just twenty minutes left, she begins packing her bags as quickly as she can as the time ticks down.

She can't get out of here fast enough.

A notification pops up on Jules Winter's phone that someone is making changes to the travel itinerary she's set up. Sitting in a dimly lit snug hidden from view in the manor house bar as she nurses her second vodka soda, Jules taps through to find Sloane's modifications.

Jules catches the bartender's eye and motions for the check. She signs for her drinks and, feeling prying eyes watching her, calmly walks out of the bar. Once out of view, Jules hikes up her dress and begins to run toward the Conservatory Suites before her older sister can disappear into the foggy Oxfordshire evening, thereby launching Jules into a far more uncertain future. An uncertain future she would have to face alone.

Out of breath from the run, Jules pounds on Sloane's door. Again and again. Again and again. The door finally wrenches open.

"What . . . what do you want?" Sloane asks. Flustered from Jules's relentless knocking, Sloane's face drains of color as she realizes the state of her room—open luggage, clothes taken down from the closet, phone charger strewn across the bed.

"Where are you going?" Jules says, pushing her way into Sloane's suite.

"Home. I'm going home." Sloane takes a deep breath and goes back to packing up her suitcase.

"There are no flights tonight, so—"

"I'm booked on the first flight out tomorrow," Sloane says, dropping her fully packed toiletry bag into her suitcase.

"What is this? What are we doing here? Walk me through how this is not you being insanely dramatic? And then let me remind you that that's usually my job," Jules says, plopping down next to Sloane's suitcase on her bed.

"I just want to go home. That's it. I just want to go home," Sloane says, not wanting to tell the whole truth to Jules just yet. Sloane takes out the last of the items she hung up in the closet one by one and folds them up tightly into her suitcase.

"Can we just stop for a second here? Can you stop? Are we allowed to talk about this or . . ."

"No! I'm done talking about this. All we do is talk about *this*. Do you remember when we used to talk about something other than *this*?" Sloane slams the top closed. She struggles to zip it up. Jules stands up and sits on top of the suitcase. Just like they did when they were kids. Sloane tries to keep from crying as she zips the suitcase around Jules's body.

"Can you at least tell me how far you are planning on taking not talking about *this*," Jules says, hopping off the zipped suitcase.

"I don't want to do this anymore. I can't . . . Every lie seems to produce ten more lies; every terrible thing we do breeds ten more terrible things . . . I thought—ugh, I was so stupid . . . I thought we would get to a point where we could go back to being . . . good. But we're just staying bad and becoming more bad," Sloane says, growing more and more emotional.

"We're not bad," Jules says.

"Oh, honey. Yes, we are," Sloane says.

"You always forget this," Jules says, handing Sloane the phone charger off her bed.

"Thanks," Sloane says, wrapping the charger around itself and dropping it into her purse.

"And we're not bad," Jules says.

"You know what really bothered me about that quote?" Sloane asks. Jules shakes her head. "I meant it. For the first time in a long time, that was me being honest. I was happy Mom did what she did to Athena. What kind of person . . ." Sloane's voice catches.

"We just have to play this game a little longer, and in order to win, we have to do some things that might be categorized as bad because that's the game Mom is playing. Being good won't win this fight, Sloane."

"Then I don't want to win."

"We're too close—"

"Come with me."

"What?"

"Come with me. We've got money saved up, and I have ideas and you have ideas, and we can start our own thing. We don't have to do this anymore," Sloane says, taking Jules's hand.

"We had a plan. We *have* a plan. If Mom blew it at tonight's gala, we were going to the board of directors. One vote of no confidence and it's ours. It's all ours. The worst is almost over. We're so close," Jules says, gripping her sister's hand back.

"Do you like you right now?" Sloane asks.

"No, but I never like me," Jules answers honestly.

"Oh, honey." Sloane's entire face softens, but Jules stands firm—pushing past her momentary slip of honesty.

"Just . . . Sloane, please. Don't do this . . . We have a shot here at having it all," Jules says.

"But it's Mom's all! Do you even want Central Trade? Do you want Heather Osborne? Do you actually want those things?"

"We can fix them now. You. And. Me. We can fix it."

"But why? Why don't we let Mom fix what she broke for once?" Sloane asks.

"But we're so close," Jules repeats, her voice growing desperate.

"I know you see the summit. I can see how close it is, too. And I know that you want to stand on top more than anything. But we're going to die up there, Jules. We're going to die up there. It's not worth it. None of this is worth it."

"I thought you didn't like me," Jules says. Sloane smiles.

"I may not like you sometimes, but I've always loved you."

"You do?" Jules asks, breathless.

"Yes," Sloane says. Jules pulls away, suddenly overcome. Sloane lets out a little, aching yelp, thinking she's lost her sister. "Jules, please—"

Jules waves her hands in a desperate gesture for Sloane to just give her a second. Because finally . . . *finally* . . . after all these years . . . someone sees her. Someone finally sees her. Someone wants her. Chooses her. And it's not for her game playing or for what she can do for them. It's not because she's beautiful and perfect and says all the right things. It's because Sloane sees her and loves her. The real her.

"Okay," Jules squeaks.

"Really?"

"I'm scared," Jules blurts out.

"Me too," Sloane says, taking Jules's hand. Jules squeezes tight.

"Okay," Jules says again. Sloane pulls her in for a hug. It's bumbling, chaotic, and absolutely beautiful. They break apart, laughing at their own awkwardness.

Sloane checks her watch. "The car will be out front in fifteen minutes."

"Then I'll meet you out front in fifteen minutes," Jules says.

Sloane lunges into her sister for another hug. And this time, they get it right.

"Okay, but this hug can only take less than a minute. You saw how much I have to get packed," Jules says, smushed into the crook of Sloane's neck. Sloane laughs, feeling weightless.

"Out front in fifteen minutes," she says, finally letting go of her sister.

"I'll be there." Jules nods and rushes out of the room.

And for the first time, Sloane believes her.

✳

As Dame Jocasta's words weigh heavy, Maren Winter is sitting all alone in her lavish Conservatory Suite when she receives Sloane's and Jules's resignations. They've cc'd the board of directors and have alluded to ongoing conversations with counsel in order to "make this split as amicable as possible." As Maren drops her phone to her lap, the first thought that crests her riot of a mind is that she's still wearing the expensive formal gown she wore to the ceremony. And without the help of one of her daughters to unzip her, she'll be stuck in this expensive gown until she swallows her pride and calls for a discreet Glass House staffer to free her.

What has she done?

CHAPTER FIFTEEN

In the weeks following the Banquet Conference, the adrenaline from stealing away in the dark of the Oxfordshire night and sending their resignations had all but worn off for Jules and Sloane Winter. But in its place was something extraordinary and brand new. Unable to name it or even understand its borders or composition, Jules and Sloane found this new element spreading uncontrollably to other things that were, on their face, seemingly unrelated to the Winter empire at all.

Their mother responded to their resignations with very little fanfare. And the Winter empire attorneys handled all the rest of the communications as dryly and lawyerly as possible. All Jules's and Sloane's personal effects still at Northern Trade were neatly packed into boxes and sent to them via messenger. It was all so very civilized. And while Jules and Sloane navigated their own complicated feelings about their mother's seemingly shrugging dismissal of their leaving, they never regretted it. In fact, the painlessness of their escape almost confirmed that what they did was right. And however hard that was to digest, it was what it was.

They believed their mother hadn't fought them at all. She hadn't apologized or run after their car in the rain begging for forgiveness. Maren Winter simply added her own personal attorney to the resignation email and typed, See below.

See. Below.

The only two words their mother had to say on the matter.

Sloane and Jules had heard rumors—or more accurately, Jules had extracted certain facts from those in the know—about the fallout from Lola's article, the drama at the Banquet Conference, and the impact of their own resignations. But she needed more. So she suggested to Sloane that they invite Odette Bankolé and her husband over for dinner. On top of being a representative for the staff on the board of directors, Odette was always at the center of all gossip that moved through the Winter empire—probably something about her pouring just enough wine to make people get a bit loose lipped. Sloane agreed, unable to deny that she wanted to know all the gory details, too. And even before the fish course hit the table, Odette began to regale them with the tales of Heather Osborne's unceremonious firing in exquisite detail.

According to Odette, Maren started her conversation with Heather, "I'm sure this will not come as a surprise to you," which was when Heather Osborne pounded her fist on the wooden table and yelled, "I am exceptional!" Something the entire kitchen staff heard—half because Heather Osborne yelled it, but also because they were all leaning up against the door fully eavesdropping.

But just after Heather told the world she was exceptional, Maren Winter started laughing. And didn't stop. Like, for a long time. Eleanor Zhou, who was crouched at the top of the stairs watching the whole thing, told Odette later that Maren cackled for a good two minutes, tears streaming down her face as she struggled to catch her breath. Everyone thought the laughing had finally died down, and Heather Osborne thought that'd be a good moment to interrupt with, "This is *my* domain and—" But before she could finish her thought on her *domain*, Maren barked out a laugh so loud it made Heather flinch. After the "this is my domain" line, Maren put both of her hands on the table and just hung her head while she continued to laugh.

When Maren Winter finally gathered herself, she looked up at Heather Osborne and simply said, "How did I not see you for what you really are?"

And because Maren's question was not about Heather's domain or her exceptionalism, Heather couldn't muster a response. In the expanding silence that hung between them, Maren finished off her choice for head chef with, "Hiring you will go down as one of the low points of my life." And with a wave of her hand, Maren turned away from a stunned Heather Osborne, craned her neck up the stairs, and called to Eleanor, who she apparently knew was sitting there the whole time, "See her out, will you?"

Maren Winter walked out of Northern Trade's main dining room and didn't look back. Eleanor later told Odette that Heather Osborne monologued about how unfair this was the entire time she was being removed from the premises. As Sloane filled her wineglass again, Odette said that Heather Osborne had already added "head chef, Northern Trade" to her website along with several "candid" photos of her on the Northern Trade grounds. So, not so unfair that Heather didn't still milk it for all it was worth.

Odette went on to say that Hana Ahn told her later that Maren had come down to the gardens and asked to speak with Penny in private. Hana nodded and quickly exited, only to position themselves just outside the greenhouse so they could hear Maren confess everything Dame Jocasta had said to her after the lifetime achievement award ceremony. Maren had apparently talked about how cruelly she'd treated Athena and then admitted that when she got Jules's and Sloane's resignations, she'd never felt so alone. But it wasn't until Heather Osborne screamed "I am exceptional" in her face that she saw how truly far she had fallen. How did she not see it? And if she didn't see that level of arrogant idiocy, what else was she missing?

Maren paced as she spiraled, imploring Penny to answer her as she asked how she was any different from Heather Osborne? Because wasn't that what she'd been doing for the last few months . . . years? Screaming "I am exceptional" in everybody's faces and reminding anyone who challenged her that this was her domain?

Which was when Penny Ahn finally told her oldest friend the truth.

That over the course of the last ten years, Penny had gone from being a partner and collaborator to just a prop in Maren's origin story. And after far too many failed attempts at trying to pull her dear friend back from the edge, Penny had made the wrenching decision that she needed to start disentangling herself from Northern Trade and, more painfully, Maren Winter.

She pitched the television show, she wrote the gardening books, she got agents and managers, and built a life for herself where she wasn't just some faceless blob seated on the smallest blanket in the world in the middle of Golden Gate Park, whose sole job was to witness Maren Winter's great genius.

"You broke my heart," Penny had said.

Odette took a long drink of her wine, set the glass down, and continued her story to a stunned Jules and Sloane. Apparently, on New Year's Eve, Penny had to make the agonizing decision not to step in and protect Athena. Because she knew that what was best for the little girl she'd known her whole life was to get as far away from Maren Winter as possible. She knew this because it was what she had to do, too. And moreover, Penny knew that in firing Athena, all hell would break loose. And if Maren couldn't see what she'd become then, there truly was no hope.

Stunned, Sloane asked Odette what her mother had said to Penny's confession.

"Nothing," Odette had said. Maren collapsed onto a garden bench and let her head fall into her hands. At this revelation, Jules drank the remainder of her wine in one long gulp.

When Odette and her husband left that night, Jules and Sloane were quiet for a long time. They'd wanted to hear the gossip. They'd yearned to hear that their mother was hurting after their resignations. They'd planned the dinner just so they could relish the crumbling of an empire that no longer included them. But when Odette delivered everything they wanted, all they felt was deep sorrow. Because among the rubble and ruin of the life they'd once lied and cheated to protect, there was now a tiny green sapling of hope. And for people raised in the brutality of a family like the Winters, it wasn't the rubble or the ruin that unnerved Jules and Sloane. It was the little green sapling.

In the days following their dinner with Odette, Jules and Sloane continued their cautious crossing of whatever this rickety bridge was from the life before to whatever it was going to be on the other side. Regardless of what Odette had told them, they had yet to hear from their mother. So, officially, all they had were the words "See Below" and just this dangerous hope that that little sapling survived. And among the swirling gossip, the plans for the future, and the stepping over the boxes with their personal items from Northern Trade, this newly discovered element seemed to buoy Jules's and Sloane's hopes despite the stomach-dropping heights at which they were traveling.

Quite simply, Jules and Sloane Winter were starting to see another side of themselves. The good side. For real this time. And that feeling guided them to weather the uncertainty and stay curious a little bit longer. Because if they could change, maybe there was a glimmer of hope that Maren would look beyond herself for once and finally be a mother to them. Especially now that they were starting to believe that even they were worthy of it.

Jules meets the first day of February sitting in one of her uncomfortable dining room chairs, looking out over Stinson Beach's rugged coastline just below her multimillion-dollar modern home. Absentmindedly pushing a little pile of crumbs from her morning toast back and forth, Jules sips the bitter dark-roast coffee Richard has a subscription to and insists on making as elaborate pour-overs one single mug at a time. He also frowns on any kind of coffee condiment, as it would *sully the cup quality*" of the brew.

Truth be told, Jules has never liked this coffee. But then again, she's never liked a lot of things. What she liked was how cool these things looked. Joy for Jules Winter came from taking a perfectly framed photo of a black coffee in a handmade mug and posting it to social media with a caption about loving her coffee black blah blah blah, something about purity and cup quality blah blah blah. Watching people in the comments eviscerate the uncool was as delicious to her as drinking her coffee the way she actually liked it. Or so she thought. Bitter coffee, uncomfortable chairs, cold modern houses, too-high heels—Jules found herself getting inconveniently and dangerously less okay with it all.

Jules wonders why these inconvenient observations have only flooded in since coming back from Oxford. She thought by doing the right thing, she'd naturally feel better. Instead, she's felt trapped inside a fun house of a life in which she no longer fits. But it's the growing desire to break free from this fun house that worries her the most. She fears the future that lies beyond these contorted and mirrored walls will be so changed and new that she'll be unable to understand how to even begin.

As Richard comes in from his run, Jules sets her mug down and, with just the right blend of the old and new Jules Winter, finally confronts him about an issue that she could no longer be silent about.

"I don't like this coffee," she says, standing and facing Richard.

"Did you weigh it out on the scale? It could also be the grind . . . Did you make sure the grinder was on the right setting?" Richard strides over to the "coffee station," as he calls it, and checks all the dials and elaborate mechanics that go into making a "simple" cup of coffee.

"I want to get a regular old-timey coffee maker, and I also want those creamers that taste like candy canes or whatever," Jules says, deciding to bravely bring peppermint back into her diet. Richard slowly turns around as if he's just heard an intruder cock their gun behind him.

"What did you just say?" Richard asks, as if he cannot even begin to understand what Jules just said.

"I like peppermint," Jules says, pushing her shoulders back.

"Why?" Richard asks, his mouth contorted in a disgusted snarl.

"I also hate these chairs," Jules says, pointing to the uncomfortable straight-back dining room chairs.

"Those chairs are Panton," Richard says, nearly breathless now.

"They're uncomfortable," Jules says, crossing her arms across her chest.

"You picked them out?" Richard's voice trails up despite his comment not being a question.

"I know, but they don't feel good to sit in, and now I hate them," Jules says.

"And what else do you hate in this house that you're just now telling me?" Richard asks, semijoking.

The clarity of Richard's question pierces through all Jules Winter's defenses and guards. Every quip, every jab, and every joke she could make in this moment disappears from her brain as one word inflates bigger and bigger inside her head until she can't not speak it.

"Us," Jules says.

"What?" Richard asks, his temper rising.

"Us," Jules repeats.

"So, you hate us now?"

"Well . . . no, not—"

"So, you don't hate us?"

"No, I just don't hate us *now*. I've hated us for a while."

"Oh good, yes, thank you for clearing that up."

"I think I probably did like us at some point, or maybe it was the idea of us. Could be that I just liked being part of an us," Jules says.

"You literally posted a photo yesterday saying how much you loved being married," Richard says, tugging his phone out of his shorts pocket and pulling up the photo as evidence.

"I know," Jules says, unable to look at the photo.

"And?" Richard asks.

"I really wanted to love being married to you," Jules says, looking up at him.

"So you lied?"

"No . . . no, not really. I wanted to love you so badly. And when I didn't, I thought there was something wrong with me," Jules says.

"I think that's still up for debate," Richard says, cruelly.

"See, the thing is you can't say anything as mean as I say to myself," Jules says.

"I don't . . . I don't know how we got here. I'm still in my running gear for Chrissakes! You liked the photo I just posted from my run and commented with a bunch of hearts!" Richard says, showing Jules that photo as well.

"I know, but I can't . . . I can't do it anymore," Jules says, searching for the words.

"Are you serious? Are you actually serious?" Richard asks.

Jules is quiet. Her brain explodes with the usual tangle of manipulation and lies. They come easy to her. Too easy. She sifts through the noise, pushing away that biting one-liner, the dismissive joke, and the easy cruelty of her not-so-recent past, finally revealing the simplest of truths cowering beneath the storm.

"Yeah," Jules says.

"Yeah? That's all you're going to say? Yeah?"

Jules stumbles on her response, trying not to answer his question with another "yeah."

"Richard—"

"How can you be so cavalier?"

"This has been really hard to say. I'm not being cavalier. I just . . . This is the truth of what I'm feeling. And it's simple and doesn't take a lot of words," Jules says, with a long exhale.

"I can't believe you," Richard says, his face flushed and angry.

"I'm sorry," Jules says, marveling at how the one time Richard can't believe her is when she's actually telling the whole truth.

"No. Don't be. It's just like you to think you're the only one who hates it here," Richard says.

"But—" Jules starts, taken aback.

"How did it never occur to you?" Richard asks, stepping closer to her.

"What?" Jules asks, growing uncomfortable.

"That I hate you, too," Richard says, his mouth pressed into a thin, cruel line.

"I said I hated us, not—" Jules rasps, emotion choking her throat.

"Yeah, well," Richard says, cutting her off.

The old Jules Winter would have known exactly how to play this. She would have already planted little bombs around their entire future, looming over the rubble of their marriage like a chess master. She would have lied. She would have told him whatever he wanted to hear. She would have smoothed things over and swallowed the truth. She would have kept up appearances.

But the new Jules Winter—the one who's just starting to like herself for the first time in her life—can only feel sorry for the old Jules Winter. That this was the best she thought she could do. That this is what she thought love was. Seeing it so clearly breaks her heart, and in that moment, she knows there's nothing she could say that could possibly be worse than spending one more minute in this house with that man.

As Richard lazes back onto the kitchen counter, settling in for what he's sure is going to be a full twelve-round, knock-down drag-out fight, Jules instead turns back to the dining room table. Wordlessly, she picks up her half-full coffee mug and sweeps the little pile of toast crumbs into its murky depths. She walks over to the kitchen, turns on the tap, and quickly washes the mug, finally setting it carefully down onto the dish drainer once it's clean.

Unable to just do nothing, Richard shifts around in his breezy stance, unsure whether he should recross his legs or lean back more on the counter or bait his wife with another dig, so he kind of does all three. And as Jules dries her hands and tucks the kitchen towel back onto its bar, Richard recrosses his legs, casually leans just a little bit deeper, and spits, "Great job washing a mug you hate." And the minute he says it, he knows he's blown it.

Jules turns around, looks Richard dead in the eye, and lets the moment hang. And hang. And hang. He clears his throat, crosses his arms across his chest, and looks down at the kitchen floor. With a heavy sigh, Jules grabs her phone, her keys, and her purse and walks away from the marriage she hates one final time.

Sitting in her car moments later, Jules muses at how such a short conversation could be so world ending—how the words poured out of her. How long had they been waiting for that opportunity? It's still hard to believe that it took just two minutes to tear down everything she built.

But Jules Winter has no time to dwell on the tectonic shifts of the last few minutes. She has an appointment. And as always, life has an exquisitely banal way of carrying on even when you're being cracked open. So she finds a little package of tissues in the bottom of her purse and tries to wipe away any remnants of showing actual emotion. Because the only thing worse than having unruly feelings is having them in public. Jules texts Sloane a hilariously truncated version of what happened this morning—told Richard I hated his coffee and us, think we're done?—gathers herself just enough so she can drive, and sets off toward Tiburon.

Sloane gets Jules's text right in the middle of the chaos of the school run. Unable to get actual shoes onto Krister, she's allowed him to wear the plastic sandals usually reserved for a beach day or an afternoon at a pool. But it was either those or bunny slippers, and at least she talked him into wearing socks with the plastic sandals. Sloane was able to drop Minnie off at school without incident, but the two little ones have a way of knowing that when their morning routine is off, their mommies are off. Sloane did bedtime, not breakfast. Sloane did baths, not the school run. And Sloane never came to get them on half days; she was always at work. In the DNA of their childhood routines, they sensed something was different.

After several very intense conversations, Sloane and Lærke decided to go to couples therapy as well as planning a getaway with just the two of them. What Sloane was finally able to see was that the events of the last month only amplified aspects of her marriage that had long been strained. Sloane's issues with her mother had been eroding the very fiber of her marriage for much longer than she was aware. This was just the straw that broke the camel's back.

As they took those first steps to work through their issues, Sloane promised Lærke that she'd be better about balancing her work and life with her and the kids. Lærke had heard this before, of course, but . . . she wanted so badly to believe that Sloane could change. So they found a great therapist—conveniently located right next to an ice cream parlor—and booked a cottage at the Mill Valley Inn that had a burbling stream running through it, access to Mount Tam, Muir Woods, and a bunch of other beautiful hikes that they'd lie to themselves and say they'd do. Sloane and Lærke also booked a family trip to Denmark so they'd all be able to spend the summer running around Lærke's parents' beach house just like she did when she was their age.

Sloane drops Freja and Krister off at the co-op and gets just enough side-eye about Krister's little plastic sandals to send her reeling about not being a good enough mother. By the time she gets to the appointment with Jules, she's fully spiraling. Sloane pulls up in front of the storefront in Tiburon, slams the door, and strides over to Jules, who's perched on the small ledge of the main window.

"First thing we need to do is put a little bench or something out front," Jules says, pushing herself up from the uncomfortable roost. "Maybe an awning." She shields her eyes from the sun.

"Am I a good mom?" Sloane asks, coming to a stop in front of her sister.

"You're going to have to catch me up on how we got here," Jules says, gesturing to the whole of Sloane's person.

"Krister wouldn't put on shoes this morning, but he would wear those little plastic sandals you gave him for his birthday last year—"

"Those are super cute, though."

Sloane presses on, not listening to Jules. "I got socks on him, but when I dropped him off at the co-op, the woman gave me a look." She peers inside the storefront.

"The real estate agent isn't here yet," Jules says. Sloane nods and steps away from the window. "What kind of look?"

"A judgy one," Sloane says, trying to re-create the look.

"That could just be her face," Jules says.

"So I am a bad mother," Sloane says, throwing up her hands.

Jules lets out a long sigh. "Okay, what are you looking for here? A pep talk? Some advice? You want to gossip about the school? Or do you just want me to listen and nod along?"

"I don't know," Sloane huffs.

"Can I also ask why this is somehow more pressing than me leaving my husband this morning?"

"No, your text said you just hated his coffee—"

"And us. That I hated the marriage," Jules finishes.

"Ah, okay . . . yeah, I didn't catch that part," Sloane says, gathering herself.

"I really thought it would feel good, you know? Doing what feels right and . . . I don't know, all of it, I guess. But no one tells you about how much it hurts having to face it all. Wondering if you've actually left that other you in the past, or . . ." Jules trails off.

"I know. That's what got me thinking about how selfish I've been and whether I was any better than Mom," Sloane says.

"Me too," Jules says, her voice barely a whisper. They are quiet for a long time. Not knowing what else to say, Jules steps close to Sloane and gives her a very awkward half shake half hug. "We . . . God, I really hope we get better at the displays of affection thing."

Sloane pats Jules's back stiffly and they both laugh, just as their real estate agent pulls up and parks behind Sloane's car. The woman steps out and greets Sloane and Jules warmly. Within minutes, they're let into the little Tiburon storefront and the real estate agent has given them some "poke around time," which sounds way dirtier than it was meant to be.

This storefront is where Jules and Sloane want to open up their own little place. A market that would highlight the relationships with the fresh food vendors that they've built over the years working for their mother. Something that feels new and different enough that Jules and Sloane can call it their own.

The idea came out of an afternoon Jules and Sloane spent day drinking. They got to talking about this one sandwich they remembered having as teenagers. It was only made at this small family-owned market over in Corte Madera. The bread was baked right there—sourdough, if memory served—and you'd pick whatever lunch meat you wanted—ham, turkey, roast beef, or all three if you were feeling yourself—and they used sweet pickle chips and shredded lettuce. What really got Jules and Sloane going—outside of the massive amount of Long Island Iced Tea they'd made—was that when you deconstructed the sandwich into its individual parts, it didn't sound extraordinary at all. In fact, it just sounded like a boring old sandwich. But to Jules and Sloane, it was the stuff of legend.

That's when they started realizing it was more than just the sandwich. It was the field trip they took over there. It was the tiny shopping carts with the adorably earnest regional ads on the little seat. It was the '80s music they piped in just a little too loudly, and how you'd see the same people every time you went. It was also that they sold local, smaller brands that you never saw anywhere else. Small-batch everything, some jam their grandma made, and there was that whole year they got really into cloudberries, so there was cloudberry jam, thumbprint cloudberry cookies, and that one sandwich where they tried to pass off cloudberry jam in a Thanksgiving cranberry–adjacent thing that, to be honest, didn't work at all. However, that was the sandwich that Athena liked the most, but she liked spumoni ice cream (something else they could only get at this market), so . . . who knew.

What Jules and Sloane finally got was that the little market could do whatever they wanted—carry the foods they wanted and play the music they wanted. Sloane was really stuck on the fact that they baked their own bread. Economically it's never a wise decision, at all. They should have partnered with a local bakery and used their baked goods, but that's not what they wanted to do, so they didn't do it. Because that old market knew there was something particularly magical about home-made bread—and having the smell of it constantly wafting through the little market far outweighed whatever money was being lost in the process. And because it was their own market—and not a large corporation or some conglomerate crunching numbers—they could bake their own bread and find other ways to make ends meet.

This is what Jules and Sloane want to do. They want to open up a little mom-and-pop market with a bakery and amazing, fresh prepared foods that would be in these smaller towns—like Tiburon—and fill it full of everything from local small businesses and fresh food vendors. And yes, they are going to bake their own bread and pipe in '80s music just a little bit too loudly.

As they walk around the storefront, Sloane points out where the butcher will go and the fishmonger and the fresh produce and the cheesemonger and the coffee outpost and the prepared food section and, of course, the bakery. And every time she points something out, she gets a little bit more excited, and every time she gets a little more excited, she gets a little more scared. When the real estate agent gives them a second to themselves, Sloane sees her opportunity to pick back up her conversation with Jules and hopefully alleviate some of her anxiety about this new endeavor in the process.

"Do you want to talk about what happened this morning with Richard?" Sloane asks, holding the other side of a measuring tape that Jules is holding out.

"I just couldn't take it anymore," Jules says, calling out the measurement. Sloane reaches into her purse, takes out her little notebook, and writes down the numbers as Jules calls them out.

"Take what anymore?"

"I got it wrong. I just . . . couldn't admit it, I guess," Jules says. Another measurement. Sloane scribbles in her notebook.

"What exactly did you say?" Sloane asks.

"That I hated his coffee—"

Sloane interrupts, trying to preemptively soothe her sister. "Well, that's not—"

"And that I hated us," Jules finishes.

Sloane is dumbstruck. "You said you hated 'us'?"

"I know. It came out so wrong. I did say that I wanted to love him so badly. I made sure to put it on me, you know? Do you know what he said?" Another measurement. Another scribble.

"No," Sloane says, gently.

"He said that he hated me. Not us. Me," Jules says. Sloane stops writing.

"Oh, honey," she says.

"I am . . . *was* pretty hateable," Jules says, her voice shaking.

"Sweetie—"

"Don't be nice to me, because what happens when you're nice to me is I feel worse about what I did and who I was and I don't deserve people being nice to me and it's this trash compactor of a feeling and I just feel crushed by it . . . Do you ever feel crushed—" Sloane walks over to her little sister and pulls her in for a hug. The measuring tape snaps back with a thunderous clang. Jules and Sloane laugh, but soon Jules is crying. Sloane holds her tighter and tighter.

"I'm so sorry," Sloane says, smoothing down her sister's long blonde hair. Jules cry-talks into the crook of her sister's neck, and Sloane can only get about every other word.

"I knew . . . He was always . . . didn't love him . . . What was I thinking . . . He wasn't even that . . . Did you know he would . . . You tried to tell me . . . Athena hated him first . . . She always knew . . . didn't even want a dog . . . Who doesn't want a dog . . . That stupid coffee . . . Why can't I have creamers that taste like candy caaaaaaanes." Sloane pulls her sister in tighter and tries not to laugh at her earnest but pretty hilarious sobbing monologue.

Sloane peers outside, where the real estate agent is now watching them with a look of deep concern.

"She's watching us," Sloane says.

"Let her watch," Jules says, finally pulling away from her sister.

"We're doing great, real estate lady!" Sloane says, laughing.

"This is what it looks like when you decide to become a better person!" Jules says, her mascara trailing down her face.

The real estate agent mistakes Jules's and Sloane's jokes for a request to come back in. Pushing the door open, she quickly pivots and pulls a package of tissues from the depths of her purse. She offers it to Jules. This makes Jules cry even more.

"You're so nice," Jules says, taking the tissues.

"We're just really happy with the space," Sloane says, stepping in front of her wreck of a sister.

"Oh good. Yes, I think it will be perfect for you. Good parking out back, a rarity around here. And I have my eye on a few more spaces in some nearby small towns for when you decide to expand," the real estate agent says.

"Expansion is definitely something we're excited about, too," Sloane says.

"Have you thought about a name?" the real estate agent asks.

Jules and Sloane share a meaningful look. Currently, two names have risen to the top of the list. And each name brings its own emotional gauntlet to their decision-making.

Sloane pitched the name the Trading Post. An obvious play off the tradition of naming Winter restaurants Something Trade. Sloane liked the name. But she liked what the name promised even more. If the market was called the Trading Post, then Jules and Sloane would still be perceived as a part of the Winter empire. And not out on their own. If the market was named the Trading Post, everything would be as it was. And maybe even better, if what Odette Bankolé said was true—that their mother was having exactly the epiphanies she needed to be having so they could all be one big happy family again. Or, more accurately, for the first time.

Jules pitched the Winter Sisters Fresh Market. But the issue with that name was either they'd have to be okay with it being just two of the Winter sisters or they'd finally have to actually have the conversation both Jules and Sloane have been dreading. But now the timing is all wrong. They'd not only have to make amends with Athena but explain why it took them so long to reach out while also selling her on joining their business—which, let's face it, didn't go so great the last time. It's hard enough to convince someone you've changed—in a mere matter of weeks, no less—but it's a whole other thing to then expect them not to question the timing of this heartfelt atonement and its proximity to you trying to hook them back into the family business.

"We haven't quite decided yet," Sloane finally says.

"Well, what I always tell my clients is that it's like a wedding dress or your first home . . . When it's right, you'll just feel it," the real estate agent says with just enough forced positive sentimentality to make Sloane recoil.

Jules can't help thinking that both her wedding dress and her first home were things she ended up hating, so she's hoping her ability to "just feel it" has improved as of late.

The trio exits the storefront in Tiburon with talk of next steps, timelines, and budgets. They'll all be in touch and their lawyers will be in touch and then they and their lawyers will be in touch and then the small talk and farewells get so awkward and repetitive that Jules starts pulling Sloane away and waving goodbye to their real estate agent.

While more than three hundred miles away, Athena Winter is hours from being fired by Rafael Luna.

CHAPTER SIXTEEN

Athena is sitting on an overturned produce crate in a back alley in Altadena, California, positive she's about to be fired by someone she thought was a friend. Just when she thought being fired by her own mother was bad . . . but she'd be lying if she didn't admit that she kind of saw this coming. In fact, she knew on the drive down here.

She'd arrived in Southern California a couple of weeks ago, after limping down Interstate 5. After the first incident happened on Highway 1, Athena, in all her Winter Way glory, decided she would push through whatever had happened on that vista point and prove that she was fine. This time would be different.

She read all the books, listened to all the podcasts, and had her little anxiety bag of tricks all packed and ready for her drive down to LA. She was going to be grounded in her body, touch her fingertips to one another, breathe, and rest her nervous system as she tried to achieve a state of nothingness. She was going to count five things she could see and four that she could hear and then count all the way down until the anxiety subsided. She had books she was going to listen to, calming meditation sessions and spa music queued up for just the right moment. She'd thought of everything. She was ready and prepared. She was in control.

And for the first three hours of her drive, everything went great. Better than great. She stopped for road food at a glorious farm stand, stretched her legs, and played with a pair of pugs at a rest stop. She texted their picture to her brand-new group chat with Lola, Valentina, Rafael, and Jenn. She rolled her window down and actually used the time to talk out all that had happened since the Banquet Conference. It felt good. She felt free. She felt as though this were the new beginning she'd talked about in her speech. She was starting to feel like herself again.

But just as she got to Harris Ranch—the halfway mark between Northern and Southern California—her mother called.

Athena watched in sheer panic as the photo of her mother meandering through the Northern Trade gardens lit up her phone. At the last minute, Athena pulled off the freeway and answered the call.

"Hello?"

"Thank you for picking up," Maren said. Her voice was . . . like home.

Athena was quiet. Maren was quiet.

Athena found a parking space in a large gas station lot and turned off her car. Still waiting for her mother to say something, Athena finally asked, "Mom, was there something specific you needed?"

"Yes," Maren said. Athena waited. Again. Was this an apology? Was this a chance at everything going back to the way it was? Was this . . .

"Mom?"

"I want you to come back. To Northern Trade." Maren's voice was clipped and tight.

"You want me—"

"Yes. As head chef," Maren said.

"But—"

"It's where you belong."

"Mom, I—"

Athena cut herself off, unsure of what she wanted to say. She just needed the conversation to stop for a second.

"I'm heading to LA to work with Rafael, but—" Athena stopped again.

"But what?" Maren asked. Inside Athena's head were screams to say no, to tell her off.

"But I can give you an answer when that's done," Athena said, deflating from her inability to stand up to her mother. Even now.

"And when will that be?" Maren asked.

Athena gave her the date and listened as her mother sighed and searched for something to say that wasn't impatient, disappointed, or critical.

"We'll talk soon then," Maren had said.

"Yes. That sounds fine," Athena said.

And they hung up without another word.

Athena sat in her rental car in a daze until she started feeling a growing weightlessness. The feeling like she was almost being lifted up out of her driver's seat by her spine.

"No . . . please no," Athena said as the tingling in her feet and hands, the pinholing vision, the muffled sound, the fluttery chest, and the shortness of breath all came roaring back.

Jumping into crisis-mitigation mode, she told herself that this was just because she felt uncertain about her mother's offer. And that that was okay. That didn't work either. She frantically counted her breaths, but each failed half lungful only panicked her more. She tried to feel grounded in her body; she listened to the meditation sessions. But nothing worked. In fact, it was getting worse.

She was losing control.

Athena got out of the car and walked around. She then drove around Harris Ranch trying to trick her body into not noticing that she was inching ever closer to the on-ramp. In a final pitch of complete unraveling, Athena Winter bought a bonsai tree at a dirt lot across from the main drag, explaining to the lovely man who worked there that she'd be "happy for the company" on her long drive and could use a little good luck.

The pressure alleviated just enough for her to get back on the freeway. But within thirty minutes she was sitting in a gas station parking lot asking the bonsai tree why this was happening to her when she was so excited about this trip and didn't she want to go back to Northern Trade? And by the third stop, Athena had started calling the bonsai tree Darlene. Buying a bonsai tree in a fugue state was a low point, but surely naming and talking to it was rock bottom.

This was how Athena made the remainder of the drive down to Los Angeles—one rest stop at a time, one conversation with Darlene at a time, and one raging howl at her brain for not being able to fix this at a time. So Athena Winter was officially spiraling by the time she arrived at Rafael Luna's friend's house where she'd be staying while she worked at Wolf Cub.

But who could she talk to about this other than Darlene? She hadn't really talked to her mom or sisters since New Year's Eve, and Rafael and Valentina were beyond busy with the pop-up. She thought about her conversation with Lola after the awards gala and decided that one slightly funny story about not being able to catch your breath on the side of the road was fine. But an ongoing issue with anxiety was something else altogether. Not that this reasoning held up when Athena thought of Lola. Which she did often. But this, too, was an area where Athena wasn't sure her feelings were good or bad. They just felt scary.

So she just tried to move on. Losing herself in Wolf Cub and existing in a safe state of nothingness, desperate not to wake the sleeping dragon that had apparently taken up residence in her chest.

She told herself it was okay because the pressure subsided when she was working Wolf Cub's grill. And after a long night of work, she slept well and was able to keep the anxiety at bay throughout the day. She hadn't had another full episode like the one on Interstate 5 for weeks, telling herself that it happened because she was feeling uncertain about her mom's offer, but that once she accepted it, this would all calm down. Northern Trade was her home. Her mother was right; she belonged there. Everyone would understand why she went back.

Wouldn't they?

On the night Athena Winter thought she was going to be fired, she'd had a normal day. She slept well, had coffee and breakfast at the same little diner she went to every morning, and arrived at Wolf Cub an hour early, as she always had. Second on the grill with her was a young chef Rafael had asked Athena to guide and teach. The young chef was driven and talented but lacked experience in a kitchen. Athena had taken this mentorship very seriously and made sure to make every moment an opportunity for learning, slowing down her process to explain every nuance. She had flourished under Athena's tutelage.

But on that fateful night, Rafael Luna noticed a slight tweak in one of his dishes. Thinking it was the young chef and that Athena had just not felt comfortable with confronting her, Rafael began to watch more closely in preparation for having that hard conversation, without putting Athena in that difficult position. Which is when he saw that Athena was behind the tweak, and not the young chef. The tweak wasn't inexperience; it was intentional.

He weighed all his options. They had two more weeks in Los Angeles at Wolf Cub, and then it was back to the Bay Area to go over all that they'd learned. Once they'd processed it, they'd decide whether they wanted to pursue opening up Wolf Cub as its own permanent restaurant or if they'd have to go back to the drawing board. Since this pop-up was more of a lab for Rafael than any kind of moneymaking endeavor, he needed his dishes to stay as close to his original recipe as possible so he could decide which dishes worked and which ones didn't. Athena's tweaks meant that some customers would be eating a dish—however delicious he was sure it was—that wasn't part of what he originally pitched, and therefore he'd be unable to weigh the efficacy of the tweaked recipe. He also wondered how long she'd been doing this. And even more concerning, since a majority of the dishes utilized the grill in some way, how many dishes she had been tweaking without his noticing. He'd trusted her intrinsically and was now regretting that choice.

But more than all that, Rafael was upset and disappointed. He and Athena had talked about these recipes before they opened and she'd said nothing. She knew how hard he'd worked on them. She knew his past. She knew what he was trying to do. And yet here they were. Eating a pork chop instead of pork belly. And while Maren Winter most certainly had her flaws, Rafael Luna was beginning to understand more and more about what she felt that night.

So, at the end of service, Rafael Luna pulled Athena aside and asked her to wait for him in the back alley so they could speak privately. When she pressed him, fearing the seriousness in his voice, he tried to hold her off as much as he could. But with every evasion, Athena grew more and more positive that she was on the cusp of being let go. Which is why she is now sitting on an overturned produce crate in a back alley in Altadena, California, at twelve thirty in the morning, positive that she is about to be fired.

Every sound coming from just inside makes her flinch, and every hit or tap of the back door causes her to turn around. The waiting is excruciating. What is even worse is that she isn't quite sure what she did.

Finally, Rafael pushes open the back door holding two cups of hot tea. He hands one to Athena, looks around the back alley for another crate to sit on, and settles in across from her. Athena waits, the warmth of the tea helping to calm her nerves.

"Talk to me about the tweaks you've been making," Rafael says. Athena's stomach drops.

"Oh," she says. Rafael lazes back on his crate against the opposite wall of the alley. He stretches his long legs out, crosses his feet, and sighs. He looks exhausted.

But what the darkness doesn't allow Athena to see is the rhythmic tensing of his jaw as he bites back the things he really wants to say in this moment. Because contrary to how it appears—Rafael Luna is pissed. It's the kind of righteous anger that comes when a reformed fuckup experiences what it must have been like to deal with them at their worst. The wasted potential, just enough glimmers of genius and initiative to lure you in, and then the backslide . . . the backslide . . . the heartbreaking backslide.

"Was it just on the sandwich?"

"No, Chef," she says.

Rafael is quiet for a long time. Athena picks and pulls at the tag on her tea bag, finally ripping it off entirely.

"You were there when we finalized the recipes. Why not say something then?" Rafael asks.

"I don't know."

"The unfortunate thing for you is that we are a lot alike. So I know exactly why you did it."

"I thought I was helping," Athena says.

"No, you thought you could make it better."

Athena clears her throat and shifts around on her produce crate. Rafael is right.

"Sloane told me on New Year's Eve that I made the pork chop because of my ego. Jules said it was what Mom would have done."

"Maren wouldn't have done that."

"What?"

"Your mom has her own recipes. She always has," Rafael says, letting the weight of his words blanket the space in between them.

"Right."

"Do you have your own recipes?"

"Just the hot dog and this one . . . there was one around a lemon that . . ." Athena trails off.

"So you just tweak everyone else's?"

"Yes, Chef."

Rafael shakes his head. "Do you have your own restaurant?"

"No."

"Do you want your own restaurant?"

"I don't know."

Athena has never seen Rafael like this. She's used to his intensity. But not when it's directed at her.

"So I'm going to do for you what no one did for me. Or at least I was too much of a dipshit to listen. I'm going to give you some consequences and hope that it makes you so uncomfortable that you'll at least think twice before you continue down this path."

"You're firing me."

"I am. I'm firing you because you know better. I'm firing you because I asked you to mentor a young chef, and you took that opportunity to teach her to undermine the head chef and his recipes. I'm firing you because you would rather feel sorry for yourself than face what's really going on with you. I don't want you to go down like I did." Rafael leans closer. "Do you get that?"

"Yeah," Athena says.

"Do you?"

"Yes, Chef."

"You're brilliant."

Athena is quiet.

"Truly singular. But right now you've got some major shit to figure out."

"I'm so sorry," Athena says.

"I know you are."

"I don't know why I did it," Athena says. Rafael raises an eyebrow. "I know you said that it's because I thought I could make it better. And I know that's true, but I didn't know that at the time I was doing it. Does that make sense?"

"Yeah."

"You see it in hindsight, you know?"

"No, I know. I've definitely been there. Hindsight is my bread and butter."

"I don't know what's going on with me. How do I not know what's going on with me?" Athena stands up. Rafael stands. They see eye to eye. A rarity for both.

They are quiet.

"Did you mean what you said?" Rafael asks.

"When?" Athena asks, her entire being exhausted.

"In your acceptance speech at the Banquet."

"I . . . That whole thing is a blur."

"You said that this was just the beginning—"

"I only said that because Mom ended her speech with that, and I . . . oh god, I guess I'm tweaking her speeches, too."

"Ah. Okay," Rafael says. He offers Athena a tight smile as his shoulders deflate.

"I really do want a beginning. I just . . . I—"

"Then you're going to have to get some skin in the game." Athena looks down at the ground, unsure. "Caring about things is hard," Rafael says, taking Athena's empty teacup from her. "Being all in is heartbreaking sometimes, but isn't it better than whatever you've got going on now?" He hesitates, waiting to see if Athena has anything else to say.

"I am new to . . . um . . ." Athena stumbles on her words, unsure of how to say this. Rafael waits. "I am new to having friends. Does me tweaking your recipes . . . uh . . . did I mess it up? If you could just let me know if we're still—" Before Athena can finish her sentence, Rafael Luna pulls her into him for the biggest hug and doesn't let go. She tucks her face into the crook of his neck and holds on tight. He smooths her hair and sways a bit, rocking her gently as she holds back tears.

"I am your friend," he whispers. She nods, still firmly nestled into him. After several minutes, Athena finally untangles herself from Rafael and gives him a weary smile.

"Thank you," she says. She holds his gaze, willing herself not to look away or down at the ground. Rafael gives a slight nod and disappears inside the restaurant.

Athena paces around the back alley. Her mind is so loud she can't hold on to any one thought. So after enough time has passed, she slips back inside the restaurant to get her things, doing her best impression of someone who has not just been fired. The rest of the kitchen staff are planning on where to go after they finish cleanup, and Athena uses that conversation as cover to quickly extricate herself before Rafael notices she's gone. She's too ashamed to face him. Too ashamed to face any of them.

She drives back to Rafael's friend's house, trying hard not to spiral into shame, humiliation, and apologies as she lets herself in through the back door. But by the time she's packed up most of her stuff and is ready to leave first thing in the morning, the shame and humiliation are gone. And in its place is something much more dangerous: an absolute tangle of feelings she can't even begin to identify.

As she tosses and turns throughout the night, she catches the tail of a bittersweet relief as she begins to lean more toward going back to Northern Trade. Somewhere around 2:00 a.m., she slips into resentment as she builds narrative after narrative where everyone is thriving but her. She pairs this chapter of her sleepless night with going back onto social media, looking up those she feels are her equal, and then enviously scrolling through their impossibly photogenic successful and fulfilling lives. But by four thirty she's just lost, and back to being ashamed for even contemplating going back to Northern Trade. And by six thirty, as Athena throws her duffel bag and backpack into the trunk of her rental car, she feels only utter defeat and exhaustion. She didn't have the courage to say goodbye to Rafael and Valentina but found a tote bag waiting for her by the back door filled with a thermos of coffee, two pan dulce, and a bottle of water. She left a note thanking everyone for letting her stay and giving her the opportunity to work at Wolf Cub.

Athena climbs into her rental, carefully places Darlene, her unwitting bonsai companion, on the passenger seat, making sure to buckle her in for safety, and finally sets off for home.

With her anxiety bag of tricks still in place, Athena decides to take US Route 101 back home. While Interstate 5 is the fastest, 101 is slower, far more populated, and postcard-worthy beautiful—sometimes tracing right along the stunning coast of California itself. Athena loves this drive. She stops for another coffee and is thankful, for once, to get caught up in Los Angeles's rush-hour traffic for the first ninety minutes of her drive. The stop and go has quelled her anxiety down to a low, distant thrum. She also keeps putting off calling her mom to tell her of her decision. She tells herself the reception will be bad or it's too early in the morning or she still needs time to think.

Once the traffic thins out right around Camarillo, Athena is relieved to find herself faring far better than she thought she would. And by the time she hits that spellbinding bend right by Ventura that reveals the full California coast and the Pacific Ocean just beyond, Athena rolls her window down and breathes in the crisp sea air. And for the first time in a long time, Athena smiles.

She turns on some music and rolls through Ventura without incident. But as she gets to the less-populated parts just north of Santa Barbara, she can feel the pressure building in her chest once more. The tingling in her hands. The floaty feeling. She closes her window and starts listening to a book. Then a podcast. Then back to the book. She concentrates on her breathing. She turns on the air-conditioning full blast, then opens the window. And for the next hour, Athena Winter actively fights to manage her anxiety—like she's trying to lasso a dragon. Usually, Athena talks to herself, monologues and dreams and fantasizes, during these long drives. She's even been known to practice an acceptance speech or two. But this time her brain is deafeningly quiet and unable to hold on to any word or phrase, instead defaulting to trying to calm down the dragon, hold the dragon . . . control the dragon.

She stops to get gas and reset her nervous system somewhere around Solvang. But by the time she gets to San Luis Obispo, the dragon is officially winning, and she is on the cusp of losing total control.

Seeing that the next off-ramp is in just two miles, Athena holds on to the steering wheel for dear life and focuses on her breath. Her eyesight now pinholing and her entire body shaking, she slows to forty miles an hour. One mile to go. She slows to thirty miles an hour. Half a mile to go, and Athena balls up her fists and shakes her hands out one by one as she inches toward the off-ramp. Thankful for a slow-moving delivery van, Athena falls in just behind it, following it down the ramp and into a gas station just at the base of the exit.

Once parked, she turns off the car and lets go of the steering wheel. Unlike when this happened on that vista point or even at the many rest stops on the way down, this time there is no Winter Way, no talking, no screaming, no raging, no counting her breaths, no grounding her body. All Athena Winter can do is sit.

And sit.

And sit.

After about thirty minutes, Athena numbly walks inside the gas station mini-mart and buys a sparkling water, hoping it will settle her stomach. She goes back to the car, not wanting to leave Darlene unattended, and takes a long drink. And another. She is calming down and her brain is finally able to form a thought. A single thought so clear-sighted and conclusive that she is unable to reason or argue with it. That single thought is that she can't keep driving and has to figure out another way to get home.

At first, she tries to see if there's a way to get home via city streets or smaller highways. But that quickly becomes a fool's errand when she learns that one of the options is the actual highway where James Dean wrecked his Porsche 550 Spyder and was killed back in 1955. The ridiculousness of this makes Athena bark out a laugh so loud that a woman filling up her tank looks over to see where that ungodly noise came from. But this burst of laughter alleviates the pressure on her chest just enough that she can finally take her first full breath in almost an hour.

Now able to think a bit more clearly, Athena investigates whether she can have the car towed or if she can dump her rental and take a train or plane back up to the Bay Area. But each of those scenarios has some part of it that doesn't quite work—whether it's time or money or her overall inability to start the car without causing yet another incident. She looks over at Darlene.

"It looks like we're stuck," she says. Darlene is quiet. Athena nods and steps out of the car. Closing the door behind her, she leans back. It's just barely nine o'clock in the morning.

As Athena watches the world go by, resigned to her fate of living at this gas station in San Luis Obispo forever, she starts pinning some of the highlights from the last couple of months to a metaphorical corkboard inside her brain in a desperate attempt to do what Rafael Luna told her to do.

She is going to try to figure out what is going on with her.

She pins New Year's Eve. She pins making the pork chop. She pins nothing . . . nothing . . . nothing. She pins Rafael and Valentina's kindness. She pins that terrible yellow hotel in Sausalito. She pins her sisters' silence. She pins her own silence. She pins her dinner at Hills and Valleys. She pins Jenn's scribbled "what do you want?" She pins the Banquet Conference. She pins her conversation with Lola. She pins the converted garage and the rental cars. She pins that perfect day in London with Valentina, Jenn, and Rafael. She pins Rafael's words to her: *Then you're going to have to get some skin in the game. Caring about things is hard. Being all in is heartbreaking sometimes, but isn't it better than whatever you've got going on now?* She pins every article about her that compares her to her mother. She pins her own marginalia in her mother's cookbooks. She pins how good it felt to be the head chef at Northern Trade. She pins *this is just the beginning.* And that's when the pressure in her chest begins to build. Athena brings her hand over her heart and repeats, *"This is just the beginning."* The pressure swells in her chest.

"Come on. You can do this," Athena whispers to herself. "One more time." Another exhale. Another count to six. "Good girl . . . good girl . . . there you go . . ."

And it's not the fear or the desperation that makes Athena Winter start crying in that moment, but the gentle kindness that she finally shows herself when all is lost. Because sometimes it's not a person who tells you the hard truth; it's your own body.

As Athena finally lets herself cry, she understands that while the last couple of months have certainly been hard, it's the ambiguity of where she goes from here that's causing her to come undone.

Because who is she without her mother?

Who is she without Northern Trade?

Or even just . . . who is she?

After several minutes, a woman walks over to Athena and offers her a napkin from a fast-food restaurant. Athena looks up. The woman is tiny, maybe five feet. She's dressed in a fast-food uniform with a name tag that reads CARLY. Her curly black hair is pulled into a tight bun and held back by the bright-red visor that finishes off the fast-food uniform.

"Thank you," Athena says, taking it.

"Did you break down?" Carly asks, gesturing to the car.

"Technically, yes," Athena says, not expanding further.

"Is there anything I can do?" Carly asks.

"Not unless you're heading to San Francisco," Athena says, trying to force her voice to sound as light and jokey as possible.

Carly laughs. "I would much rather go to San Francisco than work a double today," she says, smiling.

"Thank you for the napkin and for . . . being nice to me," Athena says.

"Who hasn't cried at a gas station?" Carly asks. Athena nods and musters up a smile.

"Indeed," Athena says, cringing at her use of the word.

"Okay—" Carly hesitates, but then continues, "Is there anyone you can call?"

"I . . . I'll be fine," Athena makes herself say. Carly nods and smiles, then turns to walk back to her car before pulling out of the gas station with one last friendly wave.

Athena climbs back into the driver's seat and takes a drink of her sparkling water. She finds the stack of napkins in the tote bag Valentina packed for her and blows her nose, opting to use her sleeve to wipe her tears away. Which is when Athena looks down at what she's wearing and realizes that she dressed for a solitary car ride and not whatever this epic journey is turning out to be. Braless, she's wearing a pair of heather-gray sweatpants that she slept in last night and a lumpy brown cable-knit sweater. She's finished off this Outfit of Someone Clearly Having a Breakdown with a pair of old Pumas and a giant scrunchy that's bigger than the hair it's holding. She pushes her filthy glasses further up her nose and turns her giant gray G-Shock watch around on her wrist. She's officially fidgeting. Finally, she pulls her phone out of her sweatpants pocket and dials.

Sloane Winter looks down at her phone and sees that it's Athena calling. No matter what's happened between them in the last couple of months, getting a call from out of nowhere on a random Tuesday at 9:30 a.m. sends Sloane into full Big Sister Mode. Everything that's gone down between them disappears and she answers on the first ring.

"Are you okay?" Sloane asks. This breaks Athena. The tears come back.

"No," Athena squeaks out.

"Where are you?" Sloane asks, her voice urgent but even.

"At a gas station in San Luis Obispo," Athena answers. Looking around at where she's ended up is surreal.

"Are you hurt?"

"No, but I had . . . I've been having these anxiety attacks. I drove to LA to work at Rafael's pop-up, but he fired me. He fired me and I deserved it. So I was driving home . . . or back, I don't have a home . . . but I had a bad attack. A really bad one, so I can't drive anymore. It's not safe. I'm stuck. I don't know what to do. I don't know what to do," Athena says, the shame washing over her.

"Okay," Sloane says. Athena hears her typing on her computer. "Looks like there's a flight from SFO to San Luis Obispo leaving in about an hour and a half. The flight's an hour, so can you sit tight until then?" Her voice is muffled from tucking her phone into the crook of her neck as she furiously types.

"Yeah," Athena says.

"Okay. You're going to be okay." Sloane waits. "Athena?"

"Yeah?"

"You're going to be okay."

"Okay," Athena robotically repeats.

"Text me the address where you are, and I'll be there as soon as I can," Sloane says, still typing.

"Sloane?" Athena says, tears now streaming down her cheeks.

"Yeah?"

"I missed you," Athena says.

Sloane inhales, trying to stave off the rush of emotion. "I missed you, too," she says.

Athena signs off, letting her hand fall to her lap. Within seconds, she slides painlessly into a liminal space where her psyche becomes this fog of every feeling and emotion—each one moving with the other like a school of fish. Since she can't grab onto any one without all the others following, she sits back and watches them swarm.

Athena remembers a day she spent at the beach with her family. As the youngest, she was always the one who wanted to play in the water longest, go out deepest, and adventure farthest. Sloane would play just long enough to tantalize Athena and Jules with her oldest-sibling, elegant presence. Then she'd quit right when things were getting good, labeling whatever they were doing as something that was "for babies." Always wanting to follow her eldest sister, Jules would parrot whatever Sloane said, inevitably leaving Athena to play by herself for hours.

On this day, Athena was playing out in the ocean as she always had. She liked to pretend she was a dolphin diving in and out of the waves. She'd just come up from diving under one wave when another much larger wave crashed over her, pushing her under. She was spun around, twisted, and pulled deeper still until she didn't know which way was up. And just twenty feet from where Athena was fighting for her life, her entire family lazed and laughed on the shore.

Because what no one tells you about drowning is how quiet it is.

After she'd slammed one too many times into the gravelly and rocky ocean floor, Athena finally pushed herself off from it and burst through the water with a desperate gasp of air. She swam to shore and collapsed onto the family's laid-out blanket with her fantastic tale of survival.

As Athena sits dazed in the driver's seat of the stupid rental car in a gas station she hopes to never see again, she remembers back to that day at the beach. How she sat shivering with a towel around her as she looked out over the ocean and marveled at how there was no other life or world outside of the column of ocean water in which she was being tumbled. And how once she made it to shore, everyone expected her to be fine.

But everything is not fine. Everything is so very not fine.

But she could make it fine. This could all be over. And from here on out, her being stuck at this gas station could become one of those funny family stories that's told and retold at Christmas every year. As Athena sits in that driver's seat, the siren's song to move on continues to call to her. That way feels more like something she can control.

The Winter Way.

All she has to do is bandage up the wound and walk on. Then she won't have to admit how afraid she still is, how broken and lost she feels, and how exhausted and weak she is in her bones. Who wants to see that in themselves? It's such a better story to say that you went through something hard, but now you're through it—stronger than ever and safely back on shore. *And here are the three inspirational things I learned along the way.* No one wants to hear about someone who went through something hard and is still struggling.

Athena takes a long drink of her now-flat sparkling water and looks over at Darlene.

"I don't know what I'm going to do," she says. Darlene is quiet.

Athena nods and looks out the window, continuing to watch the world go by. Which is when she sees Sloane and Jules stepping out of the back seat of a car that's just pulled into the gas station. It doesn't seem real, as Athena can't believe she's been sitting in this car for however many hours had to pass to make this be a thing that is happening right now. But before she can think or make a choice that would be more fitting of a Winter or answer the siren's song of fineness, she jumps out of the car, runs over to her two sisters, and crumples into them, crying like she's never cried before.

"Okay . . . It's okay," Sloane says, smoothing Athena's hair.

"We've got you . . . we've got you, Teeny," Jules says, wrapping her arm around Athena's waist and pulling her in close.

Cars pull in and cars pull out. People exit the mini-mart with candy bars and cans of soda, and every single person watches three grown women hugging and crying in the middle of it all without a word.

Because despite what Athena thinks, sobbing and hugging in a gas station is something everyone understands on some level.

CHAPTER SEVENTEEN

The car ride home is both a glimpse into the future and a memory from long past. It is by no means perfect and frustratingly messy at times. Waves of long-held grudges abut new and naked emotions see the light of day for the first time in years. It is a high-wire act, a ballet in three acts, and a boxing match in twelve rounds.

But at its core, for the first time in decades, it is real.

When Athena chose to lean into not being fine, she set the tone for the rest of the trip. And this allowed Sloane and Jules to meet her where she was. Which, of course, was exactly where they were. Not that they would have opened with that.

As the little rental car with a trio of broken sisters speeds through Paso Robles and then on to Salinas, the downloads and more general subjects became fewer and fewer, pushing the sisters into the minefield of material that could threaten their fragile cease-fire.

Sloane and Jules told Athena everything Odette Bankolé had told them, as well as their own resignations and breakthroughs. They spent at least twenty minutes on "See Below" alone.

Athena finally admitted that Maren had offered her her old job back as head chef at Northern Trade. Sloane and Jules couldn't hide their shock. And when they pressed her about her answer, Athena just kept saying that she didn't know. That it was tempting. And that she would "probably say no." Sloane and Jules understood. In fact, Sloane and Jules both fought deep and complicated feelings of envy that they weren't the ones Maren called home.

It felt good to tell each other that they'd been brave. That they saw the light and they were finally on the right side of this thing. Or at least that's what they hoped. Because lingering in the pauses and breaths in between their conversation was a sticky doubt as to whether they could sustain this bravery through what was looking like a rougher and far more uncomfortable road ahead.

There was a lull in the conversation then. Finally, it was Jules who broke the silence, and as was her role in the family, she said The Thing—

"Why hasn't Mom reached out to us? Why hasn't she apologized?" Jules asked, as they sat on low wall at a rest stop just outside Los Gatos.

"I'd like to think it's shame, but—" Athena starts.

"I doubt it." Sloane's voice is clipped.

"How could she go around and have all these deep conversations and not reach out to us?" Jules asks.

"I don't think she went into either of the conversations with Aunt Penny or Dame Jocasta thinking she was going to get told off," Athena says. Jules nods.

"Best case? She's trying to right her wrongs—starting with giving Athena her old job back—before she reaches out so she can show us that she's walking the walk," Sloane says. Jules and Athena look over at her wordlessly.

"Worst case?" Jules asks.

"That Mom is still looking out for herself and only fixing the things that stabilize her empire rather than . . ." Athena trails off.

"Work on building back any kind of relationship with us," Jules finishes.

"Right," Athena says.

They are quiet.

"Would you . . . were you going to ever reach out to me?" Athena asks, unable to look at her two sisters, already hating that she's the one who's going to ruin what's been a lovely and long-over-due few hours.

"Now, that? That was shame," Jules says. Sloane nods.

"Oh," Athena says.

"Reaching out to you meant facing what I'd said—" Sloane starts.

"You were right, though," Athena says, looking down at her bitten and bloody fingernails. "About me."

"No, I wasn't. I'm so sorry," Sloane says. Athena gives a curt nod of acceptance.

"What we did was . . ." Jules trails off.

"Terrible," Sloane finishes, just before excusing herself to take a very interestingly timed trip over to the vending machines.

An incredibly loud family walks by on their way to the large outdoor bathroom, rumbling past like a pack of semitrucks. Jules and Athena are thankful for the noise. But among the welps, howls, and yips of the family's correspondingly loud pair of huskies, the silence between Athena and Jules grows. And in that quiet, Athena begins to doubt. Shrink. Disappear. Jules reaches over and takes Athena's hand. It's awkward, but earnest.

"I realize I'm bad at the touching thing—" Jules starts, but Athena laughs. "I'll get better." Jules gathers herself as Athena waits. "But I . . . I am . . . I'm so sorry. I'm just so sorry."

Athena grips Jules's hand as her eyes well up once more. The woman taking the huskies for their bathroom break glances over with a concerned look. She's caught, so she switches to eyeing Jules and Athena with a series of furtive, sneaking glances disguised as a one-sided yet somehow escalating conversation with the otherwise engaged dogs.

"I'm sorry, too. You tried to tell me not to do the pork chop, but I wouldn't listen. I thought you were just being an asshole—"

"I mean, I was an asshole . . . am an asshole," Jules says.

"But that doesn't mean you weren't also right," Athena argues.

"Hm," Jules says, perking up just a bit.

"Two things can be true," Athena says in her best game show host voice.

"Welcome to *Two Things Can Be True*! The game show where we test whether . . . two things can be true. In our first round, we'll answer the question: Can your mother both hate and love you at the same time? Let's welcome our guests!" Jules announces, her hand outstretched in a robotic, presentational way. Athena laughs, but the truth of that hurts.

"Oof," she says, shaking her head.

"And for our second round, we'll dig into how a woman can hate the man she's married to, but love flaunting being married to him in front of other women to make herself feel better!" Jules says, her voice breaking. Athena looks over at Jules, who lets out a long exhale and can only shake her head, looking away.

"Jules—"

"Did I ever tell you how much I hate black coffee?" Jules asks, trying to find a place to unwind all that's happened.

"Black coffee is delicious. Those pour-overs you were making were great," Athena says.

"Ugh, you would say that," Jules says.

"Got us some snacks," Sloane announces as she walks back carrying an overflowing armload of candy, snacks, and beverages for everyone. She doles out each person's exact favorites from memory. Jules gets a box of Hot Tamales and a Diet Coke. Athena gets a lemonade and some pretzel sticks. Sloane has a real Coke and Doritos Nacho Cheese. She plops down next to Athena, setting her Coke down carefully on the low wall.

Jules and Athena look down at their bounties. The kid versions of them would have lost their minds if they were ever presented with this magnificent, intricate combination of their most favorite treats.

It's the Road Food Holy Grail.

As Athena, Jules, and Sloane Winter sit on that low wall at a rest stop luxuriating in their snack-food plunder, passersby would have gotten a glimpse of what the trio looked like back when they were kids. Dangling feet, sticky fingers, and just enough chip dust at the corners of their mouths to let you know where they've been. It's a moment so free and unplanned that it defies time and space.

But as the Winter sisters continue to sit on that low wall, what they don't say is without their mother telling them what to do and who to be—or more accurately, telling them what not to do and who not to be—they're completely at a loss about where to go from here and who they even really are. Sure, they've made plans and looked at storefronts in Tiburon, but they've yet to actually make any of that a reality. This new life, this new path, this new world without Maren Winter is still only academic. And when pressed, none of the Winter sisters will even state outright whether if their mother should ask them to come back . . . if they wouldn't say yes.

"I think I'm going to be sick," Jules says, putting down the empty box of Hot Tamales.

"I know, but it tasted so good," Athena says, breaking a pretzel stick in half and putting them in her mouth like walrus tusks. It gets a laugh out of Jules, as it always has.

"Do you know how long it's been since I've had any of this stuff?" Sloane asks, holding up her empty can of Coke.

"Too long," Athena says.

With all the snacks now eaten, the sisters linger in the beautiful, almost drunken haze. No one wants to break the spell of this moment. Because deep down each of the Winter sisters believes that as soon as they get back into that rental car and drive the last hour into the Bay Area, everything is going to change. Including them. And regardless of how deeply they now understand how corrupted they were, it doesn't make it any less sad to leave behind and have to mourn the life they once lived.

"It wasn't all bad," Athena finally says.

"Not at all," Sloane says with a sad smile.

"I mean, a lot of it was pretty terrible," Jules says.

"Yeah," Athena agrees.

"But not all bad," Jules allows.

They are quiet.

Finally, Sloane reaches out her hand and both Jules and Athena know to hand her their trash. They've been doing just that for as long as they can remember. But before she goes to throw everything away, she stops. Overcome with this new but somehow old feeling, she looks back at Jules and Athena and can't find the words. She wants to let her little sisters know that they're going to be okay, that whatever happens, they'll stick together. That she'll protect them as she always has . . . or should have. But all she can find are bigger and bigger feelings, and that makes her feel further away from the words. Sloane's mouth is just far enough open that maybe if she's still, the right words will slip out.

"I know," Jules says, looking up at her. Sloane exhales. "We know." Sloane smiles. While Jules doesn't know exactly what Sloane is feeling, she's certain it's in the same overwhelmed, gooey, terrified ballpark where she is right now.

Sloane continues on to the trash can as if on a cloud. But this weightlessness only adds to her discomfort. Sloane has always favored the utility of a ballast, the beauty of being grounded, and the divinity of order. And she's confident that, if she's brave enough, she'll somehow be able to find her old friends in the new life she's now committed to forging.

The rest of the drive back north is one of traffic, rain, and—despite living in the Bay Area their whole life—Sloane somehow getting on the wrong freeway ending in 80. But as night falls Sloane insists they stop by Athena's temporary converted garage apartment to pick up her things and, along with a now house-less Jules, convinces both sisters to stay with her and Lærke until they figure out where they want to live. The kids are barely able to contain their excitement when both aunts walk in that night and announce that, not only is Athena making dinner for everyone, but she and Jules are staying for a sleepover.

Fending off a real hard-sell pitch by Minnie and Freja to have Jules and Athena sleep on the trundle beds in their room, Sloane instead puts Jules and Athena up in their own personal guest rooms. Guest rooms that are all but personally designed for each of her sisters. Although she never said anything, it's clear that Sloane prepared for this very instance—however subconsciously—well over ten years ago, when she and Lærke first bought the house.

Using ingredients already in Sloane and Lærke's house, Athena makes a simple carbonara for the family. She serves the lush pasta with steaming garlic bread and a fresh side salad. It's home cooking at its finest and every ounce of love Athena put into the meal warms each and every person seated around the table.

Dinner is a raucous affair. And it's all Sloane and Lærke can do to get the kids bathed, read to, and tucked in just a bit past their bedtimes. Which is when Lærke breaks out the good bottle of wine and pours everyone a glass while they share cleanup duty. As Sloane washes the dishes and Jules dries, Athena puts the dishes away—always the Winter sister who could reach the highest cupboards and cabinets. Everyone is being cordial, but still guarded and on their best behavior. And no one really knows how to broach the subject of even one of the several elephants in the room, until finally—

"Have Sloane and Jules told you about the market?" Lærke asks Athena. Sloane brings over another bottle of wine and sets out an after-dinner cheese board with mouthwatering offerings from the Marin Fresh Cheese Company and Point Reyes Farmstand Cheese. Now, segueing from buzzed to downright drunk, the four women settle in around the dining room table, all half-masted eyes, sniggering giggles, and loose lips.

"No," Athena says, picking at the cheese board.

"Well, I'm sure they'll tell you in due time," Lærke says with a long, weary sigh.

"Is this an errand for tomorrow? I can go before I return the rental. I'm fine on city streets," Athena says.

"Sloane and me—" Jules starts, popping a dried apricot into her mouth.

"Sloane and I," Sloane corrects and immediately purses her lips. Everyone looks over at her. "I'm sorry. I'm tired, and when I get tired, I correct people's grammar." The room loosens. But Sloane's admonition has peeled back a layer of the chummy atmosphere, revealing a tension humming just underneath today's loveliness.

Jules continues, "Me and Sloane want to open up a neighborhood market. You know like that one—"

"That sold the spumoni ice cream," Athena finishes, her face lighting up.

"Ugh, you and spumoni ice cream. We were remembering those great sandwiches they made," Sloane adds.

"Do you remember how they used to squeeze fresh orange juice? So the whole place smelled like fresh oranges?" Athena asks.

"I'd forgotten about that," Sloane says.

"Me too," Jules says.

"And the peanut butter—" Athena starts.

"Oh my god, I hated that peanut butter," Jules says.

"They would grind the peanuts right there and then add the oil, but then you'd have to stir them both together. . . and every damn time, that oil went all down your arm," Athena says.

"I never remembered why exactly I hated peanut butter so much, but—" Sloane starts.

"Yeah. It's because we ate terrible peanut butter for the entirety of our childhood," Jules says.

"I was actually thinking that a funny amuse-bouche at my new restaurant would just be offering a jar of peanut butter to the table and letting everyone take a spoonful," Athena says. Everyone in the room freezes.

"Did you just say *your* restaurant?" Jules asks.

"I mean . . ." Athena struggles to find the words or if she did or . . . "I still don't know about, you know, what I'm going to say to Mom, but yeah . . . I guess I'm kind of thinking about it now?"

"You've never talked about your own restaurant before," Sloane says.

"Now, don't spook her. Maybe if we leave a cardboard box out on the porch with a blanket in it, the little stray cat will sit in it and tell us all some menu items," Jules jokes, elaborately sneaking a reach back over to the wine bottle to top herself off. She holds out the bottle. Lærke takes her up on her offer.

"A scoop of peanut butter out of a jar is hardly a recipe," Athena says.

"No, but it's a start," Sloane says, sounding a little too much like Jenn Nishimura.

"It's a start . . ." Athena trails off.

"But?" Jules asks.

"I've been thinking a lot about what Rafael said about my not having skin in the game," Athena says, her words slurring just a bit.

Jules pulls out her phone.

"'Skin in the game' sounds like it came from Olde English or maybe something naval. It's always something naval. Let me—" Jules gets lost in her phone, just drunk enough to find the etymology of the phrase the most important thing she needs to understand right now.

"It's actually from the '80s. It's a finance thing," Athena says.

"What?" Athena nods. "Well, that's super boring," Jules says, dramatically putting her phone away.

"No, I know. I've already processed my disappointment," Athena says, laughing. Her teeth are turning a deep purple from the red wine.

"So, as you were saying?" Sloane asks.

"To have skin in the game, I have to care. Which means I have to find and develop recipes that mean something to me. I have to envision an idea of a restaurant that's personal. I have to choose the location and build a menu and what the waitstaff will be wearing and what the gardens will grow and which vendors to work with. And then I have to hire each person who will work there and train them up how I want them to do the job. It must mean something. All of it. And once I have all that, then I have to put my name on the restaurant. *My* name, not Mom's. I have to stand in front and not hide out in the kitchen."

"That sounds heavy, *min kære*," Lærke says. Athena smiles at Lærke's constancy and kindness.

"It is, but it is a weight I have to carry if . . ." Athena trails off.

"If what?" Jules asks.

"I don't even know. Oh my god, I don't know what all this is for," Athena admits.

"Purpose?" Jules asks, with a drunken shrug.

"Peace? Contentment?" Lærke serenely offers.

"Joy and family," Sloane throws out, thinking of what she herself is striving for.

"Nah, no." Athena thinks. The table is quiet. "I don't think I'm even there yet. I . . . I have to get to know myself first." She nods to herself. "Yeah, that's it. I want to know myself, so that I know what my purpose is, not Mom's. I don't even know what peace looks like for me. I've seen flickers, but . . . and I . . ." Athena looks around the home and family that Sloane and Lærke have built. "And I wouldn't even know where to begin with actual joy and my own family."

"So, what does . . . what does this all mean?" Sloane asks.

"I don't know—but mostly I . . . need to find my voice. I need to figure out what I like and what I want," Athena says.

"Yeah, I want that, too, sure mmmmm yep, voice and self and traveling . . . shhhh, skiiiiin in the gaaaaame . . . but I also and another thing—" Jules waves her drunk jelly arms around and closes her eyes as she searches for the right word.

"Okay, this is—" Sloane says, laughing and sliding Jules's ever-full wineglass away from her.

"I want to win. Is that so bad? I want to fuckin' win. Wait, oops. Sorry to your babies and my bad language. I know shhhh, but—I know it's petty, I know . . . it's . . . but I'm pffffffflt—workin' on it, you know? Nothin' wrong with it," Jules says, sitting straight up.

"However far we get, us apples never fall that far from the tree," Sloane says.

"Apples and trees," Athena says, raising her glass to toast the hyper-competitive DNA gifted to each one of them at birth by their mother.

"That's not a bad name for the market," Sloane says, scribbling the words down on a nearby notepad before her drunken mind permanently forgets them.

"I want . . . I see this . . . moment . . . future moment in my head where I'm probably . . . okayyyyyyy, obviously I look amazing and we're someplace nice and there's fancy people and—" Jules takes a swig of her wine. Forgets that she's talking. She continues, "We're doing great and everyone is 'ohhh JulesandSloaneWinter are the best at markets and groceries; what they're doing is amazing, and oh ho ho, look at Maren Winter being so sad she was mean and there's . . . they're clapping for us . . . oh, us yes you and she . . . Mom gets it, you know? She gets how much it hurt . . . how much it hurts . . . I want her to get how much it hurts," Jules says, growing melancholy. Lærke reaches over and pulls Jules in close. Jules melts into her.

"She may never get that, sweetie," Sloane says quietly.

"But if she did, maybe she wouldn't do it anymore," Jules says.

"Maybe," Sloane says.

"Maybe," Jules repeats in a whisper.

"Have you thought about what you'd say to her?" Athena asks.

"I have a speech," Sloane says.

"She practices it," Lærke adds.

"Obviously we need to hear it," Jules slurs.

"Little dress rehearsal?" Athena asks.

"Wouldn't hurt," Lærke adds.

Sloane Winter stands up, sways a bit, and realizing how drunk she is immediately plops back down in her chair.

"It's all fun and games until Jules is not the drunkest one," Jules says.

"It's all fun and games until Jules starts referring to herself in the third person," Athena jokes.

"Jules thinks that's funny," Jules says, giggling.

Sloane steadies herself on the dining room table, pushing herself up into a standing position. Sloane fixes her clothes, gathers herself, and steps to the head of the table, positioning her hands like she's holding something.

"She's holding a trophy," Lærke clarifies.

"Oh, we know. I knew exactly what that was," Jules says. Athena nods in agreement.

"Obviously," Athena says, laughing.

They are quiet. Sloane pushes back her shoulders and locks eyes with their invisible mother.

"Oh, hi. Thank you, it was quite a surprise." Sloane pauses as invisible Maren says something. "Please stop crying. I accept your apology, and I forgive you because you gave me the greatest education of my life. You taught me how not to be a mother. You taught me how not to be a sister. You taught me how not to be a wife. You taught me how not to be a friend. You taught me how not to be a mentor. And you taught me how not to be a leader. You taught me everything I'll ever need to know about what not to be, and for that I am forever in your debt." Sloane waves to an invisible person across the invisible room. Jules looks to see who it is. Sloane continues, "Have a good night."

Jules, Athena, and Lærke quietly applaud as to not wake the kids up. Sloane smiles and bows. But giving the speech has taken its toll on her, and as she sits down across from Lærke, she empties her wineglass.

"What if we fail?" Sloane asks, looking down at the table.

"We won't," Jules says.

"We have to show her. That we can do this without her," Sloane says.

"We will. Don't worry," Jules says, reaching across the table to awkwardly take Sloane's hand.

"Do we, though?" Athena asks.

"Do we, though, what?" Jules asks.

"Do we need to show her?" Athena asks.

"I know I'm supposed to say no, but—" Jules trails off, unable to confess the hardest truth of all—that it's permissible to be cast out and to fail only if you rise from those ashes stronger and better than ever. That you "show them all." Because a great loss is only noble if it's followed by an even greater win. But to fall and stay down? To fall and admit you're hurt and need some time to heal? It's just not done.

"Haven't we spent enough of our lives using her as our sun and moon?" Athena asks.

"She's not our sun and moon," Sloane says.

"Then what is she?"

"That, but meaner," Jules says.

"What?"

"I get what you're saying, but the sun and moon are beautiful and she's not being beautiful," Jules says, slurring even more now.

"I think what Jules is trying to say is that, like my dumb little speech—"

"Your speech wasn't dumb," Lærke says. The two share a tender moment. It breaks Jules's heart and begins to pull her under.

"That she's a cautionary tale. Someone we compare ourselves to as a reminder," Sloane says.

"So we're just going to continue to carry her throughout our lives?" Athena asks.

"No, it's not like that," Sloane says.

"And also aren't you the one who's going back to work for her?" Jules slurs.

"Maybe not," Athena says.

"Still pissed she didn't ask me," Jules mumbles to herself.

"I know, sweetie," Sloane says.

"As hard as it's been, we've finally freed ourselves, and now we're saying we have to keep our shackles on to remember what being caged felt like. Can't we just be free?" Athena asks.

"Free is scary," Jules says under her breath.

"What?" Athena asks.

"It's easier . . . come onnnnnn . . . Maybe it's easier to trade a little freedom so we can just see how good we're doing," Jules says, filling her glass again. "Just have her in our pocket for measuring purposes." She elaborately mimes taking a tiny Maren Winter out of her pocket, measuring something against her, and then giving a big thumbs-up.

"But don't we . . . or aren't we trying to have that in here?" Athena asks, putting her hand on her chest. Jules and Sloane are quiet. "I'm not saying we walk away or ignore her or don't forgive her or not have her in our lives, but I refuse to have my entire life be about what goddamn Maren Winter thinks of me." Lærke smiles at Athena and nods. This is clearly something she and Sloane have talked about.

"I'm not strong enough," Jules says.

"The hell you aren't," Athena says. Jules is taken aback by Athena's intensity. "You survived. Do you know how strong you had to be to get here?"

"I'm only here because Sloane asked me to come with her in Oxfordshire," Jules says.

"But you said yes," Athena says.

"I said yes," Jules repeats.

"You said yes," Sloane repeats. Jules smiles.

"We can do this," Athena says.

"I don't know, Teeny," Jules says.

"It's one thing to be strong enough to beat Mom. It's a whole other level to be strong enough to not need her. And I'm not sure . . ." Sloane trails off.

"Together," Athena says, reaching out her hands to her two sisters. They take them. Lærke brings her hand to her chest, overwhelmed at seeing Sloane accept Athena's proposition. It's all she's ever wanted.

"Together," Jules says.

"Together," Sloane says.

CHAPTER EIGHTEEN

"Wake up. Honey, wake up," Sloane says, shaking Athena awake. The room is pitch black.

"What time is it?" Athena rasps, squinting her eyes open.

"It's just after 2:00 a.m.," Sloane says.

"Why are you in my room?" Athena asks.

"Because you're the only sober one and we need to drive somewhere," Sloane says.

"I don't know if you've heard, but me and driving are in a fight," Athena says, turning over onto her side and away from Sloane. "Also, it's late and you're drunk. If you want a snack or something—"

"Teeny, we gotta go and you gotta take us," Jules says, turning on the flashlight on her phone and shining it right into Athena's face. Athena bolts up, shielding her eyes from the blast of light. Jules drunkenly tries to keep the flashlight on Athena's face as she moves around. Finally, Sloane closes the door to Athena's guest room and turns on the lights.

Looming above Athena are Sloane and Jules, both wearing their winter coats, purses slung over their shoulders, and car keys tightly grasped in Sloane's fingers. Athena leans over to her nightstand, finds her glasses, and puts them on.

"What is wrong with you two?" Athena asks, sitting up in bed.

"We got a call from the security guard at Central Trade. He says he hears glass breaking inside," Sloane says.

"Did you tell him to call the police?" Athena asks.

"He can't call the police," Jules says.

"Why not?" Athena asks.

"Because it's Mom inside breaking the glass," Sloane says, extending the keys out to Athena.

"What?" Athena asks.

"Just come on. Please," Sloane says. Athena takes the keys, slips on her shoes, and follows her two drunken sisters out of Sloane's house and to the driveway, where she's the only one sober enough to drive over to their mother's new restaurant to see why she's breaking glass at two in the morning.

The drive to the Ferry Building is taken up with Sloane and Athena trying to keep Jules from eating the little cookie and cracker crumbs shoved into the back seats. Apparently, Jules found half a Goldfish cracker as they crossed the Golden Gate Bridge, and from then on she was dead set on finding "some more where that came from" because she was "feeling a bit noshy." As Athena pulls onto the Embarcadero, she sees the lit-up Ferry Building in the black of night. Because she didn't go to the Central Trade soft launch, tonight will be the first time Athena sets foot in the doomed eatery.

They find amazing parking—something they all comment on, no matter how wasted Sloane and Jules are—and see the security guard standing just outside the two large front doors of Central Trade.

"Thank you so much for calling us," Sloane says, approaching the man.

"I didn't know who else to call," he says, looking worried.

"We really appreciate it," Athena says.

"'ppreciate it," Jules repeats.

"She's been in there for about an hour. We talked for a bit, but then I started hearing the glass breaking and—"

"You did the right thing calling us," Sloane says. The security guard nods, pulls his large key ring from where it's connected to his belt, and unlocks the two large front doors as quietly as he can.

"Good luck," he says, backing away once the door has been unlocked.

Sloane, Jules, and Athena step inside Central Trade just as a huge shard of chartreuse glass hits the light wood flooring with a crash.

"Holy shit!" Sloane yells, throwing out her arm to protect Jules and Athena from the debris.

Looking up high into the rafters, the three Winter sisters see that the giant green orchid glass installation has finally been installed only to now be destroyed elegant shard by elegant shard. It still looks like an orchid, but with slightly fewer petals. Just below the nineteen-foot chandelier is an assortment of green glass shards, and what looks to be an accumulation of every kitchen tool and/or appliance in the entirety of Central Trade.

"Sloane?" Maren calls out from the balcony.

The three Winter sisters look up and see Maren Winter standing on the balcony, a meat cleaver in one hand and a heavy ceramic mug in the other.

"Mom?" Sloane asks, calling up to Maren.

"You'd think the meat cleaver would be better at this, but—" Maren holds the heavy ceramic mug in her hand, cocks her arm back, and throws it right at the giant green orchid. Sloane grabs Athena and Jules, pulling them out of the danger zone just as the mug hits one of the lower petals and causes a brand-new explosion of glass. "Actually I've found these mugs are really the best for this."

"Mom, what are you doing?" Athena yells up.

"What does it look like I'm doing?" Maren asks, throwing another mug. The glass hits the floor with another crash as Sloane, Jules, and Athena step farther back.

"She's got you there," Jules says.

"Mom—" Sloane says.

"That is my legacy!" Maren yells, pointing at the orchid.

"What?" Athena asks.

"This is my legacy!" Maren yells, throwing another ceramic mug. Another crash as two giant petals peel off the installation and crash to the floor.

"Mom, that's not your legacy—" Sloane starts.

"It's just a giant glass flower," Jules adds.

"No, that's where you're wrong," Maren says, throwing another ceramic mug. It misses the chandelier but hits the lovely wooden flooring with a crash.

"How many mugs does she have up there?" Athena asks.

"Literally all of them. That's where the coffee bar is," Sloane says.

"Really? That's a weird place for it," Athena says.

"Right?" Jules asks.

"Can we focus up here?" Sloane asks.

"They just got finished installing it tonight. Had to fly technicians in from Italy. Took them hours. And I was just sitting watching them do it. They thought I was being quiet because I was in awe. Kept saying 'Bellissima!' over and over again. But I just kept thinking, What kind of asshole orders a nineteen-foot orchid made out of glass?" Maren says, hurling another mug, hitting it dead center and causing another explosion of glass.

"You did," Athena says. Sloane and Jules look over at her.

Maren falls silent. She lets her arm drop to her side. "I did," she says.

"Mom, please come down here," Sloane says.

"Leave the mugs," Jules adds.

"Mom, please." Sloane's voice is soft.

Maren sets the ceramic mug onto the railing, and it immediately slips off and falls to the ground just below.

"Saw that one coming," Jules whispers to Athena.

Maren looks down to where the mug fell and shakes her head. She stands back up, neatly tucks her hair behind her ears, and with a sigh, makes her way down.

As Maren Winter gets to the bottom of the stairs, she walks behind the counter and crouches down so Sloane, Jules, and Athena can no longer see her.

"Is she . . . is she hiding?" Sloane asks.

"I mean, we know where she is," Jules says.

"Mom?" Athena calls out.

Maren pops up behind the counter with a bottle of red wine in one hand and a corkscrew in the other. She shakes them both around like she's just arrived at a wild bachelorette night out and she's brought the drinks. Maren comes out from behind the counter, picks her way through the broken glass and mugs, various cutlery, and pots and pans that litter the entire ground floor of Central Trade. She stops at a table just next to where her daughters are standing. Far from the destroyed glass orchid. She puts the wine bottle on the table and deftly opens it. She offers the cork to the girls. Jules takes it.

"Mom—" Sloane starts.

"Anyone want any?" Maren asks.

"Yeah, all right," Jules says, reaching out for the bottle. Sloane gives Jules a look as Maren passes the bottle to her. Jules takes a long swig and passes it back. Maren takes an even longer swig.

"So, you were sitting here watching them install the orchid," Athena leads.

"It's one thing to read that something is nineteen feet high. It's a whole other thing to actually see how big nineteen feet is," Maren says, wiping her mouth of any leftover wine.

All three of Maren Winter's daughters look up at the giant orchid. Even in its half-destroyed state, it's still a massive installation. And even though Central Trade was designed to be light and airy, high rafters and minimalist—the giant green orchid seems to drag everything into it like a black hole. It should be beautiful. It should be awe inspiring. But all it is . . . is big.

"So you started throwing mugs at it?" Athena asks.

"No, actually. I was just sitting here and something fell off it. A screw or probably a tool that one of the technicians left on one of the rafters. It hit one of the petals and a little tiny sliver of glass hit the floor with a . . . *tink* sound. I don't know why, but hearing that glass break felt good. And I haven't felt good in a long time. So I wanted to do it more," Maren says, taking another long swig of her wine.

"Mom, you can't just break things—" Sloane starts.

"Can't I, though?" Maren asks, making very pointed eye contact with each of her daughters. They are quiet.

"Why don't you just say you're sorry?" Jules asks finally. Sloane and Athena look from Jules to their mother.

"For what?" Maren asks.

"What?" Jules asks.

"For what?" Maren asks again.

"Are you kidding me?" Jules asks.

"For what?" Maren asks again.

A long moment passes as Sloane, Jules, and Athena all look to one another. Overwhelmed by the question.

"Mom—" Sloane begins.

"It's terrifying getting older. I think you think you understand— with your cute little backaches and obsessing about that one time some kid called you 'ma'am,' but I'm becoming invisible. Me. Maren Winter. Is becoming invisible. I haven't been invisible a day in my whole life. And now, every day I disappear a little more." Maren looks around the full expanse of Central Trade. "This was supposed to . . . I just wanted them to see me. I needed to be seen. If only"—Maren takes a long swig of her wine—"one last time."

Everyone is quiet. For a long time. Then—

"Nah," Athena says.

"What?" Maren asks, whipping around. Sloane and Jules look over at Athena.

"You don't get to dim all of us so you can shine brighter. You don't get to cut everyone else down so you're taller. And you sure as hell don't get to erase everyone who built and worked to lift you up so only you get to be seen. Your obsession with yourself has corrupted you. *Is* corrupting you," Athena says, stepping forward. Behind her Jules reaches across and takes Sloane's hand.

"You've been a real asshole, Mom," Jules says.

"An asshole who's given everything so you three could have a better life," Maren argues.

Jules barks out a laugh. "You're such a liar. You've given everything so you could have a better life. You. It's always been about you."

"No. No, honey, it hasn't," Maren says, her voice a bit softer.

"Well, then that's what it became. What you became," Jules says, standing her ground.

"It's interesting," Maren starts.

"I really doubt that the next thing you say is going to actually be interesting," Jules says.

"For three people who are apparently so disgusted by their own mother, you sure have learned a lot from me," Maren says, draining the bottle.

Both Jules and Athena look to Sloane. A tentative, crooked smile curls across her face as she steps forward, just as Maren shambles back over behind the counter in search of another bottle of wine.

"Oh, hi. Thank you, it was quite a surprise." Sloane's voice is a whisper as she begins the speech she's practiced a thousand times in the mirror. Maren ignores her eldest daughter.

"You got this," Jules says. Sloane takes a deep breath and, just as she had earlier that evening, positions her hands like she's holding something. Maren gets another bottle from behind the counter, pulls the cork free, and starts walking back over to where Sloane is standing.

"Please stop crying. I accept your apology—" Sloane robotically says.

Maren looks over at Jules and Athena in confusion. No one is crying. No one has apologized.

The Winter Way.

Sloane presses on, her voice a little bit louder. "I forgive you because you gave me the greatest education of my life. You taught me how not to be a mother. You taught me how not to be a sister. You taught me how not to be a wife. You taught me how not to be a friend. You taught me how not to be a mentor. And you taught me how not to be a leader. You taught me everything I'll ever need to know about what not to be, and for that I am forever in your debt." Sloane waves to an invisible person across the invisible room. Maren looks to see who it is. Sloane continues, "Have a good night."

"I also taught you how to be cutthroat and make a pork chop instead of pork belly. Taught you how to be shrewd and give Lola Tadese unlimited access to a crumbling empire so you could sit on the throne all by yourself. And I even taught you how to lie to yourself and say that all these bad things you're doing would be worth it in the end. Didn't I?" Maren asks.

Sloane, Jules, and Athena all nod.

"Well, you're welcome," Maren says, raising the latest bottle of wine in a toast before taking a long swig.

"Great, so we're all assholes. What happens now?" Jules asks.

"Well, what happens now is Aunt Josephine and the CEO of East Bay Soups led the board of directors in a vote of no confidence just after being informed that my overspending on Central Trade—and neglect of everything else—put the Winter Group in danger of bankruptcy. Lola's article was all she needed," Maren says. Jules and Sloane share a knowing look. Fucking Aunt Josephine swooping in with their goddamned plan.

"Lola's article told the truth," Athena says.

"I know, but it doesn't mean it wasn't painful," Maren says pointedly.

"Not just for you, Mom," Sloane says.

Maren looks at the broken glass that covers the floor.

"Well, maybe Aunt Josephine can clean all this up, including my legacy," she says, kicking a large shard into the pile.

"We're also your legacy!" Jules yells.

Everyone looks at Jules.

"We're also your legacy!" Jules yells again.

"And Aunt Josephine can't clean that up," Sloane says.

"That's on you," Athena adds.

"You three have already made it abundantly clear that you want no part of my legacy," Maren fires back.

"You're still not hearing me," Jules says.

"I've heard everything loud and clear," Maren says, kicking another shard of glass.

"Okay, let me put this as plainly as possible, so even you can grasp what I'm trying to say here." Maren's gaze hardens as Jules holds up both of her hands. "So, over here is all of the truly amazing things you've achieved in your professional life. More women in kitchens! Innovation awards named after you! Smashing the patriarchy and revolutionizing the entire culinary world." Jules circles her hand around. "This legacy? All good."

"Julienne, this is becoming—" Maren's voice is a low growl.

"Over here, however," Jules says, circling her other hand around. "Threatened by your own daughters! Erasing Aunt Penny from the DNA of Northern Trade's success! Being an all-around egomaniacal tyrant who is so insecure that she not only fires her own kid on New Year's Eve but then takes potshots at her after she had the audacity to win an award." Jules shakes that hand around violently. "This. This is what I'm talking about. This is the legacy that's broken." Athena looks over at Jules, tears welling up in her eyes. Jules steps back, standing almost in front of Athena, as if to protect her from whatever Maren retaliates with. Athena reaches over and takes her hand. Jules tightens her grip around Athena's as she pulls her closer.

"Does that legacy even matter to you, Mom?" Sloane asks.

Maren looks down. Surrounded by broken glass. She picks up a shard with a long, weary sigh.

"How does one even begin to clean that up," Maren says, her voice an angry whisper.

"Do you mean how do *you* even begin to clean that up?" Jules corrects.

"Yes, fine. How do I even begin to clean that up?" Maren asks.

Jules lets go of Athena's hand and walks over to her mother. She takes the shard of glass out of her hand. She holds it up.

"You can thank Sloane for giving you your first green orchid." Jules bends down and picks up another shard. "You can apologize to Teeny for not even trying her pork chop." Jules reaches over to a nearby table and picks up another shard of glass. "And you can acknowledge that the photo you sent to Dame Jocasta to end your retrospective at the Banquet—a photo you've said time and time again is your favorite—was taken by me. That I was there." Jules carefully hands the three shards of glass to her mother. Maren looks down at them as Jules steps back next to her sisters.

The four Winter women are quiet. For a long time. Maren shifts the shards of glass in her hands, finally setting them down on a nearby chair. Sloane, Jules, and Athena watch her every move, tension buzzing through them like high voltage. Without saying a word, each of the Winter sisters vows to stay quiet, to not offer any help or consolation or break the tension in any way. Whatever happens next has to be up to Maren Winter and Maren Winter alone.

Maren grabs the wine bottle off the table and takes a long swig, swiping her mouth with the back of her hand. She holds the bottle limply as she looks upon each of her daughters individually, noticing for the first time they defiantly hold her gaze.

Maren recognizes the things Jules has asked her to say are fair. Which is why she's growing frustrated for being unable to say them. Every time she tries to drag the words out, they claw their way back down to the shadowy corners of herself in a desperate attempt to stay hidden and keep the truth of what she's done buried along with them.

Maren scans the thousands of shards that litter every inch of Central Trade, realizing now that each one symbolizes something reprehensible that she's done to someone she supposedly loves. Becoming overwhelmed, Maren looks high up into the soaring rafters of the restaurant. Away from the shards of glass. Away from the defiant gazes of her daughters. Away from the broken legacy that lurches ever closer to the sharp edge of a cliff.

Time stops.

Maren Winter clears her throat.

"Thank you," she says, looking at Sloane. Sloane's face softens, but the slight furrow in her brow lets Maren know that Sloane's guard is still very much in place.

"You're welcome," Sloane says in a choked whisper.

"I'm sorry," Maren says, unable at first to meet Athena's gaze. Athena is silent. Waiting. Finally, Maren looks up and the pain in her youngest daughter's eyes sends a jolt through her. She lets out a ragged exhale. Not yet trusting herself to let her mother off with unearned words of absolution, Athena chooses to simply nod in acceptance.

Jules can't help but lean forward, starving for her mother's long-awaited words. She forces herself to lean back, wobbling slightly in the process. Sloane reaches out to steady her.

"I see you," Maren says, nodding.

Jules takes in an urgent, raspy breath, her shoulders touching her ears. Tears spring to her eyes as she struggles to keep her composure. "Thank you," she says with a breathy exhale.

The Winter women stand amid the ruins of Central Trade, firmly in uncharted territory. The moment sags around them as they grow uncomfortable.

"So, what happens now?" Sloane asks, always the one to put the train back on the rails.

"They're going to shut down Central Trade. We can't lose Northern Trade, so I'm going to sell my house and a few other assets to make up the losses," Maren says.

"Where will you live?" Sloane asks.

"Well, I've heard there's a pretty nice little studio on the grounds. I can live there until I get off whatever probation Aunt Josephine's got me on and I figure if you're not going to come back as head chef," Maren says to Athena.

"What would you do?" Athena asks.

Maren smiles. A real smile. "I would open my own restaurant."

"Me too," Athena says.

"Then Salma can step in as head chef and—"

"And then what?" Sloane asks.

"I mean, my publisher has been asking for me to write a memoir," Maren says.

"Mom, you can't be serious," Jules says.

A large shard of glass crashes to the floor inches from where they're standing. Maren looks from it to her three daughters.

"Who doesn't like a little comeback story?" Maren says with a wink.

"Well, you'll have plenty of time to write it now, I guess," Jules says.

"After you clean up your legacy, of course," Athena adds, motioning at the glass. A tight smile curls across Maren's face as she turns to walk toward the utility closet in search of trash bags, brooms, and dustpans. But before she gets a few feet, Sloane cuts in.

"We'll leave you to it then," she says, surprising everyone.

"You're not—" Maren stops herself. "Of course. Right."

"You'll let us know when you're ready to talk more," Sloane says.

"Yep," Maren says. Her clipped response lets each of her daughters know that there was more than a little sliver of Maren Winter who thought her sincerity over the last few minutes might fully exonerate her.

Sloane nods and shoots a pointed look over at both Jules and Athena. Falling in behind her like little ducklings, they follow their eldest sister as she strides out of Central Trade, leaving Maren Winter alone with her broken legacy.

As Sloane, Jules, and Athena walk along the Embarcadero, they continue to turn back toward Central Trade, watching their mother move around the restaurant, sweeping and clearing up the glass.

"Should we be worried about this whole memoir thing?" Jules asks, her breath puffing out in front of her in the freezing early-morning air.

"We'll cross that bridge when we get to it," Sloane says.

"Together," Athena adds.

"Together," Sloane and Jules answer.

"But not Mom," Jules says, her voice playful and arch.

"No, not Mom," Sloane says, laughing. Even Athena cracks a smile.

But as they pile into Sloane's car, each one of the Winter sisters secretly thinks, *Maybe*.

Just maybe.

ACKNOWLEDGMENTS

I am writing these acknowledgments on my birthday. I didn't plan it; it just worked out that way. I couldn't be happier, because for me this book is magic. It made me rediscover myself. It taught me about creativity and slowness. It gave me something to live for as I fought cancer. It gave me hope as I wrote in the early-morning hours of each day before I had to wade into my day job.

In short, this book saved me.

It's humbling as someone who calls themselves a writer to be unable to put into words the sheer gratitude I feel for my family and friends who stood by me during this time. And to Haley and Danielle and the entire WME and Lake Union teams, I constantly wonder what I did to be so lucky to get to work with you.

I am simply in awe and beyond thankful.

ABOUT THE AUTHOR

Photo © 2006 Edwin Santiago

Liza Palmer is the author of *The Nobodies*, *The F Word*, and *Nowhere but Home*, winner of the Willie Morris Award for Southern Fiction. A two-time Emmy-nominated, internationally bestselling tea enthusiast who gets to write for Marvel sometimes, Liza lives in Los Angeles, where 95.3 percent of people call her Lisa. For more information, visit https://lizapalmer.com.